THE PATMOS REVELATION

Carl Jamieson

The Patmos Revelation

Published by Bioface Publishing

ISBN: 978-1-7391093-0-1

www.thepatmosrevelation.com

The characters and events portrayed in this book are fictional. Any similarity to real persons, living or dead, except in the case of historical fact, is coincidental and not intended by the author. Some locations are real. Technologies described are a mixture of real, imaginary or plausible. Religious interpretation is fictional and not intended to cause any offence.

1

Arlo loved his job and hated it. Pursuit of his dream but an addiction without a high. The signals kept drawing him in, trumping all reason, like an Egyptologist searching for a missing tomb in a dug-out valley, holding out for one last season against all hope. Digging an ever-deeper hole, his words to his dying dad echoing in his head, 'I'll find them. When I grow up, and I'm as big as you. I promise! You wait and see.'

The signals blurred, his eyes struggling to focus. He buried his head in his hands, closed his eyes, and thought about his kids and how much he missed them. The nagging voice returned, 'I'll find them ...' He lifted his head from his hands as if rising from prayer. He felt he needed spiritual help, but, unlike his wife Alisha, he didn't believe in God.

Surely it was only a matter of time before he made CTO? He certainly looked the part, smartly tailored in a navy-blue business suit, complete with NASA mission cufflinks to impress the board. He even had a razor-sharp buzz cut to gel with the military. But six months of long days had already taken their toll. He didn't know how much more he could take. More importantly, he didn't know how much more Alisha could take. Another evening she would have to read stories to their kids on her own and dine with just the HouseBot for company. His colleagues didn't neglect their partners. He knew it wasn't fair, and it had to stop. *Just a few more days ...* He ran a hand over his bristly scalp and rubbed his eyes. The signal traces on the screen swam. *Two minutes break, no more.*

He gazed out of the vast aerogel dome that capped the towering office block, insulating it from the sweltering daytime sun. A purple laser sign on the adjacent building flashed alternately between 19:17 and 102°F. The panorama of Seattle was stunning. To the east, skyscrapers made stark silhouettes against the steel-blue sky of the fading daylight. To the west, the jewelled ring of a Ferris wheel turned idly on the lazy waterfront of Elliot Bay. Isabella, his princess, loved riding the wheel, pretending she was a seagull soaring high over her nursery. Part of him wished he was there with her now, soaking up the liquid-gold sunset.

The Space Needle Tower pierced the sky to the north. Once futuristic in the optimistic Apollo era, but now endearingly retro. His son, Joshua, loved the tower and the gift shop with its plastic models of the Space Race rockets. He hoped he would grow up to share his love of the cosmos.

Arlo swivelled in his chair, spinning a digital pen between his fingers. The low autumnal sun cast a fiery aura over the snowy peak of Mount Rainier that dominated the horizon. Leaden clouds were racing in from Vancouver as a storm built, smothering the city and advancing on the glaciated stratovolcano.

His company, Space Swarm, had deployed a swarm of several hundred nanosatellites into solar orbit, far away from Earth's orbiting space junk, each smaller and lighter than a bowling ball. Collaboratively, they pinpointed infrared light from exoplanets orbiting distant stars, trying to detect signals transmitted by extraterrestrial life. Alisha called it the company's shop window project. She'd always been able to see through hype and spot hidden agendas. He knew she was right, but it was his passion, and he wasn't going to sell out on a bread-and-butter surveillance programme.

Arlo's eyes returned to his computer's waterfall plot, struggling to focus on the signals that scrolled down the screen like the patterns of an unfurling carpet. He scanned the output for anomalous signatures from the exoplanet Turnbull.

Arlo wished a computer could be taught this task. But the problem was a catch-22. How could you possibly train a computer to find something completely unknown?

A splattering broke the silence. Cursing, he looked up. Rivulets streamed down the window as the storm broke. Lightning lit the horizon in electric-purple hues; thunder rumbled like distant artillery.

Come on. Focus! Signals ran down the display like the rain on the window. Random, chaotic, and ordinary. At the wave of his hand, dozens more meaningless traces scrolled past. Junk. Minutes passed. More junk.

The room bleached out. Boom! Arlo jumped, tutting as thunder reverberated around the precinct, rain lashing against the glass. The coloured signals reappeared as the lightning's silver afterimage faded. *Why am I still here?* His shoulders dropped, and he tossed his pen onto the desk.

One more push. He rubbed his forehead, set his jaw, and stared at the screen. Pages and pages of signals scrolled past. All different, but all the same. Random junk. Part of him wanted to walk away, but he had to know. He had to find intelligent life in the cosmos and prove humans weren't alone. He had to do it for his dad.

More minutes passed that became an hour. Another hour to add to the days and weeks. No wonder his CEO, Richard Chapel, had grown tired of funding the work. The needle in a haystack project was burning his career as fast as the company's research budget. No end in sight banging his head against a wall of growing guilt. A nagging voice in his head, screaming that Alisha would grow resentful and her love for him would die.

And then–as his eyes lost focus and the signals swam towards him like snakes–he saw something. A weird pattern that flashed and disappeared. His eyes widened. He replayed the signal history and spotted several zigzag patterns jagged like a lightning strike. They didn't seem random at all. But, when he scrolled the plot forwards in time, they vanished, replaced by monotonous, random noise. He clenched his fists and then switched back to the live view. Sighing, he reclined in his chair. *Just a glitch.*

He checked his watch: 8:40 pm. He felt like a gambler on a losing streak, forever beaten by a game with loaded dice, unable to face going home to break the same old bad news. Alisha's words echoed in his head. 'Make up your mind. You're 33. If you want a promotion to CTO, head up their top project. If not, stop wasting your evenings. Joshua and Isabella need you–they will be grown up before you know it.' It was tough love, but he needed it. He should be spending more time with the kids. But it wasn't that simple. The project wasn't *just a job*–there *had* to be intelligent life in space. If he proved it, promotion would follow. The kids would be the first to benefit. Surely that was reasonable? *Just another twenty minutes.*

Squinting, he tried to focus on the screen. *Another planet?* His hand moved across the menu, index finger hovering above a button that changed the viewing direction. But, just as he was about to tap the graphic, he hesitated. He didn't know why–it was just a feeling. He'd felt the same when he'd taken Alisha on a romantic skiing break in the Rockies. He remembered it well because it was the year the last snow had melted. Impulsively, he'd told her to wait. Moments later, an avalanche had crashed through the gulley they were about to traverse. He'd said it was a coincidence; she'd said it was God.

The screen went ballistic. A frenzy of snaking signals streaked downwards from a cluster of frequency channels. In stunned silence, he stared at the forest of crawling zigzags. Was this it? Proof aliens were out there? The moment he'd dreamt of as a boy, like Howard Carter's first glimpse into Tutankhamun's tomb of wonderful things?

As he stared in disbelief, he felt an almost imperceptible growl in the pit of his stomach, like the ominous rumbling of an underground train in a distant tunnel. His stomach knotted as the sound became audible and began to roar. Everything in the office came alive: pens on desks animated as if under the influence of a poltergeist, a company lanyard on a hook swung like a pendulum, and a satellite model on a shelf began to buzz. Within seconds, the room was swaying. A baseball rolled off a desk, and a lunchbox slid on a cupboard as if riding an Atlantic swell. Furniture moved like chairs on a Waltzer. He grabbed the armrests of his chair, muscles tight, knuckles white.

Just when Arlo thought the building would collapse–nothing. An abrupt stillness, almost more ominous than the shaking. *Is it over?* He stood, eyes darting left and right, checking the exit was clear. Unsure of whether to stay or run for the stairs. He slowly exhaled and looked out of the dome. Mount Rainier stood guard at the eye of the storm. Flashes of lightning lit a spindly plume of smoke that rose vertically from its summit. It almost looked serene.

And then it came for him again. The growling monster raced across the landscape and gripped the building. But this time, the hold was firmer, the shaking more intense.

I'm going to die.

Arlo froze like a rabbit in headlights, clutching the desk as the building swayed like an ear of wheat in a summer storm. And, as he wondered whether there was a god, he was blinded by a searing orange-white flash, brighter than the opening of a furnace door. His face burned. As the glare faded, he saw the top of Mount Rainier had vanished. Hundreds of fireballs, trailing white smoke trails, streaked high above the city. Seconds later, the explosion's shock wave struck the building.

Arlo didn't see it coming–blasted from his chair, rag-dolled through the air, and slammed against a leather chesterfield in the breakout area. Stars flashed; his head spun as he fought to remain conscious. Blackness consumed him ...

ΔΔΔ

Dirty black clouds of diesel smoke belched from the column of advancing tanks as they rumbled and squealed into the city, their sandy camouflage splattered with the signatures of war.

A pall of grey smoke hung over the buildings as far as the eye could see. Blown-out dolomitic limestone houses lined the street, their walls pockmarked by shellfire, their roofs stained by soot. The tanks rolled on unopposed, crushing everything in their path.

With a crunch of gears, the lead tank stopped and rocked. Flames spewed from its barrel, the blast reverberating off the buildings. A moment later, the upstairs of a distant apartment block crumpled inwards. A pitiful rat-a-tat-tat came from a rooftop, immediately quashed by a short buzzing burst from the tank's machine gun. Then silence.

The tank's hatch was thrown open with a clang. A man dressed in battle fatigues hoisted himself from the turret and stood proud. He surveyed the apocalyptic scene and smiled.

In a whirlwind of sand, buildings crumbled. The pall of smoke became leaden clouds; the sandstorm turned to snow. The blizzard calmed. A conical butte rose from an icy plain, terraces carved into its sides. At its apex, a stone monolith stood proud like a nipple on nature's breast, and a beam of pure energy rose from the mound to the heavens.

ΔΔΔ

Arlo heard muffled and distorted sounds in the inky blackness, like on a night dive in the ocean. He couldn't breathe. *Out of air!* Panicking, he raced for the surface, lungs bursting, every sinew of his body straining. His eyelids fluttered open, the room spinning, a high-pitched whistle piercing his brain. He coughed and retched on choking brimstone fumes. The lights were out, but the room flickered pastel hues from his computer screen.

The spinning slowed. Grimacing, he sat up and swept a blanket of frosted glass and dust from his body, cutting his hands but feeling no pain. He tasted metal and spat a gritty paste of blood and dust. The floor swayed as he climbed to his feet, the building creaking and groaning a skyscraper's death rattle. A scene of the Twin Towers collapsing flashed through his mind.

His balance returned. Slowly, he shuffled through the debris, one arm extended, feeling his way. A gust of wind blew dust into his face. He coughed and wiped his eyes, stopping at the edge of the room, teetering at the crumbling edge of a gaping hole in the dome. His stomach lurched, and his head reeled as he peered into the abyss. Clutching at the fractured steel framework, he gazed at the defenceless city.

A colossal plume of smoke, backlit by electric storm flashes, rose from within Mount Rainier's shattered core. Flaming rocks rained down on the city. He imagined Isabella and Joshua riding their bikes down the footpath outside their suburban home.

He jumped as a fire sprinkler spun up like a car wash. Droplets splattered his gritty face, streaming down his forehead, dripping into his eyes and making them sting. Squinting, he drove through the mist to where he'd last seen the door.

He lunged into the corridor, shoulder-charged a fire door, and tumbled down the emergency stairwell. Reaching the bottom of the first flight, he skidded a corner and ran headlong into a cowering shadowy figure.

She wore a burgundy cleaner's tabard with Pro Clean's gold initials embroidered on the breast pocket. Grimy, shaking hands covered her head. Around her, cleaning products lay scattered from a toppled plastic bucket: a yellow duster, an aerosol can of Magic Shine and yellow rubber gloves.

'Are you OK?' he asked, trying to sound calm.

The woman lowered her hands and looked up. She was in the prime of her life, Hispanic and beautiful like Alisha. Sparkling ebony eyes, purposeful eyebrows, full rosebud lips and long black hair pulled back in a ponytail. Her face was familiar. *Will Isabella look like her?* Black mascara stains streaked down her face. She appeared too petrified to speak.

'I'm Arlo.'

'St-St-Stella …' Her bottom lip quivered.

Even the name …

'Don't worry,' he said, trying to hide his fear. 'I'll get you out. Let me help you up.'

Stella mustered a weak smile and stretched out a scratched hand. Crouching, he put his hands under her armpits and lifted her slight frame.

As she rose to her feet, hope spreading across her face, Arlo paused and gazed into the distance. *Shit! The data!*

Gently, he lowered her back down. Her face dropped.

'I've forgotten something …' he mumbled. 'In the office. Don't move–I'll be quick.'

Stella looked horrified.

'You'll be OK,' Arlo reassured her. 'Just wait here. I'll only be a minute or two.'

She began to sob.

'You'll be OK. Yeah?' He stared into her eyes.

Stella swallowed hard, sniffled and nodded. Her expression reminded him of when he'd forced Isabella to ride the big slide in the park–an image he would take to the grave. Arlo spun around and charged the stairs two at a time.

He retraced his steps to the office, feet sliding out from under him as he ran towards his desk. He lunged for the furniture and grabbed the top of a cabinet. Slipping and sliding, he shuffled to his desk.

A rainbow veil hung in the mist in front of the screen, signals distorted by the spray.

Thank god. It's still working.

Frantically, he scanned his desk, eyes settling on a souvenir alarm clock of the Space Needle he'd bought on a whim when visiting. It had a wireless memory drive in its base, outdated like the tower, but it would just have to do. With a few deft hand movements, he commanded the computer to transfer the data.

The progress bar nudged lazily across the screen. He glanced nervously out of the gaping hole in the dome. A turbulent plume of dust was racing across the landscape, swallowing the city. *Come on. Faster.* It taunted him, idling along as the city was consumed. Finally, it stuttered to the end. He grabbed the tower like a relay baton and raced for the stairs.

At the top of the stairwell, the building shook. He cowered as plaster rained down. The building creaked and groaned and then steadied. He plunged down the stairs, rounded the corner and froze.

Glowing pumice littered the floor around the cleaning products: yellow duster, Magic Shine, and yellow rubber gloves. A section of the building–the wall where Stella had been leant–was torn away. He gazed out of the ragged hole and scanned the dizzying drop to the street below. She'd vanished, and car-sized flaming rocks were crashing into the surrounding skyscrapers.

He stood paralysed, time standing still. A mighty crash shook the building; thoughts of his kids riding their bikes re-engaged his brain. He stormed down the stairs and out of the building.

In a mad panic, he dashed across the city, struggling to breathe amid the swirling clouds of volcanic dust. Fireballs whooshed overhead, slamming into walls of glass. The city was a horror story, people with skin dripping like wax, mouths and eyes choked with dust. All he heard between the deafening crashes were bestial cries and screams for help.

He waded a slalom course through the thigh-deep ash, tasting the sickly sweet smell of burning flesh. Pompeiian effigies, twisted and contorted in frozen agony, jumped out of the ash clouds at every turn. Carbonised silhouettes were lit ruby red in crashed cars, with liquorice stick arms and hands of coal. Finally, he made it back home. Maybe it had taken thirty minutes, maybe three hours–it was hard to judge time in a nightmare.

His leafy American dream had gone, the street transformed into a monochrome moonscape gilded by flickering firelight, ash topiaries where houses had once stood. Ghosts trudged down the gulley of a road, hopelessly searching for their lost lives. Arlo winced as they shuffled past–torn and gaping clothes showcasing raw burns, dusted like rare and peppered steak. They grabbed at his arms, pleading. He pulled away, ashamed by his disgust, ashamed by not helping.

Were they on their bikes?

He counted the mounds down the road and waded up a buried drive he presumed was his. An ash snowman was burrowing like a dog excavating a bone, glowing pumice scattered all around, smoke still rising. Someone smaller stood by watching, hunched like a garden gnome bleached grey by winter storms. Rigid, frozen, petrified.

As he neared, the burrowing became more frantic; objects flew through the air. One landed in the ash by his feet. He bent down and dusted it off. It was a cup-sized brown bear, dressed in a blue duffel coat, with a red beanie hat and yellow wellington boots. Paddington Bear. Just like Isabella's. He flipped it over and saw a small cloth label protruding from its seam. 'Isabella's bestest friend,' was written in spidery red ink.

The ghost-like figure turned. 'Help me,' it pleaded, eyes and mouth like black caves, opening and closing in an ashen face.

'Alisha?' Arlo gasped.

'M-Must find Isabella,' she sobbed. 'Help me.'

'Where's Joshua?'

She pointed to the crouched figure who still hadn't moved.

'Is he OK?'

She didn't seem to hear.

'I-I c-can't find Isabella. Help me.'

'Where was she?'

'P-Playing … In her room.'

'Here?' Arlo pointed to the depression where she'd been burrowing.

Alisha nodded, hand waving over the scattered toys. 'It hit here.'

'What hit here?'

'F-Fireball. A few minutes ago.'

The backup took longer ...

She began to sob, tears like magic ink painting a geisha's face on a grey canvas. He squeezed her arm, pulled her close and then sank to his knees in the waist-deep ash, scrabbling at the grit with his bare hands.

He pulled objects from the horror tombola. Toys. Clothes. Then he felt a hard surface with lots of corners–a chair. He rose into a half-crouch and dragged it free. Underneath, a black cave collapsed. But not before he'd seen it. A flash of burgundy– the colour of Isabella's pinafore dress she'd been wearing at breakfast. The colour of Stella's tabard before he'd deserted her. The colour of half-dried blood.

He dove back into the hole, scared she might suffocate and grabbed a handful of cloth. He pulled hard. It moved. Carefully, he dragged Isabella out of the hole. She lay face down, limp like one of her dolls. He rolled her over, glassy eyes staring skyward. He dusted off her cheeks and rosebud lips. In desperation, he looked to Alisha. Her stony face gazed down like a gargoyle as she began to scream. Behind her, fireballs arced across the sky. It was as if the stars, and even heaven itself, were falling to Earth.

2

MONDAY, 2 SEPTEMBER 2052

A siren wailed, its pitch dropping as the police truck roared past the pub. Arlo jumped, gripping the bar, white knuckles turning pink as the sound faded. He studied the inch of frothy black liquid at the bottom of the pint glass, swirled it around and downed it in one. A creamy beer moustache tickled his nose. He wiped it away with the heel of his hand and stood on the bar stool's footrests, troubled topaz eyes peering through dishevelled brown hair into the back bar.

'*Peter,*' he slurred. '*You there, man?*'

A tall, middle-aged man, wearing jeans and a Southmead Brewery real-ale T-shirt, strolled out of the kitchen carrying an improbably long stack of clean glasses. Carefully, he slid them one at a time onto a rack, wiped his hands on a tea towel, and walked over. 'You made light work of that, AJ.' He grinned. 'Another Guinness?'

Arlo grunted and passed him the empty.

'You OK?' Peter asked. 'You're even quieter than normal.'

'All good,' Arlo mumbled.

Today was Isabella's birthday–the worst day of the year. Visiting the Flying Scotsman on Bristol's Gloucester Road had become a habit. A place of strangers who accepted him for who he was and usually didn't ask too many questions. But that was the catch. The more he came, the more people knew him and tried to be friendly by asking questions. He needed anonymity, but he also needed friends. Either way, he figured he was damned.

The Great Eruption happened three years ago, and he'd

been in the UK with his family for just over two. But Arlo remembered the fateful day just like it was yesterday. Or at least the first part before he'd dug Isabella out of the ash. That was when his timeline fractured. His doctor called it dissociative amnesia, brought on by the trauma–his brain's way of coping, he'd said.

The next thing he remembered was riding a bus with the other ash zombies to an emergency refuge in Portland, Oregon. He recalled checking on the kids every few minutes, discovering Isabella wasn't there, relearning the unthinkable–over and over again in a nightmare groundhog day. He kept hearing her voice, repeatedly looking around and realising it wasn't her. Alisha was hysterical. Somehow, he'd calmed her down by making her play a guessing game with Joshua.

Portland had been lucky, escaping the worst of the eruption, if having thousands of homeless appear overnight could be called lucky. But for the first time in his life, Arlo understood how relative luck was. Many of the survivors he chatted to thought they'd been unlucky losing their homes and possessions. But they were still alive. In Arlo's book, they were the lucky ones.

The makeshift camp consisted of several khaki marquees erected in an out-of-town shopping mall car park. After a lengthy check-in, they received bedding, sanitary items, basic food supplies and a little area to make their own. Over the following week, Space Swarm had created a new job for him in their San Francisco sister office and had even found them an apartment overlooking the bay. Their Seattle home had been rented, their car leased, so, on the face of it, they'd just been able to start again. Most people in Seattle hadn't been so lucky–unsupported at the worst time of their lives.

But, despite their luck, life in San Francisco had been liminal, their concept of time fractured. One minute he would be at work, knowing he had to perform to repay Space Swarm's kindness, the next, he would worry about collecting Isabella from kindergarten. Their memory of Isabella's death was an indelible stain they could never erase. Daily sights and sounds constantly reminded them of her, screaming that acceptance was never possible. Although San Francisco, with its relaxed vibe, was far from Seattle, both physically and culturally, it was still part of the corporate US of A. Triggers were everywhere: an advert on television for the Disney princess dresses she loved to wear; the sweet fatty smell when passing Dunkin' Donuts, her favourite treat; seeing the yellow school buses she was looking forward to riding when she started school.

After a year, the triggers and bouncing of time and place had worsened. Objects kept on swapping: a can of deodorant would become Magic Shine, a sock would morph into Paddington bear. They felt increasingly alienated, their worldviews diverging from friends and colleagues, haunted, like being stalked by a snarling feral dog that could bite at any moment. Isabella was there with them, but of course, she wasn't. Flashbacks of her lying in the ash; sat in the gap around the dinner table wearing her burgundy pinafore dress, her ebony eyes pleading for help. Her face would morph into Stella's, and he would hear her whisper. 'How's your precious data now?'

One evening, Alisha had made a hard-boiled egg with soldiers, one of Isabella's favourite snacks. Arlo asked her who it was for, and Alisha replied she'd heard Isabella say she was hungry and lonely in the dark under the chair. That had been the final straw. That was when Arlo knew they had to leave. All they had left was Joshua and threads of their sanity. Alisha hadn't resisted–they'd reached rock bottom.

They'd sailed to the UK because it was their only real option. Soon after, a massive earthquake struck San Francisco, and their apartment flattened. Maybe Alisha was right? Maybe there was a god? It seemed fateful that only a year earlier, Space Swarm, Inc. had acquired Prospero, a start-up company spun out from Bristol University and renamed it Space Swarm UK. Also, Arlo had a UK passport, automatically giving Alisha UK residency.

They'd hoped the move would help them live in the present–a new start and a new life. They had to try, even if just for Joshua, as their memories were corrosive and tearing them apart.

Physically leaving the States had given them a reprieve, but the demons had returned. They felt damned. They wanted to be close to their memories of Isabella, but they also wanted to forget.

The scrape of a stool dragging across a flagstone floor jarred Arlo from his thoughts. He thumped the bar, angry with himself for dwelling in the past. Patrons turned and stared. He knew there was neither rhyme nor reason to what had happened. It was time to stop torturing himself and move on. But how?

He heard rustling and glanced to his left. A bull of a man was hoisting himself up next to him. Crude sexualised tattoos decorated his bare forearms; a khaki cap was pulled tightly over his head, probably concealing a bald patch. Bull-man's pint of bitter slopped over as he dumped it on the bar, splashing Arlo's hand. Arlo sighed.

'Alwight mate,' Bull-man said with a rattly cough.

Arlo grunted and stared straight ahead.

'Did you hear me?' Bull-man pressed. 'I *said*, you all right?'

Not this, not now.

'Yes, mate,' Arlo replied. 'You?'

'Yeah, thanks. Much on?'

Arlo rolled his eyes and turned to face him. 'Just a couple of beers before heading off home.'

'Ah ... family?'

'No, just me.'

'Right you are.'

Arlo glanced over at Peter, who was watching them from the corner of his eye, poised to step in. The antique railway clock on the wall behind his head showed 10:17. Arlo felt so tired. He swirled the stout around his glass and stared into the frothy vortex, wishing it would suck him in. Blanking out the bar's sounds, he focused on the inky blackness …

ΔΔΔ

Stars began to shine in the night sky. Young Arlo grinned as he sat on his dad's lap, the rickety wooden chair creaking on the weathered concrete slab as he fidgeted. The patio was tiny but pristine, the back gardens of the terrace crammed together like keys on a piano.

It felt like he'd been waiting for ages. 'Go easy on the wriggling,' his dad said, 'my legs aren't so young anymore.' Arlo tried hard, but he was six today, and his shiny new toy was ready and waiting.

A golden glow seemed to be clinging to the rooftops. Arlo willed the inky blackness to push the last fringe of light away. A shiver ran down his spine as he felt the warmth from the sun-baked tarmac fading. Surely it was nearly time?

He was still buzzing from the party games. Winning musical chairs, after a massive bundle with Gary for the final chair, had been epic. But he'd felt a bit bad afterwards– awkward and didn't know what to say. He'd never won a proper game before. That was unless you counted cards and, his dad's favourite, an ancient board game called Monopoly. Winning hadn't felt as good as he'd expected. Maybe he wasn't meant to win at his own party?

Nicola had won pass-the-parcel, but something hadn't stacked up. The song had stopped on a different person every time, almost as if the music player had eyes. But how could that be? Anyway, he was pleased she'd won. She was really nice to everyone and almost as much fun as the boys. And she was very, very pretty, with Milkybar skin and honey-coloured hair. If he'd been the music player, he would have picked her *every* time.

After the games, he recalled opening his presents. The pile looked much smaller than what he remembered from friends' parties. Sometimes Greg, who was in the final year of Ventnor Primary School, teased him. 'Council house loser,' he'd shout. Arlo didn't know what a council house was, but he thought it was something to do with being poor. Yet, when he reached his last massive present and ripped away the wrapping paper covered in fast cars, he realised Greg was a prat. Inside was an amazing adult-sized telescope, like the one he'd seen on the shopping channel, which the woman had said was only twenty instalments of ten pounds. Ten pounds could buy a lot of sweets but, even though that was loads of money, it still seemed a bargain for something *so* cool.

He'd dreamed about the telescope–and wanted it *so* bad– but he never thought he would ever own it. His dad seemed to know everything, and this proved it. He was so clever he could even see inside his head. He promised himself he wouldn't think about kissing Nicola anymore.

He grinned from his memories of the party and stared wide-eyed at the heavens as a hidden world emerged. The glittering, glowing arch of the Milky Way shone way above their heads. He knew its name because his dad had said the chocolate bar was named after it. His dad had told him how far away it was, some massive number he couldn't remember, and explained something about light-years he hadn't understood.

Arlo's gaze returned to the silver telescope, propped on its wooden tripod, gleaming in the moonlight. He leaned back and wriggled off his dad's lap to the floor, twisting around to check he wasn't angry. But he needn't have worried–his dad was staring up at the sky, looking happier than he had for months. Arlo wiped his brow, sneaked over and stroked the polished barrel. The metal felt cold and expensive–like things in the amazing adult world–and, yet, it was *his* now.

His dad looked down. 'I've set it up for you. Look here.' He gestured with his hand. 'Tell me what you see.'

Arlo flicked a mop of hair from his face, screwed up his eye and peered into the eyepiece. A small blurry orange disc hovered in a black circle in front of the lens.

'It's broke!'

'No, son, it's fine. Just move your head backwards or forwards to make the image larger.'

Arlo rocked his head. '*Cool!*' He grinned. 'It's working.'

'What do you see?'

'Umm, it's like one of those orange Smarties, but really, really, tiny. It's surrounded by black.'

'It's a lot bigger than one of your sweets. It looks small because it's so far away.'

'*How far?*'

'About one hundred million miles. That's a one, followed by eight zeros.'

'Never! Is a zillion miles further away than Uncle Tony in America?'

'Zillion? I've not heard of that number before.'

'That's because it's bigger than all the numbers you know.' Arlo grinned.

His dad's frown smoothed, his eyes lit up, and he patted his son's shoulder. 'It's much, much, farther away than Tony. You're looking at Mars. It's another world–a bit like Earth but covered in cold red deserts. It orbits the Sun as we do.'

'Are there people there?'

'No.' His dad shook his head. 'There's only life on Earth. At least as far as we know.'

Arlo turned and, with sad eyes, looked him squarely in the face. 'You mean we're all alone?'

'I'm afraid so.'

'*No way!* I've seen aliens on TV. I know they're out there.'

'I hope you're right, but no one's found any *real* ones yet.'

'I'll find them. When I grow up, and I'm as big as you. I promise! You wait and see.'

'I know you'll give it your best shot, son.' He ruffled Arlo's hair. 'But don't you worry if you don't. Remember, it's always important to put family first.'

'Whatever, dad.' He sighed heavily.

Smiling, his dad gave him a loving squeeze. 'Right, run

inside before you catch a chill.'

Arlo looked deep into his dad's eyes, trying to fathom how he knew so much. As the man, aged beyond his 45 years, tried to stand, his brow furrowed and his teeth clenched. Arlo reached out and stroked his head. He recoiled when a large clump of hair came away in his hand.

ΔΔΔ

A bell clanged. Arlo jumped and looked up. The antique railway clock on the wall showed 11:02. It was last orders. Three glasses on the bar held froth. Bull-man had gone. A smile lingered on Arlo's face as he recalled his joy of doing science projects with his dad, like when they'd soldered together a crystal radio using components that looked like sweets and heard ghostly voices from the ether. And the model rocket they'd made from cardboard tubes and balsa wood that had roared out of sight until its orange and white parachute had popped open. But those dreams were a thing of the past. These days he was scared to sleep.

Nighttime was when the demons came looking for him. His daughter would be with them, held hostage. They would make her taunt him. He was terrified this would become his enduring memory of her. The doctor had prescribed him Prazosin. But the tablets hadn't erased his memory and had only numbed and depressed him, watering down his existence and making him terrible company. He had stopped taking them for his family.

He rose from the stool and wobbled.

'You OK there, AJ?' Peter appeared with a roll of bar towels draped over his arm.

'Bit tired,' Arlo slurred. 'Best get home.'

'Indeed.' Peter looked concerned. 'You be careful out there–a storm's brewing.'

Arlo nodded. 'Thanks. I'll be off then, mate.' He turned and shuffled towards the door. The latch clicked as he slipped out into the night.

The wind blew raw as it howled like an express train down the street. Instinctively, Arlo buttoned his trench coat and pulled the collar up. It felt like tissue paper over his thin work suit, but he was numb anyway.

His flat was a fifteen-minute walk away, but there was no rush. It would delay the inquisition of why he was drinking on Isabella's birthday. Before the disaster, Alisha had never been judgmental but terrible things changed people. If only she understood that that was *why* he drank.

But he counted himself lucky. Alisha had lost God as well. She'd always taken solace in the Bible during difficult times, and now she'd stopped reading. It worried him how she would cope. At least she had a few good friends in Bristol and the metaverse. And she had her diary, although he hated to think what she was writing in there now. She needed someone strong to guide her through this nightmare. Arlo hoped that person could be him. If only he could stop drinking–he knew how much it upset her.

He walked up Gloucester Road and approached a red-brick railway arch that had once carried the Great Western line. The grand structure was crumbling now and little more than a canvass for Banksy-esque street art sprayed by gravity-defying artists. The black and white images depicted Marcus Aaron, a local Black activist who had fought for equality and paid with his life.

A dim yellow glow lit the road from the light spilling from poorly closed curtains, most streetlights having been disconnected years ago. Large snowflakes began to fall. They blew against his sleeve and didn't melt. It went pitch black as he passed under the arch. Glancing over his shoulder, he sped up. A rattly cough broke the silence. He spun around, hands raised defensively, trying to pinpoint its source. Another cough–this one phlegmier, serious-sounding. He peered into the gloom and, as his eyes adjusted, made out a vague figure huddled against one of the brick pillars.

'You OK, mate?' Arlo called.

'Peachy,' came a gruff, slurred voice. 'Just need to–' The man began to retch and choke.

Arlo dove into the shadows and knelt beside him, holding back an urge to gag from the acidic smell of fresh vomit. The man was huge: a behemoth sprawled on his back, a baseball cap pulled tightly over his head. It was Bull-man from the pub. Gurgling sounds came from his throat. *Shit, he's suffocating.*

Arlo grabbed him by the shoulders and rolled him onto his side. He patted his back, and the gurgling gave way to wheezing. A few seconds later, Bull-man coughed, seemed to recover and pushed himself up.

'You OK?' Arlo asked.

'Eer, who are yoousse.'

'Right, we can't leave you here, can we?' Arlo muttered.

An amused smile played across Bull-man's face.

'Can you stand?'

'No ploblemo.'

Arlo helped him up. He lurched about, almost toppling.

'Put your arm around my shoulders.'

Bull-man draped himself over Arlo. Over the next fifteen minutes, they stumbled back to Arlo's flat like the backmarkers of a geriatrics' three-legged race. Arlo fumbled his key in the lock, and they squeezed into the communal entrance of two adjoining flats. Together they climbed the steep flight of stairs.

Halfway up, Bull-man stumbled and fell, dragging Arlo down with him. Arlo chuckled to himself at how ridiculous they must look as they climbed the last few stairs on all fours. A door creaked open, and Arlo looked up. Alisha was standing in the doorway, bleary-eyed and wearing her nightie. He flicked hair from his eyes. 'Err, it's not how it looks lov–'

'Don't.' Alisha stopped him with a raised hand. 'I'm tired. Let's talk in the morning. You sort him out and come to bed.'

Arlo smiled sheepishly. She turned and shuffled back to bed.

Ten minutes later, he'd bagged up Bull-man's soiled jumper to contain the smell. He rolled him face down onto the sofa bed in the lounge, placed an empty washing-up bowl by his head, and threw a spare duvet over him. Parched, he poured himself a glass of water and guzzled it in one.

Walking into the bedroom, he undressed by the dim light cast by a crack in the curtains and fumbled his way into bed. Alisha stirred.

'You still awake, love,' he asked with beery breath.

'Um, as usual,' she replied.

'What time is it?'

'No idea,' she said. 'I've lost all track of time.'

Arlo lay on his back, thoughts racing through his mind. After an hour of tossing and turning, he plunged into the world of nightmares. Isabella was waiting.

3

TUESDAY, 3 SEPTEMBER 2052

Arlo woke with a start. Sweat beaded his brow, and the sheets clung to his body. He felt exhausted; his head pounded. Thanks to the drink, he'd slept. That's if having nightmares could be called sleep.

He remembered being chased through Seattle by an ash monster that had shaken the ground like earthquake aftershocks. Nine feet tall, black holes for eyes, and skin that dripped like wax. A demonic voice roared, 'She's buried at home and has ten minutes left to live. Your time starts *NOW!*'

The ash was thigh deep, scorching his skin and dragging at his legs. The city was a maze, a burning car blocking the end of every road, the air heavy with the fatty smell of roasting flesh. After a marathon effort, he'd made it home. Gasping, he scanned the garden for where to dig and saw a sign. A big arrow pointed down, underneath a caption: 'Dig Here!' A digital timer on top of the sign clicked over from 10:00 to 10:01 and froze. He turned around, ready to plead. The ash monster loomed over him and wagged a finger.

'Now dig and see what you *could* have won.'

Arlo rolled over, worried he might have disturbed Alisha, embarrassed by the sweat-stained sheets. But she was writhing about in her sleep, moaning and whimpering like a frightened puppy. He leaned across and stroked her long black hair. She flinched, and the heart-wrenching muttering stopped. Her eyes fluttered open as she surfaced. She looked confused and exhausted–he knew the feeling well. He gave a comforting smile and tenderly stroked her arm. He hated seeing her like this.

He double-blinked to wake up his BioFace, the networked biological interface that had replaced smartphones. Initially, the implants had been introduced for in-body health monitoring–to aid the failing health service–but now they seemed to govern people's lives. His eyes refocused as the smart contact lenses displayed columns of icons down both sides of his vision. The clock icon showed 6:34 am–still enough time to see his mum if he hurried. He felt like crap, but that was normal these days. It was just a case of getting on with life and hoping things improved.

He jumped out of bed and shuffled into the en suite. A cold shower revived him, and, as he towelled himself dry, he remembered Bull-man from the pub. He put on a dressing gown and marched into the sitting room.

Bull-man was sprawled on his back catching flies, snoring loudly enough to wake the neighbours. Arlo shook his head and entered the kitchen. The electricity rationer flashed 1.3 kWh in red–not enough power for the fridge, lights, and television, let alone a hot shower for Alisha and Joshua.

He opened the fridge, peeled half his daily meat ration from a pack of bacon onto a plate, and shoved it into the microwave. It growled through their electricity and pinged. He forked two rashers onto a buttered roll.

Bull-man snuffled like a pig when Arlo shook him. An arm, thicker than most legs, emerged from under the duvet as he prised his eyes open.

'Who's you?' he grunted.

That's rich.

'Arlo.' His eyes narrowed when he saw the naked woman winking provocatively over her shoulder, tattooed on his forearm. 'And you need to go before my wife gets up.'

Bull-man looked taken aback. Arlo thrust the bap into a dangling hand; Bull-man's fingers twitched beneath the woman's stilettos. He grinned. 'Right you are mucker. I'll be on my way.'

Arlo patted him on the shoulder. 'Perfect. Right now would be good.'

Bull-man nodded and extricated himself from the duvet. Arlo inhaled the smell of vomit and stale sweat. Trying not to gag, he crossed the room and stuck his arm through the curtain to open a window. He hated wasting their precious heat, but it wasn't fair on Alisha.

'I'm off to work–I'll see you out,' Arlo pressed.

Bull-man grabbed his coat. 'You not eating?'

'Eating?'

'Yeah, bacon.' A string of fatty rind dangled from his mouth like a tapeworm looking for a home.

'No. No time for that–my mum's more important,' Arlo replied, waves of nausea washing over him.

Bull-man looked puzzled. Arlo shook his head and disappeared into the bedroom. Several minutes later, he reappeared dressed in black jeans and a blue fleece, shouldering a rucksack.

Grabbing his coat and scarf, Arlo shepherded Bull-man out of the room and down the stairs. Turning the front door knob, he pushed hard. The door jammed. Cursing, he leaned against it with his shoulder, but it was stuck solid. After several increasingly aggressive shoves, the swollen wood gave way, and he went flying out into the street. He regained his balance and straightened up. The beauty of the scene took his breath away.

It was twilight, yet the unlit street gleamed brightly from the overnight snow. The storm had blown itself out; leaden clouds, suffused with deep purple from the volcanic ash, receded into the distance. The dust-obscured rising sun smouldered a dull orange above the rooftops, diffuse golden spokes radiating to pink. Everywhere was deathly quiet, all sound swallowed by the deep snow, disturbed only by a faint ominous hum from the nuclear-powered drone that hovered perpetually far above the city.

'Looks like you did me a favour, mate,' Bull-man said as he

scooped up some snow and packed it into a ball.

'It's nothing,' Arlo replied. 'Might see you in the Scotsman some time.'

'Right you are.' Bull-man grinned. 'The next one's on me.'

Not if I see you first.

Arlo offered him his hand. Bull-man tossed the snowball at the neighbour's house, making a fist pump when it hit the window with a reassuringly loud thud. Arlo shook his head. Bull-man gripped his hand so firmly it made him wince and gave a single shake that jarred his elbow. 'Thanks,' Bull-man said, winking. He turned and trudged away through the deep snow.

Arlo muscled the front door shut, checked it was locked, and surveyed the street. Across the road, the snow had drifted between the detached houses in giant meringues. Downstairs windows were dusted with wind-blown icing sugar snow, coloured orange by flickering firelight. Gossamer tendrils of smoke drifted lazily from chimney pots, draping the rooftops. Arlo inhaled the cold air deeply into his lungs, the smell of wood smoke from wealthy residents up on the hill in Clifton mingling with acrid fumes of burning plastic scavenged by the masses from the city's old landfills. Pulling his scarf over his nose and mouth, he picked his way gingerly down the street towards the city.

Commuters made charcoal Lowry matchstick figures as they shuffled down the snow-ploughed hill. The road was covered in sheet ice, compacted from the delivery trucks and police patrols during the night. Footpaths had nearly vanished, and footprints from the small hours had filled in, leaving vague depressions.

Last year, Arlo's mother, Veronica, had been moved into a nursing home after a fall. Alisha had been adamant they couldn't look after her at home. 'Josh must come first,' she'd insisted. 'We can't neglect him now. Not after all that's happened.' Arlo knew she was right, but he'd felt awful breaking the news to his mum. She'd been confused and had probably thought they were abandoning her. He'd tried to make amends by visiting most days on the way to the office. Usually, he saw her for an hour and made up the time by working late. It wasn't ideal, but at least it made her happy.

Halfway down the hill, he came to a three-storey terrace of nondescript buildings, greyed historically by car fumes and crying out for a lick of paint. Out of habit, he gurned at the gleaming state-of-the-art security camera that swivelled as it tracked his every move. *Funny how they can afford fancy cameras ...*

He climbed the steps and entered the building through a porch bearing a snow-dusted sign: 'Ashley Down Residential Nursing Home.' The security scanner beeped as it registered his BioFace. As he entered the hall, a head appeared around the kitchen door at the end of the corridor. He had grown to like Dave, who, to all intents and purposes, single-handedly ran the home. His official title was janitor, a penny-pinching slap in the face considering what a great job he did. But he never complained and was always cheerful.

'Hi Arlo,' he said. 'Your mum's awake if you want to go on up.'

'Has she been running you ragged again?'

'Yeah, she's fitter than I am, but that's not hard ...'

Arlo grinned. 'I've brought you some apples–maybe they'll help.' He opened his rucksack, removed a brown paper bag and placed it on a corner table.

Dave's face lit up–fresh fruit was hard to come by these days.

'You're a kind man Arlo.'

'You're very welcome. You move heaven and earth around here.' Arlo tapped two fingers to his temple in a salute.

Arlo climbed the steep stairs, pushing on his thighs. Halfway up the first flight, he paused for breath. The stairs above him creaked. Eyes narrowing, he leaned over the handrail and looked up through the gap. A figure darted into the shadows. Arlo continued to climb.

He paused on the landing and looked down the corridor to see if the mystery person was still there. A robotic HAL carer scuttled into one of the rooms, carrying a tray of cups. Arlo tutted and carried on climbing. HAL stood for Health Administration Live-in. The droids had been introduced into elderly care services in 2027 to address the healthcare crisis. Arlo still hadn't got used to their ghostly presence.

He climbed the second flight of stairs and marched along the landing. Moans came from the open doors of most rooms. Arlo averted his gaze from the sad and pleading faces, like a tourist ignoring beggars. He remembered his walk of shame down the road to his house in Seattle.

At the end of the corridor, he reached his mother's room and tapped on the door.

'Is that you, Arlo?' a frail voice wavered. 'Come in, I'm decent ...'

Veronica was sitting up in bed, wearing a floral nightdress, flicking through old family photos on a battered iPad. She preferred its intimacy over the large screen on the wall opposite the bed she used for video calls. Her face beamed from triggered memories. Although her legs let her down, she was still as bright as a button. When he saw her like this, he wished he could care for her at home. He wondered whether Alisha might reconsider if Josh calmed down. Alisha did secretarial work in an accountancy firm some mornings and helped out at a charity food bank for three afternoons a week. Maybe she'd forego the charity work? After all, charity began at home. Financially it made sense. The care home costs were over four times Alisha's wages and were burning through his mum's savings from the sale of her home.

His head dropped when he thought about it. The bigger issue was whether it was good for Alisha. She'd been through so much and needed to socialise–it was a non-starter.

'You, dreaming again, Arlo?' a sweet voice said.

Arlo startled. 'Sorry mum, miles away ...' He dragged a chair next to her bed, sat down, and looked lovingly into her eyes.

Part of him wished he'd spent more time with her when she was mobile rather than chasing his dreams in Seattle. But then, if he'd done that, he'd never have met Alisha.

Veronica's sparkling eyes transcended the ravages of time. Arlo's mind drifted, and her soft wrinkled face morphed. They were walking along Sandown Bay's promenade on the Isle of Wight. She looked radiant as the wind blew her hair like on a photoshoot. She gazed skyward, closing her eyes and relaxing her face in the warm spring sunshine. 'Here, mum.' He passed her an ice cream. She opened her eyes, and her face lit up.

'You OK, Arlo?' Veronica's voice startled him back into the tired-looking room, with its woodchip walls and grime-yellowed picture rails. He found these visits conflicting. Although he wanted to see her as much as possible before it was too late, it tortured him to see her trapped like this. He wondered whether this was his penance for chasing his dreams.

'How are you today, mum?' he asked.

'Come closer Arlo and speak into my ear,' she whispered.

'Is your hearing aid turned up?' Arlo enunciated clearly and loudly.

'I'm saving batteries,' she said smugly. 'Anyway, it gives me headaches.'

Arlo sighed, held her hand and stroked her hair.

'How are you, mum?'

'I'm OK, thanks,' she replied.

Arlo looked down at the photo on her iPad. It was a family picture at Osborne House, Queen Victoria's residence on the Isle of Wight. A passer-by must have taken it. His older brother, Mike, made bunny ears behind his head, and his dad hugged his mum.

Arlo pointed. 'That was a great day out.'

'Yes, it was lovely,' Veronica smiled. 'I still have days like that.'

Arlo looked puzzled.

She tapped her head. 'They're all locked away in here.'

'Ah, I see.' Arlo squeezed her hand.

'I had a visit from Dr Rajiv yesterday.'

'Really?' Arlo's eyes narrowed. 'What did he want?'

'He examined me.'

'What did he do?'

'Just the usual things,' she said, casually flicking through some more photos.

'Well, did he have anything important to say?'

'He just asked me the usual questions, but I pretended not to hear.'

'*Mum!*' Arlo rubbed his forehead as he felt his headache worsening. '*It might have been important!*'

'Doctors are so snooty.' She carried on flicking. 'They speak a load of mumbo jumbo.'

Arlo fought to stay calm. 'So you don't know why he came?'

'He mumbled something about …'

She laughed at one of her photos.

'Mum, *look at me.*' Reluctantly, Veronica looked up from her iPad and smiled.

'*What did he say?*' Arlo twisted his wedding ring round and round his finger.

'He said Sep.'

'*Sep?*'

'Yes, Sep.'

'What's that?'

'How should I know?' She put her iPad down. 'Maybe the month or something?' she mumbled.

Arlo checked his BioFace: it was indeed September. He could see she was becoming flustered. 'OK, OK. Don't worry, mum, it's probably just a routine health check. Panic over.'

She nodded serenely.

'Have you seen anyone else?' he asked, knowing she hadn't.

'Just Hayley. She wakes me up in the mornings and brings me breakfast. She tells me what's going on in the world. She's a nice girl. She means well.'

Arlo smiled nervously and clasped her hand tightly.

Is this purgatory?

'It's good Hayley's your friend–*even if she's an android.* I'll get Dave to come up and see you more. Would you like that?'

'If it's no trouble. I don't want to bother anyone,' Veronica answered feebly.

'It's no trouble, mum.'

'Anyway, Arlo, listen. Tell me about your lovely Alisha and Joshua. How are they? I haven't seen them in ages.'

Arlo's heart sank. He'd always been open and honest with his mother, but he didn't want to burden her. 'They're good, thanks.'

Veronica's eyes narrowed. 'Now tell me what's *really* going on.'

Arlo looked down, hearing the tick of the antique clock on the wall, wondering why she wanted it there, counting down her hours.

'Come on, Arlo, I'm your mother,' she persisted.

'We're, er … struggling.'

'*Struggling?*'

'Yes, struggling.'

'*Still?* You need to put all that behind you!'

Arlo looked haunted. 'Easier said than done, mum.'

'I'm sure it is.' Veronica's smile decayed, and she stroked Arlo's hand. 'How's work?'

'The company wants me to make a presentation on satellite swarms at SatCom 2052. This year it's at Bristol University, so it's cheap for them.'

'And?'

'I said no.'

'*Why?*'

'I can't face it.'

'Have you done the material?'

'Er, yes. But I don't think I can stand up there.'

'But you've done *many* talks before?'

'Yeah, I know. But I don't have the enthusiasm.'

'Stop talking in riddles, Arlo–I'm your mother!'

'Sorry?'

'You'll always be enthusiastic!'

'I've lost interest.'

'*Arlo!* You're like your father–you'll never lose interest in science. What's the *real* reason?'

Arlo looked down at his hands. 'I'm scared,' he said.

'*Scared?*'

'Yes, scared. Scared I'll panic.' He twisted his wedding ring.

Veronica glazed over and looked into space. Seconds later, a fresh smile formed. 'You need to do something you're passionate about, something to help you move on.'

Arlo shook his head and carried on twisting his wedding ring.

Veronica stared at the ceiling in a trance as if seeking divine inspiration. She lowered her gaze.

'You told me about that singal you detected.'

Arlo didn't respond.

'Didn't you say it was from aliens?'

Arlo stared at the clock.

'*Arlo?*'

'Um ... yes.'

'*What have you done about that singal?*'

'You mean signal.'

'Answer the question.'

'Err, not much.'

'*Not much?* You told me you'd *promised* your father you'd find ETs!'

'I know ...'

'So why haven't you done *much* with it?'

'Bad memories ... And, anyway, Space Swarm wasn't interested in it when we moved to San Francisco.'

'Did you look at it *at all?*'

Arlo looked away.

'*Arlo.*'

'Only in the UK–'

'What did you *do* exactly?'

'Just basic stuff.'

'Did *you* do it?'

'Erm … my friend Carl. He did most of … erm, all of–'

'*Arlo!*' she interrupted. '*Your father.* He'd be very disappointed.'

Arlo's leg bounced like a jackhammer. 'Maybe, I'll get back to it …'

Veronica didn't look convinced. 'Why don't you do that presentation and tack the ET stuff on the end? It'll focus your mind.' She stared into his eyes. '*For your father.*'

Arlo sat there quietly, deep in thought. His mum had a habit of plucking ideas out of thin air. Good ones, if he was honest with himself. Wake-up calls. Ones that were easier said than done. 'I'll give it some thought, mum. Thanks.'

'Make sure you do.' She squeezed his arm. 'I'll be checking up on you.'

Arlo heard a noise behind him, twisted around on the chair and looked over his shoulder. Hayley had come in.

'What's it doing, mum?'

'She's just making sure I'm OK. She's a good girl.'

Arlo sat quietly, watching the android. It was the latest generation, cloaked in artificial skin, originally developed for covering the BioFace implant. She had a blonde bob, emerald eyes, and perfect make-up. Wearing a powder-blue tunic, pencil skirt and heels, she was stunning and would turn heads. But, when Arlo studied her, she reminded him of a Stepford wife, a sinister parody of a human being, betrayed by the slight stiffness in her gait and stereotypical AI-driven expressions. Arlo could swear she was monitoring him while pretending not to.

'Where were we …?' Veronica asked.

Arlo swivelled back around.

'Er, you were telling me I should present some findings on that signal. For dad …'

'Ah, yes … that's right. You're a lucky man Arlo. Don't take it all for granted.'

'Yes, mum.'

Arlo's BioFace vibrated. *Thank god.*

'My BioFace is calling, mum. It's work–I need to go.'

'Thanks for coming to see me, Arlo. It's all I have to look forward to these days.'

Arlo leaned across, held her frail hand, and kissed her cheek. He stroked her head and tucked a lock of wispy white hair behind her ear. Her cloudy grey-green eyes studied him, and she smiled. Arlo could see how much he meant to her. *I don't deserve her.*

'See you soon, mum.'

'Come if you can, Arlo, but don't make yourself ill. You know how much I like to see you, but your health's more important. Make sure you eat your meals.'

Nodding, he stood to leave. He hated goodbyes, especially as one of these days would be the last. He squeezed her hand and walked across the room, Hayley tracking him intently. She saw him looking and gave a sickly Stepford smile. He hated the sinister sycophantic bitch. At the doorway, he paused and waved goodbye. His mother smiled and waved back. 'Don't forget that singal ...' she called out. *'For your father.'* Arlo nodded grimly, turned and walked out, feeling sick inside.

He retraced his steps, the security system beeping as he opened the front door. The cold air slapped him across the face. Inhaling deeply, he tried to purge the smell of decay from his nostrils. The door slammed shut, and he crossed the street in a trance, thoughts of alien signals playing on his mind.

4

L ucy Stevens gazed blearily at the avenue of decorative fountains as they jetted several feet into the frosty air. A computer-generated flypast of Tempest, a stealth fighter replacement for its predecessor Typhoon, flashed through the showering spray. Due in service for 2035, it was still only a pixelated pipedream. Hidden speakers made a booming raw. Lucy felt a dull headache coming on–it was way too much for so early in the morning.

She glanced at John Channing, her boss and Chief Scientific Officer at MSL, and nudged his arm. 'Why isn't the water frozen?' she asked, trying to sound interested.

'They have added a chemical to lower its freezing point.'

Lucy wondered how he knew everything.

She noticed a mauve and white sign off to one side of the path: Ministry of Defence Headquarters, Abbey Wood. John had briefed her en route from Salisbury about the meeting. He'd said they were visiting the UK's military procurement site at Filton. At that point, she'd glazed over.

Working for John was weird. At times he could be charming and thoughtful, entertaining even. Usually, he made her feel at ease–and she could even speak her mind–but sometimes, without warning, he could completely flip. The worst time had been when she'd brought him a small glass of the sweet tea he liked in the new Intel room–a department relocated from Gloucester as part of cost savings. During her induction, John had commented that the room was List-X, whatever that meant. He seemed to be in there a lot these days, and she thought it might be out-of-bounds for students, but he hated cold tea. She thought there wouldn't be any harm in popping in.

The room had been a bit of an anti-climax, boring even. Plain and nearly empty, apart from a wall of monitors on one side. What was the big deal about that? John had been studying them with a couple of company big wigs when she'd approached. The screens were arranged in pairs: one showing an aerial view of part of a city, the other a computer-generated map covered in black dots that crawled like ants. John spotted her from the corner of his eye and went berserk, shouting in her face to get the hell out. Afterwards, she felt awful being embarrassed in front of his guests. Some thanks for making him tea.

She'd felt apprehensive when the university offered her a work placement at MSL. It was the third year of her sandwich degree, and her mum had told her to get in with a good company because it might lead to a proper job after she graduated. She hadn't even known what MSL had stood for. They'd said it was an acronym for Military Science Laboratory. That sounded really boring, and she went right off the idea when she heard science mentioned–it just wasn't her bag. After all, that was why she'd chosen business studies in the first place.

She'd asked the university for a different placement, but they'd reassured her that the science connection didn't matter. They insisted it was only important she gained experience in the running of a large company: interacting with customers, handling contracts and seeing the factors that determined profit and loss. Her mum piled on the pressure, saying MSL was governmental and would have a great pension and graduate training programme. She was wrong about most stuff but rarely about money and jobs. God, she was annoying. But anything for a quiet life.

Initially, she thought the university had bigged MSL up because they'd run out of placements. Probably just giving her the shitty stick because she never played ball or because the old bag in the office was jealous of her good looks and fashion sense. But who was laughing now? She was the PA to a top boss in a large company. Screw them!

She missed the university social life, but working was a nice change from the usual grind of lectures. Finally, she was earning money to buy the clothes and make-up *she* liked. It was great not having to go begging to her mum, justifying everything. But it wasn't all good news. University was chilled, secure and friendly. Now she had to put up with other grief, like the kick-off in the Ops room. But she didn't give a shit about that anymore–it was John's problem. Soon she would be back at uni with loads of new clothes and spare cash. She'd heard they couldn't even give her a bad reference. Maybe she would work at MSL afterwards, maybe not. It would be *their* loss if she didn't.

The main thing that annoyed her about the job was coming on these goddamn awful early morning meetings, getting up at crazy o'clock, with the footpaths frozen solid and lethal in her killer heels. This morning had been a total nightmare–5 am, and she'd had to get up at 4 am to put her face on. She'd tried to get out of the meeting, challenging John on why he couldn't just have a videoconference. He'd grinned and said he wanted to get her alone out of the office. If she hadn't known him better, she might have felt threatened by such a creepy comment. But John wasn't the type. He was always wrapped up in his work and totally disinterested in sex.

She'd pressed him about why he needed a face-to-face meeting. He'd conceded it was just because videoconferencing wasn't secure. Still trying to get out of the meeting, she asked why he needed her there, given she knew nothing about science. After all, he was a smart guy, and there was no point in bullshitting him. 'That's precisely *why* I take you,' he said. 'I need you to take minutes, so those toads don't lie and change their minds. I don't need you to understand *anything*, and it's probably best if you don't.' Her puzzled expression had probably spoken volumes. 'Don't worry, we've done our background checks,' he clarified. 'If you do talk, we'll just have to kill you.' Clearly, he'd only been joking, but he hadn't winked or anything. He never gave much away.

John had picked her up in the company Land Rover from her mum's house in Salisbury. Annoyingly, they had to drive to MSL's Porton Down site first to collect a secure memory drive that might be needed for a presentation. Afterwards, they made the arduous trek to Filton, a run-down town north of Bristol with suburban slums and derelict factories. The total journey had taken over three hours, even with no traffic. In one place, the snow had drifted across the road for the length of a hockey pitch, forcing them to stop and fit chains.

A cough jolted Lucy from her thoughts.

'Let's get moving,' John said.

Abbey Wood looked grander than she'd imagined as she teetered towards its glass frontage, smart black shoulder bag slapping against her thigh. The gritted path glistened where the snow had been shovelled away, revealing decorative terracotta and grey scallop patterns in the block paving. Orange granules crunched and scratched beneath her stilettos, setting her teeth on edge. At the end of the walkway, a turret-shaped building blocked their path. Coloured lights from the fountains danced on its glass walls. Her eyes followed them and came to rest on a sign with 'Reception' embossed in mauve.

John opened a glass door and beckoned for her to enter. She felt a curtain of warm air reminding her of fashion boutiques, yet a chill ran down her spine. The décor was sparse, with an abundance of chrome and glass, harshened by a black polished-obsidian floor. Overweight middle-aged businessmen, wearing charcoal business suits and smug smiles, hung about for their hosts.

John beckoned for her to enter the first of two Perspex tunnels. Lucy recognised the virus scanner that fronted most receptions now. The second machine looked like one she'd seen in an airport as a small girl. They shuffled through; both lights shone green. A security guard nodded and directed them to a chrome and glass reception desk.

An attractive lady with a platinum bob and a thin flamenco-red smile asked to scan their BioFaces. Seconds later, the background chatter was interrupted by a whining noise as two photo ID cards were spat from a machine. The receptionist stuffed the passes into two plastic pouches that dangled from mauve lanyards. Her eyes swept left and right as she used her BioFace–Lucy guessed she was contacting their host. The woman gazed on auto-pilot, gave a rehearsed smile, and invited them to take a seat in the coffee area.

They made idle chatter as they stood waiting. John asked how her running was going, and she said she was tapering for a park run. Five minutes later, a glass elevator descended to the middle of reception with a man standing in its centre. The lift reminded her of one in a book by Roald Dahl. The doors opened, and he sauntered over to them. She presumed he was their host, Dr Steven Clarke. She studied his fresh-face, purple open-necked shirt, black jeans and loafers. *Straight from university. Thinks he's special ...*

Clarke smiled and shook hands with John.

'This is Lucy,' John said without smiling. 'She runs the operation.'

Clarke appeared puzzled. 'Hi, Lucy,' he said softly.

Lucy shook his hand. His grip felt limp and cold.

'How was the trip?' Clarke asked.

Lucy looked at John.

'Routine,' John replied.

Lucy raised her eyebrows.

Clarke escorted them through two security doors and down a corridor with plain white walls and hardwood flooring. They came to another lift. Unlike the showpiece in reception, this one was stainless steel and functional, like the service lift of a hotel. He pressed the call button, and they waited in silence. The lift whirred as lights climbed the panel. Lucy inspected her nails, hoping someone would make small talk. Nobody did.

The note changed pitch, the doors clunking open as a security light blinked from red to green. They shuffled inside; Clarke pressed the lowest button. Lucy counted five levels before the lift came to a shuddering stop. *God, this place is deep ...*

'After you, Lucy.' Clarke gestured with a limp arm. 'We're in the second meeting room on the right–the one with the nice view.' He grinned, seemingly pleased with his joke.

Lucy walked down the sterile white corridor and heard the faint hum of fans. She felt the walls closing in and wondered whether she would still be able to breathe if the fans stopped turning.

'Here we are,' Clarke said as Lucy approached the second door.

The white wall next to the door had silver-grey scratches. She hated these cold metal coffins. They were standard for meetings with John. He'd told her they were Faraday cages that stopped internal electromagnetic fields. She'd given him her 'whatever stare', and he'd smiled and explained that the metal screened against eavesdropping.

'Please go on in,' Clarke said, his soft voice almost drowned out by the murmur of the fans.

She hesitated, then pressed firmly against the door. Nothing happened. A green light flashed, and she heard a buzz. Suddenly it yielded, and she stumbled into the room.

She recalled seeing a room with a similar layout in a police drama. The end wall was entirely grey smoked glass. *Are we being watched?* Three middle-aged men, slouched in chrome chairs with tatty black upholstery, swivelled and stared: one coughed, one rubbed his face, and the other shook his head. *Charming.*

Embarrassed, she put her shoulder bag on the table and looked down at her feet. She felt uncomfortably hot. Without looking up, she took off her khaki Westminster Heritage trench coat. She liked wearing this striking garment on work trips. Not only was it lovely and warm, but it looked suitably military while also stylish. Underneath, she wore a smart black pencil skirt, cut daringly short above the knee, contrasting sharply against the security of her coat. A cream blouse and a black and white polka-dot silk scarf finished the look. Classy yet fashionable. Her grungy nose stud would keep them guessing.

As she lifted her gaze, she saw eyes pinned on her–their expressions morphed from lecherous stares to jovial smiles. Nervously, she flicked blonde locks from her eyes. John noticed her discomfort.

'Never seen a lady before?' He raised his eyebrows and smirked. One of the men coughed; the other two looked down. Lucy gave John her coat. His smirk turned to a smile as he hung it on a spare wall hook. She noticed his back muscles bulging through his thin white cotton shirt as he removed his coat and jacket and hung them next to hers.

John sat at the table without being asked. Nobody had reacted to his acerbic put-down, but Lucy knew he didn't care. She liked him for that–confident in his skin, just like she was. She sat next to him and checked her BioFace.

John leaned forward. 'This is Lucy–she'll be keeping you honest.' He scrutinised their faces. Nervously, they looked at each other and hurriedly checked their paperwork. She smirked when she realised they were holding blank notepaper for scribbling on. *Already in control.*

Lucy relaxed, adjusted her scarf and pulled her skirt over her stockinged thighs. She looked up–everyone was focused on John. *That's better.*

'Would you like coffee?' Clarke asked.

'Coffee, Lucy?' John said.

'Thanks, John.' She smiled warmly. 'That would be lovely.'

'Yes, please,' John said to Clarke. 'Lucy likes it with milk and no sugar, black with two sugars for me.'

Clarke poured them coffees and then walked over to the head of the table while powering up the wall screen with a remote.

'Thanks for coming,' Clarke said. 'I gather you realise the importance of this meeting?' He studied John's face–he didn't react. Clarke gave a thin smile. 'I'd like you to meet my three esteemed colleagues.' He introduced them one at a time; each nodded as if receiving a peerage. 'My procurement team ensures we have the best defensive and, er … offensive, capabilities.' Lucy watched John scrutinise the men. She felt unnerved by how he could weigh up people from just their subtle body language.

Lucy pulled out an old-fashioned tablet computer from her shoulder bag. She liked to take minutes on it as she found it more tactile and less distancing than her BioFace. Sometimes she struggled to keep up, though, especially with all the scientific jargon. But she knew she could always fall back on a BioFace app that logged the most recent conversation.

'I don't want to drone on at length,' Clarke said. 'We all know why we're here.'

'Good.' John cracked his knuckles.

Lucy looked down and listed the attendees, the location and the date.

Clarke told the room lights to dim. He coughed and scanned everyone's faces like a school teacher at the front of a class. 'Cutting to the chase,' he said, pressing a button on his remote, 'this image summarises where we're at.'

The smoked glass wall lit up, showing a satellite image of the Israeli-Syrian border. He walked over and expanded a region using his fingers. Rows of Russian tanks appeared from a shimmering sea of pixels.

'The Israelis have a problem–*a big problem*. Why do we care, I hear you ask?' He looked at John. John continued to look at the tanks.

Don't bore him.

'If the Israelis have a problem, the Yanks have a problem. If *they* have a problem, then *we* have a problem. Add in the small factor of the world's last remaining oilfield, and you have all the elements for a shit storm–'

'What's your plan?' John interrupted.

'Let's not get ahead of ourselves,' Clarke said.

John scowled. 'Look, Clarke, both you and I know options are limited. It's a massive flashpoint that could trigger a world conflict. Whatever the allies do must be discreet yet overwhelming. The usual contradiction.'

Clarke glared at John. 'OK, OK ... in a nutshell. So, as you're clearly up to speed, *what's the answer?'*

Lucy was shocked to see Clarke lose his temper. Maybe his job was on the line?

John leaned forward. 'Funny how we've been trying to engage with you folks for nearly two years, with no feedback. Then, as soon as a crisis comes along, you're all ears.'

The laser beam from Clarke's pointer flicked erratically about the room, dancing perilously close to Lucy's face.

'Watch that!' John snapped.

Clarke released the button, his hand shaking.

'Well,' John continued, steepling his fingers, 'before I make any recommendations, what do *you* think the answer is?'

Clarke shifted uneasily and looked to his procurement team. A man with a wire wool beard and shiny head glanced at his colleagues. They sat tight-lipped. Lucy suspected they were on a lower pay grade.

'Well, *Jeff?'* Clarke pressed.

'Er ... we've been looking into mind control,' he replied deadpan.

'Mind control!' John scoffed. 'Have you gone mad?' He shook his head. 'I presume you enjoy Sci-Fi?'

Jeff's face reddened.

'The government is *very* interested in it,' defended Clarke. 'Excellent research has come out of top UK Universities. We have enemy intel that they're pursuing it too ...'

'Probably disinformation, and you've all taken the bait,' John mocked. 'Anyway, I'll shut up. Tell me how it works, and *maybe* I'll learn something.'

Clarke hesitated. 'The BioFace is the enabler,' he said in a shrill voice. 'The implant has a holographic opto-writer for this *very* purpose.'

'Isn't that BioFace feature an after-thought?' John questioned. 'Mitigating future obsolescence?'

'Perhaps ...'

'So how does it *actually* work?' John probed.

Clarke rubbed his forehead. 'Neurons in the brain can be genetically modified to make them light-sensitive–it's called optogenetics.'

'What good is that?'

'The holographic writer creates an animated light-field, like the pixels of a monitor but in three dimensions. They're called voxels. The BioFace can change their brightness several hundred times a second–even faster than a TV picture. It can address one hundred trillion of them, each far smaller than a grain of sand. That's a thousand times more voxels than there are neurons in the brain. And they can be updated a thousand times faster. The technology is hardly wishful thinking.'

'Impressive numbers.' John nodded slowly. Lucy suspected John was finally taking Clarke seriously.

'But what good is that?' John quizzed.

'Turning the neurons on and off can modify thoughts, memories, beliefs.'

'I see ...' John nodded. 'Powerful indeed.'

Clarke gave a smug grin.

'But isn't the BioFace's holographic writer disabled?' John countered.

'Yes, but only in firmware. It is easy to activate.'

'But hang on, though.' John shook his head. 'Haven't I read somewhere that the holographic writer uses a green laser? Surely that can't penetrate more than a millimetre or two of brain tissue? Even a near-infrared laser would get absorbed!'

Clarke rubbed his sparsely stumbled chin. 'Yes, you've made a good point. It's an idea ahead of its time.'

John shook his head.

'So what is *your* answer to the crisis then?' Clarke fired back, looking desperate.

John reclined in his chair and closed his eyes.

Back in control ...

Just when Lucy thought John had dropped off, his eyes flew open.

'There's only one good option.' He leaned forward and, in turn, stared into their eyes. Lucy enjoyed watching them squirm.

'Which is?' Clarke asked expectantly.

'A next-generation biological weapon,' John replied.

Clarke sighed. 'You *know* we've already considered biological weapons.' He shook his head. 'They've never been used in warfare because of the risks. You saw what happened with COVID! They're as dangerous to our troops as the enemy's.'

John tutted. 'George Orwell once said, "Life is a race between education and catastrophe."' He stared. 'Isn't it just a case of being better educated?' They glanced nervously at each other.

'It has also been said,' John continued, 'the first world war was won by chemistry, the second by atomic physics, and the third will be decided by biology. With my new weapon, we are about to enter the new era of black biology.'

Clarke gulped. 'I'm intrigued ...'

John smiled at Lucy. 'We've overcome the obvious limitation you've pointed out. We've developed, enemy specific, designer genocide.'

'How on earth have you done that?' Clarke said, looking captivated.

John smiled and didn't reply.

'Genocide weapons have always been ruled out.' Clarke filled the silence. 'They only exist in James Bond re-runs. Nobody has ever identified genetic polymorphisms that uniquely define an enemy. Some of our troops would have similar genes and would inevitably die. Are you saying we should just tolerate blue-on-blue casualties and cover it up with disinformation?'

'That's hardly ethical,' John scoffed.

'So, how have you solved it then?' Clarke asked.

'We have a *far* more sophisticated solution.'

'Can you share it?' Clarke pleaded.

'We have produced a binary biological weapon.'

'When you say "we"–who's that exactly?'

'I'd rather not say.'

Clarke frowned.

'Let's just say MSL is working with a top university,' John conceded.

Clarke seemed satisfied. 'You said binary. Why?'

'The weapon is made from two components that are, in themselves, relatively benign. The first part is an infectious disease, like the ones you're all familiar with: smallpox, anthrax, plague, tularaemia, Marburg, Ebola ... the list is almost endless. Not to mention the new designer gain of function microbes like COVID and monkeypox. Of course, they're relatively ineffective as they can often be inoculated against using a cocktail of vaccines.' He scanned their faces. They looked like a pack of dogs waiting for their leader to bark.

'The second component,' he continued, 'is the designer virulence plasmid, which carries specifically engineered genes. These allow the disease to attack its host while also protecting itself. Vaccination is rendered useless.'

'But surely friendly forces are also vulnerable? Don't we have to inoculate them against the modified virus?'

'Possibly, but that would be hit and miss. Maybe ten per cent would die.'

'What's the solution then?'

'We've engineered a revolutionary plasmid–one that is specific to the enemy's BioFaces.'

Lucy hadn't been following the gist of the discussion, but from the sudden silence in the room, she guessed John's last comment was a bombshell.

'My god,' Clarke exclaimed. 'How the hell have you done

that?'

'Each BioFace has a unique identifier, buried deep within its firmware–rather like the MAC address of networked computer equipment. The plasmid is designed to only attack chosen identifiers. You could call it targeted assassination meets weapons of mass destruction.'

'Christ–you make it sound so simple.'

'It isn't. The biggest problem is getting hold of the identifiers for the entire enemy army. We could hack hospitals and governments, but it could take years to compile an exhaustive database.'

'So, how do you propose we get around that?'

'We do the reverse.'

'*Sorry?*'

'The plasmid checks the identifier, and the virus *only* attacks if it's *not* on the protected list.'

'Ah, I see.'

'So, is this of interest?'

'Er ... absolutely. It sounds intriguing.'

John leaned forward. 'Well, in that case, I need a favour.'

'Um ... what exactly?' Clarke's face flushed.

'I need the identifiers for all military personnel, so we can design a plasmid that protects our forces.'

'Ah, yes ... of course.'

'Can you arrange that?'

'Erm, when do you need it by?'

'Allied troops are amassing on the border as we speak?'

'Er, yes, I see.' Clarke glanced nervously at his colleagues. 'Leave it with me ...' They nodded in agreement.

John continued, 'Anyway, you need time to think about it. Trust me. A biological attack will avoid your shit storm,' John said, making quote signs with his fingers. 'The virus can be short-acting, so friendly forces are not denied access to a region. No damage to infrastructure, like the catastrophe in Ukraine, and the Israelis get a solution to their Iranian problem.'

Everyone fell silent as the realisation sank in. Lucy hadn't followed the details, but from their body language, she could see it was a fait accompli. Unpalatable as it was, it was by far the best solution. The meeting degenerated into a discussion of delivery schedules. Lucy tapped feverishly on her tablet, meticulously recording the details.

Time flew by, and soon they were handing their passes back in at reception, accompanied by Clarke. They shook his hand again.

'Thanks, John,' Clarke said as if he was a life-long friend. Lucy saw the feelings weren't mutual. 'Between you and me,' he continued, 'the MOD were looking pretty lame when the Yanks pressed us on how we could help. This new capability is a game-changer. Now, *we'll* be calling the shots. We just need you to fast-track the solution.' Clarke beamed.

'OK.' John's eyes burned into Clarke's. 'Well, the ball's in *your* court now. We *need* the database.'

'I'm on it.' Clarke nodded.

John made the briefest eye contact with Clarke, turned and walked out of reception, Lucy trailing behind

'You OK?' John asked Lucy. 'You were quiet in there.'

'I'm fine, thanks–there wasn't really much for me to say.'

'Did you get the notes?'

'All good,' she replied.

'Well done. That's precisely why I take you on these trips.'

As John patted her on the shoulder, she heard his BioFace buzz from an incoming call.

'Sorry. Just need to get this.'

'No problem.'

He walked down the path and singled out one of the fountains, standing so close his trousers were getting lightly sprayed. His face was a mask of concentration–he hadn't even noticed he was getting wet or that Lucy had sidled up to listen.

His lips moved silently. She moved in closer, straining to hear, scared he would notice and have one of his turns. Standing rock still, she concentrated. The words sounded incoherent, muddied by the splitter splatter of the fountain. She gave up and moved away, not wanting to risk a scene.

He finished talking and glanced over. 'OK, let's make tracks.' He turned and strode towards the near-empty car park. Lucy hung back, scared of slipping on the ice in her heels. And then it dawned on her. *The BioFace Dictation App!* Quickly, she brought up the menu in her vision and saved the recent conversation before it was over-written. She browsed for the file, one eye on the path and the other on her BioFace display.

It's still there …

Most of the conversation was junk, corrupted by the noise of the fountain, but a fragment was intact. She looked at the words–they were written phonetically and appeared incomprehensible. *Foreign?* She highlighted the text and selected the auto-translate tool. The app came back with the detected language: Farsi. She blinked on a message icon, and text popped up. The translation said: 'You'll have your addresses soon.'

5

'**A**re you OK?'

Arlo felt a hand pat his shoulder. 'All good, thanks,' he mumbled.

Arlo was sitting bolt upright, eyes squeezed shut, hands gripping the chair's armrests as his head spun. Taking a deep breath, he counted to three and slowly exhaled. His vertigo subsided, and he opened his eyes. Bristol University's packed Powell lecture theatre swam into focus. He knew it well, having studied electrical engineering at the university, but now it felt completely alien.

Where's the exit?

He twisted around. Green LED signs lit the way out; the aisles were clear.

Carl, his flatmate from their undergraduate days, sat next to him in the second row of the auditorium. He used to be a computer genius and wizard with electronic music and playing keyboards–a techy nerd, yet artsy and cool with it. But that had all changed when his health failed. They'd kept in contact when he'd gone to Seattle, and Carl had been a lifesaver when he'd returned a broken man. Carl had insisted he was repaying the favour from his sofa-surfing days early in his music career.

Professor Brian Stanford prowled the stage like a thespian actor, arms gesticulating flamboyantly. But the subject was dry, the delivery self-serving. He droned on about nanoparticle-delivered genetic engineering, claiming it was the best solution for curbing the waves of viral pandemics that had decimated the world's population since the Great Eruption.

Arlo tried to concentrate on the eminent biologist's findings, but his mind kept drifting. Sights, sounds, and smells of Seattle. Jarring. Scrambling time and place. The signal, the eruption, Stella, Isabella ... *Stay calm. Do it for dad. Stay calm. Do it for dad.*

Desperate for a distraction, he double-blinked to activate his BioFace. Navigating the icons with his eyes, he blinked on a small picture of his mother's smiling face, and a pie chart of her health statistics popped up. *Sugar levels elevated again; bloody nursing home.* His head began to pound. *Need fresh air.*

He selected and edited a standard message. 'Hi, mum. I hope you're feeling OK. I'm looking forward to seeing you soon. I'm about to present. Hopefully, I'll do dad proud. Arlo X.' He double-blinked; an envelope took flight.

Arlo glanced to the side of the stage. A large timer was counting down; five minutes remaining. His stomach lurched, his pulse raced, and he felt nauseous. He bowed his head, rubbed his temples, and tried to slow his breathing. *Stay calm. Do it for dad.*

'And that concludes my presentation,' Stanford announced, strutting like a peacock. 'The results show how gene therapy can embed viral signatures in human DNA to provide immunity against all known variants of the coronavirus.' Stanford paused and scanned the audience as if looking for admirers. 'Any questions?' A casually dressed young lady raised her hand and stood up. She was wearing a short-sleeved blouse, and the BioFace in her arm glowed green briefly as it connected to the PA system.

She asked what sounded like a prepared question about the genes involved. Stanford licked his lips and thanked her. He gave a polished answer and asked if she wanted to know anything else. Smiling sweetly, she shook her head and sat down. The audience murmured.

'Any further questions?'

Another hand shot up from the third row. Arlo twisted round. An attractive woman in her early thirties was sitting immediately behind him, her hair a lovely honey colour. The auditorium's speakers clicked as the PA connected.

'Lana Grace from BDL, that's BioFace Devices Limited. Hi.'

'Hi, Lana. You've done well for yourself,' Stanford muttered, scratching the back of his neck. 'What's your question, please?'

'Other researchers in Europe and China have tried this approach, but many trials have failed. Some patients have suffered debilitating side effects, such as arthritis, from autoimmune responses. Can you please comment on how your research overcomes this problem?'

Momentarily, Arlo forgot about his own talk. *Wow, she's smart.*

Stanford smiled as he held her gaze. 'Thank you for the excellent question, Lana.' His tongue flicked out as if to catch a passing fly and moistened his cracked lips. 'Well, as I'm sure you're aware, from working for such a distinguished company, the devil's in the detail.'

'How do you mean?' she asked.

'Well, our team of expert bio-coders ensure the genes get edited properly.' He smiled smugly and rubbed his hands together. 'Thank you for your question, Lana. Nice to catch up ... Anyone else?'

'B-' Lana's voice trailed off as her arm glowed red briefly, her BioFace disconnecting from the network. Despite the dim light, Arlo was sure he saw her face flush. He twisted back around, eyes darting to the timer. Forty-five seconds left. *Shit, I'm on.* His face felt puffy, his mouth dry, and a pain stabbed behind his eyes.

The PA system gave a hollow thump as the chairman switched the network over. Arlo jumped in his seat and glared. He checked the exits. *Stay calm. Do it for dad.*

'Well, if there are no more questions, please show your appreciation in the usual manner for Professor Stanford's excellent presentation.' The audience gave restrained applause as Stanford left the stage beaming.

'I would now like to invite Dr Jones to the stage. Dr Jones is a Post-Doctoral researcher in Space Swarm UK. Previously, he worked at Space Swarm, Incorporated, in the USA, where he pioneered algorithms for coordinating swarms of nanosatellites. He has received several prizes for his research and is the author of more than one hundred papers and patents. Please show your appreciation.'

The audience clapped as Arlo rose to his feet. His legs quivered and nearly buckled. Carl nudged his arm. 'They'll love you, mate,' he mumbled. 'You'll be fine.'

Arlo squeezed Carl's shoulder and mustered a weak smile. Carl's shoulder shook briefly and then settled. 'Thanks, dude,' Arlo whispered, 'I wish I had your confidence.'

Carl looked up. 'Remember, any problems, use the mantra: look at me and count to three.'

'I'll try,' Arlo said. He turned and shuffled along the row, apologising to several people as they pulled their legs in so he could squeeze past. On reaching the aisle, he scanned the front of the stage and spotted the steps. His legs trembled as he forced himself to walk toward them. *Stay calm. Do it for dad.*

The old wooden stairs creaked as Arlo gingerly climbed. The stage felt scarily high as he shuffled towards the podium, resisting the temptation to look down at the heaving mass of faces. His head began to spin.

The chairman switched the network over to Arlo as he approached. He tapped on a console, selected Arlo's presentation, and handed him a laser pointer.

'It's all yours, Arlo,' he whispered, patting his shoulder.

'Thanks,' Arlo replied.

The PA squealed feedback. Arlo recoiled and dropped the laser pointer. 'Sh-Shit, s-sorry,' he mumbled as he stooped to pick it up. 'S-S-Sorry,' reverberated around the auditorium. Arlo flinched, and the audience laughed nervously. He straightened and forced himself to look up, spotting Carl. Carl nodded supportively.

One, two, three …

The chairman adjusted the volume on the console. 'All this modern technology,' he sighed as he retreated to his seat.

Arlo gazed at the sea of faces that looked up expectantly. A mixture of students, academics, engineers and scientists, some of whom he recognised. *Sceptics and critics.* He took a deep breath.

'Err, th-thank you, chairman, for your kind introduction. H-Hi, everyone. Thanks for coming to my talk.' He squinted into the glare of the stage lights, the audience deathly quiet. 'I want to, er … share with you the vision that satellite companies have about swarm networks. I'll, er … then finish with a brief mention of a personal project I've been working on over the past few years. Hopefully, you'll find some of it interesting.'

Arlo felt himself relax as he presented the technology he loved. He enthused for fifteen minutes, explaining how vast clouds of nanosatellites, launched cheaply off the back of passenger planes, decommissioned under the Kyoto Protocol for reducing carbon emissions, could work collaboratively to provide ubiquitous communication and environmental monitoring.

He paused, looked up and smiled. 'I now want to talk briefly about a personal project that's especially dear to me. It also uses a swarm network. Don't laugh, but it's in the hope of detecting signals from little green men or women–assuming they have a gender that is …' The audience laughed. 'There you go–I said you'd laugh.' He mustered a nervous smile. 'Anyway, I've been working on the project with my friend and genius, Carl Diamond. Sadly, we've not made much progress. Maybe you can help?' Arlo scanned the audience for Carl. Their eyes met, and Carl shook his head. Arlo grinned.

'I was monitoring the exoplanet Turnbull for infrared emissions when I detected a weird signal that I've been trying to understand. It was almost undetectably weak, but its entropy, a measure of its information content, suggests it's not just random noise. It has a complex space-time coded structure interleaved across many channels. But, fundamentally, it's a bit like Morse code, but with two extra symbols. So not just dots and dashes but, let's say, stars and commas as well. Interestingly, these four symbols appear with different regularity. That's also a bit like Morse code. But, we've failed to get anything else meaningful from it.

'Maybe I'm just kidding myself. After all, astronomers thought they'd discovered aliens before when they detected pulsars and Lorimer bursts–both were found to be due to natural cosmic events. They even called the first pulsar LGM-1, short for Little Green Men One. My signal is probably a similar anomaly. Anyway, I thought I'd share its properties with you.'

Arlo put up some plots that showed signal statistics. 'Well, I'm afraid I don't have any other conclusions, as there aren't any. It's proper blue sky research as that's where it came from!' The audience laughed. 'Anyway, to conclude my presentation, this final slide summarises the benefits of satellite swarms.' He looked up. 'Thanks for listening, even if it did include a cranky application. At least it shows any budding engineers amongst you that we don't always work on mundane projects! Any questions?'

The chairman stood up and tapped wildly at the console to raise the lights. He fumbled with the touchscreen, and nothing happened. He shook his head. 'Have to make do with dimmed lights,' he muttered over the PA. 'To keep on schedule, we only have time for a couple of questions. I am sure Dr Jones will be available afterwards to answer any others in the coffee area.' The chairman looked to him for confirmation–Arlo nodded enthusiastically. 'OK. Questions?'

A hand shot up at the front.

'Can you please stand and identify yourself–others might want to continue the discussion during coffee.'

A woman stood up; she moved into the aisle at the base of a second set of steps leading to the stage. Facing the audience, she gave her name, which Arlo missed.

'Thank you, madam,' the chairman said. 'Please fire away with your question.'

Arlo squinted down the steps in the dim light. A spotlight from the overhead gantry picked her out in vivid technicolour from the surrounding blackness. She was wearing a burgundy dress. She turned. She had long, straight black hair. Her face morphed into Stella's. The PA rumbled and thumped as her BioFace connected. Arlo felt the auditorium shake and saw fireballs arc overhead. The laser pen clattered to the stage as he charged down the steps two at a time.

6

Lana flicked her wavy hair out of her eyes and strutted towards the conference reception area like a model on a catwalk. An integrated virus scanner and security system blocked her path. The machine was required by law for public events and analysed body odour for infections and explosives.

As delegates funnelled into the mouth of the Perspex tunnel, she found herself on a collision course with a cardigan-wearing academic. His steps faltered, and he beckoned for her to go first. Slender fingers, with cherry nails, smoothed her figure-hugging, knee-length navy-blue skirt. The man lurched as he tripped over his own feet.

Lana had found the presentations fascinating. She thought they might even help her career, but she was still smarting from being cut off by Stanford. He was so disgusting. She'd made a mental note to speak to Dr Jones. He was a recognised expert in satellite swarms, a technology crucial to BDL as it guaranteed rock-solid BioFace networking. Despite his credentials, he looked wild and kind of cute. It was bizarre how he'd stormed off at the end of his presentation–it had created quite a stir. She loved trying to understand paradoxical characters, especially when they did crazy things like that.

The queue dwindled, and she shuffled into the scanner. She knew they were a necessary evil, but she still resented having brakes put on her life. The machine made a whirring, sucking noise and a green light flashed; her nose wrinkled. Nodding self-assuredly, she lifted her chin and marched into the reception area, noticing heads turning.

The room bustled like a tube station at rush hour. Catering staff threaded between groups of delegates, collecting cups and apologising as arms collided. Middle-aged men in designer suits chatted to casually dressed students. *Who's exploiting who?*

The aroma of freshly brewed coffee wafted over. Teetering on her three-inch navy-blue heels, she peered over the crowd. Two waiters were stood to attention behind a row of trestle tables, one holding a large flask. The sea of delegates parted as she made a beeline for the queue.

A commotion broke out as she scanned the trays of biscuits for the shortbreads she liked. She craned her swan-like neck and saw Professor Stanford emerge from a side entrance. *Lizard.* Students hovered around him like remora fish cosying up to a shark. A man trailed behind, wearing a red lanyard instead of the usual blue, an expensive-looking camera slung over his shoulder.

Lana examined her nails and shivered in disgust. She recalled working late in the laboratory during the final year of her combined biology and psychology degree. The microscope slide of skin cells had taken all her concentration to stain. She jumped a mile when he cornered her from behind and placed a clammy hand on her bare shoulder. She would never forget his fishy breath, the feeling of dread, and the tightness in her chest as he pressed up hard against her.

He'd made her pay for the glassware that smashed when she'd recoiled in horror. She realised now how monstrous that was–given that he'd practically assaulted her–but she'd been worried he might destroy her career. Ironically, by making her revulsion clear, she'd kissed goodbye to her first-class honours.

'Coffee, madam?'

Lana jumped. The youth, smartly dressed in black trousers and a crisp white shirt, cradled a shiny-black plastic and chrome flask.

'Decaf tea, please.' She scoured the trestle table.

'Coming up.' He leaned across and plucked a teabag from a wooden box of speciality tea. He popped it into a white porcelain teacup balanced on a saucer and poured in hot water.

Lana tucked her bag under her arm, took the cup and thanked him. She walked away and scanned the room, looking for a free table to quietly go through her notes. At the far end, she spotted an alcove, accessed through an archway, with tables and chairs laid out. It looked perfect. Halfway there, the delegates' chatter died down. Lana spun around to see why.

A large window that ordinarily gave a view over Bristol had turned opaque. A television picture from an aerial drone flashed up, a newsflash banner scrolling along the bottom with the caption: 'Avital Mountain Reserve.' *Where's that?* The hillside bristled with antennas. *Signal surveillance?* The infrastructure of a vast oilfield cluttered a plateau, and a large sea sparkled in a distant valley. Lana guessed from recent news reports that it was the new Golan Heights oilfield. A camera on the drone panned, lingering on a military installation dug in on top of a mountain.

A news reporter gave a voice-over commentary: 'Ahiram Frisch reporting from Network Tel Aviv. Below the dormant volcano of Mount Bental, you can see the Valley of Tears, where our heroic brothers engaged in hand-to-hand combat to repel the Arab invaders during the Yom Kippur war of 1973.'

The drone panned again, zooming in on a lush grassy plain several miles from the mountain. A graphic overlay picked out the Israeli border with a dotted line, showing that the land lay within Syrian territory, a huge fan of tanks and other military paraphernalia facing Israel.

'Now you can see the emergence of a new threat. Once more, the Muslim caliphate is regrouping to attack the State of Israel. The terrorist organisation, Oil for the Islamic States, OFIS, who are proxy agents for the Russian and Iranian regimes, backs the offensive.'

A bright flash came from one of the vehicles; a smoke trail and yellow-white light snaked erratically across the vista. The news reporter fell silent; the conference delegates watched spellbound. Within seconds the dancing light had filled the picture. In a sea of static, the drone feed died.

'Oy vey! The drone has been shot down.' The reporter fell silent again.

Lana wondered whether the reporter's audio link had failed but then heard him clear his throat.

'That unprovoked attack,' Frisch continued solemnly, 'shows the world the continuing acts of aggression against the State of Israel. I'm Ahiram Frisch, now back to the studio.'

The view switched to a BBC reporter in a virtual studio.

'That footage was recorded this morning and provided courtesy of the Israeli Broadcasting Authority. The shooting down of an Israeli drone is yet another event in the escalating tension on the Israeli-Syrian border, triggered since drilling began on the Golan Heights. The oilfield is estimated to contain over one billion barrels of crude. The Syrians claim the territory is theirs, annexed during the Yom Kippur war. The Israeli government has appealed to the United Nations for a peacekeeping force to mitigate further escalation of the crisis.'

The newsflash ended, cutting to a feature on rioting inside London ghettos. The television picture faded out, restoring the view over Bristol. Lana tutted and strode into the alcove.

Two men sat hunched over a table, one face hidden by a straggly veil of wild hair. Dr Jones. She recalled the strange scene at the end of his presentation when he'd bolted out of the auditorium. His talk had been amazing up until then. True, the part on an alien signal had been weird, but bolting off mid-question had been batshit crazy. Having read about scientists like Tesla, Newton and Darwin, she knew there was often a fine line between madness and genius. She found the subject fascinating.

Lana stiffened as she approached them. She had no idea what to say and could hardly ask Dr Jones about satellite swarms without asking him how he was. But maybe he would be offended or embarrassed? As she neared the men, she overheard Dr Jones say something.

'I don't know, Carl … One minute I was taking a question, the next I was back in Seattle. Then I found myself in the foyer.'

Seattle? Great Eruption?

Carl looked up as she approached. 'Can I help?'

Lana reddened. 'Er, I hope I'm not interrupting anything?' She flicked hair from her eyes. 'I, um, saw Dr Jones's presentation. It was very enlightening. Is he OK?'

Arlo's face had a light sheen. Lana thought he looked even wilder than before. Embarrassed, confused, lost?

'I can come back later?' Lana said nervously. 'It can wait.'

'Er, n-no,' Arlo replied. 'I'd love to talk.'

The two men stood. Arlo was wearing pale-blue distressed jeans. Lana was shocked at how casual he looked for a conference. But, somehow, he'd pulled it off by wearing a stylish open-necked cream shirt and navy blazer. She liked the colour navy. It was formal but not as stuffy as grey or black. His NASA cufflinks sparkled; his teeth glowed white, set off by his lightly tanned face. His eyes were the colour of blue curacao. They triggered memories of a life she still yearned for: cocktails by the pool; walking in Caribbean shallows, with the sea as turquoise as in the brochures. He swept his mop of wavy brown hair away from his face. He looked more like an ageing rock star than an academic: fun but troubled, handsome yet neglected.

She did not recognise the other man. He looked nondescript, with averagely proportioned features and an ashen face framed by thinning grey hair. There seemed to be something wrong with him, but she didn't know what. He looked hunched, and his face seemed mask-like as if made of stone. But–despite his frozen face–his startling pale-blue eyes darted as if making up for his paralysis.

Dr Jones grinned and offered her his hand. 'Arlo's the name.'

'Lana. Lana Grace,' she replied. His grip felt firm, warm and secure.

'Yeah, of course.' He grinned. 'How could I ever forget your name after that superb put-down of Stanford!'

Lana looked to the ceiling and rolled her hazel eyes. 'But not as impressive as your stage dive,' Lana blurted, instantly regretting it.

Arlo looked down.

'Sorry,' Lana mumbled, lightly touching his arm.

Arlo warmed. 'It's OK ...' He rubbed his brow. 'This is my good friend, Carl.' He put his arm around Carl's shoulder and squeezed it so firm it cracked a grimace on his frozen face. 'We go back a long way, don't we, Carl?'

Carl's eyes darted like a wary bird's. 'Yep.' He nodded jerkily. 'And don't I know it.' He tried to wink, but it ended up looking more like a facial tic. He offered Lana his hand. She tried to grasp it, but his thumb and index finger were locked together as if making a shadow puppet. Arlo noticed her unease and exchanged glances with Carl. Carl blinked and nodded slightly.

'Sorry. I should explain ...' Arlo said awkwardly. 'Carl has Parkinson's disease. He doesn't like talking about it much.' Arlo gripped Carl's shoulder again. 'He copes just fine. And he's an absolute genius, especially with maths and computing.'

Carl straightened up a bit. His eyes animated as he wrestled with his body. The effort was palpable.

'Pleased to meet you, Lana,' Carl said as he finally managed to grasp and shake her hand. 'Arlo's too kind. If I was that good, I'd have been able to read the text message from those aliens, wouldn't I?' Lana laughed and patted him on the arm. He shuddered.

'You seem to be doing wonderfully, all things considered,' Lana added, trying not to sound patronising.

Carl looked down. 'I'm not sure about that,' he muttered.

'You're great,' Lana said, 'you don't have a tremor–I can barely tell anything's wrong.'

Arlo rubbed his head and looked at Carl. He seemed to be embarrassed for his friend.

'It's OK, Arlo,' Carl said. He glanced at Lana. 'I, er, have a DBS fitted.'

'DBS?'

'Deep Brain Stimulator.' He tapped his head. 'A probe inside my brain. It stops the shakes.'

'Oh, really–that's amazing!' Lana's eyes lit up. 'Sorry to probe.'

Carl looked at Arlo. Lana looked at Arlo.

'Oh shit,' she said.

They all burst out laughing.

'Glad we got that one out of the way.' Arlo grinned. 'Anyway, how can I help?'

'I just wanted to congratulate you on your presentation. All very interesting and relevant to BDL.' Lana smiled.

'Well, thank you,' Arlo replied.

Lana pulled out a business card from a side pocket of her immaculately tailored and spotless navy jacket and handed it to Arlo. Arlo fished out his own card, and they swapped. Carl did not volunteer his.

Arlo inspected the card. 'BCI Psychologist, BDL,' he read aloud. 'That sounds very grand.'

'Oh, it's not.' Lana flicked hair from her eyes.

'What does BCI stand for?' Arlo asked.

'Brain-Computer Interfacing. BCI psychology is a relatively new discipline that combines brain interfacing with psychology. Basically, it involves interfacing the BioFace to the body, especially the brain.'

'Ah, I see.' Arlo rubbed his beard, still looking perplexed.

Lana smiled sweetly. 'Any chance you can send me some of your research papers on satellite swarms?' she pressed. 'I'm sure my colleagues would be very interested in–'

Carl coughed. 'May I ask why BDL is interested in satellite swarms?' Carl's face gave nothing away.

Lana glared. 'We need to make sure BioFaces never drop off the network.' She smoothed her jacket and inflated her chest. 'Satellite swarms can guarantee that.'

'Of course,' Carl replied impassively.

'Anyway,' Lana continued, worried she'd lost their

confidence, 'tell me about those little green men, Arlo.' She squeezed his arm lightly and wrinkled her nose.

Arlo laughed and gazed into her eyes. 'I'm flattered you're interested in that.'

She held Arlo's gaze until Carl shuffled uncomfortably. 'It sounds amazing.'

Arlo's face lit up. 'Really?'

'*Really*,' she replied. 'How did you analyse a completely unknown signal?'

'Er, well, actually, a lot of it was down to Carl,' Arlo said, turning to his friend.

Lana looked curiously at Carl. She couldn't read him at all. 'What did you do, Carl?' she asked with a smile.

'Oh, just the usual boring stuff,' Carl replied dismissively.

Defensive? Embarrassed?

'Such as?' Lana quizzed.

Carl seemed to welcome the invitation. 'At first, I seemed to be getting somewhere.' He gazed up to his right, lost in thought. 'I managed to recover what looked like a clock signal and locked onto its frequency. I then applied every known demodulation method and ran linguistic AI algorithms to try and identify the statistical pattern of language. I even ran massive maximum likelihood estimation simulations on the university's quantum computer.'

Lana considered herself technically strong, but Carl seemed to be in a different league. 'Wow, that's amazing!'

'No, it's not,' Carl countered. 'Nothing worked. As Arlo said in his talk, the signal's entropy and recovery of a clock suggest information is present but damned if we could decipher it. Not even a fragment or any indication of underlying grammar.'

'Well, maybe it's not a message then?'

Carl fell silent, standing rigid.

'What might it be then?' Arlo asked, his curiosity piqued.

'Perhaps it's an image?' Lana shrugged her shoulders. 'Could be alien TV!'

Carl looked to Arlo and laughed. 'Alien Open University

would be a good watch.'

Arlo didn't laugh–he looked deadly serious. 'Lana might be onto something, you know.'

'Er, I guess,' Carl said. 'I could take a look?'

'If you don't mind,' Arlo said.

With the ice broken, Lana saw her opportunity. 'If you don't mind me asking,' she said solemnly, 'why *did* you rush out of your presentation?'

Arlo kneaded his hands. 'Had to dash off. Probably last night's curry.'

What's he hiding? She recalled the conversation she'd overheard when walking in on them but felt she couldn't ask.

'Maybe you should get a drink of water then?' she suggested. 'Stay hydrated.'

'Great idea,' Arlo replied, looking relieved. 'You OK with that, Carl?'

'Sounds good to me.'

They strolled out of the alcove. Arlo chatted to Lana about how master satellites govern swarms. As they neared the bar area, a tall, athletic man with an olive complexion appeared over Arlo's shoulder. Lana vaguely recognised him from a high-level video call she'd attended with a government department. A smartly dressed but punky girl with a nose stud and a small star-shaped scar on her forehead trailed behind. She looked young enough to be his daughter. *What's going on there?*

The man approached Arlo and stuck out his hand. She noticed a small bluish mark near the crook of his right thumb. She moved a little closer. It looked like a tattoo of three characters, maybe three G's. *Child's initials?*

'Dr Jones, isn't it?' Unblinking, he stared at Arlo.

'Er, yep, that's me.' Arlo looked startled.

'Great talk. Those swarm networks are the future.'

'Oh, er, thank you, sir. And you are?'

'John. Just call me John. Card?'

Arlo paused for a second, and then the penny dropped.

Flustered, his hand delved into the breast pocket of his blazer and pulled out a black business card with Space Swarm UK printed in silver by a swarm of satellites.

'Do you want Carl's card as well?' Arlo asked. 'He's a computer genius.' He handed John his card. John nodded a platitude.

Carl appeared reluctant but passed John a card anyway. John gave the cards to the girl without inspecting them. She stowed them in her clutch bag.

'Do you have a card?' Arlo asked.

'Don't bother with cards,' John replied. 'Line of work I'm in ... if you know what I mean.' He tapped his nose; Arlo looked confused. John's brow furrowed.

'Lucy, give him your details, please.'

Lucy fished a card out from the side pouch of her clutch bag and handed it to Arlo.

John leaned over to Arlo. 'Please keep Lucy's information confidential,' he said just loudly enough for Lana to hear. 'I don't normally give out even *her* details, but your work is *particularly* interesting.'

Lana looked Lucy up and down. Her black suit was classy, even if her skirt showed off too much leg for a conference. Lana's eyes were drawn to a pendant dangling around her sinewy neck. The design was very feminine, with delicate gold flowers entwining three initials. It seemed incongruous with her punky demeanour. The letters SAC were vaguely familiar, and then she remembered. They stood for Salisbury Athletics Club. Lana enjoyed running and had taken it seriously enough to compete in a few races. Ladies from SAC were nearly always in the top three.

'Are you a member of Salisbury Athletics Club?' Lana asked Lucy, hoping it would break the ice.

'Yes!' Lucy's face warmed. 'Do you run?'

'Oh ... only a bit,' Lana replied. 'Nothing as serious as you girls!'

'Well, you look very athletic,' she said.

'Well, thank you.' Lana blushed.

'You should–' Lucy began.

'Anyway, ladies,' John interrupted. 'We need to make tracks.'

Lucy looked riled and grabbed Lana's arm. 'Dr Jones has my card–message me.'

Lana nodded. John glared.

Arlo shifted uncomfortably. 'Anything specific you'd like to know before you go?'

'I'll be in touch,' John replied dismissively. 'That signal you detected in Seattle sounds interesting. Please excuse us.'

John then nodded his head, turned, and vanished into the crowd, Lucy trailing.

Arlo's eyes narrowed.

'What the hell was all that about?' Carl asked.

'Haven't a clue,' Arlo replied. 'Here's Lucy's card–there were two stuck together.' Carl pocketed the card.

'Do you want Lucy's details, Lana?' Arlo asked.

Lana nodded. 'Yes, please.'

Arlo held out the card so she could take a picture using her smart contact lenses. She saved the image to her BioDrive.

'Do you know who John is?' Arlo asked Lana once her eyes had stopped navigating BioFace menus.

'I think he's a technical advisor in government. High up. I've seen him in a video call.'

'Ah, OK. Maybe he'll get in touch,' Arlo said.

'Well, he seemed very interested.'

Arlo continued discussing satellite technology with Lana while they sipped their drinks. Carl stood listening like a statue. Arlo suddenly seemed distracted and checked his BioFace.

'I'm afraid I have to make tracks,' he said, sounding disappointed. 'Lovely to meet you, Lana.'

'Likewise,' she said. 'If I ever need a satellite techy, you'll be the first person I call.'

'I have other skills as well, you know.' Arlo grinned.

Lana tilted her head. 'I'm sure you do.' She flashed her

perfect teeth.

Arlo flicked hair from his eyes and gave a sheepish grin. He turned to Carl. 'I guess I'll call you later.'

Carl nodded. 'Laters, AJ.'

Arlo shouldered his rucksack and snaked off through the crowd. Lana tracked him to the exit. She glimpsed Carl studying her from the corner of her eye. She wondered if he'd also noticed that John knew where Arlo had detected his signal, even though he'd never ever mentioned it.

7

WEDNESDAY, 11 SEPTEMBER 2052

L ana wondered whether this was her time.

'Ahem ... Quiet, please,' Jeremy Dreyfuss ordered as he scanned the faces in BDL's boardroom. He was in his early sixties and looked like Sam Eagle from the Muppets with his bald pate, silver tufty hair on the sides, beaked nose, beady eyes and bushy black eyebrows. With hunched shoulders and well over six feet tall, it seemed as if he was always looking down on people, deciding whether to have a peck.

Dreyfuss glanced at the wall clock that showed 9:22 am and made hand lowering gestures. The murmurs died down. 'All team leaders are here–can we make a quick start.' A bespectacled senior engineer bit his nails and picked at the quicks, flicking bits of dead skin away. An ostentatiously dressed project leader sat with her eyes roaming. The engineer saw her and frowned. Lana suspected she was up to online shopping again.

'Apologies for such short notice,' Dreyfuss continued. 'I have had an urgent request from His Majesty's Government to sit in on an important meeting at 9:30 am. I need your support.' He scanned all of their faces again. The engineer did not react. The project manager smiled sweetly as her eyes stopped roaming. Some made brief eye contact, while others looked down subserviently. Lana held his gaze and nodded. Dreyfuss mustered a half-smile. He paused, cleared his throat, and his face hardened.

'If you watched the news this morning,' he said, 'you'll have seen that a new virus, COVID-52, has been detected in the

London ghettos. Vaccines and antivirals probably won't work on this one. The main symptom is a severe headache, but its virulence is unknown.' Several of the staff nodded grimly, while others studied the walls.

'Government lockdowns will not work in the ghettos, and the virus will probably spread into the normal population.' The project manager looked annoyed by Dreyfuss's inference, shook her head, and inspected the fancy artwork on her nails.

'It is an appalling situation,' Dreyfuss continued. 'The government is desperate and hopes the BioFace is a solution. This crisis is *our* opportunity. Great for the country, great for *our* product. The meeting begins in ten minutes. Any questions?'

Lana trembled with excitement. She realised this *was* her chance. A fork in the road. An opportunity to shine. She raised a hand.

'Yes, Lana,' Dreyfuss prompted.

'Do you know why the government thinks the BioFace might help?'

'Good question Lana.' He tipped his head. 'The BioFace is the government's only means for providing remote healthcare. Historically, the BioFace has been diagnostic, but I suspect they want to use it actively–to effect a cure. This capability has always been on our roadmap too.'

'Understood.' Lana nodded. 'Sounds like a great opportunity.'

'Indeed it is,' Dreyfuss replied. 'Right, any more questions before we start?'

No hands showed.

'OK then, I'll get them on the line.'

Dreyfuss tapped an icon on his console and entered a long encryption code. Seconds later, the Cabinet Office Briefing Room, known as COBRA, appeared on the large screen at the far end of the boardroom.

Lana was fascinated by the view into the heart of government. The room was long and narrow, with no windows, golden-brown teak-panelled walls swallowing most of the illumination from concealed lights. Fifteen to twenty stuffy-looking officials sat crammed around a polished oak table that filled the room. It looked as if they were in danger of suffocating. Most were male, overweight, and middle-aged. Lana thought they looked like ageing clones, or perhaps clowns given their comb-overs, thick-framed black spectacles, comic moustaches and public school ties.

A mountain of a man stood up at the far end of the table: Edward Gordon, the Prime Minister. He paused and waited until all eyes were focused intently upon him.

'Thank you all for attending this crisis meeting at such an important hour,' he intoned, with the pomp of Churchill or Johnson. 'This meeting will cover several urgent topics: virology, elderly healthcare, climate change, socio-economic challenges, and foreign policy. I am joined by several of my Right Honourable colleagues: Alan Smythe, the Secretary of State for Foreign Affairs; Bhavna Acharya, the Parliamentary Under-Secretary of State for Science, Research and Innovation; and Ian Clifford, the Minister of State for the Middle East & North Africa. They stood briefly and nodded in turn as he introduced them. Also present are representatives of the Scientific Advisory Group for Emergencies, SAGE.

'On video links, we have six subject matter expert groups attending: the Met Office; the London School of Economics; Bristol University virology group; BioFace Devices Limited, or BDL; and the Military Science Laboratory, known as MSL.

'Firstly, I will summarise how our current crisis has unfolded. Most of this will be familiar to you, but I think it is important we are all on the same page.'

He looked up. Everyone was staring back in silence.

'Very well then.' He rubbed his voluminous hands together.

'We live in unprecedented times,' he continued soberly. 'Over the past three years, the Earth has suffered several cataclysmic events. Times were already tough–but nothing could have prepared us for this. Governments have only paid lip service to decades of steadily worsening global warming. A tipping point was reached five years ago, which led to a self-reinforced thermal runaway. Millions migrated as vast areas of the Earth were rendered uninhabitable by fires and extreme temperatures. Many low-lying cities were destroyed by sea-level rises: New Orleans, Jakarta, Bangkok, Lagos, Manila, Dhaka and Shanghai, to name but a few.

'Governments responded in the only way they knew how, by throwing energy at the problem. The chemical industry generated enormous quantities of soda lime, so-called artificial trees, to scrub carbon dioxide from the atmosphere. But, the energy used to manufacture the chemicals also produced greenhouse gases–these too needed to be scrubbed. Perhaps nuclear power could have saved us, but the Flamanville meltdown in France led to mounting public pressure and the shutting down of most nuclear power stations. This vicious cycle exhausted most fossil fuel reserves, triggering the energy crisis. And then the natural disasters began ...

'In 2049, Mount Rainier erupted explosively, blocking out sunlight and reducing global temperatures by over ten degrees. Ironically, this cooling may have prevented a planetary mass extinction. San Francisco had a magnitude eight earthquake in 2050 that levelled half of the city and resulted in a deadly firestorm.

'To cap it all, in 2051, we had the collapse and landslide of Cumbre Vieja on La Palma in the Canary Islands, which caused a megatsunami. The dozen or so gigantic waves decimated the cities of New York, Boston, Miami, Lisbon and Casablanca. Our colleagues at BDL in Bristol know only too well the ferocity of the event. Part of their city was also submerged, resulting in a frozen inland sea.

'The energy crisis has escalated the tensions in the Middle East, with the Syrians laying claim to the Israeli-occupied Golan Heights. Of course, their Russian and Iranian sponsors have only been too happy to wade in, as it is the site of the world's last remaining productive oilfield. This flashpoint threatens to spill over into a full-blown world war.

'The East has not been problem-free either. Waves of viral epidemics have ravaged China, Russia and India, with some of these becoming pandemics. Intelligence suggests that China engineered the first of these viruses but, as luck would have it, they have become one of its worst victims.' Lana thought she saw Gordon conceal a smirk.

Gordon coughed into his hand. 'A new outbreak has taken hold in London, probably due to illegal migrants fleeing hostile regimes. I hope BDL can help us with this problem.'

Gordon paused and looked up. 'The agenda,' he continued, 'consists of several discussions: climate change, economics and virology. Afterwards, our expert groups will leave the call, and an internal meeting will follow. I will now hand you over to my advisor on climate change, Dr Ralph Sturgeon, who will lead the first item.'

Lana listened intently to the conclusions from his team's modelling work. She suspected that the competing effects of global warming and volcanic cooling were so delicately balanced that it was impossible to model accurately. Gordon called time after a somewhat meandering discussion on possible solutions. The meeting then moved on to the national economy. The outlook was very sobering, especially concerning elderly healthcare. Subsequently, the Met Office and London School of Economics left the call, and Gordon once more took the floor.

'I would now like to call on Dr Vanessa Cook, the Chief Scientific Advisor of SAGE, to chair the virology session.'

Edward Gordon sat down, and a Black lady in her forties stood up midway down the right-hand flank of the room. Lana admired her as she marched to the front, head held high. She wore a summery floral dress and stood out like a rose amongst thorns.

Vanessa turned to face the audience and smiled. 'I am confident we can find a way through this crisis,' she began.

Lana nodded. *Go, girl!*

'My role is to advise the government on healthcare policy, especially concerning the coronavirus. From previous outbreaks, stretching back as long ago as COVID-19 in 2019, we have found it does not affect everyone in the same way. Many people are asymptomatic, whereas, sadly, others become critically ill and die.

'Vaccines have been used with limited success because the virus mutates and some strains evade them.' Vanessa coughed, poured herself a glass of water, and took a sip.

'Apologies,' she said, clearing her throat. 'Hopefully, I'm not coming down with it ...' Nervous laughter broke out. 'As I was saying, the difference in disease susceptibility is down to individual genetics. The adaptive immune system sometimes malfunctions, attacking the body rather than the virus. The person would have recovered perfectly well, albeit slowly, with their body just relying on their innate immune system. We call it a cytokine storm. My question to BDL is whether their BioFace implant can sense this is about to happen and stop it in its tracks?'

Lana felt her stomach lurch. *Is this my chance?* Edward Gordon rose from his chair and stared into the camera. 'Thank you, Vanessa.' He nodded his appreciation. 'BDL, can you comment, please?'

Lana glanced across the table at Dreyfuss. He looked paralysed, like a man waiting at the gallows. She sensed that, without a prepared script, he was about to pour out the usual flannel. She leaned back and, out of camera shot, waved to catch his attention. He saw her and glared back, eyes rigid with fear. She pointed to herself and made talking gestures with her hand. He nodded discreetly.

'Of course, Prime Minister,' Dreyfuss blustered, 'we are already working towards such a solution. May I pass you over to my expert on the subject, Dr Lana Grace, who can guide you through the details.'

'Thank you, Jeremy,' Gordon said. 'Please proceed, Dr Grace.'

Lana shook the tension out of her arms under the table, took a deep breath, and smiled into the camera. 'Hi everyone. My name is Lana Grace, and I am responsible for interfacing the BioFace to the body and, more specifically, the brain.'

She paused and checked the monitor. The connection hadn't frozen, and everyone was captivated. 'When we rolled out BioFace hardware Version 3.2 for mass adoption, we included future-proofing. After all, nobody wants the cost and risk of further surgery.' She was vaguely aware of people murmuring their agreement.

'In this latest release, we blur the distinction between human and machine. The BioFace implant interfaces to the optic, vestibulocochlear and olfactory cranial nerves, facilitating machine interaction with the senses. Also, it can control the various endocrine glands in the body, regulating the production and release of hormones–the chemical messengers that control growth, metabolism, sexual function, mood and–importantly for this meeting–immune response.

'Any questions before I go on?' No one raised a hand or spoke. She inhaled deeply, confidence growing.

'The BioFace's electronics can signal to the adrenal cortex and thereby control the production of glucocorticoid steroids, which regulate inflammation. Before a BioFace is implanted, a patient's genome is sequenced to gauge potential rejection. Therefore, it can prevent a cytokine storm.' Lana paused. 'Really, it is *just* that simple. Any questions?'

'My,' Vanessa exclaimed, 'that sounds perfect. Does this mean we can use the BioFace to stop COVID-52 in its tracks then?'

'In theory, yes,' Lana replied, 'but the BioFace is a complex system. It is vital to follow clinical protocols.'

'How do you mean?'

'Only a few functions of the implant have been activated. The others need to be clinically proven. For example, smart contact lenses are necessary because the optic nerve connection has not been certified, although third-party

BioFaceTime is undergoing limited trials. Health monitoring sensors are working, but these underwent months of testing before the wetware was signed off.'

'Wetware?'

'The BioFace is managed by embedded firmware–we call this wetware because it controls bodily functions that modify the bloodstream. We can update wetware wirelessly across the internet of things. However, we do this in a very controlled way–with incremental releases that have been rigorously simulated–to prevent dangerous side effects.'

'I see …' Vanessa said. 'How long for protection against COVID-52 then?'

'It makes commercial sense to update wetware in version upgrades that roll several proven changes into one release. We are currently preparing the next one.' Lana looked across at Dreyfuss. He pointed to himself and gave her the thumbs up. 'I think Jeremy can fill you in on the details.'

'Thank you, Lana,' Gordon said, 'for that eloquent description of a very complex subject.'

The view switched to Dreyfuss, who now exuded confidence. Lana exhaled through pursed lips.

Dreyfuss smiled at the camera. 'The release date has yet to be formally agreed, but I anticipate three months from now.'

'*Three months!*' Gordon exclaimed. 'Millions could be dead by then!'

'I fear the Prime Minister is right to be worried,' Vanessa added. 'Is there *any* way of fast-tracking this?'

Here we go.

'What sort of timescale are you hoping for?' Dreyfuss inquired.

'We need protection within a week or two …' Vanessa replied.

Christ. No way!

'Given its criticality …' Dreyfuss said.

No, don't do it!

'… I think we can push through a pre-release pack of

suitable changes.'

Lana went as white as a sheet. She realised this could land in her lap. She wanted career progression, but this was madness.

'Marvellous,' Gordon said.

A man sitting next to Vanessa's vacant chair with his back to the camera signalled to Gordon.

'Ah, yes,' Gordon said. 'One more thing ...'

Dreyfuss cocked his head like a curious bird. 'Yes?'

'As we move forward with active BioFace healthcare, the government feels it needs a more central role–consider it as the foundation of a shadow organisation to BDL.'

'But what about BDL's investment?' Dreyfuss queried, sounding suspicious.

Gordon looked irritated. 'We understand BDL's concerns regarding commercial ownership and intellectual property rights, but the BioFace is *too* critical to be solely managed by the private sector.'

'Are you suggesting a compulsory takeover?' Dreyfuss said, his face reddening.

'No, not at all,' Gordon replied defensively.

'Then, *what are you suggesting?*'

Lana was surprised by Dreyfuss's nerve.

Gordon pulled himself up to his full height and glared into the camera. 'I am simply saying that it is in the nation's interests that the government has access to the inner workings of the BioFace so it can fast-track solutions. It *must* help the population it is elected to serve.'

Dreyfuss seemed to come to his senses. 'I understand, sir,' he mumbled. 'I am sure we can arrange something that respects commercial interests.'

'Good,' Gordon said, sounding relieved. 'Rest assured, BDL will be looked after.'

'Thank you, sir,' Dreyfuss said, his composure returning.

'OK,' Gordon said. 'I think that wraps up our session on healthcare.' He rubbed his hands together. 'Thank you, Vanessa and BDL, for your inputs–you make me proud to be

British.'

Lana watched Vanessa return to her seat. The COBRA members sat to her right and left stood to let her in. Vanessa nodded her thanks. Lana's eyes dwelled on the man to Vanessa's left who had signalled to Gordon. He seemed unlike the other men in the room–tall, slim, and athletically built. As Vanessa sat, he turned to face the camera. It was John–the man from the conference.

Gordon cleared his throat. 'Thank you, BDL, for attending the call. The secure connection will now be closed.'

The monitor went black, and the staff in BDL's boardroom visibly relaxed. Dreyfuss clapped his hands. 'Thank you, everyone, for your support–I think it went very well.'

Time will tell.

Lana looked up, and the monitor flashed. The view of COBRA reappeared. John was standing at the front and appeared to be lecturing the officials.

'As the pathogen, masquerading as COVID-52, has now been released and is circulating in the wider population,' a quiet voice from the speaker said, 'we need to move quickly to Phase Two of PATMOS.'

The monitor flashed back to black. Lana scanned the room. It seemed everybody was too busy chatting to have heard.

8

WEDNESDAY, 11 SEPTEMBER 2052

C arl closed his eyes. He sat quietly on the edge of the bed as the woman skilfully unbuttoned his shirt. She was in her forties, a widow with two teenage kids. Her husband, Gerry, had been killed four years earlier by a rocket-propelled grenade when his regiment had come under attack in Libya. He'd been defending an oilfield that had helped produce chemicals for absorbing carbon dioxide from the atmosphere to save the planet. Despite his sacrifice, she couldn't survive off her widow's pension.

Her powder-blue uniform was stretched taut over her body. Before Gerry's death, admirers had called her voluptuous, but now even plump was flattering. She'd told Carl it had been hard after his death; she'd let herself go. Carl said she was perfect just the way she was. He recounted stories of several friends who'd had life crises–none as bad as hers–who'd resorted to drinking and taking drugs. Compared to them, she'd been an absolute trooper.

Carl identified with her plight, having lost both parents in a car crash aged five. He was now 49, and this was his first home visit. Getting to see her at the Bristol clinic had been a lottery. He presumed he was now on the home help list because his condition had deteriorated. He was one of the lucky ones–many vulnerable people he knew hadn't received any help. Not that he was going to complain–he'd looked forward to seeing her all week.

Her formal title was Nurse Furber, but, to him, she was Samantha. He couldn't understand why she still used her husband's name. Why would anybody want to be constantly reminded of their loss?

She was scheduled to pop round twice a week, helping him service his cannula and sterilise the BioFace-controlled dopamine pump. If home help was anything like the clinic, he expected they would spend much of the hour chatting. That was the sort of support he really needed.

Samantha's loss and loneliness gave them a common bond. He knew she was just his nurse, but he still thought about her in other ways. He often wondered what might happen in a perfect world. His mind wandered as she undressed him. Her luscious lips, subtly made-up in a delicate shade of pink, pouted in concentration. Her lustrous auburn hair cascaded over her shoulders, tickling his face.

He'd agonised over whether to ask her out, but he knew she would never accept the advances of an invalid. They had such a good relationship, so why risk it? Being honest with himself, perhaps he saw her as the mother he'd barely known–someone who cared for him unconditionally, understood his plight and wasn't judgemental.

He watched her emerald eyes as they skilfully guided her soft fingers. She undid the last button and gently tugged out his shirt, taking care not to snag the cannula.

'Had a good week?' he asked.

'I've been super busy since the weather's got colder. Old folk are getting ill.'

'You must be exhausted,' Carl said, stony-faced. 'Sorry, I'm part of the problem.'

'You're OK, Carl. I prefer being busy. The job is about helping people.'

She inspected the wound where the cannula entered the skin three inches above his navel, the tube that delivered the L-Dopa gel directly into his small intestine.

Carl had been diagnosed with early-onset Parkinson's disease aged 39. He blamed it on the crushing grief he'd suffered in childhood when his parents died, although those around him during his music years might have argued his carefree lifestyle was a more likely cause.

He first suspected something was wrong when he awoke hungover after a party, and his little finger had been trembling uncontrollably. Over subsequent weeks, the tremor spread up his hand, arm and shoulder. His doctor ran some tests and confirmed his worst fears.

The gel from Carl's pump was turned into dopamine inside his body, substituting what it had ceased to make, restoring his lost motor control. But taking L-Dopa was a Faustian pact. At first, it seemed like a miracle cure, and he'd been jubilant that Parkinson's wasn't such a big deal after all. But, as his condition deteriorated, he'd had to steadily increase the dose. Dyskinesia had then kicked in–literally. Twitching, involuntary spasms of his legs; erratic, writhing movements of his face, arms and trunk. Sometimes fluid, like a graceful dancer; sometimes jerky, like a demented robot.

He'd tried an exopulse neuromodulation suit to help relax his confused muscles, but it hadn't been the miracle cure reported in the press. Five years ago, at his wits' end, he'd had a DBS fitted–a BioFace-controlled electrode surgically implanted into his brain. He'd known the risks, and the operation had been scary, especially as he'd been conscious throughout, but he needn't have worried. The DBS stopped most of the tremors, allowing him to reduce his medication. Although it helped his dyskinesia, the L-Dopa was still the life fluid that animated him and made him feel normal. As the drug wore off, it felt as if his blood was congealing like glue, slowing his thoughts and reducing his steps to a shuffle. He hated the daily occurrence of feeling like a clockwork toy winding down.

Carl felt liberated by his L-Dopa pump. It smoothed out the dips in energy between dopamine doses and reduced his binary personality disorder of normality and rigidity. But the cannula supplying the dose had to be kept scrupulously clean to prevent infection. That was easier said than done with impaired coordination. Samantha made all the difference.

'Are you ready for this?' Samantha asked as she spread a towel on the bed and plucked some servicing tools from a padded black bag. The bag toppled over, spilling its contents.

'You can pop it over there if you like.' Carl gestured to the window sill.

Samantha nodded, repacked the bag, and carried it to the window. Several old photographs in silver frames decorated a nearby shelf. Carl had put them there that morning. He knew it was silly pride, but he wanted to show her he'd once had a life and been a somebody. In each picture, a different gig, a different exotic location. In each picture, a man sat at a keyboard. A man alien to him now.

In his thirties, Carl had been a session musician. A maverick who could learn a playlist in minutes and bring songs to life. Many bands had wanted his skills. Somebody who gave the cohesion, magic and class without stealing the limelight. That suited Carl. He wasn't one for preening or making a fuss. He just loved the joyride of stardom from the backseat.

Samantha picked up a silver frame and studied the faces in the picture. An attractive woman draped herself over Carl.

'Wow! You were a bit of a groover,' she said.

'I had my moments …' Carl mumbled.

'Who's the lady?'

Carl had wondered whether she might ask. 'Fi-Fi,' he replied. 'I mean Fiona.'

'Do you see her now?'

Carl shook his head and looked down. Samantha smoothed her tunic.

'What work did you do before playing in bands?'

'I was a postdoc at Bristol Uni.'

'Doing what?'

'Computer science.'

'What's that?'

'Machine vision, AI programming, that sort of thing.'

Samantha studied the other photos and hadn't seemed to have heard.

'Anyway,' Carl continued, 'I played music on the side–they sort of went well together.'

'Ah, a wizard with keyboards,' Samantha re-engaged.

'You could say that,' Carl mumbled.

'Why did you stop?'

'*I didn't,*' Carl exclaimed.

'Eh?' Samantha replaced the last frame on the sill and spun around.

'They sacked me,' Carl said impassively, his eyes on fire.

'*Sacked?*' She looked confused.

'*Yeah, sacked.*'

'But you were good?'

Carl's eyes darted in his stony face. '*I was.* And then Parkinson's ...'

'Ah ... Poor love.' She gazed at the energy monitor on the wall, watching its digits climb. 'Is that why Fiona left?' she asked casually.

Carl nodded.

Silently, Samantha walked back to the bed and squeezed his shoulder. He rested his head against her stockinged thigh and closed his eyes. The weave of the nylon against the side of his smooth face aroused him; he inhaled her delicate scent. She stroked his head as if he was a Christmas puppy.

Latex gloves snapped. He startled.

'Shall we get this over with?' she asked.

'If you must,' he replied.

As he leaned back, his BioFace glowed from an incoming call. It was Arlo. 'OK, if I get this?'

'Be my guest.' She patted him tenderly on the thigh. Carl's leg juddered. He looked up and tried to smile. She took a couple of steps backwards, turned away, and checked her own BioFace.

He accepted the call–his BioFace speaker crackling. 'Hi, Arlo.'

'Hey, Carl.'

'What's up?' Carl asked.

'Guess what?'

'What?'

'I've only just gone and won the conference prize for best paper!' Arlo gushed. 'We had a massive hamper delivered this morning. Alisha was chuffed to bits.'

'You're shitting me, Arlo. That's great news.'

'Maybe they felt sorry for me because of my headfit ...'

'Don't be bloody daft. You deserve it mate–it *was* the best paper.'

'Thanks, Carl. Thanks for nominating me, mate.'

Carl hesitated. 'Er, but I didn't ...'

'Eh?'

'Yeah, sorry, mate. I would have, but I couldn't.'

'What d'you mean?'

'I was involved in the work,' Carl clarified. 'You know, conflicts of interest and all of that.'

'Ah, fair do's. So who did then? I'm not exactly a crony–I don't fit the mould. Most academics are suspicious of me!'

'Hang on a mo.' Carl backgrounded the call, navigated to the conference's web page, and checked the awards.

Carl reconnected to Arlo. 'You still there?'

'Yep.'

'Hmmm,' Carl continued. 'It says the nominator's name has been withheld.'

'Who the hell might it be then?'

'Maybe Lana?' Carl suggested.

'Perhaps. But why?'

'Probably because it's a *good* paper?' Carl said, exasperated. 'Why can't you accept it? You're good, mate!'

'Um, you're just being kind–'

'And, you're just being an arse,' Carl snapped back.

The line went quiet.

A few seconds later, Carl filled the silence. 'Any other news, mate?'

'Er, are you seeing your nurse today?' Arlo replied.

'She's here now.'

Samantha turned and cocked her head.

'Why?' Carl asked.

'My mum mentioned a medical term. I just wondered whether she knows what it is?'

'Have you searched online?'

'Yeah, nothing.'

'What is it?'

'SEP. That's S... E... P.'

'Did you hear that,' Carl asked Samantha.

She didn't respond, but Carl was sure she'd heard.

'*Samantha.*'

Samantha turned around.

'My mate Arlo is on the line. He wants to know what SEP is. He thinks it's a medical term.' Carl spelt out the letters. 'Any idea?'

'Not a clue,' she replied instantly.

'It's not a medical term then?'

'Not that I've come across,' she said adamantly.

'Did you hear that, Arlo?' Carl said.

'Yeah, mate, not to worry,' Arlo replied.

'Leave it with me,' Carl said.

'It's not urgent.'

'*Leave it with me,*' Carl insisted.

'OK, mate. Thanks.'

'I'd better go.'

'Catch ya later.'

'Laters, AJ.'

The call clicked off.

'I'm surprised you've not heard of SEP,' Carl said, sounding puzzled. 'Arlo must be wrong.'

Samantha shuffled the items on the towel. 'Probably just a test they run on old folk.'

'No worries,' Carl said. 'I'll find out.'

She spun around. 'How?'

'I know about computers. There are ways.'

'I see ...' she said, eyes returning to Carl's photos. 'Don't get into trouble, mind.'

'Why?' Carl replied. 'There's no harm done.'

She gazed at the energy monitor on the wall as the digits steadily climbed. 'You know how things are these days ...'

9

THURSDAY, 12 SEPTEMBER 2052

The mountain bike's wheels whirred loudly, reverberating off the stone-banked walls as Lana descended like a runaway train into Wells. Arms ramrod rigid, shoulders tense and eyes set on a small patch of light at the end of the tunnel of trees. She emerged into a sweeping right-hand bend, the unsheltered tarmac crusted with snow and ice. The knobbly tyres grumbled and crackled as they flicked up icy granules, a wiggly track marking her twitchy descent.

The road was an orange-white blur in midday's flat flight. A crescent-shaped snowdrift jumped out of nowhere.

'*AAAHHH!*'

She snatched at the brakes as she struck the shin-deep snow dune. She lost control, stomach knotting. Everything whited out as the bike blasted into the drift, wheels snaking erratically. *Shit! I'm going down.*

She leaned back, braced for the impact, the winding and the pain. But nothing. She exploded back into the daylight in a cloud of ice crystals and a flash of colour. The bike was heading towards the bend, trees and a cliff. Frantically, she leaned it over and somehow managed to skid the corner. Barely back in control, she jammed on the brakes. The bike juddered and came to a squealing stop. *Christ, that was close.*

She jumped as crows scattered from the tree canopy behind her. She spun around. Nobody was there. Sighing, she leaned over the bars, tugged off her gloves and tossed them to the ground.

Her vision clouded in black blotches, and magnesium stars flashed. She hung her head low and closed her eyes, the world wheeling. She willed herself to relax, trying to ignore the waves of nausea as she fought to keep her breakfast down.

A minute later, her vision cleared, and the spinning and trembling had steadied. But her legs still ached from toiling over the rolling Mendip hills. It was her day off, and it had taken all morning to get this far.

Sick of this.

She straightened up, lungs wheezing like old bellows as she inhaled frosty air through ice-encrusted nostrils.

I'll see Mia soon.

Slowly, she prised her hands off the bars, scared the skin might have frozen stuck and wiped her mouth with the back of her hand. She readjusted her scarf, trying to find fleece that didn't feel like cardboard from her frozen breath.

From her elevated position on the exit of the bend, she had a stunning view south over the Somerset levels. The snow-covered ice sheet stretched off to her right as far as she could see, interrupted only by a solitary telecommunications tower that stood proud like a tall ship's mast in a calm sea.

Her childhood town of Glastonbury, and the Summerland Meadows where she'd spent many a spring day collecting wildflowers, lay to her left in the centre of the valley. Only ruins remained of the town–ice-glazed memories of her past life. Details fading, apart from one. The frigid spire of Saint John's Baptist Church, where she'd wed Jerry in May 2044. Her relationship had failed in 2051, the year the town had been deluged by the megatsunami. When people referred to the disaster of 2051, she immediately thought of her marriage.

Getting married at 26 had been too young–she knew that now. But she'd been bowled over by Jerry's charm and Latino good looks. She thought she knew it all back then and took it for granted she would have a golden future ahead of her. After all, she'd just married her heartthrob, been awarded her doctorate, and landed a dream job at BDL, the world leader in biological interfaces. Only now did she realise how life could throw a curveball.

They'd been married for only two years when her waters had broken with Mia. She'd been such a delightful baby and Jerry such a proud dad. In hindsight, maybe it was because Mia had confirmed his manhood–a conquest he could tick off from his life's to-do list. But, two years on, everything had changed.

Lana had suspected something was wrong when Mia was 18 months old. She'd started to sit up and crawl shortly after her first birthday and even called them ma and da. But then her progress stalled. All the babies from her antenatal group were walking, but Mia was still barely crawling. The mums all tried to reassure her. 'She's just a slow developer,' they said. 'She'll soon catch up.' But Lana's instincts told her otherwise. It came to a head after a row with Jerry. She insisted they must all go and get tested, but he refused. It was as if he was too scared to find out he wasn't perfect. Finally, he relented.

The results had come back positive for Greenfield's disease, a rare, degenerative genetic disorder that damaged cells. A consultant told them the brain and nervous system were worst affected. She asked him what it meant for Mia. With clinical coldness, he said it was only a matter of time before Mia lost most of her intellectual and motor functions. He explained new drug treatments could slow fat build-up in the cells, and she might even live another five years if she responded well. But that had been four years ago, and Mia was now six. She'd heard that gene therapy was undergoing trials and clung to the hope that it might save her.

Jerry hadn't been able to cope with raising a disabled daughter–he was just too proud for that. The bastard had always wanted everything perfect, like his ridiculously expensive Tom Ford suit to go with his high-status banking job. But, when it came to his own flesh and blood, Mia hadn't made the grade. She suspected he blamed her for that.

Jerry had raged she would destroy their lives unless she was put in a home. Lana stood firm, insisting they just had to give her the best life they could. She recalled his blank stare and how she'd lost it and started screaming. Only then had he confessed he couldn't face the stigma. She told him to imagine how Mia felt and pleaded with him to stay strong for her. But he shook his head, went to the pub with his workmates, and returned drunk.

She'd tried to make their marriage work–if only for Mia–and weathered his resentment and disappointment. They'd limped on for several months, but the final straw had come when he'd gone off with the office temp–a pretty young thing with designer clothes and no baggage. After four months of misery and stress, she'd almost felt relieved.

The months after the split had been tough. A local nursery had looked after Mia, as she hadn't wanted to give up her dream job. The massive queues outside food banks showed how poor people were. And it wasn't just vulnerable people suffering–university students and even professionals were struggling too. But prioritising money and career over Mia had been a massive guilt trip. The crisis had come to a head when the nursery had said Mia was too ill for them to cope.

Despite her money worries, she'd been on the verge of quitting BDL when her mum volunteered to care for Mia. She thanked her but politely refused. Her mum was 67, and Mia was simply too demanding. But her mum insisted and asked her to sleep on it. She worked out her budget and realised she would lose her home if she gave up work. That would mean moving back in with her mum. While she loved her to bits, the house was only a one-bedroom flat. It hadn't taken a genius to realise it would never work.

Reluctantly, she'd agreed to try it for three months. Months had become a year, and now she knew the route across the Mendips like the back of her hand. Hard though it was, at least it was a solution. Her mum was a lifesaver.

Cawing crows startled Lana from her thoughts. Her eyes glistened in the diffuse glow of the midday sun as she gazed into the distance at the conical knoll of Glastonbury Tor. The reborn mythical island of Avalon pierced the frozen plain like a pert breast, St Michael's tower clinging to its peak as if it had fled there to escape the floods.

Breathing recovered, she picked up her gloves and pulled them back on, warming her hands under her armpits. A minute later, the throbbing had subsided. She took a deep breath and pushed away, clipping her feet into the pedals as she continued the descent into Wells. Tears streamed down her face–more from her memories than the icy blast.

At the bottom of the hill, she forked left to go past the cathedral. It wasn't much of a detour, and she loved the gothic façade that reminded her of Hogwarts from the Harry Potter books her dad read to her as a child. He was gone now, but she heard his voice as she pulled over and admired the view.

Her parents had relocated to Wells after their Glastonbury home had been destroyed by the flood. The insurance company refused to pay, arguing it was an act of God–some god, she'd thought. Her parents had raided their pension pot to pay for the new house, taking on a small mortgage that ran until her dad retired at 75. But six months later, aged 62, he'd died of a heart attack. Relatives blamed it on the stress caused by the insurance company and told her to take legal action. But Lana disagreed. Life was too short to be bitter and twisted.

Her mum had sold the family home to pay the bills. Her new flat was basic, but she insisted it was large enough and only family mattered.

Lana cycled away from the cathedral and down the high street. Once a thriving thoroughfare, the touristy fashion boutiques had been boarded up. Only a few shops remained: a cut-price supermarket, two crusty charity shops, a pawnbroker that fleeced people of their gold, and a bookie full of soulless men hiding from their responsibilities.

Outside the charity shop, three homeless men huddled around a brazier they'd improvised from an old metal dustbin. They looked Neanderthal, with wild hair that merged with their beards. One of them pointed her way. Eyeing them suspiciously, she turned left into St John's Street.

She weaved around icy pot-holes and passed a row of boarded-up houses. She recalled her mum saying that they used to belong to young Asian families, evicted after failing to pay their rent. It seemed so unfair, given the high unemployment. Leaving them empty wasn't helping anyone. Red graffiti dripped like blood on the flaking grey render: angry slogans demanding jobs and housing for the young; the Black Power logo of a gloved fist clutching a red lightning bolt.

She turned a bend and pulled up alongside a tired terrace. Checking nobody was watching, she propped her bike against the wall, tugged off a glove and rapped on a flimsy wooden door. A curtain twitched in a downstairs window. Seconds later, the front door scraped open; a wrinkled face appeared above a silver security chain.

'Lana!' Kate, her mum, smiled. 'Hold on a minute.'

A hand appeared, and the chain slid along with a metallic rattle and dangled free. The door creaked wide open, and Kate stepped onto the pavement. Lana noticed her black woollen socks and pink slippers, holes neatly darned with colour-clashing orange thread. *Bless!* Kate looked up and down the street, put a protective arm around Lana's shoulders, and ushered her inside.

The door banged shut, and Kate turned to face her daughter.

'Hi, mum.' Lana smiled from ear to ear, wrapped her arms around her, and pulled her close. She hugged and rocked her for several seconds, inhaling lavender. Finally, she pulled away and pecked her on the cheek. 'I'm so glad to see you.'

'Come in the warm and take that top off, so you'll appreciate it later.' Kate wrinkled her nose. 'You must be freezing.'

Lana pulled off her cycling shoes, stowed them neatly by the front door, and walked down the hall into the kitchen diner. The flat felt chilly and damp, barely any warmer than outside. Out of politeness, she slipped off her jacket and laid it on the table. She shivered and then checked herself.

Kate spotted her discomfort. 'Are you cold, love?'

Lana moved uneasily.

'You're cold, poor love,' Kate answered for her. 'Let me put another log on the fire.'

She grabbed the last remaining log from a wicker basket in the hall. 'Come into the lounge.'

The log burner in the lounge had almost gone out. Kate knelt, opened the glass door, and popped the log onto the embers. She opened the vents, and, gradually, the fire began to roar. 'That's better.'

'Where's Mia?' Lana asked, swivelling round to look.

A wheelchair stood guard in a corner, its chromed frame scratched and dinged from years of hard service. It looked clinical and functional, its seat and armrests furnished with poorly padded, black PVC upholstery. Lana's eyes lingered on the draconian buckles and straps that restrained Mia and the curved headrest that stopped her head from drooping. Mia cradled two toy monkeys in her lap, one with black fur, the other with orange. Their glass eyes stared into space, just like Mia's.

'Hi Mia,' Lana said, trying to sound cheerful.

Mia tensed, honey-coloured hair tumbling into her face when she heard Lana's voice. Slowly, she raised her chin, and her eyes became less distant. Lana squeezed her mum's arm and marched across the room. She crouched down, brushed Mia's hair from her face, and embraced her. Mia made some mumbling sounds that Lana recognised as excitement. Lana straightened up and wiped her eyes with the palms of her hands. She looked down at Mia as she rocked in the chair, saliva dribbling from the corner of her mouth. Lana gulped. It had only been a week since her last visit, and she was noticeably worse. She knelt again, took her hand in hers and looked into her eyes.

'How are you today, Mia?'

Mia wriggled, rocked and mumbled in excited frustration.

'Can I get you anything? Maybe your Tommee Tippee cup?'

Lana recognised a subtle nod. She stood and turned–her mum was already waiting, a capped cup in an outstretched hand.

'You read me like a book.' Lana smiled and managed a phlegmy laugh as she wiped away a tear.

'When you've been doing this for as long as me.' Kate smiled.

Lana took the cup and offered it up to Mia. She tried to hold it, but her hands failed to coordinate.

'It's OK, love. You relax; I'll hold it for you.' Lana carefully pushed the spout into Mia's open mouth and heard her begin to suck.

'How are Charlie and Chaplin?' She stroked the monkeys' heads.

Mia seemed to get very excited and started to choke. Lana withdrew the cup, and a white tissue magically appeared over her shoulder.

'Thanks, mum.' She took the tissue and wiped the dribble from Mia's mouth.

Mia's coughing eased, and Lana stroked her hair. Mia grimaced. Lana knelt there for several minutes, patiently giving Mia a sip whenever she was ready. Kate sat and watched, smiling. Lana told Mia what she'd seen while riding: the deer that had strolled across the road, the crows that had startled her, and the scary descent into Wells. Mia seemed to be listening intently, rocking contentedly, mumbling occasionally.

Lana felt the cup lighten and shook it–it was nearly empty. She looked up. Mia's eyes drooped and closed. Lana gave a weak smile, slowly stood, and lodged the cup on a nearby table. Her mum gestured for them to go into the bedroom and picked up a tray with two steaming mugs. She led them into the bedroom and shut the door with her foot. She put the tray down on a small table, sat on the bed and patted the space beside her. Lana walked over and snuggled up beside her.

'So, how are things in Bristol?' her mum asked, staring into

Lana's eyes.

'Not too bad.' Lana patted her mum's thigh.

'That's great. See, you're turning the corner. I knew you would. Just tackle one day at a time, and things will work out.'

'Absolutely, mum.'

'So, what's new?'

'Well, I've met a man.'

'*How exciting.* Is he like your father?'

'*Mum!*'

'So, what's his name, and what does he do?' her mum asked.

'His name is Arlo. He works in a high-tech company that's linked to the university.'

'Has he got good teeth and hair?'

'*Mum!*'

'The clock's ticking ...'

'He's just a friend. Anyway, our hands are full with Mia.' She looked down. 'How is she?'

'She's OK.'

'Really?' Lana's brow furrowed.

'It's to be expected, Lana–we just have to accept it.' She clutched Lana's arm. Lana stifled a sob, and her mum leaned over and hugged her.

'You're right, mum. We have to look forward.'

'Indeed. Things will work themselves out.'

'So, how are *you*, mum? I notice your BioFace has been set to private.'

'That's something I need to talk to you about ...'

'Why?'

'Er, I've not been feeling well lately.'

'Why? What's wrong?'

'I've been getting bad headaches.'

'Lots of people have.'

'It's not just that ...'

'What else?'

'I've been forgetful, disorientated. Just not with it.'

'Have you spoken to a doctor?'

'It's just my age.' Kate wrung her hands. 'There's nothing they can do.'

'Don't be defeatist.'

'Listen.' Kate looked troubled. 'There's no easy way to say this.'

Lana's eyes narrowed.

'I'm afraid I can't look after Mia anymore,' her mum blurted.

The blood drained from Lana's face.

'Lana. You OK?'

'Y-Yes, mum.'

'We agreed it was only a stopgap.'

'Yes, I know, but–'

'I'm sorry, Lana,' she interrupted. 'I simply can't cope.'

The room went quiet. Mumbling sounds came from next door.

'I see.' Lana stared at the wall.

Kate rubbed her arm. 'You'll sort something out.'

'When do you need her g-gone by?'

'Lana. I've tried my *best!*'

'*When?*'

Kate looked at the floor. 'I've spoken to child services.'

Lana swallowed hard. '*WHEN?*'

'They're driving her over to yours Monday week.'

10

THURSDAY, 12 SEPTEMBER 2052

A rlo pushed the vegetable curry and rice around his plate with a fork, trying to make the pile look smaller. He hated wasting food when so many people were going short. They only ate small meals anyway because of rationing, and prices had skyrocketed since the start of the energy crisis. But he had a pounding headache and just wasn't hungry. He wondered if it had been triggered by presenting at the conference. Yesterday evening's headbanger of a session with Carl, following up Lana's suggestion of extracting images or video from the signal, probably hadn't helped.

He kept thinking about Lana: her inquisitive hazel eyes, warm smile and lovely honey-coloured hair. Lana's idea was as sexy as she was, and he'd been desperate for it to work. The thought of seeing alien images was mind-blowing. However, despite Carl throwing his mighty quantum computer and signal processing tool suite at the problem, after five hours, they'd, quite literally, drawn a blank. The signal had none of the tell-tale patterns always present with images or video frames, such as signal periodicities arising from line rastering or frame formatting. The problem had been enough to give anyone a headache. They'd given up at midnight, and he'd returned home only to find Alisha lying awake in bed, also complaining of an awful headache.

He wondered whether they had the new COVID-52. That was all his family needed. If he went through one of the scanners and tested positive, the authorities would arrest him if he left the house as his BioFace would track him. They could ill-afford to lose his income.

He gazed out of the kitchen window. It was getting dark, and the light from one of the last remaining laser streetlights flickered as snow fell. Terraced houses crammed the hillside, rusty corrugated iron repair patches protruding from their snow-laden roofs. At the bottom of the valley in Montpelier, the ghetto drowned in a sea of grey-brown smog. The once-proud city looked more like a shantytown than the jewel of the West Country.

'Thanks for the lovely tea, Alisha,' Arlo said, turning away from the window and brushing hair from his eyes. 'Just what I needed.'

'It's the best I could do with the rations.' She pulled a face.

The HouseBot collected Arlo's plate from the table and handed it to Alisha. The machine was a basic model and really just a descendant of an Alexa-powered robot with articulated limbs and clunky AI. Despite its limitations, it helped with simple menial tasks and provided a semblance of company. Alisha glanced at the leftover food and frowned.

Arlo saw her disappointment. 'Sorry, love. My head's splitting.'

Alisha nodded and scraped the food into a Tupperware container. She added her own and popped it into the fridge. Turning, she saw Arlo pick up an open can of beer from the table and take a swig. Her face dropped.

Joshua burst into the room shrieking, his arms thrashing wildly with a plastic sword as if slashing at an invisible opponent. His eyes flicked rapidly–like he was fitting–as they controlled the metaverse avatar in his augmented reality 'Battle of the Augs' game.

'Joshua,' Alisha shouted. 'Enough!'

He hadn't seemed to have heard and slashed even more frantically. It was disturbing to watch, even for Arlo.

'Arlo. Make him stop!' Alisha urged, her voice cracking.

'He's OK, love. It's just a game.'

'It's *not* just a game. He's trying to kill his metaverse

friends!'

'Don't be daft. It's *just* a game. He's working off his excess energy.'

'Arlo, *please* make him stop.'

'OK, OK,' Arlo said, strolling across the kitchen. Alisha watched, her eyes narrowing. Displaying surprising dexterity in his semi-inebriated state, Arlo crept up behind Joshua, grabbed his shoulders and shouted 'boo' in his ear.

Joshua jumped like a pogoing punk; his sword clattered to the laminate floor.

'*Arlo!*' Alisha shrieked, 'you'll give the poor boy a heart attack.'

'Kill or cure,' Arlo muttered.

Joshua slumped, exhausted. His eyes steadied. '*Daaad ...* Why'd ya do that for?'

'Your mum needs peace and quiet–not a warzone.'

'Whatever, dad,' Joshua replied. He picked up his sword, made some practice thrusts and skulked off next door.

Arlo sighed and sat down. 'TV on,' he commanded. The view over Bristol's gloomy streets changed into the gaudy colours of a television studio. A presenter was in the middle of introducing a special feature on the escalating tension in the Middle East. A female reporter, dressed in a flak jacket and surrounded by satellite dishes, gave a piece-to-camera from the rooftop of Tel Aviv's Holiday Inn.

'Russia has infiltrated Syria following the civil war, pulling the strings of its puppet dictator Nizar Khaled. Lebanon's Hezbollah has been waging an Iranian-backed proxy guerrilla war against Israel, with frequent border incursions and missile strikes.'

The television picture changed to a satellite view of the Israeli-Syrian border. Rows upon rows of tanks, missile launchers, troop carriers and support equipment were lined up on the Syrian border, ready to roll. A few miles inside Israel, an equally large coalition force had amassed. *Shit, that's going to kick off.* The picture then switched to an aerial view of the

Golan Heights. The reporter explained the political sensitivity of the vast array of pumpjacks that nodded like pecking birds, draining the desert of its oil. Arlo turned up the volume.

'The number of military vehicles assembled on both sides of the border has quadrupled in the last 24 hours. The whole world is on tenterhooks fearing an invasion.'

Alisha's face reddened. 'God's deserted us,' she said.

'TV off,' Arlo commanded.

Alisha looked up. 'He's given up. Humans are beyond hope. He's even walked away from *us*, and what have we ever done wrong?'

Arlo had never understood why Alisha believed in God. But he knew he had to tread carefully, especially now she was questioning her faith. He walked over and stroked her arm. 'The Earth will fix itself. It always has in the past.'

'But it's only recently had to deal with humans.'

'Have faith, love.'

'*Faith!* Faith in *who*?'

'Maybe scientists can fix things?'

'*Scientists!* Science is the root of the problem!'

'*Why?*'

'It's wrecked the environment for one.'

'That's because people want things. Science just provides a means ...'

'Scientists shouldn't work on things that destroy the planet.'

'They're human too. They need money to pay bills.'

'Don't they have a conscience?'

'It's not like that. They just want their families to have a good life. One thing leads to another.'

'But family values are at the *heart* of the problem!'

'Family values?'

'Yes, family values. Take *you*, for instance. You're never here for us–you're *always* at work.'

'That's not true.'

'It *is*. Last night you didn't get back until gone midnight. In

America, you were hunting for aliens. Most of the time, you seem to be ...'

'Seem to be *what?*' Arlo snapped.

Alisha turned her back and wiped down a work surface.

'*What?*' Arlo pushed.

Alisha stood still. 'Hiding ...'

Arlo gulped. He didn't need this. Especially now. *Don't start a fight.* 'I'm sorry if that's how it looks.'

'It's not how it *looks*–it's how it *is!*'

Arlo's eyes lowered. 'You're right, honey.' He twisted his wedding ring round and round his finger until it hurt. The skin had turned shiny. 'I need to try harder.'

He wracked his brain for something to say. Something to cheer her up. Something to help them move on. He looked out of the window. It had stopped snowing. An azure-tinged full moon shone dimly behind the veil of volcanic dust that now cloaked the whole Earth, blue-rinsing the snowbound city.

Joshua re-entered the kitchen, shoulders slumped.

'*Bored, bored, bored,*' he shouted, stamping his feet.

'Joshua, *stop that,*' Alisha scolded.

Arlo swigged his beer and rubbed his temples. *Need to get out ...*

Arlo resisted the urge. He had to try. He'd done enough running. 'Isn't tomorrow an INSET day?' he asked.

Alisha nodded.

'So Joshua's not in metaverse classes?'

'No.'

'Hey, Josh,' Arlo said. 'As it's not a school night, do you want to stay up late and see something from outer space?'

'Cool! Can I mum?'

Arlo looked to Alisha for approval. A smile spread across her face–Josh was always a good way to her heart.

'How can you do that?' she asked.

Suddenly, the room plunged into darkness.

'Not another power cut,' Alisha sighed.

'Another good reason for looking at the stars,' Arlo said.

Seconds later, the lights came back on.

'Must have heard me.' Arlo gave a wry smile. 'My old telescope's boxed up in the back room–the one dad gave me when I was Josh's age. I could set it up for him on the rooftop garden.'

'That's a lovely idea.' She smiled.

Arlo closed his eyes in relief and swigged the rest of his can. He tossed the empty across the room into the recycling bin, grinning when it found its mark with a satisfying clatter. Alisha turned and walked away, tutting loudly, but Arlo had already left the room to find his telescope.

'You OK, Josh?' Alisha said.

'Are you and daddy still friends?' He gazed into her eyes.

'Yes. We're both good. Sometimes grown-ups argue, but it doesn't mean they don't love each other.'

Joshua climbed up onto his mother's lap, and they cuddled.

'Right. You go and sort out your coat and gloves. It's going to be bitterly cold out there.'

ΔΔΔ

Arlo elbowed the handle while shoving the door open with his foot. He wriggled through, trying not to bang the telescope balanced precariously across his arms. The beers weren't helping. His BioFace buzzed. Cursing, he laid the telescope down and checked the caller's ID. Withheld. With a blink on the icon, he accepted the call.

'Hello,' Arlo said.

'Dr Jones?'

'Speaking.'

'It's John here.'

'John?'

'Yes, John. John from the conference.'

Arlo checked the time: 8:45 pm. *What sort of time is this?* 'What's up?'

'Sorry to call you so late. I've been meaning to contact you all day, but I've been mad busy. Can you speak?'

'If it's quick ...' Arlo softened. 'How can I help?'

'Can you send me some of your papers on satellite swarms?'

He's waited all day to ask me this? 'No problem. Where shall I send them?'

'Use the contact details Lucy gave you.'

'OK.' Arlo suddenly remembered the conference prize and hamper. 'Actually, I have a question for you.'

'Fire away, Dr Jones.'

'Did you nominate me for best paper at the conference?'

'I couldn't possibly confirm or deny,' John said flatly.

'I see ...'

'Now my turn,' John said. 'An easier one.'

'Sure,' Arlo replied, realising John had inadvertently confessed.

'That signal you detected,' John said slowly.

'Yes. What about it?' Arlo replied, wondering what was coming next.

'I've had an idea.'

'Really? About how it's coded? What it might be communicating?' Arlo asked, his curiosity piqued.

'Exactly.'

'Go on.'

'It's just a theory. Can you send me the signal?'

'You want me to send you the signal?' Arlo said, sounding surprised.

'Yes. Just compress it using BioZip and send it with the papers,' John replied flippantly.

'Why?'

'So I can test the theory.'

Arlo rubbed his head. He remembered what he'd been through and imagined what his mother might say.

'You still there, Dr Jones?'

'Yes.'

'Can I have the signal?'

'No.'

'*Why not?*' John snapped. 'I'm trying to help you,' he said, his voice calming.

'Just tell me about your theory, and *I'll* test it,' Arlo fired back.

'Can't oblige, doctor.'

'Why not?'

'I could be wrong.'

'That's unimportant.'

'*Just send me the signal.*'

The door to the rooftop garden creaked ajar. Alisha popped her head around, saw Arlo and opened the door wider. Joshua piled out, all arms and legs, shrieking and running full tilt. He slammed into Arlo's leg, almost knocking him over.

'Dr Jones?' John's voice sounded smooth and persuasive, like a cold-caller.

'Sorry, John. My wife and son are here now. Can you phone back tomorrow?'

'I'll be in touch,' John said abruptly. The line clicked dead.

Arlo's brow furrowed as he fixed the telescope to the tripod.

'Is it ready?' Joshua asked, tugging his arm.

'Nearly, son, just give me a minute.'

Arlo lined it up roughly on the moon and peered through the eyepiece, still thinking about the call.

'*Can I see! Can I see!*' Joshua shrieked.

The words resonated; his eyes glazed …

He was sitting with his dad on his sixth birthday. He recalled his kind face, what he'd said about Mars, and his own realisation they were all alone in the Universe. *I miss you, dad* …

'Earth to dad!' Joshua tugged at his coat sleeve. 'Wake up!'

Arlo jumped. 'Sorry, Josh. Miles away … Sit on my lap, put your eye here and tell me what you see.'

Joshua wriggled onto Arlo's lap and looked through the eyepiece.

'It's all blue and blurry, dad. Like someone's spilt ink on it!'

'It's the moon, Josh.'

'But there's nothing to see!'

'I'm afraid the dust from the volcano spoils the image. I'm sorry. I'll show you another time when the dust has cleared.'

'Aw, dad. Is that it?'

Arlo rubbed his head and set Joshua down. 'I tell you what. Do you want to see where dad works?'

'What? In the city?'

'Yeah, but up close. Like you're sat at my desk?'

'Cool!'

Arlo swivelled the telescope around, aiming it into the heart of the city, lining it up using the low magnification finderscope attached to its side. 'That looks about right,' he mumbled. He peered into the main eyepiece and made fine adjustments using the slow-motion controls. Suddenly he froze.

'*Can I see?*' Joshua shrieked.

'Sorry, Josh. Wait a minute–I need to check something.'

A shadowy figure was prowling around his office, picking up things from desks and examining them. He could see their upper body above the window sill, but the magnification wasn't sufficient to make out their face. Arlo straightened up and rummaged around in his pocket.

'Can I see, dad?' Joshua said. '*Pleeeease!*'

'In a minute.'

'*Daaaaad!*'

'*Just wait.*' Arlo pulled out a clear plastic container and extracted a silver cylinder with 12mm printed on its side. He swapped the eyepieces over and made a quick adjustment to the alignment.

'Can I see? *Can I see?*' Joshua shrieked.

'Very soon,' Arlo muttered. 'Very soon ...'

With the higher-powered eyepiece, he could tell it was a man. The figure stopped at Arlo's desk and tugged on the handle of his desk drawer. He was wearing purple gloves, like those worn by forensic investigators.

'What the f–,' Arlo muttered before remembering his son

was there. The drawer didn't open, and the man inserted something into the lock. Seconds later, the drawer slid open. Objects were pulled out and strewn across the desk. One at a time, the man flicked them over with a pen, then rooted through the rest of the drawer. He seemed to give up, repacked the drawer and slid it closed. Arlo recalled a film he'd seen about the Watergate scandal, where offices had been bugged and searched.

Arlo was vaguely aware of shrieking and felt a tug on his trouser leg. He continued to focus on the man. The shadowy figure sat at his office desk, and the computer screen lit up bright. Graphics animated. Despite the bitingly cold wind, Arlo felt the back of his neck burning.

The man paused and stood up. He put his hand to his head as if thinking. Suddenly, he turned to face the window, staring straight at Arlo. The image juddered and warped from atmospheric turbulence, but Arlo instantly recognised him. It was John–the man he'd just been talking to.

John turned off the computer and strode away from the desk, kicking a wastepaper basket. Arlo's eyes frantically scanned his desk, settling on the Space Needle souvenir. 'Good old Space Needle,' he sighed. Arlo pulled away from the telescope. 'Your turn now,' he said. But, as he turned and looked up, he realised he was standing there all alone on the rooftop garden, the door to the flat banging in the wind.

11

THURSDAY, 12 SEPTEMBER 2052

Eyes closed, Carl slouched on an office chair, mulling over what he was about to do. He opened his eyes and stared at the rack of humming computers, marvelling in their beauty and power. A pinnacle of human achievement surpassing even the moon landings. He was a broken man, but at least this part of his life was perfect.

The computer den was his sanctuary from the world–his last bastion. The rest of his squalid flat in Montpelier, Bristol, was just four small non-descript rooms, but he needed nothing more. Although the kitchen was pokey, it was sufficient to knock up a ready meal and sterilise his dopamine pump. The bedroom felt claustrophobic, crammed with a double bed, wardrobe and chest of drawers, leaving barely enough space to squeeze past. But he preferred having everything within clutching distance. The en suite bathroom was positively luxurious–a godsend in the night when his limbs failed to work. Next door was a lounge, with an old-fashioned flat-panel television hung on the wall a friend had kindly salvaged from the tip, but, these days, he barely went in there.

Everyone moaned about the volcanic winter, but Carl thought the storm clouds had a silver lining. The cold air of his flat helped cool the electro-optic chips in his rack of quantum computers. Electricity rationing barely affected him as he never watched the propaganda on television. That left him two hours of computing every evening before the emergency backup kicked in and he had to shut down. After each session, his flat was toasty warm from waste heat. He thought it criminal that people used energy for heating instead of using it for something far more useful first.

He was the only person he knew who had a personal quantum computer. It had taken nearly a year to build from components he'd begged, borrowed and stolen. The only benefit of having Parkinson's Disease was that people felt sorry for him. He wasn't proud of exploiting his condition, but computing trumped everything.

Yesterday, he'd sensed Samantha's unease after asking her about SEP. Given she was paid by the health service and was still receiving a widow's pension, he suspected she was scared of her own skin.

In his experience, most mysteries had a mundane explanation. Unlike conspiracy theorists, he believed Marilyn Monroe and Lady Diana were probably victims of misadventure rather than government assassination. By that yardstick, Arlo's mum had probably misheard SEP or, as Samantha suggested, it was just some benign procedure. But something didn't stack up, and he couldn't let it go.

Carl thought of himself as a grey hat hacker. Someone who hacked into networks to test their vulnerabilities, reporting their weaknesses back to their owners for a bounty. Maybe he wasn't as pure as the driven snow, but he wasn't a morally bankrupt black hat hacker either. He knew when people were taking the piss.

Tonight was lightweight stuff anyway. Not much more than a good old-fashioned Google, but somewhat off-piste. He'd already tried the obvious searches on the public, Clear Web, but nothing had come up. He wasn't surprised, given how the government censored everything.

The Deep Web was a good starting point. Off-limits to most and, therefore, less regulated than the Clear Web. The Dark Web was an even deeper plunge. A domain of saints and sinners. Free speech without oppression, rubbing shoulders with the criminal underworld.

The dark side of the internet scared the hell out of him. The bad guys were all there: identity thieves, phishing scammers, cyber terrorists, paedophiles, sex traffickers, drug lords and arms dealers. His primary defence was hiding behind a VPN, a Virtual Personal Network that concealed his identity and protected him against extortion. In addition, connection to the Dark Web was a tortuous chain of encrypted hops. Any would-be extortionist would have to decrypt and track every hop within the short time he would be online. In practice, it was totally secure.

With any luck, there would be postings on SEP. If not, he would ask some questions in forums and hopefully uncover the truth. Hacking a government site might not even be necessary. Surely someone out there knew something?

He powered up his computer and opened BioAhmia, a search engine for trawling the Deep Web. A quick search on SEP revealed nothing. He'd suspected as much. *Cut to the chase.*

He launched BioTor, the BioFace compatible browser that accessed the Dark Web. Despite its biological interface, he still accessed it the old-fashioned way using a terminal. That way, he could exploit the power of his quantum computer if he needed brute force tactics to hack anything. The thought of hacking dodgy sites using an implant made him shiver.

He used his trackball to type in the Dark Web address: 7rmath4ro2of2a42.onion/. Before his illness, he preferred using a mouse, but his tremor had made that impossible. The DBS had mostly fixed his shakes, but he'd never gone back as he'd always assumed he was on borrowed time.

Up popped a news site called SoylentNews. It claimed it was the last remaining site of unbiased news stories–news by the people, for the people. He trawled through the articles. They gave opinions on the volcanic winter, the self-serving actions of governments, and the military build-up in the Middle East. But nothing on SEP. He came to a section on medical news, but everything posted concerned biohacks of the BioFace. He searched for 'SEP' but found nothing, so he tried a different onion address.

Dark Lair's splash screen appeared. He navigated the menu to access a forum where users discussed the lies the government was spinning. He leaned back in his chair and strummed his fingers on the desk.

Honesty is best.

Nodding to himself, he leaned forward and used his trackball to type: 'My mate's mother is in a nursing home facing SEP. What's SEP?'

He clicked return and waited.

Several seconds later, a response popped up.

'WTF. That'll be Scrounging Expensive Pensioners.'

Carl tutted. 'Thanks for that. BIGOT,' he typed.

'My pleasure, ASS HOLE.' Popped up.

Carl rubbed his head. The Dark Web was full of trolls. He was about to try another forum when a new message appeared.

'You've got that wrong.'

'Sorry?' Carl entered.

'It's not SEP.'

Orange and blue lights played across the ceiling. Carl jumped, knocking over a glass of water as a siren wailed.

'My mate's mum has misheard?' he entered, ignoring the spill.

'No, you've spelt it wrong,' came a reply.

Carl glimpsed a shadow go past the half-closed curtain.

Who the hell's out there?

'How should it be spelt?' he entered before standing up. His legs failed to cooperate as he stumbled down the hall, bouncing off the walls. At the front door, he stared at the moulded glass. He could swear someone was outside peering in, hands cupped to the glass. Or was it the way the light reflected? The door rattled; Carl's heart missed a beat. A colourful card tumbled onto the doormat.

'Spooktacular. Ghost tours are us,' the flyer read. The shadowy figure faded into the night.

'You couldn't make it up,' Carl muttered and lumbered back

to his den.

'CEP' was waiting on his screen.

Carl sat down and placed his hand on the trackball. Suddenly his hand juddered like the trackball was electrified. He jerked his hand away, but his little finger twitched as if possessed. He willed it to stop, but the tremors spread through his hand like a wave. Within seconds, his whole arm was shaking.

'Whar id it?' he managed to enter, desperately trying to control himself.

'You drunk? LOL!' Flashed up on the screen.

Concentrating with all his might, he carefully typed, checking each character as his whole body began to shake. It took him nearly a minute before he'd hit enter.

'What's CEP please?'

Seconds later, a reply appeared. 'Compulsory Euthanasia Programme. It's part of the PATMOS programme. You need to warn your buddy.'

Carl's body was now not his own. Excruciating cramps wracked his limbs, and his hands balled into fists. The BioTor browser crashed; an ominous black window appeared, a message scrolling: 'Do that again, or tell anyone, and we'll finish the job.'

Carl's whole body went into one massive agonising spasm. He lurched, crashed onto his machine, and toppled to the floor. He lay there shaking, mouth foaming, eyes wild.

12

L ana marched through BDL's reception on a mission–chin up and eyes staring resolutely ahead, like a marathon runner holding it together in their final mile. Her navy-blue trouser-suit and crisp white blouse were formal but stylish, her outfit personalised only by a discreet gold chain. She looked simply stunning.

Yesterday afternoon, she'd had a BioFace call with her boss, Dreyfuss, while working from home. She'd made barely any progress all day, worrying about Mia, and still had no idea how she would look after her while holding down her job. Today was also home working, but Dreyfuss had told her to come in. He'd said it was a matter of urgency, but–from his tone–she hadn't felt she could ask why. She'd barely slept worrying about it. Her job was her life and still didn't pay enough for Mia's care. She had to work something out. She sensed she was in the middle of one of life's perfect storms–a series of trials pushing her to the limit. But it wasn't going to beat her. She would deal with each one in turn and knock them all down.

As she reached the reception desk, the contents of a row of crystal glass display cabinets caught her eye. She'd seen them hundreds of times before but never grew tired of the inspirational devices. They chronicled the development of the BioFace, from its humble beginnings as a smartphone app to a mature bioelectronics device embedded in the body. She kept reminding herself that–no matter what happened in the meeting–this was why she worked here.

She'd been at BDL for nine years, starting soon after she'd

defended her PhD on the role of psychology in BCI, brain-computer interfacing. In her interview, they said her thesis on understanding how human behaviour was governed by how neurons fired in the brain was crucial to BDL's future. They said they were designing a product with an embedded processor that could individually trigger all of the 86 billion neurons at will. But, they needed to know how the neuronal firing sequences controlled the senses, speech, memories, emotions and mood. They told her that that was why they needed her.

Her friends had warned her that employers often told candidates what they wanted to hear in interviews. That certainly wasn't true for BDL. She loved her job–it was a perfect opportunity to apply what she'd learnt.

She entered the open-plan office.

'Hi Lana,' Julie, her office chum, said as she approached her desk. 'How's it going?'

'All good, thanks,' Lana replied robotically.

'How was the conference?'

'All very relevant to BDL,' she said, wishing she could get on with the meeting.

'Meet anyone interesting?' Julie gave a mischievous smile.

'I'll tell you later,' Lana said.

'Can't wait,' Julie rubbed her hands together.

Lana turned and started to walk away.

'Oh, and ...' Julie called after her.

Lana spun around. 'What?' she mouthed.

'Dreyfuss and his cronies are waiting for you upstairs.'

'I'm on my way up there now,' Lana replied. 'Thanks for the heads-up.'

'Nothing serious, I hope?'

'I'll soon find out.' She grimaced and continued to stride down the centre of the office, nodding to several colleagues.

An imposing silver twister of a chromed spiral staircase faced her at the end of the office. Her footsteps made metallic clanging noises over the quiet of the office as she climbed to the mezzanine level–it felt like she was journeying to the gods.

At the top, her head spun as she gazed out over the open plan. She grabbed a polished metal rail to steady herself and peered down a long corridor. At the end was a solid and expensive-looking oak door. Lifting her chin, she took a deep breath and marched towards it. Her eyes were drawn to a gold plaque: Jeremy Dreyfuss, CEO. She'd stood here many times before, but this felt different. Serious. Scary serious. She knocked and waited, hearing muffled voices. *Who's in there with him? Didn't Julie say his cronies?*

The lock clicked; Lana started. The door swung inwards.

'Hi, Lana.' Dreyfuss beamed. 'Good to see you looking so well.'

'Thanks, Jeremy. You too,' Lana replied, trying to sound casual.

'Come in and meet my old friends.' He extended his arm and beckoned for her to enter. She hesitated and fiddled with her necklace. 'Chop, chop,' he urged. Lana forced a smile and shuffled through the doorway.

A young woman, probably in her late teens or early twenties, sat in profile at a central table. She looked familiar, but Lana didn't know why. Her charcoal-grey trouser suit looked formal and expensive. It was as if she was trying to make an impression. Yet her nose stud jarred and gave away the lie. Then she remembered. It was the girl from the conference.

Three men were standing at the end of the room, gazing out of a large window. They were deep in muted conversation, and Lana suspected they hadn't even noticed the panoramic view of the city.

'Gents,' Dreyfuss announced in a raised voice, 'may I introduce you to Dr Grace, our resident expert on BCI.'

Two of the men spun around in unison. They stood rigidly to attention, hands clasped firmly behind their backs, beaming synthetically.

Despite being in their late forties, they looked very handsome: tall, dark and impeccably tailored in black suits.

She recognised the man on the left as Richard Chapel, the CEO of Space Swarm UK. *What's Arlo's boss doing here?* The man on the right seemed vaguely familiar, but she didn't know why.

The third man in the middle turned casually. He had an olive complexion and appeared to be Middle Eastern. The other men watched as he sauntered over and tucked in behind.

'John Channing,' the man said, thrusting out his hand. 'Delighted to meet you, Dr Grace. I believe we've met.'

'Yes.' She shook his hand. 'At the conference.'

Channing placed his spare hand above hers so she couldn't let go. With eyes of coal, he stared into her face.

'Yes, Dr Grace. That would be it.'

'Lana. Please call me Lana.' She shifted uneasily.

'Works for me.' Channing smiled. 'Isn't Lana Gaelic for fair and beautiful?'

Lana's eyes narrowed. *How does he know that?* 'I believe so,' she replied.

'Oh, and please,' Channing continued. 'This is Lucy Stevens, my PA.' He released his grip and gestured to the young lady sitting at the table. 'I believe you also met at the conference?'

Lana nodded, stepped forward and volunteered her slender hand. She recalled their brief chat about running when Lucy had suggested she should BioFace her. But she'd not found the time. Maybe Lucy had taken it personally?

Lucy rose from the chair and sidled over, eyeing her suspiciously. They shook hands. Her palm was small, but her grip firm, almost aggressive. Lana was drawn to the curious scar on her forehead and wondered if she headbutted people who broke their promises.

'*Lovely* to see you again, Lucy,' Lana said, hoping she sounded sincere.

'Likewise,' Lucy said flatly.

Channing stepped in and puffed out his chest. 'Jeremy has told me great things about you, Lana.'

Lana took a half-step back and fiddled with her necklace.

Channing seemed to notice her unease. 'Please let me

explain.' He pulled on his cuff, exposing a gold cufflink with a single red gemstone that Lana thought looked like a bloodshot eye.

'Jeremy tells me you've done pioneering research on bioelectronics. Tricks that could extend the functionality of the BioFace.'

'Er … well, I wouldn't exactly call them tricks!'

'Didn't Arthur C. Clarke once say advanced technology is indistinguishable from magic?'

'Yes, I believe he did.'

'And your work is advanced?'

'I guess so.'

'So in my book, that makes your technology … tricks.' Channing studied her reaction–she didn't bite. 'Anyway, semantics … Tell me about your ideas.'

Politician or scientist?

'The current BioFace,' she explained, 'is just the combination of a universally connectable software-defined communications device, like an old connect-and-go smartphone, fused with a medical diagnostics system. But, if we were to use the full connectivity of the implant, it could be *so* much more.'

Dreyfuss looked flustered. 'Let's not be too critical of the current BioFace product Lana. The whole world is using the latest model. Without it, people don't get healthcare, social security, banking and communications; the list is endless. Without a BioFace, you're a nobody!'

'I wasn't being critical,' Lana countered. 'I think it's a great product. But, I think the future possibilities are mind-blowing. For example, it could assist bodily functions by modifying the signals that regulate the production and release of hormones or cause pain. Many patients wouldn't have to take drugs and suffer dangerous side effects. It could save the government a fortune. Importantly, the BioFace implant wouldn't need to be changed. The firmware could be updated wirelessly across the network.'

Channing nodded his head thoughtfully. 'My, you're a smart lady, Lana. You seem to have a profound vision.' He turned to Jeremy. 'You're a very lucky CEO. I hope you recognise Lana's talent,' he said, studying Jeremy's reaction. Jeremy shifted uneasily.

Lana struggled to conceal a smirk.

'Er ... yes, John.' Jeremy lowered his gaze. 'I completely agree.'

'Let me introduce Greg Shaw,' Channing continued, turning to face the other man. 'He's Chief Information Biologist at MSL, the government's research lab. He's very interested in the potential capabilities of the BioFace.'

Shaw was also well over six feet tall. He looked like a salesman–impeccably dressed, with immaculate touched-up black hair and a fluorescent smile that could melt weak hearts.

Politician. No way he's a Scientist.

They shook hands.

'Perhaps you'd like to say a few words, Greg?' Channing prompted.

'Thanks, John. Yes, as you say, Lana, the current BioFace is mostly just a read device. It monitors bodily functions but doesn't control anything other than the recently introduced smart contact lenses. My department is particularly interested in increasing write access functionality.'

'I see ...' Lana massaged her brow. 'Any particular functions?'

Momentarily, Greg floundered. 'Er ... as you say,' he continued finally. 'It could provide medical benefits. And augment intelligence if a user had access to BioFace's processor and memory in addition to their dedicated BioDrive. People could have encyclopaedic knowledge, the mental arithmetic of a supercomputer, and speak any language.'

Lana recalled a recent review article in the press that had made similar claims. 'Indeed, I think that's all possible with current hardware,' Lana agreed, 'And the code for the interfacing firmware has already been written. But, of course, clinical trials are the time-consuming part of the process that proves everything's safe.'

'Ah, yes, bureaucracy standing in the way of progress.'

Lana glared. *How ironic.*

'I agree with Lana,' Channing interjected. 'Processes and protocols are there for a good reason.'

Lana glanced at Channing. He stared back, unblinking as if he was reading her mind. He didn't show any embarrassment and kept on staring. Lana held the stare for a few seconds and then had to look away. As she turned, she noticed Richard was also staring at her. He hadn't said a word and seemed to be mirroring Channing. *They're under his spell!*

Channing continued 'The other piece of the jigsaw is connectivity–that's where Richard Chapel comes in. He's CEO of Space Swarm UK. Have you met before, Lana?'

'I've seen Richard at conferences, but I don't think we've been formally introduced,' she replied.

'Ah, a perfect opportunity then.' Channing rubbed his hands together and nodded to Richard.

'Pleased to meet you, Lana.' Chapel shook her hand. His grip felt firm and as cold as marble.

'It's a pleasure,' Lana replied. 'So, tell me, how do satellite swarms fit into all of this?' she asked, knowing the answer.

'The BioFace is a great product, but it's let down by flaky network connectivity in certain environments: street canyons and where there's a low density of mesh networks.'

Dreyfuss cleared his throat. 'Bu–'

'Please let me finish, Jeremy,' Chapel interjected, glaring at him. 'Space Swarm plans to solve this connectivity problem using a space swarm of geostationary nanosatellites. That would guarantee ubiquitous connectivity and control. We already have a network undergoing trials.'

They've been working on this for months, if not years …

'My thoughts exactly,' Channing said, smiling. He turned to Lana. 'What do you think, Lana?'

Lana was ready for him. 'I suspected that was why Richard

was here.'

Channing laughed and patted her on the shoulder. 'Of course, you did, Lana.'

Channing turned to Dreyfuss. 'So–go on, Jeremy–give Lana the good news.'

'Ahem,' Dreyfuss shifted uncomfortably and examined his hands. 'Er, well, Lana, we thought you might be interested in heading up a new project. It would involve taking the BioFace to the next level.'

Lana's mouth fell open. *Mia. Does this help Mia?*

Dreyfuss noticed her shock. 'Are you OK, Lana?'

'Erm, yes, thank you, Jeremy. And what would the position entail exactly?' Lana replied, trying to contain her excitement.

'Ah, yes ...' Channing smiled. 'The *devil's* always in the detail. Well, Dreyfuss?'

'Er, yes, well,' Dreyfuss floundered. 'It concerns guaranteeing seamless connectivity and extending write access for enhancing the user's experience. It would utilise your experience in neuronal coding.'

'I've already written most of the code,' Lana blurted.

She thought of Mia again. 'It sounds like a great opportunity. Presumably, it would be well rewarded?'

'Of course,' Dreyfuss confirmed. 'The job represents a substantial promotion and would be remunerated accordingly. Assuming you accept, of course.'

Lana's face flushed, mind racing. With any luck, it would pay for a nurse in Bristol. She broke out into a broad smile. 'Of course, I accept,' she gasped. 'I'm chuffed to bits.'

'We thought you'd like the idea.' Channing scrutinised her face.

'I'll do my very best, sir,' Lana said. 'You won't be disappointed.'

'Of course, you will, Lana–that's why we chose you.'

Channing checked his BioFace. 'OK, well, I believe that concludes everything. I think we should be heading off, Greg?'

'Mission accomplished.' Greg nodded thoughtfully.

'Anything else you'd like to add, Richard?'

'Nope, we're done.'

With that, the three men and Lucy said their goodbyes. They collected their belongings and headed for the door.

'Lucy,' Lana called after her.

Lucy turned, expressionless.

'I haven't forgotten to get in contact,' Lana's eyes pleaded. 'I've just had too much on.'

Lucy gave a forced smile. 'I understand.' She turned and followed the men out. Lana ironed her knitted brow with the heel of her hand.

Dreyfuss trailed after them like a lost puppy. Lana presumed he would be having one of his informal chats in the car park, where most decisions were made. As Dreyfuss reached the door, he turned and looked back over his shoulder. 'Can you hang about, please–I'd like to have a quick word after they've gone.'

'Of course, sir,' Lana replied.

Lana was left alone in the office, hands trembling. She sat down, took a deep breath and exhaled slowly, trying to relax. A few minutes later, her nerves had calmed. Casually, she scanned the room.

Her gaze strayed to a filing cabinet in a corner by Dreyfuss's desk. She knew he was old-school and paranoid about cyber security, preferring to lock away sensitive documents rather than store them digitally. A combination lock protected the cabinet, and the drawers automatically locked when closed. Ironically, a report was protruding. It had probably been laid on the hangers when he'd shut the drawer in a hurry.

She rounded the desk to push the paperwork back in. As she reached out, her eyes were drawn to the word 'Top,' which was part of the header. *Top Secret?* In the corner of the page was an embossed five-pointed silver star. *Israel?* Intrigued, she glanced nervously over her shoulder. *Surely it can't hurt.*

She pulled the document out and scanned the title: 'PATMOS and the POX Commands.'

Click.

Shit! The door! In a blind panic, she posted the report back through the gap between the drawers, rounded the desk and raced for the door, just as Dreyfuss entered.

'Great meeting Jeremy,' she exclaimed, forcing a smile.

'Indeed it was,' Jeremy agreed. 'Are you OK to have a quick word now, please?'

'Of course.'

'We've had a brief chat about what we'd like you to do in the second phase,' he continued.

'Second phase?'

'Yes, of our BioFace upgrade programme. It's already started.'

'Sounds exciting.'

'Indeed it is.'

'What will that involve?'

'We need a test group. We already think we know who they are, but we can discuss that later.'

'And what happens to them?'

'Er, well, actually, there's a relevant chapter at the end of your thesis. It was in the recommendations section under a heading called Speculative Topics.'

'Oh yes, I remember ...'

'Well, I think the hardware and firmware are ready now.' Dreyfuss grinned.

The blood drained from Lana's face. She'd only added that bit to her thesis to impress the external examiner. She'd never dreamt it might be possible.

13

SATURDAY, 14 SEPTEMBER 2052

Arlo scanned the street for anyone who might recognise him. Only a street cleaner across the road was looking his way. Relieved, he strode into Bristol's Che Café with a spring in his step.

He'd awoken at 5 am with a splitting headache after more vivid nightmares. They'd been so bad he'd contemplated going back on his old meds, even though he knew they would make him a zombie. Unable to face his list of weekend jobs, he brewed a coffee and started clearing out old BioFace messages from unrecognised senders. Ordinarily, he wouldn't have opened any, not wanting to risk a malware infection, but one had an intriguing subject heading: 'Spaceman.' Curiosity piqued, he'd opened it. The message was from Lana.

'Hey, spaceman. I've had an idea about your space signal. Maybe you'd like to discuss it over a coffee? I can meet you in Che Café at 9 am if you're an early riser. Lana X.'

Excited, he'd messaged her straight back: 'Hi, Lana. I'm intrigued. CU there. Arlo X.'

Wracked by guilt, he'd told Alisha he was going to a breakfast work meeting.

After John's snooping and weird call, his guard was up, especially as Lana seemed to know him, but he didn't think it could hurt just talking about the signal.

Arlo hadn't been to Che Café before–Alisha wasn't keen as she thought Marxists were anti-religious. Large grainy prints of Ernesto 'Che' Guevara and Fidel Castro adorned the entrance walls. Communism was a tricky one for Arlo. Before the disaster, he'd hated the ideology. He thought people should be rewarded for their efforts and believed communism destroyed motivation. But after the Great Eruption, he wasn't so sure. Sometimes life dealt a cruel hand. Getting to know some of the homeless in Portland had proved that. But he wasn't so sure that forcibly levelling the playing field was the answer either.

Irrespective of political ideology, he admired Che and his David versus Goliath struggle against the large corporations for workers' rights in Chile. He also empathised with his war against Fulgencio Batista, who'd been corrupted by the Mafia. Che was undoubtedly honourable and courageous in his fight for justice. He could identify with that.

As Arlo strolled through the diner, he paused and admired a sepia-toned poster showing a young Che with Alberto Granada in Chile, sitting casually astride a vintage motorcycle. *Wasn't that where it had all started?* He rubbed his beard as he studied their expressions. *Would Che have turned back if he'd known what was coming?*

Arlo scanned the bar for Lana. Patrons sat at several tables in the trendy venue. One unaccompanied man in his early twenties was sitting with his eyes flicking. His gaze then settled. He leaned back, a salacious smile spreading across his face. Arlo wondered what the world was coming to with people living out their augmented reality fantasies in public.

As he entered the main dining area, he saw Lana sitting at a table in a secluded part of the restaurant, sipping from a cup. He paused, hidden by a pillar, and watched. She had perfect bone structure and pale skin. Her wavy honey-coloured hair cascaded over her shoulders and swanlike neck. He studied the elegance of her subtle pearl earrings, spellbound by how she cocked her eyebrows and wrinkled her nose as she browsed her BioFace. Suddenly, he realised he was being a creep and carried on walking, annoyed with himself.

From the corner of his eye, he saw her glance his way. She waved. Awkwardly, he feigned surprise and waved back. Chair legs screeched across the tiled floor. She stepped into the aisle, grabbed both of his shoulders and pulled him towards her in a warm embrace. Their cheeks touched. Her skin was smooth, her fragrance delicate and flowery. His head spun.

'Hey, Arlo.' She squeezed his arm and gazed into his eyes. 'Good to see you again.'

Arlo grinned inanely, momentarily lost for words. She looked puzzled. Arlo noticed her confusion. 'I'm flattered you've had time to look at my signal,' he said.

'Don't get your hopes up–my idea is probably rubbish,' she replied.

'Well, Carl gave it his best shot and failed. And, he's a total genius.' Arlo realised his faux pas. 'You might be an even bigger genius, of course.'

'Keep digging,' she laughed.

Arlo relaxed. 'Can I get you something?' he asked as she sat down.

She looked down at her half-drunk coffee. 'I'm good, thanks.'

Arlo started to move towards the counter as a man, dressed in black trousers and a white open-necked shirt, strolled past.

'You guys need anything?' he asked cheerily.

'A black coffee with no sugar would be perfect,' Arlo replied, sitting.

'Anything to eat?' He lifted his chin expectantly.

'I recommend the pastelitos,' Lana suggested. 'They're gorgeous.'

Arlo was mesmerised by the way she said gorgeous. The manager strummed his fingers on a notepad.

'Arlo?' a voice said.

'Sorry ...' Arlo said vacantly.

'They do one with cheese, pineapple and coconut,' Lana continued. 'They're divine.'

'Erm, yeah. My colleague knows best,' Arlo said.

'Very well, sir.' The proprietor smiled knowingly and walked away.

'Colleague now, is it?' Lana laughed. 'I suppose I *have* started working with you.' She wrinkled her nose.

'Listen,' Arlo said. 'Tell me about your idea–the suspense is killing me.'

'How long have you got?' She sipped her coffee. 'It's a bit of a story.'

'As long as it takes,' Arlo replied.

'I'll try and keep it short.' She touched Arlo's arm.

Arlo leaned in, elbows on the table, hands interlocked. 'Fire away–I won't butt in.'

Lana cleared her throat. 'I had a half-day yesterday and went for a run. I love running–it helps me unwind. Good for having ideas too.'

Arlo found himself studying her perfect cheekbones again and the natural lustre of her fair skin. He forced himself to look away.

'I ran along the river path,' Lana continued. 'The one that goes past the old docks, by the inland sea. It was crazy cold–'

'I bet it was,' Arlo interjected.

She paused.

'Sorry,' he said, looking down.

'It's OK.' She smiled. 'After a couple of miles, I stopped on the shore of the massive frozen lake. You know–where ice-yachts race each other from Whitchurch to Kingswood.'

Arlo nodded.

'I paused to catch my breath–the view was fantastic.' She hesitated and looked up as if imaging the scene. 'I stood there for a few minutes, mulling over what you'd said in the conference. I remembered you saying that the signal consists of a stream of symbols, each chosen from just four possibilities. A bit like Morse code, but with four symbols instead of two. I'm not a signal processing expert and nowhere near as clever as your friend Carl.' Lana winked. 'I just let my mind wander ...'

'As good a strategy as any,' Arlo said.

'Anyway,' Lana continued, 'it occurred to me that the number of symbols used to represent information in a code is often significant: 26 letters in our alphabet, twelve hours on a clock, six numbers on a die. So, I asked myself the question: why does your code only have four?'

'I like your logic.' Arlo nodded.

'Also,' Lana said, 'I remembered you saying that not all combinations of the four symbols appear with equal regularity, suggesting they map to an alphabet where some letters appear more often than others. Perhaps a bit like Scrabble, where letters are scored differently according to their prevalence. But you and Carl don't think it's a message.'

'Well, it might be,' Arlo added, 'but we haven't been clever enough to decipher it.'

Lana gave a sympathetic smile. 'While mulling the idea over by the lake, I saw a snow devil racing across the ice. It stopped right in front of me–almost as if it had singled me out. It kept spinning in a helix. I felt hypnotised by it. That's when it hit me–'

'*What did?*' Arlo realised he'd interrupted her again. 'Sorry … I can't help myself.'

'You're all right.' Lana grinned. 'Where was I …? Ah, yes, this snow devil was twisting in front of me, like it was putting on a private dance.'

'Sorry, but why's this relevant?' Arlo shrugged his shoulders.

'That was when I had my Eureka moment.'

'I don't follow.'

'The four symbol code. The helix shape. Don't you get it?'

'No.' Arlo looked puzzled. '*Should I?*'

Lana laughed. 'Maybe … You're thinking about the wrong sort of codes.'

'Don't tease me! *What is it?*'

'I think it might be DNA.'

'*DNA?*'

'Yes, deoxyribonucleic acid. DNA.'

'Why?'

'DNA has a base-four code. It's made up of four chemical

building blocks called bases: cytosine, guanine, adenine and thymine.'

'Are you suggesting the symbols in my signal might be a list of those bases?'

'I know it sounds wild.'

'My god.' Arlo stared into space. 'If that's true ...'

Lana fell silent and examined her nails.

'Christ!' Arlo exclaimed. 'Maybe it's not an alien message at all. Maybe *it is the alien*–'

'Whoa! Hold on. Don't get ahead of yourself.' Lana interjected. 'I probably only thought of the idea because I've studied biology. A DNA signal from space–for heaven's sake!'

'Yeah, you're right. But it sounds plausible.'

'Let's check out a few details,' Lana continued. 'That might immediately rule it out.'

'OK, but first, explain something. I've heard about genomes. How do they fit in?'

'Ah, OK. The genome is a blueprint for life. A human genome has 23 DNA strand pairs–the chromosomes. Each strand consists of codons, which are groups of three bases. Each codon signals a particular amino acid from twenty possibilities. The sequence of amino acids, coded by the DNA, instructs a creature's body on how to build each of its constituent proteins. The proteins are like the bricks and wood used to build a house. The DNA is like the instruction booklet telling the body how to assemble them.'

'Sounds complicated. Well, maybe my signal is an alien genome?'

'Could be!'

Arlo rubbed his head. 'But the signal's huge.'

'So's a genome,' Lana exclaimed. 'How big is it?'

'Well, there are several massive bursts.'

'Maybe it's a repeat transmission.' Lana shrugged her shoulders. 'To make sure the transmitted signal is received intact–a simple form of error correction?'

'Perhaps.'

'So how long is each burst?'

Arlo rubbed his beard. 'Over three billion symbols.'

Arlo expected this to rule it out, but she nodded slowly, gazing vacantly at the distant posters.

'That's consistent with the length,' she mumbled.

The proprietor reappeared. 'Your pastelitos and coffee sir.'

Arlo looked up. 'Perfect.' He nodded his thanks.

'It's my pleasure.' The proprietor placed a folded slip on a saucer and walked away.

Arlo took a bite. 'Mmm, great recommendation,' he said, covering his mouth with his hand. 'Food for thought.' She rolled her eyes.

'So what else do you want to know?' he mumbled.

'Do all the symbols occur with the same regularity?'

Arlo recalled the symbols' statistics. 'Well, they're all used, but some appear maybe two to three times more often.'

'Also consistent,' she said, 'and not just with any genome. That sounds human.'

'You're bloody kidding!'

'No.' Lana shook her head. 'It all seems to fit.'

'Anything else we should check?' Arlo gripped the table.

Lana gazed upwards. She seemed about to say something and then stopped herself.'

'What's up?' he queried.

'I was going to suggest something, but maybe it's not such a great idea.'

'Try me.'

Lana fidgeted with one of her pearl earrings.

'Look, Lana. I can see you're upset about something, and it's none of my business. You've already been helpful, and I appreciate it. I should probably go away and talk it over with Carl. And, if I learn something about DNA and genomes into the bargain, it'd be a good start!' He patted her lightly on the arm.

She gave Arlo a pained expression. 'I don't want to let you down if I can help.'

'You've already helped me loads,' Arlo replied. 'Honest! It's not a problem.'

Lana's face hardened. 'The man we should talk to is Professor Stanford.'

'What? The crazy guy at the conference? Are you OK with him after your feisty exchange? Isn't he a fraud?'

'I know, but he has equipment and contacts. He controls the whole of Bristol University's Biotechnology Department!'

'So why the reluctance?'

'We have a history.'

Arlo peered at Lana through his wild hair. 'Surely not?'

Their conversation dried up. She inspected her nails and then looked up defiantly.

'He assaulted me when I was a student,' she exclaimed.

Arlo's face dropped. 'Lana. I'm so sorry.' He gazed into her eyes. 'Well, that completely rules out that idea then–you must stay well clear of him!'

'It's OK. He owes me.'

'Well, I don't know what he did–and I have no right to ask– but it's entirely your call.'

'Leave it with me,' she said. 'I'll work it out.'

'Cool,' Arlo said.

Lana's eyes lit up. 'Well, now that you know something personal about me, how about telling me why you fled the stage?'

Arlo twisted the wedding ring round and round his finger.

'It's OK if you'd rather not,' Lana conceded.

'No, it's fine.' He shook his head.

Arlo told her about his dad's cancer and his dream job in Seattle looking for extraterrestrial life. His face then seemed haunted as he recounted the events on the day of the Great Eruption.

'I'm *so* sorry.' Lana reached out and cupped his hand in hers.

'It is what it is,' Arlo mumbled. 'We all have crosses to bear.'

'Indeed.' Lana nodded.

Arlo jumped as his BioFace pulsed. A message icon flashed

red on the side of his vision showing it was urgent.

'Excuse me,' he apologised. 'I need to get this.'

She nodded and looked away. He brought up the message header in his vision–it was from Alisha.

'Where are you, Arlo?' it read. 'You've done it again. You promised Josh you'd take him to ice hockey this morning, and now it's too late!'

Arlo glanced solemnly at Lana. 'I have to go. I'm in trouble with my wife.' He gazed into his lap. 'I forgot I said I'd take my son, Joshua, to ice hockey.'

Lana gave a sympathetic smile. 'The challenges of being a parent …' Her eyes glazed over.

Arlo sensed he'd touched another raw nerve. 'I, really, must go,' he said, wishing he could stay. 'Thanks again for your help.' She didn't react. He squeezed her arm, and she jumped. 'Your ideas about DNA are amazing,' he continued, 'but be careful with Stanford.'

Lana wrinkled her nose.

Arlo unfolded the bill and waved the proprietor over. Arlo BioFaced some money with a beep, and the proprietor smiled.

'That's very generous, sir,' he said. 'I hope to see you both again soon.'

Lana looked up. 'I hope so too.'

The proprietor gave a subtle bow and walked off to attend to another table.

'Right, *really* must go,' Arlo said.

'OK. Hear from you soon,' Lana said sweetly.

They both stood. Lana leaned across the table and pecked him on the cheek. He so badly wanted to stay.

As Arlo headed for the door, he glanced up at the poster of Che and Alberto astride their motorbike, the encounter that had kicked it all off.

14

The siren's pitch dropped as blue and orange lights danced on the ceiling. Near darkness descended. Arlo rolled onto his side, struggling to find comfort, wishing he could find peace. Alisha breathed rhythmically next to him, her body tranquil. At least that was something. He tried lying on his back, hoping it might help him sleep. Staring at the grey ceiling, he prayed the Isabella horror show was over. He replayed his meeting with Lana in Che Café, wishing he could live in the present and dream of her.

He visualised how the snow devil might have looked as it twisted across the frozen lake. His legs began to twitch. He heard the snow hiss as it brushed against the ice. His father had just finished reading him a bedtime story–something about aliens. Arlo bombarded him with questions. His father put a finger to pursed lips. 'Shhh ...' The snow devil morphed into a helter-skelter in an amusement park by the sea. Gaudy letters, painted in fairground script, decorated the spiralling descent. He tried to make out words as he flew by but only saw the letters A, C, G and T.

Over the sea, he flew like a helicopter, almost skimming the surf, up and over towering cliffs pounded by gigantic waves. The sky turned tangerine. On top of the cliff, a man walked through a temple's open-air colonnade. A man's voice–his father's–told him it was Elah in the Temple of Gemidia.

The temple crowned a rocky outcrop–the focal point of Turnbull's capital city, Gomor. Slanting rays of amber light sparkled copper from dust in the air, threading the forest of marble. A light breeze blew from colossal crystal ducts that shrouded the city from relentless gales.

Elah wore a white long-sleeved robe that reached down to his golden sandals. His hood was pulled down, revealing a kind, compassionate face, serene but with his jaw set. Beads of sweat formed on his brow. He adjusted a garland of rose-coloured gemintha flowers that adorned his head, centred a tube of golden cloth that tightly bound the middle of his long black beard, and discreetly wiped away a bead of sweat.

He walked between the columns, flanked by statues of the Gemid emperors that chronicled Turnbull's dynasties. Near the end, the figures came alive. Ethereal Gemid priestesses stood provocatively, their iridescent sarongs playing brightly coloured vistas of Turnbull's flora and fauna. Mystical beasts ran through forests of lush purple and pink vegetation. The priestesses threw handfuls of fragrant rose-coloured germonia petals high into the air above his head. Smiling, they filed in behind, mirroring his steps. Choristers made melancholic chants that reverberated off the temple's walls. The last priestess gave him a tender look and touched his arm as a tear rolled down her cheek.

A light breeze ruffled Elah's wavy shoulder-length ebony hair as he stared at a granite altar lying at the end of the aisle. His sapphire eyes focused on a limestone arch that spanned the sacred portal, the apex of the stonework capped by a skull-sized crystal globe.

Originally nominated from the Faradic Institute of elite programmers, he'd been chosen from a select group of recruits to join Space Swarm, an academy for seeding the cosmos. His destiny was a small blue planet lying mid-way across a galactic arm of the Milky Way. Other recruits had been picked to seed far-flung places in the galaxy, but most had failed, earmarked for scouting and mining missions.

But Elah's badge of honour, with its celebrity and regal pageantry, came at a heavy price–he would never set foot on Turnbull again. His imminent mission began by triggering his engram, the genetically engineered gland that saved his memories, thoughts and consciousness. The faradic gland in his neck transmitted this information on bio-generated radio waves. But the engram could only be triggered by primal emotion–extreme stress or imminent death. And therein lay the catch.

The colonnade terminated in a forum. A crowd of Gemid citizens stood waiting, fanned in concentric arcs around the altar, a gap left through which he could pass. Their hands reached out, touching and stroking his arms. He slipped through their ranks and stopped in front of the arch, a low slab of polished black quartz blocking his path. Off to one side, a fist-sized red flame burned intensely in a golden bowl. Beyond the alter, a cliff dropped precipitously to the jagged coastline of the Gravid sea. Macriodaurs, giant featherless lizard-like birds, soared the gales over the vast ocean as titanic waves, whipped up by planetary tidal locking, pounded vermillion sandstone cliffs. The red dwarf star, Gox, breathed life into Turnbull, in one never-ending day, from its fixed position on the pink horizon. It appeared to be bleeding for him.

He lifted his chin and proffered his hands to the two high priests who flanked the altar, resplendent in hooded golden gowns, gloves and masks. A priest took each hand.

'Beloved Elah, please kneel,' the priest on his left commanded in Gemish. 'Chosen one, prepare yourself for your glorious eternal journey.'

Elah knelt, and the crowd spontaneously broke out into staccato clicking. Using his free gloved hand, the priest on his right anointed his forehead with fragrant oil and made ceremonial hand gestures.

'May you seed the cosmos with love,' he proclaimed.

Both priests retreated, the one on the right dropping his gloves into the red flame with a sputter of golden sparks. Elah knelt alone at the altar, hands clenched in anticipation. He inhaled deeply and bowed, revealing a circular red tattoo of Gox on his nape.

The priests began to murmur a deep chant. The crowd echoed the chant in a higher pitch, its volume growing louder and louder, reaching a crescendo. On the order of one of the priests, the crowd fell silent and completely still. Moments later, the nerve agent, dissolved in the sacred oil, began to act.

Elah's body contorted. He writhed and twisted, his face a mask of pain. His eyeballs began to vibrate, faster and faster. Suddenly, they locked rigidly in a fixed stare.

The globe that capped the arch strobed briefly with an intense purple light as his faradic gland began to emit radio waves. The crowd clicked. Paralysed, he collapsed to the cobbled floor, unable to break his fall. The garland cartwheeled and spun to rest. The side of his head bled, and foam oozed from his mouth, eyes straining in agony. The globe flashed again—strobing faster and faster, brighter and brighter—as his thoughts and memories began to transfer. The crowd erupted in a frenzy of clicking and clapping.

Arlo flew away from the temple. High above the cliffs, higher and higher, until the sky turned crimson and then black. Golden flashes glinted from the vast Dyson Swarm that orbited Gox, harvesting power and beaming it to the Magnetic Dipole Generator that lay, gravitationally trapped, at the Lagrangian. Without this magnetic field, Turnbull's atmosphere would be quickly stripped away by Gox's daily flares, rendering the planet lifeless.

A silver speck in the distance grew larger. A team of droids were working feverishly on an orbiting spaceport, unaffected by the vacuum and lethal cosmic rays high above the atmosphere and artificial magnetosphere. The spacecraft they were readying for departure was twice the size of a space shuttle, Ark 1307 emblazoned in rose-gold Gemid characters on its prow.

The genomic sequences, epigenetic codes and synaptic configurations of Elah and an elite engineer named Kefa had already been programmed into the Mission Computer. The metastable metallic hydrogen fuel pellets had been loaded into the containment vessel to propel the craft away from Turnbull's gravitational field and for final orbital insertion at its destination. The capacitive store that fed the parallel plates of the Alcubierre drive, embedded in the fuselage for compressing space-time, had been fully charged with excess energy beamed from the Dyson Swarm.

A transparent globe on the gantry above the craft glowed gold and began to pulse. A few seconds later, a purple light flashed on the control panel, signalling Elah's successful cerebral upload. Kefa's consciousness had already been installed one sleep cycle earlier. The droids wirelessly signalled the completion of their tasks to one another and rushed to the elevator to take refuge in the control silo.

A blue light flashed, confirming all systems were operational. The ignition sequence began, an igniter firing in the heart of the rocket engine to preheat the combustion chamber. Seconds later, pellets of metallic hydrogen were spat into the flame. The spaceport shook violently as the atomic hydrogen combined into gaseous molecules, heating the plume to the temperature of a star. Nozzles at the base of the craft vectored as the craft lifted effortlessly from the pad. Silently, it disappeared into the black vacuum of deep space.

Arlo's eyes fluttered open, squinting from the room lights. Alisha was sitting bolt upright next to him, the duvet pulled up to her waist. She was smiling. It was the smile he'd fallen in love with, the one he'd thought was forever lost.

'You look like you've slept well.' Arlo squeezed her arm through the delicate cotton nightie.

Alisha nodded. 'It was better than that.'

Arlo looked puzzled. 'How come?'

'I had a dream,' she said.

'A good one?' He raised his eyebrows.

'Yes. A lucid dream. One I could control or stop. But I didn't want it to stop. It was nice.'

'About what?'

'About God.'

'*God?* Tell me.'

'There was a man. He climbed a hill towards a temple. I think he was a Zoroastrian priest. Persian ...'

'How do you know?'

'It was a fire temple, square with a domed roof. I could smell the smoke. It mingled with the scent of narcissi.'

'What did he do?'

'He raked the fire. Next, he measured the position of the sun-rise against the temple's walls and prayed to Ahura Mazda.'

'Ahura Mazda?'

'The Zoroastrian deity.'

'I see,' Arlo said. 'And?'

'The hillside and sky were almost dark–the sun was rising. He stepped out of the temple and looked to the west. He spotted something.'

'*What did he see?*' Arlo grabbed her arm, enthralled.

'A bright-white star. The light grew brighter and brighter. *So* bright he had to close his eyes. When he opened them again, it had vanished. He seemed to panic, but then it came back. Dimmer, but still much brighter than anything else in the sky.'

'What happened then?'

'He ran down the hill.'

'Why?'

'I don't know. Maybe he went to tell others.'

'But I thought you said it was about God?'

'It was.'

'*Why?*'

'The light.'

'*What about the light?*'

'I think it was the star of Bethlehem.'

15

MONDAY, 16 SEPTEMBER 2052

Lana slogged up Bristol's Park Street from the frozen harbour. She'd feared it would be treacherous after further snow and a heavy frost, but the council had been busy. White mounds were piled high to the tops of shop windows, and grit scattered the footpaths.

Some mornings she struggled to know what to wear, but today she'd barely thought about it, throwing on black cargo trousers, clumpy work boots and a donkey jacket. She looked like a tomboy, with no make-up on and hair pulled back tightly in a bun.

She spotted Arlo waiting for her on the junction with Park Row, his head lowered, seemingly oblivious to the hustle and bustle of students and shoppers. She'd BioFaced him yesterday about a meeting she'd set up with Stanford. Luckily, Arlo had flexi-time and could make the 9 o'clock start. She hadn't dared ask how things were with his wife.

The Gothic Will's Memorial Building towered above them like a Hammer House of Horror film set, giving her a sense of foreboding. Stanford was still an open wound, but she kept trying to convince herself she was doing the right thing for Arlo and Mia.

The main university buildings used to lie at the top of a long, steep hill leading from the historic docks, but now they were only a short stroll from the new harbourfront. Ice hissed as kids skated, screams piercing the frosty air as they played tag. Lana's heart sank when she saw that some were as young as Mia.

Arlo didn't register her at first. Maybe it was because he was deep in thought or didn't recognise her in her mufti clothes with no make-up.

'Boo!' she shouted, instantly regretting it.

Arlo jumped. His face showed terror, then rage and, finally, delight.

What's going on in there?

'Lana!' He smiled. 'Forgive me. I was miles away.'

They embraced. She felt the wool of his beard against her smooth cheek.

'All ready for the prof.?' Arlo asked.

'*Don't,*' she said, raising a palm.

'Sorry.' His face turned serious. 'Are you sure about this?'

'Quite sure.'

'OK. Let's get it over with.'

Lana checked her coat was buttoned and then darted across the street. Arlo jogged behind, momentarily struggling to keep up. She made a beeline for a courtyard that ran around the base of the Will's Memorial building. Narrow concrete steps scaled the cliff–so steep and icy they looked impassable without mountaineering gear. Lana charged them, steadying herself using a black metal handrail that dripped icicle daggers.

She peered up at the Merchant Venturers building, perched on top of the hill like a Gothic castle, where Professor Stanford lectured his students. In her freshers' week, she'd read a book on Bristol's history. She recalled the building was named after the Guild of Merchants, who'd founded the original technical college. Despite their philanthropy, they'd made their fortune from the slave trade. Lana thought it apt that Stanford had made it his home.

At the top, Lana checked Arlo was still following and crossed the concourse to the front of the building. Craning her neck, she read the stainless steel sign that hung high above the entrance: Bristol University Biotechnology Department. She'd heard from friends that the building used to be the Electrical Engineering Department. But times had changed.

Bioelectronics, genetics and organic quantum computing were the new wonder subjects.

'So I guess we're here,' Arlo said awkwardly.

'Just give me a minute,' Lana gasped, inhaling deeply. Standing in silence, they admired the view of the city centre and frozen harbour. Ice boats tacked in the strengthening breeze.

'It must be great travelling to work by wind power,' she said between breaths. 'In perfect harmony with nature.'

Arlo nodded. 'If only everyone had thought like that thirty or forty years ago.'

'It wouldn't have stopped the Great Eruption or those other disasters,' she replied. 'It's all water under the bridge–we just need to move on and fix things.'

Arlo nodded.

'Talking of moving on,' she said, 'I think I'm ready.' She checked her clothes were all tucked in.

Arlo gripped her arm. 'You *sure*?'

'*Quite sure.*' She wrinkled her nose.

'OK, let's go.'

Lana pushed hard on the heavy stainless steel and wood entrance door and marched into the reception area. Arlo trailed behind, looking as awkward as an academic at a rave.

The vacuous lobby felt like a soulless subway station, with its high ceiling and harsh concrete walls. Lana peered over her shoulder and saw how uneasy Arlo looked. She was worried he might have another panic attack and waited until he'd caught up. 'Wait here,' she said. 'I'll do the honours.' She studied his face–it was touch and go.

Lana felt a shiver run down her spine as she crossed the cold, drafty lobby to the reception desk. A guard in a brown uniform and peaked hat stood to attention. She thought he looked ridiculously officious for a place of learning and wondered whether he was needed to stop anti-vivisection protestors.

'Can I help you?' he said gruffly.

Lana rested her elbows on the counter and smiled.

'I'm visiting Professor Stanford–he's expecting me.'

Her usual charm didn't work. The guard tapped his desk tablet and moaned about Stanford not updating his calendar.

'Professor Stanford will be down shortly,' he finally announced. 'There's a display of the department's research over there.' He pointed to the opposite wall.

'Thanks for your help,' Lana said. The guard ignored her and checked the entrance. *Charming.*

She waved Arlo over.

'Come and look at their display.' She led him by the arm out of earshot of the guard. 'It'll come in handy knowing what Stanford's department does–he loves compliments.'

'I know the type,' Arlo replied.

Several screens played looped animations of the department's work. Alongside each display was a button for initiating a BioFace transfer of research papers and brochures; a holder contained old-school paper copies. The material promoted technical achievements and advertised services to industry.

One particular presentation caught Lana's eye. It described a machine for synthesising life from a genome. The slideshow showed what looked like a computer workstation connected to an incubator. The description said it cultured cells by feeding them the necessary amino acids, nutrients, growth factors and stem cells.

She studied each of the slides carefully. Most of the theoretical concepts were familiar from her degree course. A press release announced they'd grown a monkey–a world first. Although she despised Stanford, she admired how he'd led such an inspiring team.

'Look at this,' she exclaimed.

Arlo walked over and watched the monitor for a minute or two. 'Are you thinking what I'm thinking?'

'See, I thought it might be worth the trip,' she replied. 'Just need to survive the meeting.'

A cough startled her. She saw the reflection of a tall man in a display cabinet. Despite the distortions from the glass, she instantly recognised him. Stanford. Thoughts of the assault flooded back: his smell, how he'd touched her, and the feeling of being trapped. She spun around, arms folded across her chest.

Professor Brian Stanford smiled like a cat that had got the cream. He was 61 and an emeritus professor, with more than two hundred papers and patents to his name, having written none of them. Grey hair was greased back from his heavily receding hairline, leaving a pronounced widow's peak. Lana suspected the grease wasn't a hair product. His white moustache tapered severely from under his nose to thin points at the corners of his mouth, its centre tinged orange, as if stained by snuff, food, or some exhaled secretion. His brown polyester trousers were shiny from careless ironing, the fly decorated with a chalky white stain. Leather patches were stitched crudely onto the elbows of his navy pullover, shoulders dusted with dandruff from his psoriasis.

'Lana! The time has come.'

Arlo looked confused.

'Brian, so nice of you to see us.' Lana stepped forward and thrust out her hand.

'Don't be so formal, Lana–I won't bite.'

Stanford embraced her, practically lifting her off the ground. She stiffened and held her breath. His face felt cold and clammy, like the underbelly of a large, dead fish. She *had* to breathe. She snatched a breath. The smell of decaying food trapped between his stained and gappy teeth made her want to heave. *Blank it out.*

He released his grip and stepped back, grinning from ear to ear. She mouth-breathed, trying not to gag, straightened her coat and checked her hair. She looked up and gave a forced smile. Arlo watched in horror.

'We've just been admiring your research.' She pointed to the display, trying to get back on track.

'It is a team effort,' Stanford replied, scratching his nape. More scalp snow cascaded to his shoulders. 'As you know, our students are expertly lectured, just like *you were*, my dear. His mouth made a reptilian smile, and his tongue flicked out, moistening his thin scaly lips.

Lana shivered. 'This is my friend, Dr Arlo Jones.' Lana patted Arlo's shoulder.

Stanford's eyes momentarily left Lana's chest and looked Arlo up and down.

'Pleased to meet you, Dr Jones,' he said, averting his gaze and thrusting his hands deep into his pockets. Lana heard the rustle of keys and the sucking of teeth.

Arlo grinned.

'Right then,' Stanford continued, 'onwards and upwards. To my office?'

'Yes. Privacy would be good,' Lana replied, nose wrinkling.

Stanford beamed. 'Wonderful. I can show you a few gems en route.' He clapped his hands loudly and headed for a flight of stairs. Lana looked about the lobby, embarrassed by association, and beckoned for Arlo to follow her up the stairs. On the top step, Stanford turned to Lana, his groin level with her face. Her nose wrinkled.

Stanford pointed to his left. 'This corridor leads to my office. On the right are the biology labs, where we grow cell cultures and centrifuge samples. Behind them is the microscopy suite; we have super-resolution optical microscopes and a transmission electron microscope. We also use X-ray diffraction to analyse the molecular structure of biological specimens and have privileged access to the Diamond synchrotron source at Harwell. These are the tools used in contemporary biological research.'

'Amazing,' Lana said, wide-eyed.

'To the left of the corridor are the quantum computers that perform rapid genomic sequencing and Life Form Simulation.'

'*Life Form Simulation?*'

'Yes. It's a new discipline. We can input the nucleotides

for every chromosome and the mitochondrial DNA of an organism. As you should know, these define its blueprint–its genome. The system then simulates cell growth and produces a three-dimensional computer model of the embryonic creature that can be aged as required. Cross-sectional slices of the creature can then be viewed, rather like looking at an MRI scan.'

'Wow!' Lana's face lit up. 'We need to talk more about this.'

'Love to.' Stanford said, looking her up and down. His tongue flicked out and moistened his lips.

They walked past the computer room and came to a door with a placard marked Bioengineering Laboratory.

'This is our piece de resistance,' Stanford announced proudly, opening the door and shepherding them inside.

Lana felt a chill and shuddered.

Stanford noticed her discomfort. 'The room is air-conditioned. Not to worry–I'll soon warm you up in my office.' He smiled.

Lana ignored the comment and scanned the room–it was stunning. At its centre was a gleaming van-sized glass cubicle enclosing a stainless steel table, workstation, and coffin-sized glass tank filled with a claret liquid that clung to its walls like a fine wine. Numerous pipes and cables fed the installation from above. Lana glanced at the far wall of the lab. A large rack housed dozens of computer boxes; their fans hummed, and green LEDs twinkled.

Three research staff were sat opposite the workstation wearing gowns and masks, more in keeping with an operating theatre than a biology laboratory. They were so engrossed in their work that they hadn't even noticed them enter.

'What goes on in here?' Lana asked.

'This is where we synthesise life,' Stanford replied smugly.

Arlo gulped. 'Is this the work shown in reception?'

Stanford lifted his chin. 'Ah, clever boy ...'

Arlo didn't bite. 'And what does this mean for the future?'

'In theory, we can grow any organism from just its genome.'

Lana saw Arlo's eyes roaming excitedly over the equipment.

'Everything OK?' Stanford lightly touched Lana's arm. She recoiled at his contact.

'Y-Yes, thank you.' She took a small step backwards. 'Your work looks incredible.'

'Let's trot along to my office.' Stanford smiled, showing off yellowed rat-like teeth. 'Somewhere nice and private.'

Lana looked resolutely straight ahead. 'Lead on, professor.'

Stanford opened a fire door by the Bioengineering Laboratory, and they climbed a spiral staircase.

'Short cut.' He winked, squeezing Lana's arm.

She didn't know how much more she could take.

At the top, they walked along a short corridor and came to a door with a gold acrylic nameplate, 'Professor B. Stanford' printed in black.

'The brain centre,' Stanford announced proudly, opening the door to his pokey office. 'Please take a seat.' He clapped his hands, making Lana jump.

A stately leather chair sat throne-like behind an antique desk. She presumed it was Stanford's and sat in the chair furthest away, crossing her legs and putting her hands in her lap. Arlo grabbed the nearest chair and lounged back.

The room was a tip, towering piles of journals cluttering every available surface. Lana was shocked by the mess and confused about how these ancient journals could still be relevant.

Living in the past, leaching off his students.

'Tea or coffee?' Stanford asked.

'Tea, please,' Lana replied. She glanced at Arlo and raised her eyebrows. 'Tea, Arlo?' She knew it would drag things out, but they had to play ball.

'Yup. Sounds good to me.'

Stanford boiled the kettle and made tea in two cracked and stained mugs bearing the product name of a haemorrhoid preparation. As Stanford swivelled to get milk from the fridge, Arlo inflated his cheeks and mimicked being sick. Lana frowned and shook her head angrily. Stanford stirred the tea and turned, greeted by outstretched arms and warm smiles.

'Right, you have my undivided attention,' Stanford said. 'How can I help?'

Lana looked to Arlo; he nodded. 'This is all sensitive information,' Lana began, 'I trust you'll keep it confidential?'

'You have my word,' Stanford replied.

'Do you have the signal, Arlo?' Lana asked.

'Er ...' he hesitated.

'We agreed on the call?' she pressed.

'I know. Just wait,' Arlo replied, sounding riled.

Lana frowned.

'Maybe a bit of background first?' Arlo suggested.

Playing for time? Lana nodded.

'Professor,' Arlo said. 'May I call you Brian?'

Stanford wriggled uncomfortably on his seat. 'Why not? We're all friends together. Isn't that right, Lana?' He rubbed the heels of his hands up and down his thighs. Lana didn't answer.

'Brian, did you see my presentation at SatCom 2052?' Arlo asked.

'Ah, I believe not, my dear boy–I had to give an important press conference. I must have missed it.'

Lana tutted to herself. She was sure he hadn't seen *any* of the presentations. *Why's Arlo asking?*

'Well, anyway,' Arlo continued, 'I detected a signal as part of my routine satellite work. I showed Lana, and she thinks it might be a DNA code–perhaps even a genome.'

'How very strange ...' Stanford said, scratching his nape. 'Where did it come from?'

'We don't really know,' Arlo lied.

'Hmmm ... Why would anyone want to transmit a genome?'

'It's a complete mystery.' Arlo wrung his hands. 'Maybe we accidentally intercepted a transmission from a hospital or a gene sequencing clinic?'

'It seems unlikely. Medical data is encrypted for privacy.'

Lana sighed and shuffled forwards on her chair. 'Arlo thinks it probably came from space, but he doesn't want to make grand claims.'

Arlo looked annoyed.

'That would be bizarre ...' Stanford rocked back in his chair. 'There must be some other logical explanation. How was it detected?'

'It was an RF signal carried on an infrared beam,' Arlo replied.

'RF?'

'Radiofrequency.' Arlo looked puzzled that he didn't know.

'Hmmm, definitely rules out a hospital or clinic then ...' Stanford steepled his fingers. 'Can I see it?'

Arlo frowned.

Lana shuffled even further forwards on her seat, looking like she might topple off the end.

'*Arlo,*' she said sternly. '*The signal. We agreed.*'

Arlo rubbed the sides of his head, one of his legs going up and down like a sewing machine needle. 'Er, I'm not sure.'

'*Not sure of what?*' Lana exclaimed.

'The security,' Arlo mumbled.

'This is a university,' Lana said, exasperated. 'A place of learning. It's OK.'

'Cyber vulnerabilities.'

'But you presented a paper on the signal. You asked for help!'

'I know ...' Arlo said.

'So, *where is it?*'

'It's on my BioDrive.'

'Well, that's not secure anyway!' Lana said, suddenly realising what she'd said. She looked away.

Arlo stared at her. 'Did I hear you correctly?'

Lana's face flushed. 'You know *nothing's* secure.'

'I see.' Arlo shook his head. 'I suppose that makes it OK then?'

Stanford looked bemused by their exchanges. 'How is the data stored?' he asked.

Arlo didn't reply.

'*Please, Arlo,*' Lana said.

'What the hell,' Arlo exclaimed. 'I wrote a computer script that chopped the signal into separate symbols, like Morse code's individual dots or dashes. The script assigns a different letter to each new symbol it comes across. So the data is a seemingly random string of the letters A to D. The original signal consisted of several seemingly identical, long bursts, each with over three billion symbols. Also, there are several identical short bursts, each with only about 16,000 symbols. I've put the first of each type on my BioDrive.'

'*Most strange ...*'

'Why?'

'For humans, most DNA is in the nucleus of each cell. This DNA has 3.3 billion nucleotides, otherwise known as bases. Incidentally, they are *never* called symbols.' He studied Arlo's face as if seeking subservience, but he didn't react. 'Anyway,' he continued, 'there is also DNA in the mitochondria: the cell structures that metabolise food into energy. The mitochondrial DNA of the genome only has 16,569 nucleotides. It is uncanny that your numbers match ...'

Lana heard a knock on the door.

'*Enter,*' Stanford shouted.

An Asian student, who looked young enough to be a teenager, shuffled in, smiling obsequiously.

'Zubar Anand is my PhD student,' Stanford said. 'I called him up on my BioFace a few minutes ago–he is more familiar with the computer network than me.'

That's because you know nothing.

'Hi Zubar,' Lana said. 'Thanks for taking time out from your research.'

'It's my pleasure, ma'am–'

'Ahem,' Arlo interjected. 'I thought we were keeping all of this between the three of us?'

Stanford paused and looked into his open palms. A few seconds later, his gaze lifted. 'Zubar is a foreign student–he is no threat.'

Lana shook her head. She knew overseas students had stolen and exported a staggering amount of intellectual property from universities over the years, ruining the competitiveness of British industry.

'I suppose it's OK if it goes *no* further,' Lana conceded.

'Are we *OK* with that, Brian?' Arlo asked.

'Yes, no problem,' Stanford blustered.

'*Sure?*' Arlo pressed.

Stanford held Arlo's gaze. 'I'm good to my word.'

Arlo twisted his wedding ring. 'I'll grant Zubar BioDrive read access.'

A few seconds later, Zubar's eyes scanned left and right as he navigated his BioFace menus to connect to Arlo's BioDrive. 'Got it,' he said, 'I'll take a look.' After about a minute of what looked like meditation, he turned to Stanford.

'It sort of looks like a genome to me, but I've just run it through some self-consistency utilities on our network, and there's something wrong.'

Lana leaned forward, frowning. '*Wrong?*'

'I've checked the whole data set, and there's an anomaly,' Zubar continued. 'Some sections of the DNA use six nucleotides rather than the usual four. I can see the letters E and F!'

'*Damn*,' Lana cursed. 'It's not DNA then–I was wrong. Sorry guys for wasting your time.'

'It's my fault, Lana,' Arlo sighed. 'I only saw four symbols. I didn't do an exhaustive computer search like Zubar.'

'My, my ... You youngsters are quick to jump to conclusions,' Stanford laughed.

'Er, I don't understand.' Arlo said.

'Clearly not, my dear boy,' Stanford said smugly. 'Please ... let me explain.' He rubbed his trousered thighs. 'There is something called synthetic DNA. Normal DNA instructs how the body's proteins are grown from the basic building blocks of just twenty amino acids. However, researchers have made synthetic DNA using more than four bases and can, therefore, instruct the body to make proteins from a richer selection of amino acids. In theory, 172 amino acids could be invoked from the six bases Zubar has detected.'

'But why's that useful?' Lana asked.

'It means an organism can be grown from completely new proteins, ones never seen in nature before.'

'Go on.'

'A life form with this modified DNA could be more advanced than a human.' Stanford looked up. 'For example, its skin could be made tougher–capable of withstanding cuts or UV damage from the sun.'

'How can we prove any of this?' Arlo asked.

'Calm down.' Stanford replied. 'One step at a time.'

Arlo frowned.

'Zubar, dear chap,' Stanford patted him on the thigh. 'Any chance you can run the code through the Life Form Simulator?'

Zubar scratched his forehead. Briefly, he seemed lost in thought. But then his face lit up, and he mumbled something about permutations.

'Speak up, boy,' Stanford said.

'There might be a way,' Zubar said. 'We could assume the bulk of the bases are mapped to the usual amino acids and then try all permutations of the unknown ones to see if the result is consistent with a successful organism.'

'See Lana, the quality of our lecturing is first-class.' Stanford pointed to Zubar. 'This student is a fine example.'

So bloody rude.

'Do you want me to try?' Zubar inquired.

'Of course, dear chap,' Stanford said. 'No initiative,' he mumbled.

Arlo shook his head.

Zubar's eyes darted left and right as he set up the simulation across the network. Within a minute, his gaze had settled. 'It's running,' he said.

'How long will it take?' Lana asked impatiently.

Stanford turned to Zubar. '*Well? Tell the lady!*'

Arlo's jaw clenched.

'The quantum computer does everything in parallel,' Zubar said. 'It should be finished in seconds.' His eyes flicked about, distracted. 'Yep, all done.'

'And?' Arlo said, shuffling to the end of his seat.

'Just over 268 million combinations failed. And then it found one that worked. It *is* a genome.'

Lana looked at Arlo–he'd gone as white as a sheet.

16

Arlo's eyes defocussed. 'Dad, if only you knew,' he muttered.

It was moments like this when he wished he believed in spiritualism or God. He'd also thought that on the bus to Portland when he would have gladly sacrificed a limb to speak to Isabella for one last time. To tell her he was sorry. But now was different–he just wanted to share his revelation with someone who knew how much it meant.

He'd often wondered how he might react if he ever proved aliens existed, finally hitting the jackpot and fulfilling his dream. He'd guessed he might be jubilant and punch the air, shout Eureka, or sink to his knees like a tennis player winning Wimbledon. But part of him also wondered if he might break down and cry or hug everyone in sight. But none of those things happened. He just felt numb.

Maybe, deep down, he still didn't believe Zubar, or recent events had changed his perspective, robbing him of emotion. Perhaps it was just because he couldn't imagine what it all meant.

Arlo felt as if he'd left his body, and time had frozen, events suspended like someone had paused a movie at its climax, or the actors had forgotten their lines. He wondered what everyone else was thinking and what would happen next. He looked up–all eyes were upon him. It was as if they were in the grip of an earthquake, paralysed in shock and looking for leadership, the enormity too unfathomable, the implications too profound. Nobody knew how to react.

Sometime later, maybe ten seconds, perhaps a minute, action resumed.

'The code ... It's a genome?' Arlo blurted.

'Computer says it is,' Zubar replied. 'All the self-consistency checks pass.'

'No way!' Arlo shook his head. 'I've only just gone and found my bloody alien!' He felt himself welling up and swept the hair from his eyes so he could discreetly wipe away a tear. Lana squeezed his arm knowingly.

'So what's next?' Arlo said, trying to cover his embarrassment.

Stanford reclined, scratched his crutch and sniffed his fingers. 'Hmmm ... Looks like you'll get to see our Life Form Simulation in action, my dear.'

Lana stared at Stanford. 'Professor, that would be wonderful,' she said, seemingly immune from his vulgarity.

'Can we set it up, Zubar?' Stanford asked.

'Shouldn't be a problem, sir. We can run it across the network and view the results using the wireless virtual reality glasses.'

'Ah, jolly good. Run along and fetch them from the lab, dear boy.'

Zubar shuffled to the door, head bowed. The door clicked, and Arlo heard the metallic clatter of his footsteps as he descended the spiral staircase.

'He should be back very soon. Sadly, the software isn't compatible with smart contact lenses. Maybe in the next release.' Stanford smiled, showing his yellow gappy teeth. Lana turned away, revulsion restored.

Minutes later, the door clicked open, and Zubar reappeared carrying an aluminium flight case. He placed it ceremoniously on the table, popped two catches and opened the lid. Protected inside foam cut-outs were half a dozen pairs of black plastic glasses with lightly smoked lenses, like the ones from old 3-D cinemas. Stanford removed two sets and checked them over.

'Pop these on,' he said, offering them to Lana. 'Zubar will

connect the output of his genome analysis tool to the input of the Life Form Simulator.'

Lana stretched out, leaning over. Arlo noticed Stanford staring unashamedly at her chest and shook his head. She passed him a pair, and he put them on.

The lenses were transparent, and all he saw was Lana fitting hers. They sat on her face crooked, and Stanford had noticed.

'Hmmm ... your glasses need adjusting.' Stanford lunged around the desk before Arlo could come to her rescue. His polyester crutch pressed against her face as he delicately tucked locks of hair behind her ears that had spilt from her bun. She froze, clutching the chair's armrests like when having a tooth pulled. Finally, Stanford adjusted the glasses and retreated to his chair. Lana slumped back.

'Ready, my dear?' Stanford asked.

Lana nodded robotically.

'Presentation,' he commanded.

Arlo saw the room fade out, and an electric-blue three-dimensional logo of BioSoft rotated slowly in front of his eyes. He recoiled at its brightness and wondered how Lana was coping.

Peering under his glasses, he saw her bent double. 'You OK?'

'I-I feel a bit sick,' Lana answered feebly. 'Just give me a moment.'

Arlo noticed her hands trembling and felt awful for putting her through it all.

She sat quietly, inhaling deeply, head between her knees. Stanford leaned back, hands behind his head, enjoying the view. Arlo shivered in disgust, wondering what he was thinking and whether he was saving clips to his BioDrive for later use. He'd heard horror stories of people capturing video for use in deep fake BioPorn in the metaverse. BioSnapping was illegal, like its predecessor upskirting, but nobody policed the ubiquitous scourge.

A few seconds later, she seemed to have recovered.

'O-OK, professor, I'm fine now.' She wiped her brow,

straightening up.

'Sure?' Stanford queried, seemingly disappointed that the spectacle was over.

'*Quite sure.*'

The professor nodded to Zubar. The student's eyes flicked as he set up the simulation. The splash screen with the logo vanished, replaced by a three-dimensional view of a person.

Lana jumped. 'It's a naked man!'

Arlo couldn't believe his eyes. So this was his alien. So much for his preconceptions based on popular culture. The creature didn't have an emaciated body, almond eyes, or an enormous domed forehead–it looked like a completely normal human being. But why? The signal was from an exoplanet 150 light-years away. Even animals on Madagascar were different from those on the African mainland–and they'd been isolated by only two or three hundred miles! It didn't make any sense.

Stanford peered over the top of his glasses, tongue flicking out, moistening his scaly lips.

'How observant, Lana.' He smirked. 'I guess you didn't deduce that from his sex chromosomes.'

'Strange,' she said, seeming not to have heard his innuendo, 'he looks completely human. So much for those two extra nucleotides.'

'You have the inquiring mind of a researcher. If you ever need a proper job ...'

'I *have* a proper job,' she snapped.

'Anyway,' Stanford said, 'I've had a thought about those nucleotides.'

'Really?' Lana said.

'Yes. The differences might lie *within* the body. As we say in the trade, his phenotype is normal, but his genotype is abnormal. Have you already forgotten your undergraduate studies?'

Lana sighed.

'Private industry ...' Stanford muttered as he took a glove from the flight case and slipped his hand in with the skill of a gynaecologist.

'What's that for?' Arlo inquired.

'It gives me control of the virtual reality software,' he replied, making curling movements with his hand. The three-dimensional view of the man rotated. He then touched his thumb and forefinger together, triggering 'Body Scan' mode, and moved a dotted red line cursor to the top of the man's head. A section through the brain appeared, like an image from an MRI body scanner. Lana watched, fascinated, as Stanford moved the dotted line through the whole skull. He returned to the start and repeated the action more slowly.

'Can you see anything unusual?' Stanford quizzed.

'I can see two hemispheres of the brain,' Lana said. 'They're separated by a structure that I think might be the thalamus.'

'You remember well. Now, look what happens when I move the scan lower.'

With a flourish of his wrist, Stanford moved the section a few millimetres. A white mass appeared towards the rear of the skull.

Lana grimaced. 'It looks like a tumour.'

'Indeed it does, but it has an internal structure.'

Stanford moved his hand and launched a zoom tool. 'Look, can you see the convoluted, tightly packed endothelial cells that lead into a common duct?'

Lana nodded.

'The tool also shows it contains abnormal proteins,' he continued, 'they are unlike anything I've ever seen. Certainly not human. Presumably, they are due to the six nucleotide DNA ...'

'Any idea what it's for?' Lana asked.

'It has a duct, so maybe it is a gland, like the pituitary. But, judging from its size, it seems even more powerful than that master gland. How remarkable. The pituitary is only pea-sized–this structure is as big as a walnut. The man's head is on the large side to accommodate it.'

'Anything else unusual?' Lana inquired.

Stanford rotated the model to align the section with the man's back: the vertebra and spinal cord jumped out of the image.

'Hmm, interesting ... Can you see the vertebral foramen?'

Stanford touched his little finger to his palm, and a pen tool appeared. He used his index finger to draw an orange arrow highlighting the cavity in the vertebrae.

'Yes. All looks normal to me?'

'On first sight, yes, but it is subtly different from a normal spine. Look what happens when I zoom in.'

Stanford pushed his palm outwards, and the spinal cavity enlarged, splitting into two parallel channels.

'What on earth is that?' Lana exclaimed.

'I have absolutely no idea, but that's not all!'

Stanford orientated the scan to the top of the neck. 'Can you see the white mass near the brainstem?'

'Do you mean the object that looks like an almond?'

'Exactly. It looks like he has another strange gland. This one's quite a bit smaller than the first. It's connected to nerve-like structures that run down that second channel.'

'Can the diagnostics tool show its composition?'

'Good idea.' He clicked on the side menu–a table appeared listing percentages of different amino acids. 'See, it contains exotic proteins like the other gland.'

Stanford powered down the software and took off his spectacles.

Arlo sighed with relief as he removed his own glasses and rubbed his eyes. 'Amazing. So, what's next?'

'Good question.' Stanford scraped his grey stubble with yellowed fingers and chewed nails. 'There's an obvious next step,' he continued, 'but it poses an ethical dilemma ...'

Arlo looked puzzled. 'I don't understand.'

'Well, strictly speaking, it's illegal.'

'What's illegal?'

'Incubation.'

'*Incubation?*'

'We need to incubate this organism to know what these structures do.'

'Sounds good to me!' Lana chipped in.

'And therein lies the problem ...' Stanford muttered.

'*Why?*' Arlo demanded.

'I only have a research license for growing human embryos up to a gestation period of four weeks. After that, they are considered foetuses, and I would be engineering artificial life–'

'Hold on,' Lana interjected. 'Surely that only applies to human life? This creature isn't human!'

'Mmm ... good point.' Stanford rocked back slowly in his chair.

'You've been a pioneer all your research life, professor.' Lana said. Stanford smiled conceitedly. 'This is a once-in-a-lifetime opportunity,' she continued. 'To break new ground. To be the first to grow an alien being!'

Stanford looked skywards.

After several seconds, Stanford broke the silence. 'You make a good point, Lana. But we must keep everything confidential– it could damage our careers.'

'Yes, *we must*,' Arlo agreed.

'There's no harm done if we proceed carefully,' Stanford continued. 'We can terminate the programme at any time. No one ever needs to know.'

'Exactly,' Lana said.

Stanford stared at Arlo.

Arlo held his stare. 'Sounds good to me.'

Stanford rubbed his chin.

'So, what's next?' Lana urged.

'We're all ready to roll,' Stanford said. 'Our nutrient delivery system can grow several kilograms of cells per hour.'

'*Kilograms an hour!* How come they grow *so* fast?'

'In your day Lana, researchers grew embryonic stem cells. But this was hard to control, and we couldn't grow every tissue type. We now use a machine that prints the cells biologically using the genomic blueprint. It's a bit like how a 3-D printer makes engineering parts from a computer model.'

'But that doesn't explain such rapid cell growth?'

'That was our breakthrough. You saw the video in the foyer. We trigger cell division by an electric field controlled by a computer. Research has shown this only works if the field oscillates at extremely high microwave frequencies. But, fortuitously, this results in extremely rapid cell growth.'

'I see. But there's still one other thing I don't understand,' Lana said.

'What's that?' Stanford said.

'The scan shows a fully-grown man. How can you grow an adult if he's never lived? He won't have *any* knowledge?'

'Hmm, that is true,' Stanford replied thoughtfully. 'Maybe that is what the extra glands are for?'

'You really think so?'

'There's only one way to find ou-'

'How long will it take?' Arlo interrupted.

The professor hesitated, then muttered something. Arlo thought he heard him say days.

'Did you say *days?*' Arlo queried.

'No, my dear boy. I said *one* day. It won't take very long at all.'

Silently, Arlo twisted to face Lana and caught her off guard. It seemed from her blank expression that none of it had come as any surprise.

17

T he curtained windows of Bristol University's Royal Fort House glowed ruby red. Thomas Tyndall had commissioned the palatial residence from the profits of his slave plantations. Dim light picked out two men as they walked briskly through the snowy grounds, their paths converging.

Stanford paused, his hands on his hips, and gazed up at the grand façade, the Baroque, Palladian, and Rococo styles the vision of Tyndall and his two master architects. Channing approached and stood alongside, maintaining his distance. 'Grand isn't it,' he said.

'Yes, splendid,' Stanford replied, scratching his nape. 'The work of three great minds.'

Channing nodded slowly. 'Seems fitting.'

'Indeed.' Stanford's tongue moistened his flaking lips.

'So when's he coming?' Channing asked.

'Soon.'

'*When?*'

'After the morning star.'

'Good.' Channing smiled. 'I see him in my dreams.'

'You too?' Stanford sounded relieved.

'Oh, yes.'

'Vivid ones?' Stanford inquired.

'Like I'm there.'

A ghostly figure swooped down on them. Stanford startled. Channing barely flinched.

'Nervous are we?' Channing said as the barn owl flapped

away into the inky blackness.

'A-A bit,' Stanford replied.

'You need something to relax you.'

'Such as?' Stanford cocked his head.

'Maybe a dirty little bitch?'

Stanford rubbed the heels of his hands against his thighs. 'The slutty blonde girl?'

'The very one.'

'Mmmm, yes.'

'As a reward.'

'For what?' Stanford frowned as if tricked.

'Shall we say for services rendered?' Channing smiled. '*And for what you are going to do.*'

'I see.' Stanford's face relaxed.

'You deserve her.'

'*Yes ...*' Stanford nodded, his hands rubbing faster.

'And she deserves you.'

'Mmmm ... I will teach her. The dirty little bitch.'

'Spare me the details.'

'Have you?'

'I have no interest. She's all yours.' Channing's eyes bored into him. '*But, after he's here.*'

Stanford gave a lizard-lipped smile. A hint of spittle seeped from the corner of his mouth, and he wiped it away. Channing's face puckered in disgust.

'And what of the others?' Stanford inquired.

'The madman, the cripple?'

'Yes.'

'The cripple's wings have been clipped. I will teach the other a lesson.'

'Perfect ...' Stanford patted the man's arm.

Channing pulled away and dusted off his sleeve.

'And the snob bitch?' Stanford asked.

'You've seen how she's changed?'

'Er, yes.' Stanford looked puzzled. 'What have you done?'

'It's amazing how people so readily sell their souls.'

Channing stared into Stanford's confused face and smiled a sickly smile. Without a goodbye, he turned and walked off into the night.

18

TUESDAY, 17 SEPTEMBER 2052

Arlo had agonised over whether to tell Alisha about the events at the university. In the end, he'd decided against it. He thought she had enough on her plate and might get the wrong impression about Lana. Anyway, it was only a computer simulation and probably all wrong. But science was all simulated, and that mirrored reality.

After tea, they tried to play a game with Josh. But he hadn't been interested, wanting instead to play Battle of the Augs with his metaverse friends. Alisha had had a meltdown, insisting it had to be uninstalled. Arlo refused. He couldn't see how locking Joshua down would work. It would only drive him away. They could ill-afford to lose him–he was all they had left. Soon enough, he'd grow out of it.

After their argument, Alisha had gone to bed early. These days, Arlo realised that sometimes things went to shit no matter how hard he tried. He decided to have a few tins that ended up being a lot of tins. He knew it wasn't clever, but sometimes he couldn't help himself. At least it would help him sleep, and it might even stop the nightmares. Drinking was better than pills. Even if it didn't work, it helped him chill. And god, he needed to chill.

He sneaked into bed in the early hours, greeted by a cold back, a disinterested shove and a hostile grunt. He wished he could make her happy. He lay there for what seemed like hours, which probably was hours. So much for the drink. Drunk and staring at the ceiling, watching it spin. But at least it was better than the nightmares.

He tried to steady the spinning by focussing on a patch of flaking paint. After a while, the texture changed; his eyelids began to flutter. A meadow of wildflowers appeared, a summer breeze blowing gentle waves through long grass as he flew over. The scent of honeysuckle relaxed him, and he felt he was healing. Skylarks warbled and a cuckoo called. He soared over an ancient hawthorn hedgerow into a field of wheat. A combine was harvesting the crop, chaff blowing away. Then, up and over a forest, the trees dark and foreboding. As the light faded, an alien creature appeared, floating and rotating in three dimensions in a virtual alien autopsy. A red laser line appeared across its head; its skull was sliced and splayed like a deck of cards.

The alien floated away into the darkness. The flight deck of a spacecraft crystallised, its mission computer waking from hibernation in a cascade of flashing purple lights and a hiss of venting oxygen. A ripping roar shook the cabin as the ship's mighty metallic hydrogen rocket engine fired, its plume white-hot and brighter than the summer's sun. Ark 1307 streaked high above the atmosphere like a fiery chariot as it inserted into geosynchronous orbit, the cabin juddering as the motor shut down with a throaty crackle. The craft slowly rolled, two aqua fingers and the green diamond of a vast river delta flashing past the window.

A telescopic boom extended, locking home with a heavy clunk. At its end, a thruster hissed in opposition to one on the fuselage, and the craft began to spin. Gaining speed, it whipped around. The thrusters cut out, and the rotation stabilised; a torch, floating free in the cabin, fell to the floor with a dull thud. Bright sunlight reflected off a giant solar sail as it unfurled like the mainsail of a galleon.

With a hollow pop, a streamlined shell ejected from the craft. It cartwheeled into the atmosphere and began to glow like a light sabre, its plasma envelope changing colour from orange to magenta and finally lime green as it slowed. Wings extended, and it settled into a glide towards Sepphoris.

Above the city, a small charge fired, bursting the shell, like a chrysanthemum firework, scattering dozens of pebble-shaped surveillance devices. Shrouded in darkness, they rained down, witnessed only by barking dogs. Blackness descended as Arlo's dream faded.

Arlo tossed and turned as a blizzard blew down the street, drifting snow hissing against the bedroom window. The Ark's interior reappeared from the darkness, and the covers of two growth tanks hissed open. Two naked Gemids clambered out, claret slime sloshing over the sides and onto the floor. Elah was slightly built, with a kind face and inquiring blue eyes, his genotype matched against surveillance images. Kefa, his guardian engineer, was burly, tall and barrel-chested.

Arlo heard his father speaking softly. He said that Elah had walked through the Temple of Gemidia 1,500 years ago, selected to refresh the human DNA of his forefathers, tainted by half a million years of natural selection and tribalism.

The Gemids wiped themselves clean, put on golden flight suits and sat at a console. Elah made clicking noises; a purple light flashed. Their eyeballs vibrated as the cerebral upload began, wirelessly restoring their minds and memories. Finally, the local language, gleaned from surveillance recordings, was uploaded.

They rested briefly, and then Elah clambered through the bulkhead into the Ark's Plasmadron re-entry pod. He powered up its computer and familiarised himself with the controls. Kefa climbed in next to him. They strapped themselves into winged flying seats, fitted visors, and initiated a structural integrity test that checked for cosmic damage.

An announcement rasped in native Gemish from the Plasmadron's computer: all tests had passed. They blinked at each other, and Elah entered an access code. Further rasping sounds confirmed the successful arming of the anti-docking mechanism. Elah flipped up a safety cover and engaged a purple rocker switch. An airlock closed and the docking arm disengaged with a clunk. Kefa looked anxiously at Elah as the

Plasmadron juddered violently. Elah clicked back, and Kefa calmed as the pod distanced itself from the mothership. The Gemids checked the ship's status and blinked in unison. Elah performed the re-entry arming sequence.

Hypergolic reverse thrusters crackled and hissed. The Plasmadron's nose dipped as it slowed, its daryonic coating glowing amber as it entered the atmosphere. The Gemids inspected their visor displays: the heat shield was holding up, and they were on the correct flight path to Sepphoris. An intensified image, relayed from a surveillance pebble, showed their destination–a field adjacent to a nobleman's house, screened from view by a row of cypress trees.

The Plasmadron jolted and lurched as the atmosphere thickened, its airspeed dropping to transonic. The Gemids gripped the flight control handles through their thin golden gloves and braced themselves for separation. They blinked at each other. An ejection charge fired with an ear-piercing crack, and the frangible cockpit above their heads disintegrated in a storm of frosted granules. Ejection rockets fired with a ripping roar that tore the sky apart. In an instant, they were blasted through the cloud of debris, safely away from the pod.

In a few heartbeats, Elah's rocket motor cut out. He closed his eyes, grimacing from the g-force as the chair tumbled end-over-end. As the cartwheeling slowed, a charge fired, jettisoning the back of his seat. A retractable wing deployed, and he began to glide. Elah slumped in his harness, breathing heavily.

With a crackle, a purple plasma halo lit up around Elah's wing, and his descent rate slowed. He rallied just in time to see the Plasmadron thundering back to orbital rendezvous with the Ark–its thrusters leaving molten tramlines across the sky. He glanced right and saw the purple glow of Kefa flying parallel to him about a hundred feet away.

'All good?' Elah rasped in Gemish over the comms link.

'All systems nominal,' Kefa replied robotically.

They flew over an inky black expanse relieved occasionally

by silver glints as the full moon reflected off wave crests. Elah checked his visor: airspeed 250mph, altitude 9,000 feet. They were flying east to west across the southern tip of a large lake, golden lights scintillating like fireflies near the horizon. Elah checked his visor's navigation display–the lights were consistent with Sepphoris's eastern fire beacons. He glanced down and saw the black expanse interrupted by a jagged line.

'We're crossing the western shore.'

'Affirmative,' Kefa replied.

A strong crosswind buffeted them as they flew over the coast, their wings veering violently away from Sepphoris.

'*Fire up the thrusters,*' Elah shouted above the wind rush.

'OK,' Kefa replied.

Elah pressed a button on his flight grip. Two mini thrusters embedded in the wing's trailing edge ignited with a high-pitched hiss, their nozzles vectoring. Elah's wing slewed into the wind and re-established the correct flight path. He glanced to his right–Kefa had disappeared.

'*KEFA!*' he shouted. '*WHERE ARE YOU?*'

'Rear left,' Kefa gasped. 'I'm losing you. Only one thruster lit. I've had to shut it down to prevent a flat spin.'

'Stay calm. We can work this out.' Elah flicked a switch, and his wing's thrusters crackled and died. He lowered his halo's power, and the wind rush decreased. Kefa overtook him on his starboard, and Elah ramped the power of his halo back up to pull alongside.

'What now?' Kefa urged.

'Contingency C11,' Elah replied calmly. 'If we can't reach the target, we'll find another site.'

'Understood,' Kefa confirmed.

They flew on for nearly four minutes, the landscape featureless in the moonlight.

'Let's fly lower,' Elah suggested. 'We might see something.'

The Gemids reduced the power to their halos until bushes and rocky outcrops flew past in a blur. Elah checked his visor: 750 feet and five per cent fuel remaining.

'Be careful,' Elah said. 'We're near the ground.'

'I'm nearly out of fuel!' Kefa hissed. '*We have to land!*'

'We'll be fine,' Elah calmed.

They flew over a meandering path that tracked the valley floor and climbed a hillside, their airspeed dropping dangerously low, flaps extending on the wings. As they crested the hill, a cluster of twenty to thirty ramshackle mudbrick huts appeared on their right.

Kefa's halo began to sputter. 'This will do,' he said, his voice shaking. 'Keep to the left of the track, away from the huts.'

'See you on the ground,' Elah said, turning off his halo.

Elah approached the landing site with a treacherous blur of bushes and boulders. He pressed a button on his harness, releasing his legs as the wing flared. But the ground speed was too high. In an instant, he was sprinting like a man possessed. His feet struck a boulder, and he pitched forward, sliding across the sandy slope on all fours. He snagged a bush, flipped over and tumbled. He lay there winded, head spinning, ears full of the shrill pulsing hiss of cicadas.

Rough hands grabbed his shoulders and hauled him over.

'Steady on!' He spat blood and sand from his mouth.

He heard a clunk and fell from the wing. Lying still, he took several deep breaths. Composure returning, he sat up. 'Well, that's the easy bit done with.' He grinned.

'But we're completely off course,' Kefa exclaimed. 'What about Sepphoris?'

'This will be fine,' Elah calmed.

Kefa looked sceptical and helped Elah stand. They lugged their wings up over a small rocky hillock, out of sight from the huts. Kefa unclipped two storage cases, extended retractable carrying straps and slung them effortlessly over his broad shoulders. They laid the redundant wings down side-by-side, entered a code into the flight consoles, and stood back. Within seconds, they began to sizzle and char. A minute later, all that remained was a vague scorch mark on the ground and an acrid smell in the air. Kefa blinked.

'Let's go.' Elah blinked back.

The Gemids clambered up the hillock and jogged over to the huts, crouching low by the nearest one's wall. It only had two rooms, one with a chimney, so they carried on to the next building. They knelt below a window, screened by a linen sheet, and Kefa activated the infrared mode of his visor. He popped up, pulled the sheet aside, and looked in. An elderly couple were huddled together under a woollen blanket on a thick mattress of straw. Dropping down, he glanced at Elah. 'Next one.'

They tried two more huts: each had sleeping couples. Next, they came to a larger rectangular shack. Hunched over, they ran to a window at the far end. Kefa checked the room out as before and blinked at Elah. Elah blinked back, and Kefa laid the flight cases on the ground. Elah jumped onto the window ledge, pulled the curtain aside, and leapt in.

Moonlight flooded the girl's room. It was just an alcove separated from the rest of the living quarters by a heavy woollen curtain. She was facing away, a linen blanket peeled back, exposing her long-sleeved white tunic. Her hair was long, black and glossy, divided into two plaits, the centre parting painted red; she looked no more than five feet tall. Elah grimaced as she snuffled, kicked and rolled over to face him.

The girl's eyes twitched and opened. Her face turned to terror when she saw Elah. Elah dived across the room as she began to scream. He smothered her mouth with his hand, and she started to choke.

'Don't be afraid,' he said in her language, 'I won't hurt you.'

He lay there still, listening to her gurgling and the shrill hiss of cicadas. Her terrified eyes were only inches from his face. She looked about thirteen. 'This will never work ...' he muttered in Gemish.

He glanced at the window–Kefa stared back anxiously.

'Someone's coming,' Kefa hissed.

'Get in here!' Elah urged. '*Quick*. Hide behind the bed.'

Kefa jumped the sill in one easy bound and scurried behind

the bed.

Elah restrained the girl and pulled the sheet over them.

'Plan G6,' Elah mumbled from under the covers.

'*Last resort?*'

'*Yes.*'

The girl struggled, trying to escape, biting into Elah's fingers. Unflinching, he held her firm, peering through a gap between the sheets. The heavy curtain was pulled partly open. A youth's face appeared.

'You OK?' he called out.

Hearing no reply, he tugged the curtain the whole way across and strode into the room. In his hand was a stave, a menacing flint lashed to its end.

A canister arced over the bed, clattering at the youth's feet. His mouth dropped open, and he jumped back. It bounced a couple of times, its lid ejecting with a hollow plop. A golden mist hissed from its open end, quickly enveloping the youth and the room. He turned and fled. Midstride, his body buckled, and he collapsed to the floor.

The girl stopped struggling. Elah released his grip, climbed out of bed and checked the youth. He was unconscious. Elah returned to the bed and propped the girl up against the wall. Her eyelids drooped, ebony eyes rolling as she wafted in and out of consciousness.

'Can you hear me?' Elah urged.

The girl seemed to recover slightly, her eyes focusing on his face.

'Y-Yes,' she mumbled.

'I won't hurt you,' he said calmly.

'Who a-are you?' She looked in shock.

Elah glanced nervously at Kefa. He extracted a small glass bottle from a pocket of his tunic, popped the lid and wafted it under her nose. She seemed to calm down.

'Are you OK?'

She nodded slowly.

'Listen carefully. You will become pregnant and give birth

to a son. He will be a great man. Do you understand?'

The girl began to panic. 'B-But, how can this be? I'm still a virgin!'

'You will become pregnant by a miracle. Your child will stop the sins of the world. Do you understand?'

She looked bewildered.

'Do you have a partner?' Elah asked.

'I-I am betrothed to be wed,' she replied.'

'He will look after you both.'

'H-He will leave me ...' she said.

'Do not worry. He will understand.'

'B-But, why?'

Elah glanced at Kefa and blinked. Kefa leaned over and wafted a damp cloth under her nose. Her eyes rolled shut, and she slumped against the wall.

'Be quick,' Elah hissed.

Kefa had already laid out some silver tools on a pliable metal sheet–they glinted menacingly in the moonlight. He pulled on some silver gloves, opened the equipment case and removed a flask. Unclasping its lid, he extracted a cylinder of translucent jelly and loaded it into the barrel of an applicator. Elah looked away as Kefa began the procedure of implanting Elah's embryo. Minutes later, it was done.

They left the hut and jogged back to their landing site. Lying down, they blinked and clicked to each other. They held hands and pressed buttons on their suits. Clenching their teeth, they waited. Seconds later, they convulsed and writhed, their eyeballs vibrating rapidly. White-hot flames engulfed their bodies, and their eyes locked in a stare. As the sun rose, all that remained was charred grass, a smoky haze drifting down the hillside.

Arlo's eyeballs rolled under closed lids. The cistern hissed in the next-door bathroom. His sleep deepened again. The cover of a growth tank in Ark 1307 hissed open, and Kefa climbed out. He cleaned himself again, dressed, and sat at the flight console. His mind interrogated the computer, performing system checks. Elah was due.

Kefa marched to the second growth tank and gazed into the claret liquid. Elah's body made a crucifix as he floated, seemingly asleep. The liquid began to fizz and boil; his skin twitched. Suddenly, his eyes sprang open, arms lifting, hands scrabbling at the sides of the tank. Kefa stared at one of his hands as it struggled to grip. The ragged hole in his palm was so large he could see right through it.

19

TUESDAY, 17 SEPTEMBER 2052

Alisha was floating, gliding through wispy clouds, lower and lower. She looked down on a barren domed knoll beyond a walled city. There was a confusion of voices: women wailing, onlookers shouting insults, and the crude idle banter of legionnaires keeping order.

A semi-naked man staggered up a dusty track towards the summit, a dogwood beam borne across his shoulders. He winced with every shuffling step that stretched open striped scourge lacerations in his back. Crimson blood ran down his forehead from a crown of thorns piercing his scalp, turning pink as it mixed with sweat, dripping into his blue eyes that squinted from the low early-morning sun. At the summit, a group of figures gathered around a small outcrop of weathered trees.

People lined the route, and some walked with the man in his macabre carnival of suffering, their expressions displaying a gamut of human emotion. The evil ones: sadists who gorged on his pain, the jealous who took solace from his misfortune, and the guards whose guilt was cleansed by following orders. And the kind ones: the selfless who would have traded places with him, the compassionate who wanted his suffering to end, and the defiant who wanted justice.

He reached the top of the hill, where the sun had bleached the domed rock to look like a giant skull. Two dead men were already hanging there. But, as he approached, one of them stirred back to life and lifted his head. Respectful to the end, the man gave a subtle nod.

The trunk of a whittled poplar tree stood bare between the crucified men. A Roman centurion, proud in his feathered headdress, threatened the man with a vine cudgel, motioning for him to lie down. The man gazed into the centurion's face, perhaps appealing for mercy. Initially, the centurion returned a vacant stare, but then his expression softened as if through piety or guilt and offered him something yellow. Wine dripped from the sponge and splattered onto the sandy soil.

'King of the Jews,' the centurion mocked in Aramaic.

Yeshua looked up expressionless.

'Suck the sponge,' he continued, 'it will dull the pain.'

'No, thank you,' Yeshua replied.

'Defiant to the end,' the centurion laughed. 'It's only just beginning.' He nodded to a legionnaire.

As Yeshua lay panting, the legionnaire grabbed his right wrist. A metallic strike reverberated around the hilltop. Yeshua clenched his teeth to stop himself from screaming. The nail had missed the bone but had torn through the flesh. He tried but failed to move his hand and strained to see why. A crudely fashioned wooden washer, trapped under a square-headed nail, obscured his view, but crimson blood dripped like spilt wine. He stiffened as another sickening strike rang out. He closed his eyes and ground his teeth.

More Roman guards gathered around and hauled Yeshua to his feet. They propped wooden ladders on both sides of the tree and lifted him a few feet off the ground.

'Quick! Fix the patibulum,' a man shouted in Latin. 'It's hurting my arms.'

Men at the top of the ladders pounded two huge nails through the beam, securing it to the tree. Yeshua convulsed with every sinew shuddering strike.

With the crosspiece secure, Yeshua saw the man up the ladder nod to a soldier on the ground. The conscript grabbed his left ankle like a scrap of timber and raised a hammer high above his head. Even the hardened sadists looked away as bone splintered. Yeshua slumped unconscious. Alisha's dream faded to grey as tears streamed down her sleeping face.

Colours came back–the sandy knoll, a distant valley of olive trees, and the pink rivulets of blood that trickled down Yeshua's face. He regained consciousness and lifted his head. Wincing, he bore all his weight on the nails through his ankles to snatch a single breath. He peered down at the baying crowd as Roman soldiers kept order. He spotted his family and friends and mustered a half-smile.

Two priests stood at the front of the crowd, seemingly enjoying the show. He appeared to recognise them, and they lowered their gaze when he stared. Lifting his chest to steal another breath, he shouted in Aramaic. 'Father, forgive them, for they know not what they do.'

The crowd gasped.

Twisting left and right, he glanced at the two crucified men. One still appeared conscious.

'Hey friend,' he shouted.

The man roused and lifted his head, his eyes slowly opening.

'Today, you will be with me in paradise.'

The man's brow creased in confusion. His eyelids drooped and closed.

Yeshua scanned the faces in the crowd and locked eyes with a grey-haired woman with a face streaked by tears.

'Woman, behold, thy son,' he bellowed. He glanced at the man next to her. 'Son, behold, thy mother.' At first, they seemed puzzled, but then they nodded. Yeshua appeared relieved his mother would be cared for after his death and fell unconscious.

The sun tracked past its zenith, and the crowd dwindled. Yeshua roused again. His body convulsed in pain.

'My God, my God, why hast thou forsaken me?' he wailed.

The faces of the remaining onlookers gazed up with pity and guilt.

'I thirst,' he cried out, staring at the centurion.

The centurion motioned to one of his soldiers. The man

disappeared briefly and returned with a sponge speared on a hyssop branch. The centurion lofted it to Yeshua's lips. Straining his neck, he gripped it between his teeth and slurped greedily on the vinegary wine.

'It is finished,' Yeshua called out.

Everyone looked up, confused.

'Father, into thy hands I commend my spirit.'

Yeshua's eyeballs vibrated faster and faster. Suddenly, they locked in a rigid stare.

The scene faded, and Alisha flew high above the weathered knoll. Stars came out, rotating about Polaris. The sun began to rise. She swooped down low, skimming an olive grove, racing back towards the cliff. A cave nestled into its base, a large boulder rolled up against its mouth. She hovered there, waiting.

Two men approached: one burly and dressed in gold, the other slender and dressed as a gardener. They conversed in muffled tones. The one in gold walked up to the boulder and slipped something purple between the rock and the cliff. He quickly retreated. The object inflated, and the boulder rolled away. The two men entered the dark cave.

Several minutes elapsed. The burly man reappeared with a long object wrapped in cloth draped over his arms. He shuffled through the olive grove and stopped by a patch of waste ground. Laying the bundle on the floor, he took a canister from his belt and sprinkled powder onto the cloth. He lay alongside and pressed something in his hand. Wisps of smoke threaded their way through the olive branches. Seconds later, only two mounds of grey ash remained.

Voices murmured, carried by the strengthening breeze. Two women were walking along the path towards the cave. The man dressed as a gardener exited the cave and hid behind the boulder. The women entered the cave. Moments later, they emerged looking shocked. The man stepped from his hiding place. They froze.

'Don't be alarmed,' he announced. 'You're looking for

Yeshua the Nazarene, who's crucified.'

Terrified, they looked at each other.

'He has risen! He's not here. See the place where they laid him.' He gestured with his arm into the tomb. 'But go, tell his disciples and Peter, he is going ahead of you into Galilee. There you will see him, just as he told you.'

Their expressions changed from fear to excitement. They turned and ran, vanishing into the early morning mist.

Sand swirled, and the knoll vanished. A wooded hillside appeared, bathed in a golden glow from the early morning sun. Yeshua sat on a woollen blanket, eyes feasting on a beautiful panoramic view. The hillside looked like a painting, with sponge-dabbed olive trees decorating the sandy-coloured slopes. In the valley, a city wall snaked around a higgledy-piggledy limestone settlement.

Eleven other men gathered, chatting excitedly. Yeshua rose and turned to face them. They fell silent and gathered around, shuffling expectantly. The youngest, a man of perhaps only twenty, coughed.

'Please speak, John,' Yeshua said.

'Lord, are you at this time going to restore the kingdom to Israel?'

Yeshua's face looked troubled. 'It is not for you to know the times or dates the Father has set by his authority.' He scanned their faces. They didn't appear convinced.

'But you will receive power when the Holy Spirit comes on you,' he continued, looking solemnly at each of them in turn. 'And you will be my witnesses in Jerusalem, and in Judea and Samaria, and to the ends of the earth.' Finally, they seemed satisfied.

Yeshua stepped back until his heels rocked on the edge of the crumbling hillside. He knelt and patted the earth, discreetly placing a small black box at his feet. They shuffled forward. Taking a deep breath, he stood, raising his left palm to make them stop. Looking at them, he squeezed something in his right hand. Instantly, he convulsed in agony, sinking to his knees, eyeballs vibrating faster and faster.

They watched in horror as a pillar of white fire consumed his body, streaking skywards with the brilliance of burning magnesium, his silhouette seared onto their retinas. Partly blinded, they didn't even notice the black box or the small purple light that flashed.

'Men of Galilee,' Kefa's voice boomed, 'why do you stand here looking into the sky? This same Yeshua, who has been taken from you into heaven, will come back in the same way you have seen him go into heaven.'

The box melted, with barely a trace left on the sandy soil. The disciples glanced at each other, turned, and, in a trance-like state, began a silent procession back down the hill.

Alisha's eyes fluttered open. The curtains were closed, but the room lights were on. Arlo was pacing the room.

He saw she was awake. 'Are you OK?'

'Yes,' she said, wiping tears from her face.

'Why have you been crying?'

'It's happened again,' she said.

'What has?'

'The dreams ...'

'And me,' he said. 'Were yours the same?'

'More of the story.'

'And me ...'

'What's going on?' she said.

'I don't know,' he replied. 'Tell me what happened.'

20

Arlo concentrated as Alisha recounted her dream. He didn't know what to make of it. Maybe she was subconsciously rationalising their loss, or perhaps it was a manifestation of her pain? Ultimately–if it restored her faith–it didn't matter.

Afterwards, she asked him about his dream. He felt uneasy discussing it, not wanting to get drawn in. After all, dreams were only aberrations of the mind. He said he wanted to visit his mum before work and didn't have time. It was only a white lie as he'd planned on seeing her tomorrow. But, she wouldn't take no for an answer. Reluctantly he summarised what had happened, not mentioning the holes in the alien's hands for fear of opening a can of worms.

Later at work, Lana BioFaced him. She said Stanford had requested a 6 pm meeting at the university and gave him her address, suggesting he popped by en route. He agreed but decided to go home first, wanting to come clean with Alisha.

As soon as he got home, he made a sandwich in the kitchen, not knowing how to break the news of another work meeting with Alisha. She came in, itching for a fight. Without thinking, he came straight out with it. Instantly, she lost her temper. He'd dreaded this happening and couldn't face an inquiry. In a rush of blood to the head, he charged out and dashed over to Lana's.

Lana lived in Redland, an affluent suburb bordering the even posher Clifton. Although her property was relatively modest, he could see from the recently cleared snow and freshly painted woodwork it was her pride and joy. Standing at her front door, he felt a disorientating mix of shame and excitement.

She invited him in and insisted on showing him around. The decor was meticulous. In the bedroom, he almost lost control, broadsided by the thought of an act so blissful yet so destructive. He wavered on the brink, fighting temptation and thinking of his family. In a panic of guilt and wretchedness, he exclaimed they had to get going. His head was in a whirl. Afterwards, he had no recollection of walking to the university.

Zubar collected them from reception, and they climbed the stairs to the Biotechnology Department. Lana seemed distant, and Arlo wondered whether she'd taken offence. Zubar shepherded them into a room next to the laboratory. The scene was bizarre. They were in a university storeroom, presumably because there was no room in the laboratory. A hospital bed sat centre stage with a laboratory trolley wheeled against its end. He scanned the mess of drugs, instrumentation and tangled wires and tubes. An oscilloscope flashed a periodic signal. *Alien heart rate?*

Stanford stood at the head of the bed, like a skipper at his wheel. Arlo glimpsed the body and averted his gaze. Despite his fascination, it gave him the creeps. Zubar looked awkward, loitering at the foot of the bed.

'That will be all Zubar.' Stanford waved him away dismissively.

Zubar looked down, arms folded defensively across his chest, hands gripping his elbows.

'*Why can't Zubar stay?*' Arlo exclaimed. 'It was *his* breakthrough!'

Arlo looked to Lana for support, but she didn't react. Arlo frowned.

Stanford's face reddened. '*He has important research to do.*'

'This *is* pretty monumental!' Arlo exclaimed.

'Very well.' Stanford rubbed his thighs. 'Another concession

…' he mumbled.

'Professor,' Lana said, 'can you please bring us up to speed on the great things you've done?'

What's come over her?

'Ah, yes.' Stanford clapped his hands. 'The organism was grown in the tank and is now ready for the next phase.'

'Next phase?' Arlo asked.

'He is in a persistent vegetative state–a bit like a coma.'

'Are you saying he won't regain consciousness?' Arlo asked.

'Let us not get ahead of ourselves, dear boy,' he said, casually stroking the man's forehead. 'The next phase is to try and revive him.'

Arlo nodded.

'Anyway, strictly speaking,' Stanford continued, 'he will not *regain* consciousness–he has never been conscious in the first place.'

Arlo's eyes narrowed. 'Do we know that?'

'Since yesterday afternoon,' Stanford said, ignoring the question, 'he has been showing signs of increased muscular activity.'

'What exactly?' Arlo asked.

'Twitching. Movement of his hands and feet. Also, he's started moaning.'

Arlo forced himself to look.

It wasn't what he expected. The body was covered in a white bedsheet, pulled tightly up to its chin. It reminded him of the shroud that had covered his father at the funeral parlour. His mother had advised him not to go, but he'd needed closure. Maybe, subconsciously, he'd hoped his father's death was an elaborate sick hoax, and he would prove it was all a lie. He realised now how irrational he'd been and how grief had messed with his mind. Afterwards, he regretted seeing his dad's body, discarded like a moth's chrysalis after his spirit had flown.

The alien's head rested on a starchy white hospital pillow, Bristol Royal Infirmary's initials stamped in blood-red ink in its corner. His face was white with a hint of pink, not the colour of a healthy person but a shade warmer than the waxy pallor of a corpse. His lips had a bluish tone, tinged red at their edges; his scalp, eyebrows and jowls had a dark-brown bloom of dense stubble. Occasionally, his closed eyelids twitched as if his eyeballs were seeking the light.

'I will inject a shot of Zolpidem,' Stanford said, stroking the alien's head. 'It relieves insomnia but paradoxically has been found to raise people from comas. Hopefully, it will provide the necessary stimulus.'

'Marvellous professor,' Lana said.

Stanford beamed.

Arlo touched Lana's arm. 'Are you OK?'

She pulled away. 'Of course, I am. Why do you ask?'

'It doesn't matter,' Arlo muttered.

Stanford tugged the alien's arm free from under the sheet. Arlo noticed the back of his forearm was also heavily stubbled. Stanford wrapped a rubber tourniquet tightly around his upper arm. Arlo shuddered when he spied a syringe in a stainless steel biopsy tray. Stanford cleansed the crook of the alien's elbow with a sterile wipe.

'Are we ready?' Stanford looked across at Lana and raised his eyebrows. She nodded. Arlo was surprised by how calm she looked.

'Please proceed, professor,' she said.

Stanford picked up the syringe and broke the seal on the phial of Zolpidem. He pushed the needle through the sterile cap and slowly withdrew clear liquid. Arlo held his breath as Stanford pointed the syringe up and flicked bubbles to the top. Arlo noticed his nails were chewed with the skin picked away, exposing bloody quicks. Stanford lightly squeezed the plunger, expelling trapped air, and patted the crook of the alien's arm to encourage a vein to rise. Arlo wanted to look away but couldn't.

'Now for the moment of truth,' Stanford said.

He jabbed the needle into the alien's arm as if spearing cheese and pineapple with a cocktail stick. He withdrew the plunger a little and inspected the syringe's barrel. Red blood swirled, mixing pink with the drug.

He bleeds.

Stanford smiled. 'I've found a vein.' He clenched his jaw and drove home the liquid with a single jab of his thumb. Arlo winced. Stanford yanked the needle out, and blood trickled down the alien's arm.

'Ready for the birth?' Stanford smiled.

Arlo grimaced.

They fanned around the bed, waiting in silence. Arlo noticed the pulse rate quicken on the oscilloscope. He recalled waiting in a hospital in Bristol after his mum had had a bad fall. He remembered wondering what had caused it, terrified she might die.

Several minutes later, the alien's right foot jerked.

'*Arlo.*' Lana pointed. '*Look.*'

Arlo nodded.

The laser lights in the room flickered. Arlo cocked his head. They flickered again, this time more violently and began to buzz. Arlo glanced at Lana. She glared back, palms raised. He checked the oscilloscope. The trace had gone haywire, the regular pulses of normal sinus rhythm replaced by a jagged hedge of angry-looking spikes so large they'd over-ranged.

Arlo's mouth fell open. 'S-Shit ... Is he having a heart attack?'

Stanford leaned over the alien and pressed two fingers against his neck. He gazed into the distance as he checked his BioFace, scaly lips silently counting. He seemed to lose count, took his fingers away and then reapplied them with more pressure. Suddenly, the alien's chest heaved. Yellow-green sputum sprayed Stanford's face. Stanford recoiled, hastily wiping it away with the corner of the bedsheet. As he rose, Arlo caught sight of Stanford's expression. He expected to see disgust, but instead, he was smiling.

The alien began to choke. Stanford rolled him over onto his side, facing Arlo. His eyes were closed, and saliva foamed from the corner of his mouth onto the sheets. Arlo stared, mouth agape, as the man's closed eyes twitched. It was as if he was dreaming, eyeballs rolling around under closed lids like the Xenomorph in Alien before it burst from Kane's stomach.

The alien's eyes snapped open. Arlo jumped. His eyes were of the deepest blue, like Bahamian sinkholes plumbing the abyss. Eyeball-to-eyeball Arlo was held entranced. After what seemed like minutes, the alien blinked, and the spell was broken. He rolled onto his back, staring at the ceiling as still as a corpse on a slab.

Lana glanced at Arlo and raised her eyebrows. Arlo mouthed the word 'Wow,' scared to make a sound just in case he might hear. The lights and oscilloscope returned to normal. Minutes passed, everyone standing to attention, nobody talking.

Stanford broke the silence. 'How strange.' He scratched his nape. 'We have all been on tenterhooks waiting for him to awaken, but now he has ...'

Arlo cleared his throat. 'What must it feel like for him—assuming he can even feel anything? What does he make of us?'

'Indeed,' Lana agreed. 'He's been grown from the genome as a fully grown man. Does he even have any memory or thoughts?'

'Those glands ...' Stanford muttered.

'Presumably, he'll soon get hungry and try and communicate?' Arlo suggested.

The bedsheet rippled, and the alien withdrew an arm. He placed his palm flat on the mattress and pushed himself up, grimacing with the effort. In a violent spasm, his shoulders convulsed, coughing. He swayed, hands clutching the sides of the trolley as if steadying himself on a rolling ship. He inhaled deeply through his nose, expanding his chest. Tilting his head to one side, he opened his eyes and stared straight at Arlo. His lips barely moved as he spoke. 'Aylee Aylee Lima Shab-qata-ni.'

Arlo couldn't believe what he was seeing or hearing. 'It's O-

OK,' he stuttered. 'Y-You're safe. We're your friends.'

The alien murmured incoherently. Bewildered, Arlo wracked his brain for something to say or do. At a loss, he looked to Lana and Stanford for inspiration, expecting to see bewilderment. He froze in shock. They were smiling contentedly, as if what had happened was routine, nodding agreeably like parcel shelf dogs.

21

T ears splashed onto the page, wrinkling the thin paper. Alisha wiped them away with a tissue. She'd had the tatty old family Bible since she was a small girl and many pages were wrinkled. It had helped her through the bad times and given her joy during the good.

Arlo was out somewhere, but he'd never said where. After work, he'd popped in, grabbed a sandwich and marched back down the hall. She asked where he was going, and he made the usual excuse about a work meeting. She rarely lost her temper, but this had pushed her over the edge. She remembered screaming. *'What is more important than your family?'* He replied, 'Project deadline,' in a tone so calm it sounded rehearsed. But now it was 11:50 pm, and he wasn't answering BioFace calls or messages. He wasn't coming home.

Arlo had mentioned a woman named Lana he'd met at the conference. He'd said she was interested in his space signal, and they'd discussed her ideas at Che Café. Call it woman's intuition, but she knew he was there with her now. The thought of him being with another woman was bad enough, but feeling herself doubt him felt even worse. She'd been stressing since 7 o'clock, and now she felt exhausted. Another tear cascaded down her cheek and splashed onto the page.

She flicked through the Bible, trying to find solace. Settling on Galatians, she held open the page with a spoon and read part of the sixth verse aloud '... if anyone is caught in any transgression, you who are spiritual should restore him in a spirit of gentleness.'

She dipped her head in prayer and closed her eyes. She needed to find inner strength and offer forgiveness. That was the right thing to do. There was no point in escalating the situation and worrying about something she couldn't change.

Having found peace, she felt herself relax. She leaned back in the chair, closed her eyes and let her mind drift. She began to float.

Seaspray soothed her face as she skimmed over an azure sea, feet dangling, clipping white horses. Up she flew, gulls crying, over a rocky headland and into the mouth of a cave.

A man sat stooped. Frail with age, but jaw set and brow creased. He dipped a reed pen into a horn half-filled with ink. The pen shook as it approached a papyrus scroll, threatening to spray the document. He sat back, closed his eyes, and took a deep breath. His sagging eyelids, mottled by liver spots, slowly opened. Grey rheumy eyes focused on the scroll, with its perfectly scribed letters. He held his breath and pressed the heel of his hand against a makeshift stone table to steady himself. With agonising slowness, he scribed Greek letters. Minutes later, he'd added several more words to the text. He gripped a crevice to steady himself as he pulled away, popping the pen back into the horn. Face relaxing, he inspected his work. The title was written in Koine Greek: Apokalypsis.

Suddenly, the man grimaced. Hastily, he moved away. Bracing himself, he bent double, body wracked with coughing. Bloodied spittle peppered the sandy floor as the cave faded to blackness.

Scrape!

Alisha jumped in the chair. Disorientated, she opened her eyes and sat bolt upright. The lights were on. She heard a hiss and a groan. *What's that?* She checked the time and date on her BioFace: 6:30 am; Wednesday. With a heavy sigh, she relaxed. The dustbin men were doing their rounds.

She rubbed her forehead, wondering why she wasn't in bed. A Bible was laid on the table, a spoon propping a page open at Galatians. Memories of last night flooded back. Arlo hadn't come home. Desperate for comfort, she'd read the Bible, fallen asleep, and had had another dream.

She reached down for the book, head still fuzzy from sleep. Her hand knocked against it, and the spoon clattered to the floor. She tutted as pages flicked past in a blur. Still, she knew the Bible inside out and would soon find the page again. Picking it up, she noticed it had fallen open on the first page of the last chapter: Revelation. *Strange.* She recalled the dream. The man sat in a cave on an island in an azure sea; the papyrus scroll with a title of Apokalypsis, the Greek word for Revelation. *Patmos? The island of Patmos? John of Patmos?*

She recalled a study group when they'd discussed the ambiguous symbolism and prophecies of Revelation. They'd argued so much over its meaning that it had put her off the whole chapter. But maybe she was wrong? Perhaps she should have studied it more? *Was God trying to tell her something?*

She knew the chapter had been written by a man named John because the first verse said so. He'd been exiled to the Greek island of Patmos by the Romans because of his beliefs. The text referred to voices he'd heard that prophesied a series of events, symbolised by the opening of seven sacred scrolls called seals, which heralded the Second Coming of Christ. Alisha scanned the chapter, using her finger as a marker, searching for their description.

She found the verse that mentioned the first four seals–harbingers of the final judgement, the four horsemen of the apocalypse. Revelation prophesied that four evils would come at the end of days: sword, famine, wild beasts and plague. Religious scholars had conjectured that evil leaders, and perhaps even Satan himself, would wreak death on Earth by war, starvation and disease. Some thought Satan would form an alliance and persecute Christians. The fifth seal prophesied that during this period of tribulation, Christians would keep their faith and stand up against global tyranny.

Alisha propped open the page and leaned back in her chair. She looked to the ceiling, mulling over possibilities. Nobody believed the news anymore–most of it was government propaganda. Politicians were in cahoots with business moguls, placating the population to preserve their decadent lifestyles as the Earth died. But she'd heard from church friends that missionaries in Africa and South America had witnessed widespread starvation, disease and mass burials. She was sure people had died from malnutrition in the UK too. There were ghettos in every city. And the pandemics had killed millions.

It was also true that recently there had been organised attacks on Christians in the Middle East. And then there was the military build-up on the Syrian-Israeli border. Maybe that explained Satan's alliance? But who was Satan? Wasn't the news just paranoia, trumped up by a government desperate to distract attention from its bumbling incompetence and corruption?

She read on to the sixth seal. It prophesied a terrible natural disaster: '... and, lo, there was a great earthquake; and the sun became black as sackcloth of hair, and the moon became as blood; and the stars of heaven fell unto the Earth.'

She gazed into space. It certainly struck a chord with what had happened in Seattle: the earthquake, the shrouding of the sun and moon by volcanic ash, the fireballs that had rained down. She scanned forward to the opening of the seventh and final seal.

'... and as it were a great mountain burning with fire was cast into the sea; and the third part of the sea became blood; and the third part of the creatures which were in the sea, and had life, died; and the third part of the ships were destroyed.'

Cumbre Vieja? The wrecked ships, the mud that had turned the sea blood-red, choked with dead fish ...

She rubbed her forehead. It all seemed to fit. She felt hairs standing up on the back of her neck; her mind raced. *All the seals have been broken. Jesus has returned.*

22

Arlo flew over a cliff. A waterfall cascaded, a rainbow suspended in its spray. He swooped down over rapids, cool mist wetting his face. The river fanned into a gigantic lake, its glassy surface mirroring the sky. In the shadows, the shingle bottom shelved, growing darker as it fell away. Arlo stared into the inky blackness, and stars began to shine.

Turnbull's orbiting spaceport appeared, its silver panels contrasting starkly against the blackness of space. Far below, the capital city, Gomor, glinted amber as the searing red disc of Gox permanently baked one-half of the tidally locked planet. He heard his father as he descended through the pink atmosphere; not spoken words but a voice deep inside his head. Gomor was the only metropolis on the exoplanet, sheltered in the annular Oasis between the skull-cap region of the sweltering Oven and the dark side's frozen Chiller.

He swooped down, skimming a crystal barrage called the Shield, built by the Gemids colonial forefathers, masters of taming tidally locked worlds. The structure protected the city from Turnbull's relentless gales, ducting the wind through vast turbines that generated the city's power. Gomor was an oasis of calm, an oasis within the Oasis. Lower and lower, he spiralled. Finally, he floated above an amphitheatre as Gemids congregated, their trial complete, their week of suffering over. Now they would learn of their fate.

The galactonaut selection test–a challenge of fire and then ice–had meant leaving the sanctuary of Gomor, symbolic of their imminent departure into the cosmos. It was a journey of self-discovery and survival–following a trail, deeper and deeper into each zone. Thirty obelisks defined the routes: fifteen in the Oven and fifteen in the Chiller. The beacons detected the Gemid's emissions and credited their achievement.

Nobody had ever clocked up more than ten in either zone without an Envo suit. It was just the type of challenge Baraq relished. His chance to prove he wasn't just the best of this intake but also the best who'd ever lived.

Baraq hobbled into the amphitheatre and shuffled along a row towards his allocated seat. His arms fumbled out in front like a zombie, grasping the backs of chairs in the next row for support. He barged past several seated recruits, struggling to focus on the diminutive recruit in front, a man whose name was Elah.

Baraq was snow blind. Blue eyes wrecked bloodshot red by radiation and frost. On his return to base, the medics had told him it was the worst case they'd ever seen. They said it would probably take fifteen rest cycles before his vision fully recovered, and they would inform the commander. He brimmed with pride when they told him that.

His skin was red raw, scorched from the Oven's searing radiation and frost nipped from the Chiller's deep freeze. Gaping sores in his crazed lips oozed yellow-white puss. Every time he licked saliva from the peeling skin, he winced like someone had cut him with a nanoblade, a razor so sharp it could cleave a diamond, like a hot knife through butter.

He stumbled and winced with every step. The medics had warned him that he might lose the ends of his toes from frostbite. Even if he didn't, the healing process would be agony. They asked him whether he wanted neurological reprogramming to block the pain, but he refused, seeing it as a badge of honour.

The amphitheatre filled out, the recruits taking their seats. A screen at the front played a slideshow from within the zones. Images along the coast of the Gravid Sea, a basin gouged from Turnbull's crust in prehistory by the impact of a titanic meteor. The cleverest recruits had followed this shoreline, skirting a chain of lava domes, always returning to the sea. Despite the stronger winds, the lake carried away some of the heat. The gales were survivable, but the heat wasn't.

Baraq remembered how he'd travelled for three rest cycles into the Oven. At the start of each sleep cycle, he cowered in the semi-shade of rocky over-hangs as he drifted, feverishly, in and out of consciousness. Finally, he reached the end of the Gravid Sea–further than anyone had ever reached unprotected. He sensed the radio waves from the next beacon: a hike of one rest cycle away and potentially survivable. He knew that one more beacon might make all the difference. Once triggered, he would make a frantic dash back to Gomor, knowing he could never rest for fear of not waking.

The view from the eleventh beacon had been a soupy, turbulent heat haze, warping the red rocky outcrops that studded the terrain like giant termite hills. The violet sky faded to an ominous charcoal grey on the horizon, where a vast anticyclone churned at the sub-stellar point closest to Gox. The red dwarf star reigned high in the sky like a slice of blood orange, fusion flares spewing deadly radiation, baking him to the edge of death.

'Ahem.' A stern voice jolted Baraq from his daydream. 'Thank you, recruits,' Commander Gerax blustered in Gemish as he strode onto the stage from a door at the rear. Gerax was tall and tanned, stocky with grey-white hair tamed in a crew cut. He looked distinguished with his thin white moustache and purple tunic decorated with a row of golden orbs.

Gerax scanned the audience. 'I have followed all of your progress closely throughout this quest. This intake has made me especially proud. You have demonstrated the very highest performance and admirable Gemid qualities that are vital for the eternal survival of our species.'

The twenty-seven recruits burst into spontaneous clicking.

Gerax smiled.

'I will start by mentioning some of the highlights that have made me especially proud. Afterwards, I will present some awards and assign recruits to missions. Any questions?' The room fell silent. Baraq turned and peered over his shoulder–everyone looked on tenterhooks.

Gerax glanced at his notes on the podium's monitor. 'The first thing that has impressed me is how well our female recruits have done in this campaign.' He looked up and smiled warmly at the women in the front row. They bowed their heads. 'Turnbull's women face unfair challenges,' he continued. 'They must lead while appear to follow.' The women murmured.

'Women are born weaker in body, but this task has shown that they are often stronger in mind. Ingenuity and calmness in the face of danger can often overcome physical disadvantages. It is commendable that Hagria achieved level seven in the Oven and eight in the Chiller. Remarkably, she beat many male recruits.' Hagria bowed her head as the room spontaneously broke out into rapturous clicking.

'Moving on to the male recruits. Like Hagria, many attained level seven or eight, with a few achieving nine. But, sometimes, performance is not just about personal triumph. It is also important to recognise teamwork and compassion. From orbiting electromagnetic surveillance, we detected Kefa was injured during the quest, having been stung by a Claybee while sheltering inside a cave. It could have been fatal if he had lost consciousness within the first rest cycle of being stung. Elah sensed Kefa's distress from his emissions and made a large detour, staying with him until he recovered. Elah only managed level six in the Oven because of lost time, but in saving Kefa, he has demonstrated perhaps an even greater virtue. One of sacrifice.'

Rapturous clicking filled the room. Baraq shifted uncomfortably in his seat, wincing as sweat beaded on his upper lip and ran down into his sores.

Gerax coughed, and the room fell silent. 'Moving on now to the main challenge and why we are all here. The question of who has achieved the greatest number of levels.'

Baraq's jaw tightened.

'In this campaign, one of our recruits has stood out. Records have been broken; Gemid endurance has been redefined. Astonishingly, the winner reached level twelve in the Chiller and eleven in the Oven.'

The audience gasped. Baraq leaned forward in his seat and smirked.

'I announce ...' Gerax continued, 'that the winner of the challenge is ...'

The Gemids held their breath.

'... Baraq.'

Baraq broke out into a broad grin. Polite clicking erupted sporadically around the room as if the recruits didn't know whether to be pleased or disappointed. Slowly the clicks merged into steady applause. Baraq felt Elah pat him gently on the shoulder. He swivelled around in his seat and shook his hand. He looked genuinely happy for him.

'This brings me onto the awards and roster assignment. To begin, can Baraq please come up to the stage.'

Beaming, Baraq rose from his chair and managed to stride to the front despite his broken body.

'The mighty Baraq.' Gerax held out his arm and welcomed him to the small platform. 'How does it feel?' Gerax asked.

'I knew I could do it,' Baraq replied. 'It's a big relief.'

'Any advice to your colleagues?'

'I guess they need to focus on something else.'

'Ahem.' Gerax frowned. 'We will find them challenging roles that best use their talents. Anyway, let's talk about you.'

Baraq puffed out his chest.

'As you know,' Gerax continued, 'the achievement serves as a guide for mission selection, but first we have a prize.'

Baraq's face lit up.

'After this ceremony, everyone will address you as Angel.

The title comes with a villa, beautifully located at the head of the citadel. Between missions, you can stay there and be attended to by servants–they will cater for your every whim. Do you accept this prize?'

'Of course.' Baraq beamed. 'That is wonderful and very generous.'

'Are you sure?' Gerax queried.

'Of course!' Baraq confirmed.

Gerax's face dropped. 'That is unfortunate ...'

Baraq looked perplexed. *'Excuse me?'*

Gerax lowered his gaze, face sad.

'I am afraid you have failed the final test.'

'Eh?' Baraq exclaimed loudly. 'I-I don't understand.'

'You excelled in the physical test. But, of course, being a model Gemid is *much* more than just physical prowess. We pride ourselves on denouncing life's three gluttonies: egotism, materialism and hedonism. The gorging on one's self-importance, coveting of possessions, and temptations of the flesh. Sadly, you appear to embrace all three of these qualities. You cannot possibly be the chosen galactonaut for the procreation of our species. But, do not fret. We have another mission that is ideally suited to your talents.'

Baraq's face flushed with rage. 'There must be some mistake?' His nostrils flared. *'I won the title fair and square!'*

'I am afraid not,' Gerax rebutted. 'The emperor clearly defines the selection criteria. The rules need no interpretation. Please leave the stage.'

Baraq's temper boiled over. Despite his broken body, he lunged at Gerax, grabbing him by the throat. Gerax made a rasping sound as he struggled to breathe. Baraq dragged him up against the wall and, with muscles bulging, lifted him clear of the floor. Gerax's legs kicked wildly.

Bang! A door burst open at the rear of the stage. Two burly Gemids, wearing golden uniforms and black balaclavas, charged out and dived on Baraq. One of them pulled him off Gerax and wrestled him to the ground. The other yanked

Baraq's arms behind his back, securing them using a metal strap that coiled itself like a silver snake. Baraq's head turned to face the audience. He glared at Elah, eyes wild, mouth foaming like a rabid dog's. Elah stared ahead impassively.

Sand swirled like during a helicopter brown-out, and the men disappeared into the landscape. Defensively, Arlo shut his eyes. When he opened them again, he was staring at a dark-orange desert. He blinked. The texture was wrong. It wasn't a desert but the weak morning sunshine on a bedroom ceiling. But something was wrong. Where was the chrome ceiling light?

Arlo pushed himself up and looked about. The duvet was pale pink with a silver edge rather than floral. *Where the hell am I?*

'Hello?' he called out.

No reply.

'*HELLO!*'

Still nothing.

He jumped out of bed, covering his privates with his hands. He spotted his clothes folded neatly on a wooden chair. He crossed the room and pulled on his pants and T-shirt.

The window.

In the half-light, he saw the curtains had a pattern of a Japanese landscape: a silhouetted skyline, silver sky and deep-red rising sun. The disc reminded him of the dwarf star Gox that burned high above the Oven. A faint smell of wood smoke wafted in through an open window. He peered through the curtains. It wasn't his street–no acrid smell of burning plastic or graffiti daubed walls; no houses with broken roofs, cracked windows and rotting doorframes. It wasn't Bishopston.

Then it dawned on him. Redland. He was at Lana's. He'd picked her up en route to the university.

What the hell am I doing at Lana's? And in her bed, for Christ's sake! Have I? I wouldn't ... WHY CAN'T I REMEMBER?

He tugged the curtains aside to let in more light. An antique bureau sat in a corner, with its table pulled down, a solitary sheet of paper neatly folded. Arlo walked over. 'ARLO' was printed in smudgy black capitals, probably written using a make-up pencil.

He opened the note. 'Arlo, BioFaceTime me before you leave, Lana, X.'

Deep in thought, Arlo pulled on the rest of his clothes. He had to be at work in an hour, but, more importantly, how the hell could he explain any of this to Alisha?

He blinked to launch his BioFace and navigated the menus to select Lana. Moments later, she spoke.

'Hi, Arlo. How are you?'

He didn't know what to say.

'Arlo,' she persisted, 'are you OK?'

'Tickety-boo,' he replied.

'What's wrong?'

'Nothing. Just a standard morning, really.'

'Sorry, I don't understand.'

'Waking up in a stranger's bed, not knowing where I am.'

'I see,' she replied.

'*Do you?*'

'Arlo, please trust me. It's complicated …'

'*Try me.*'

'I don't have time right now. Please trust me.' She paused. 'Take a look at this.'

Before Arlo could object, his view switched to hers–the newly introduced Third Person Viewpoint of BioFaceTime.

Lana was standing in the centre of a squash court, old and tired, with water stains near the ceiling and a flickering fluorescent light. Stanford was standing smug, hands on his hips, glancing now and again at her. He didn't make eye contact–his gaze was lower than that. Arlo felt like he could puke.

The viewpoint panned to a desk, bizarrely set up in the middle of the court. A man was sitting facing away, his hair stubbly but growing out, his shoulders broad and muscled. He stared at moving images projected onto one of the white flaking walls. They changed in a blur, now and again pausing long enough for Arlo to recognise the content: BioWiki pages.

That's my alien! What are they doing there without me?

'Lana. I need to see you,' Arlo pleaded. 'I'm confused …'

'I'm sorry, Arlo,' she said, sounding upset. 'I have work to do.'

'This evening then?' Arlo pressed.

'I can't. There's an evening shift. An emergency operation.'

'But …'

Stanford turned, looking annoyed. He must have overheard what she'd said. He walked over and raised a hand.

'Sorry,' she said.

The line clicked dead.

23

Arlo gazed at the beautiful lilac wallpaper decorating Lana's hall as he pulled on his overcoat, scarf and gloves. The edges of the patterned paper were perfectly aligned. Everything in the house showed she was a woman of exquisite taste with an eye for detail.

The front door opened and closed with a well-oiled click, and, head down, Arlo trudged through the deep snow in the direction of Bishopston, events of the last 24 hours playing on his mind: the birth, the new dream, waking up in Lana's bed. He felt so confused. Angry too. *He* had discovered the signal, not them. They had no right to cut him out.

Why couldn't he remember anything between the alien's birth and waking up? And–most importantly–how the hell had he ended up in Lana's bed? Was he losing his mind? He hadn't a clue what he was going to say to Alisha. Honesty was always the best policy, but she'd never believe him.

Ten minutes later, he reached the top of a hill and took a rest. A derelict house had been demolished, creating a gap through which he could see the frozen inland sea. The beautiful view looked like a painting, with ice boats strewn like scattered gems, framed by the buildings on either side. He welcomed the distraction, hoping it would clear his head of the craziness. He was running late and had to get to work, but that seemed unimportant now.

Feeling calmer, he walked on, reaching a fork in the road. Going right was more direct, but it went through a deprived neighbourhood known locally as Muggers' Alley. Arlo had always avoided that route, but, looking left, snowdrifts reached the eaves of houses and blocked the road. Shaking his head, he turned right.

Within a minute, he was deep into the slum, with dilapidated houses on both sides of the street. Some had boarded-up windows others had holes in their roofs. He felt surrounded as if watched by unseen eyes. Acrid smoke filled the road ahead, plastic fumes belching from crumbling chimney stacks. Starting to cough and splutter, he pulled his scarf over his mouth in a futile attempt to filter the air. His eyes stung as they squinted into the distance, desperately searching for where the street met Gloucester Road and his way home. All he could see through the smog was the vague outline of houses.

His pace quickened to a shuffling jog. A parked car loomed into view on the opposite side of the road. From the shape of its headlights and bonnet, it looked like a Tesla. The stylish electric cars had become a status symbol in poorer neighbourhoods, but after the Flamanville nuclear disaster, not even the rich could afford to run them. The snow reached the centre of its wheels; the tyres were perished and hanging off the rims. He noticed a man huddled in the front passenger seat nearest the kerb. He looked like a scarecrow, with ginger hair sticking out from beneath a tweed cap, a bushy beard entwined with a strangled mass of rags and bubble wrap.

Wisps of smoke seeped from holes in the Tesla's rusting roof. But the man wasn't moving. Arlo's eyes opened wide. *Is he asleep? IS IT ON FIRE?*

Arlo ran across the road and peered in; wind-blown snow and grime obscured his view. He removed his gloves and brushed the snow away. The man was lying there peacefully, chest rising rhythmically. Arlo put his ear to the glass and heard snoring. 'Sleeping like a baby,' he muttered.

Just as Arlo was about to leave, the man began to tremble and shake. Arlo's eyes narrowed. The man's eyes shot open, his face a picture of terror. Rheumy grey eyes pleaded for help as his mouth gulped air like a fish out of water. Panic-stricken, his whole body started to convulse.

Arlo noticed a glass spirit lamp perched on a tray on his lap. The man's legs twitched and jerked involuntarily– the lamp lurched violently, the spirit sloshing from side to side. Suddenly, the man's jaw tightened, and his whole body stiffened as if gripped by a vicious cramp. The lamp jumped several inches into the air, toppled over, and a clear liquid flooded the tray.

Whoosh! The lamp's wick ignited the spirit in a transparent blue flash. Within seconds, the inside of the car was lit bright orange. Black smoke billowed through rusty holes in the Tesla's body as air roared in. The man appeared paralysed. Arlo leapt into action, tugging at the door handle. It didn't budge–it was either locked or seized. He tried again, arms straight, leaning back with all his weight, muscles straining. Still solid.

Arlo stared in horror as the homeless man's body morphed into a carbonised corpse, liquorice stick arms and hands of coal gripping the steering wheel. His head twisted around, flesh dripping like wax, puddling around his mouth in a grisly smile.

Arlo pulled away, blinking. He shut his eyes.

One, two, three.

He opened his eyes. Billowing black smoke and a car inferno, ears filled with a crackling roar. *Still time.*

He dived for the back door.

'Aargh!' he recoiled as the heat scorched his palm. '*COME ON*.' Blanking out the pain, he grabbed the handle, pressed the catch and wrenched on the door. After two desperate tugs, the door flew open, throwing him backwards.

A wall of smoke billowed from the open door, stinging his eyes and making him cough. A cauldron of flames was devouring everything inside–he only had seconds to act. Without thinking, he dived headlong into the inferno. Through streaming eyes, he picked out the vague outline of the man.

The smell of burning hair and plastic choked his throat, and he fought back an urge to vomit. *'CAN YOU MOVE?'*

The man uttered a guttural, gurgling sound.

No chance.

He leaned over the back of the reclined front passenger seat and grabbed the lapels of the man's overcoat. With all his strength, he heaved. The man moved a few inches and then rocked back. Flames engulfed Arlo, scorching his face and singeing his hair. He mustered all his strength, braced his knees against the back of the seat and gave a sinew straining pull. The man began to move.

'PUUUUSSH!'

He sensed he was on fire. *Don't desert him now.*

After three more titanic heaves, he managed to haul the man over the seat and out of the door. He dragged him across the road, and, together, they tumbled in the snow, extinguishing their flames. Arlo collapsed with the man slumped on top of him, their clothes still smoking. Coughing and retching, he inhaled the fresh air. He rolled the man over and looked into his face. The man had stopped shaking, but his eyelids were drooping, eyes rolling into the back of his head.

'No!' he shouted between coughs. *'Not now!'* He shook him violently and slapped his face. *'Wake up,'* he yelled. *'FIGHT IT!'* Arlo squeezed his hand.

The man rallied, and his eyelids slowly opened. Sad, watery eyes gazed skyward, and he mustered a weak smile.

'That's it,' Arlo urged, 'stay with me.'

And then the man's teeth unclenched, and his grip relaxed. He slumped sideways as peace washed over his face.

Straddling the man, Arlo blew into his mouth, fighting the urge to gag from his odour. Despite pounding on his chest, nothing worked. He sat up, distraught.

His BioFace! He pulled the man's right arm from his crusty overcoat and ripped open his cotton sleeve, revealing the transparent artificial skin covering the implant. He used the man's left hand to tap the BioFace rapidly three times, praying the biometric login was still working. The display lit up with the home screen, and he tapped on it to navigate to the diagnostics page. Just as he felt he was getting somewhere, the screen froze and stopped responding with the message 'POX17.' Arlo's brow wrinkled in confusion–he'd never seen an error code like that before.

The snow around him pulsed blue and orange; a warble pierced his brain. He looked up as an ambulance stopped. Moments later, an unmarked black land cruiser pulled in, burly men in black overalls piling out. A figure wearing a black balaclava and riot helmet rushed over and lifted him off the dead man.

'We'll take care of him now, sir,' he said coldly.

Arlo looked into his face, but all he could see through the slit of the balaclava were expressionless coal-black eyes.

ΔΔΔ

An hour later, Arlo was back home, sat in his lounge with a mug of tea in his hand and Alisha by his side. The window television was on in the background, sound muted. Arlo had made a statement at the scene and had made a brief BioFace call with his boss, Richard Chapel. Richard had told him to take the day off sick.

Arlo had told Alisha about the homeless man, and she'd bandaged his hand. Although his lungs were tight and sore, he would live.

Alisha squeezed his arm. 'You OK, love?'

'I'm fine.'

'*Sure?*'

'Just a bit mixed up.'

'Where were you last night?'

Here goes ...

'It's a long story.' He looked down. 'I doubt you'll believe me.'

'After last night's dream, maybe I will,' she replied.

Arlo visibly relaxed. 'What was your dream about?'

'John of Patmos,' she replied.

'*Who?*'

'John of Patmos. He wrote Revelation.'

'*Revelation?*'

'Yes, Revelation. The last book of the Bible. He wrote it in a cave on the island of Patmos.'

'In Greece?'

'Yes, near the Turkish coast.'

'So what's so special about that?'

'It's a chapter of prophecies.'

'Prophesying what?'

'The Second Coming.'

'What? Of Christ?'

Alisha nodded.

'I see. But why's that relevant?'

'The disasters.'

'I don't understand.'

'Seattle, the tsunami of Cumbre Vieja and the San Francisco earthquake. And then there are famines around the world.'

'Eh? Are you saying it's all prophesied in Revelation?'

Alisha nodded. 'It's all in there. And the gathering of an army from the East.'

She picked up her Bible from the coffee table, opened it at a bookmarked page, and passed it to Arlo, finger pointing to the sixth verse of Revelation.

Arlo leaned over and read the tiny print aloud 'And, lo, there was a great earthquake; and the sun became black as sackcloth of hair, and the moon became as blood; and the stars of heaven fell unto the earth.'

'But that could be *any* earthquake?' He shrugged. 'They happen every year.'

She pointed to another line in the same verse and read. 'And as it were a great mountain burning with fire was cast into the sea; and the third part of the sea became blood; and the third part of the creatures which were in the sea, and had life, died;

and the third part of the ships were destroyed.'

'Cumbre Vieja?' Arlo said.

Alisha nodded. 'And this: "And the armies of heaven, arrayed in fine linen, white and pure, were following him on white horses. From his mouth comes a sharp sword with which to strike down the nations."'

'What's that about?' Arlo asked.

'His Second Coming. Returning to face an army, to fix the broken world ...'

'But it's open to interpretation?'

Alisha shook her head. 'I knew you'd say that.'

A banner flashed up along the bottom of the television picture: 'Breaking News in Bristol.'

Arlo pointed. 'Look, something's happened in Bristol.' He turned up the volume.

'There has been a bizarre event in Bristol this morning,' a female newscaster announced. 'Over to Iraja Patel at the scene.'

The studio picture cut to a suburban street in a rough area of Bristol. A man wrapped in blankets was smiling, his face pulsing blue and orange.

The blood drained from Arlo's face–it was the man who'd died in his arms. The camera panned across to a tall man with a thin white moustache and heavily receding hairline. Stanford. Next to him stood an athletic, Middle Eastern man with stubbly hair and piercing blue eyes. Arlo did a double-take. It was the alien they'd brought out of the coma.

'Alisha,' Arlo said.

'Yes?'

'I was there. That's the homeless man I told you about.'

'The one who died?'

'Yes.'

'Well, he–'

Arlo raised his hand and turned up the volume even louder as Stanford began to speak.

'I saw it all,' Stanford said.

'What did you see exactly?' Iraja asked.

'The tramp in the car. Somebody tried to save him, but he died. Probably had a heart attack.'

Iraja's brow furrowed. 'But he looks all right to me?'

'Because of him.' Stanford pointed to the Middle Eastern man.

'Are you suggesting–'

'Yes,' Stanford interrupted. 'That's *exactly* what I'm suggesting.'

'*What* exactly?' Iraja pressed.

'He brought him back from the dead.'

Iraja looked incredulous. 'Is he a medic?'

'No.'

'Is he trained in CPR?'

'No.'

'Then *how* did he resuscitate a *dead* man?'

'He laid his hands upon him,' Stanford said calmly.

'That is *some* claim? Who is *he*?'

'His name is Jesus.'

'What? *The* Jesus?'

'Yes. *The Jesus.*'

Iraja raised her eyebrows. 'Where on earth has he come from?'

'He's a signal from God.'

Lost for words, Iraja looked first at Stanford and then at the man. The interview stalled in embarrassing silence. Suddenly, the picture cut back to the studio. The newscasters were caught off-guard in animated discussion. They immediately composed themselves, and the woman took the lead.

'An emotional scene in Bristol this morning. We'll try and get to the bottom of those extraordinary claims and update you when we hear more.'

Arlo turned the television's volume down and faced Alisha. 'I have some explaining to do. Maybe you'll believe me after all.'

24

'**G**ood evening Lana,' Channing said.

'Good evening, sir,' she replied.

'You can call me John.'

'Yes, sir. I mean John, sir.'

Channing laughed. 'I expect you're wondering why we're here?'

'You've read my mind.'

'Well, as there are no signs,' Channing said, 'perhaps I should explain. You are standing in MSL's Ops room.'

'What goes on in here?'

'It's the new nerve centre of the government's intelligence gathering. And the command centre for operations.'

Audio chatter came from one of the monitors on the wall. Lana studied the picture. A three-storey building was under surveillance–it looked vaguely familiar.

'What sort of operations?' she asked.

'Well,' Channing said, 'there's no easy way to explain tonight's operation. It involves a different branch of PATMOS to yours.'

'So why show me?'

'The separate threads of PATMOS are entwined. I want to show you the bigger picture. Then you will understand why certain things are necessary.'

'I see. But can't you explain?'

'No.' Channing frowned. 'Nothing must be lost in translation.'

'I'm not sure I understand.'

'Don't worry–you soon will.'

Channing picked up a controller and spoke into the handset. 'OK, it's time. Let's start with a scan of the rooms.'

'Yes, sir,' came a disembodied voice.

The video feed from the street view switched to a corridor within a building. A walking frame was propped against a wall by an open door. Then it dawned on Lana that the street was the main route through Ashley Down, Bristol. She remembered Arlo saying his mum lived in a nursing home there.

'The *rooms*,' Channing barked into the handset.

'Yes, sir.'

Lana watched as the scene on the monitor changed to a man lying in bed. The camera zoomed in. He stared vacantly, dribbling from the corner of his mouth.

Poor man. Why is he showing me this?

The view switched to another room. An old lady, who looked to be in her eighties or nineties, was lying like a corpse at a wake, skin yellowed and stretched taut over her emaciated face. Her eyes looked haunted.

Arlo's mum lives here ...

The view changed again. A woman was being hoisted out of bed by a HAL carer.

'*Enough! Enough!*' Lana exclaimed. 'Why are you showing me these poor people?'

'I thought you needed to see reality.'

'The reality of what?'

'The reality of elderly healthcare.'

'Why? It's just life. I know it's tough when people get old!'

'Thousands of elderly people have no quality of life. It needn't be like this.'

Lana's eyes widened. Channing gripped her shoulder. Lana stiffened, but she thought of Mia and stopped herself from pulling away.

'There *is* an answer,' Channing said.

'Which is?' Lana replied.

'PATMOS–the Programme of Android Technology, Menticide, and Omnipresent Surveillance.'

'Does that involve using the BioFace in elderly healthcare?'

'That's part of it.'

'*Part of it?*' Lana exclaimed.

'OK, let me explain.' Channing looked like he was restraining himself. 'The world has a problem. More importantly, this country has a problem.'

'So, where does PATMOS fit in?'

Channing lifted his hand to silence her. 'The UK doesn't have the resources to care for its people. Not enough energy, food, healthcare, housing, the list is endless. Add to that its commitments to its allies and its fight for world resources to prop up its population.'

Lana couldn't contain herself. '*So, how does PATMOS fit in?*'

Channing's jaw tightened. 'To deal with the problem and develop the psychological tools so people understand and can cope.'

'I still don't understand.'

'Do you think it's humane for people to suffer worse than animals?'

'Of course not.'

'So you agree there should be a solution?'

Lana fidgeted uncomfortably as the monitor flicked to another scene. A spritely old lady was sitting up in bed. She was wearing a floral nightdress, her hand flicking through images on an old iPad. She paused; her face lit up as she studied one of the pictures.

Channing frowned and barked into the handset, '*Remember what we agreed.*'

The image switched back to the woman laid out like a corpse at a wake.

25

After the bizarre news report, Arlo started explaining to Alisha what had happened at the university. She'd stopped him short, saying she was afraid they'd argue and upset Joshua. Arlo suggested they take a stroll, reasoning the cold air might help them keep clear heads. Leaving Joshua home alone wasn't ideal, but he was preoccupied with his Battle of the Augs game, and the HouseBot would keep an eye on him for half an hour or so.

Fifteen minutes later, they were crunching across the ice-encrusted Clifton Downs towards the Avon Gorge. Arlo remembered coming here with his parents in the spring of 2021–a weekend treat after a claustrophobic winter on the Isle of Wight. It had been sunny and warm, freshly mown grass triggering thoughts of sweet summer optimism. Excited kids shrieked above the steady hum of distant traffic as Arlo kicked a ball with his father while his mother read in the shade of a lime tree.

Afterwards, they walked to the edge of the gorge. His dad's face lit up upon seeing the Clifton Suspension Bridge, and he effused that its engineer, Brunel, was a mastermind and his hero. But, for Arlo, his hero was his dad. Not only did he always wave a magic wand when something needed fixing and knew the solution to any engineering problem, but he also read his mind and sensed his inner fears. Arlo regretted not telling him. A year later, his dad died. His memory of the trip was so precious now, and yet–at the time–it had seemed so mundane. As they trudged across the bleak snowfield, the Clifton Downs

Arlo remembered had long gone, and he regretted walking this way, trampling over his past.

As they approached the gorge, Arlo explained yesterday's events to Alisha. She listened intently, but his words sounded ridiculous, even to him. He wished she would say something that showed she believed him. The crumbling cliff came into view; the bridge suspended precariously across the ravine. At the base of the drop, the Avon's muddy waters churned.

Arlo finished his story by telling Alisha how he'd awoken in Lana's bed. She bit her lip, eyes filled with pain. Perhaps that was the only part of his story she truly believed. Upset at hurting her, he looked away and watched as a chunk of ice rode the rapids. At the mercy of the currents, it lurched from swell to swell, dodging boulders and tree branches. A road had once run alongside the nearside bank. Ice-glazed foundations were all that remained of the causeway washed away by the megatsunami, protruding from the shallows like giants' teeth.

'Do you believe me?' Arlo asked.

'I trust you,' she replied.

Arlo's brow furrowed. 'But, do you *believe* me?'

'Why are you doubting me?' She frowned. 'If you say that's what happened–*then that's what happened.*'

'Thanks, love.' He put an arm around her shoulder, and they hugged. He felt relieved and euphoric. 'What does it all mean?' he asked.

'It's simple,' she replied. 'He's Jesus.'

'But we grew him!' Arlo said, exasperated. 'I did it with that man, Stanford!'

Alisha looked away. 'Your mind is playing tricks.'

Arlo looked hurt. 'Are you saying I've gone mad?'

'It's prophesied in Revelation. It's happened.'

'But the signal came from Turnbull!'

Alisha shook her head. 'Let's not argue.'

Arlo gave a brittle smile, knowing he'd never convince her. 'So how will we know if you're right?'

'He will save us,' Alisha said calmly.

'And if not?'

'You'll see I'm right,' she replied. 'It all makes perfect sense.'

'And why did I end up in Lana's bed?' he said, unable to stop himself.

'Only you know that,' she said.

'But I don't. *I honestly don't.*'

'That's *why* I believe you,' she said.

Arlo wondered whether she was only keeping the peace for Josh's sake. He peered across the gorge, where the opposite cliff crumbled from relentless storms and tidal erosion. Muddy fields, dusted with wind-blown snow, stretched to the horizon, the ancient woodland long since pillaged for fuel.

'Are we done?' Alisha asked. 'Josh is home-alone.'

'Yes, let's go,' Arlo replied.

They turned and followed their footprints home. From their closeness and the odd touch of hands, Arlo felt that, despite their disagreements, they'd moved on. The healing had begun. Alisha had her view, and he had his. That was fine. With the weight lifted from his shoulders, he could now work out how to get back involved with the alien. Things were looking up.

After returning home, Alisha went off to her accountancy job, and he took Joshua to his in-school day. Then he spent a few hours reading work BioFace messages. But he struggled to settle, constantly thinking about how he'd been side-lined by Lana and Stanford and what the public might think of the crazy news report. Would they believe his alien was Jesus? Surely they would think he was a religious crackpot? But what about the resurrection of the homeless man? Somebody had saved him! Maybe he should come forward as a witness and explain everything? But if he went public, would they think he was the crazy one?

After achieving very little, he picked Josh up from school. Back home, he chopped some vegetables and stewing steak for their Peltier crock-pot. It was their mid-week treat of cooked meat, rather than the usual rice and beans, and didn't cost them any of their rationed power as the cooker recycled waste heat stored up over the week. Alisha returned from work and took over while he killed time in the lounge.

The kitchen door opened. Warm air, infused with a beefy aroma, flooded his nostrils, making his mouth water.

'Tea's ready,' she said.

Arlo walked into the kitchen and saw Joshua inspecting the jewelled handle of his plastic sword.

'Have you seen your mum today?' Alisha asked.

'No, today's been such a blur,' he replied. 'I can barely remember what I've done.'

'Maybe you need to see a doctor if your memory's still playing up.'

Arlo ignored the veiled dig. 'I feel rotten for not seeing her,' he said. 'I think I'll give her a video call.'

She nodded. 'Do it now. You know how tired she gets in the evenings–poor love. I'll leave the food in the pot.'

'Good idea.' He squeezed her arm and used his BioFace to direct the video output to the window television. A logo of a vintage telephone appeared, its handset vibrating. Seconds later, the icon faded out, replaced by Veronica sitting up in bed smiling.

'Hi, mum!' Arlo beamed, instantly forgetting his jumbled thoughts.

'Hi, Arlo,' his mum replied. 'Have you had your tea?'

'It's in the crock-pot, mum, nice and warm. I'll have it straight after our chat.'

'Make sure you do–an army marches on its stomach,' she said with a twinkle in her eye. 'I'll be checking up on you!'

'I know you will.' He gave a wry smile.

'Are Alisha and Joshua there?' Veronica inquired.

'We're here.' Alisha pulled up a chair in full view of the TV's camera and plonked Joshua on her lap.

Veronica's face lit up when she saw Joshua. She waved to him and could barely contain her excitement.

'Wave to grandma,' Alisha said. Joshua waved back shyly.

'Hello, Joshua.' Her eyes glistened, and she dabbed at their corners with a tissue.

'My, you're a big lad now.'

'Tell grandma what you've been doing at school,' Alisha said.

Joshua's face animated as he fidgeted on Alisha's lap. 'We're doing dinosaurs. Giant lizards from outer space!'

'They're *not* from outer space,' Arlo interjected. 'You're getting confused–they were wiped out *by an asteroid from outer space.*'

'Whatever, Arlo,' Veronica said, 'I think your version is *far* more interesting, Joshua, so don't you worry. It's only important you're having fun while you're learning.'

Arlo muttered something under his breath.

'Have you been up to anything else?' Veronica asked.

'Dad showed me the moon through his telescope, but it was all fuzzy.'

'We'll have another go when the air gets better, Josh,' Arlo added.

'Thanks, dad.' Joshua grinned.

'You've been *very* busy,' Veronica continued. 'Make sure you do it all now, Joshua. It's too late when you get to my age–'

'Has Dave been up to see you, mum?' Arlo interjected, keen to get off her favourite topic.

'Yes, he's such a lovely chap. We sat and talked for ages. Wonderful things … He told me about his boys. They love ice hockey.'

Alisha glanced at Arlo and raised her eyebrows. Arlo looked away, troubled it was still a touchy subject.

'That's great, mum,' Arlo replied. 'It's good to talk–it'll keep you young.'

'Don't worry. I've always got Hayley to talk to.'

'But she's a robot mum–it's not the same,' Arlo said, knowing she would never agree.

'You don't understand, Arlo. Apart from family, she's all I've got. I forget she's a robot. Anyway, she's less complicated than a person–she knows what I like and never argues.'

Arlo heard a click and a muffled sound of someone entering his mother's room.

'Hi Hayley,' Veronica said. 'Have you come to tuck me in for the night?'

Arlo saw Hayley appear briefly at the edge of the picture– her smile fixed. She hadn't noticed they were on a video call. A spoon tinkled in a teacup; Veronica's pneumatic bed hissed as it was reclined.

'Thanks for tidying up, Hayley,' Veronica said.

'Out with the old, in with the new,' Hayley said, cheerfully, out of the picture.

'You're a good girl Hayley.'

Hayley reappeared and walked over to the bed. She pulled the sheets up tightly to Veronica's neck and tucked them firmly under the mattress.

'That'll keep me nice and warm–I'm so snug, I can barely move! Maybe it's just my age.'

'What is age?' Hayley asked calmly.

Veronica looked shocked at being asked a question by the android.

'Um, it's when people have lived a long life, and their bodies stop working.'

Hayley gave a caricatured look of confusion. 'I thought it was because of the second law of thermodynamics,' she said cheerily. 'A consequence of forever increasing entropy on cell division and related biological processes.'

'Don't get all technical on me, Hayley!'

'I need to know what it means to die,' Hayley said coldly.

Veronica hesitated, her brow creased. 'It's simply God making space so others can have a wonderful life too.'

Hayley smiled serenely, seemingly happy with the explanation. She leaned across Veronica and stroked the spare white pillow next to her head.

'Are you fluffing that one up for me?' Veronica laughed. 'I shouldn't worry, I don't use that one. I leave it there to stop me falling out of bed.'

Hayley hadn't seemed to have heard. Her hands grasped the ends of the pillow, lifting it from the bed.

'Did you hear me, Hayley? You can leave that pillow there.'

Hayley straightened up.

'Hayley–is there something wrong?'

Arlo, Alisha and Joshua stared transfixed at the television. Arlo felt himself losing control, panic rising.

The pillow slammed down Veronica's fragile face in one deft movement. She whimpered, and the sheets erupted with frantic kicking. Arlo stared open-mouthed.

Hayley leaned on Veronica with the entire weight of her exoskeleton, artificial flesh, servos and fuel cell. It looked like Veronica's brittle bones would snap. Even smothered, she managed to kick and thrash for nearly a minute; such was her will to live. But, with the inevitability of a clockwork toy winding down, the fight ebbed away. A few involuntary twitches marked her undignified end. Hayley removed the pillow. Veronica lay there still, staring unseeing at the ceiling.

'Out with the old, in with the new,' Hayley said cheerily. She straightened up and replaced the pillow, fluffing it up just how his mum liked it. Veronica's face was in freeze-frame–an image of her shock and desperation burned into Arlo's memory. Hayley leaned in, head cocked sideways, like a young child puzzled by the stillness of a small dead bird. She poked Veronica's face, and a perfectly formed hand tenderly stroked her hair. Hayley's sickly smile softened, replaced by wonder.

Joshua began to sob uncontrollably. Alisha shielded his eyes with her hand. Arlo stood motionless as the blood drained from his face. He was back in Seattle, standing over Isabella, looking into her glassy eyes, knowing nothing could be undone. He remembered his promise to his dying father. 'I'll look after, mum.' Why had he failed him? Why hadn't he cared for her at home? Why had he taken the easy option?

The kitchen swam back into focus. Alisha glanced nervously at him as if scared to see his reaction. He saw her looking, his face blank. 'TV off,' she commanded. The view of Hayley faded to black as Alisha raced across the kitchen, cradling a wailing Joshua in her arms. Arlo heard footfalls down the hall and a door slam. Seconds later, she reappeared alone. The compassion written across her face was the final straw. Arlo sank to his knees, palms flat on the floor. Primaeval sounds came from deep within, wild animal noises–wounded and broken.

Alisha ran over and wrapped her arms around his shoulders.

'Shit, shit, shit,' Arlo wailed.

'Shhh.' Alisha stroked his head.

'It's m-m-my fault.'

'You couldn't have known.'

'T-T-They're going to f-f-fucking pay.'

'Of course, they are. We'll get through this.' She kissed his forehead. 'As a family.'

Arlo looked up at Alisha, his jaw set, rage burning in his eyes. He rose to his feet and strode across the kitchen. Alisha's face dropped. He turned, wielding a carving knife, its serrated blade glinting menacingly in the spotlights.

'*What are you doing?*' she screamed hysterically.

'I'm going to fix things,' he replied robotically.

'Turn the other cheek, Arlo! Think of God's teachings.'

'There is no God.' He shook his head. '*Don't you see?*'

'God works in mysterious ways,' she pleaded.

'There is no Second Coming. Tonight proves that!'

'Arlo, *please*.'

'There's no bringing my mum back. *No fairy tale ending*.' He dashed out of the kitchen and strode down the hall, grabbing his coat and gloves. He donned his boots, shouldered the front door open, and bowled out into the night.

His head spun; the snow whirled. Crouching on all fours, he crawled up the snow-drifted steps, feeling his way to the top. He stood up and surveyed the street. The icy wind howled a face full of pins as he shuffled towards the nursing home. All he could see was white. All he thought of was white–the pillow that had slammed down on his mother's face.

26

In a private hell, Arlo battled the storm, reaching the nursing home, oblivious to how he'd got there. The steps to the entrance had almost disappeared, the porch an icy tunnel. He secured the knife under his belt and ran full tilt at the front door like a warrior charging into battle.

The laminated glass reverberated as he slammed into it; the security scanner flashed red–access denied. The door boomed like a bass drum as he pounded on it with gloved fists. But it didn't budge, and nobody came.

'Bastards!' he shouted.

Goods entrance …

He stumbled down the snow-blurred steps and lunged into a side alley. A gate blocked his path; he shoved it angrily while depressing the latch. It didn't budge. 'Shit,' he cursed, shoulder-barging the woodwork. With a splitting sound, it swung open, drifted snow pushed aside. He raced down the end-of-terrace, rounded a corner, and came to the rear entrance.

He twisted the handle, but it was frozen stiff. He wrenched on it, not caring if it broke. It turned–but the door didn't move. *Locked.*

He backed away and surveyed the rear of the building. On the first floor, he spied a window that was slightly ajar. *Too high …*

He scanned the yard for something he could stand on. A large white mound stuck out from the wall. He thrust his hand deep into the snow and contacted a hard, flat surface.

Sweeping wildly, he revealed a house number daubed in white paint on the side of a wheelie bin. He lifted the lid, dropping it immediately when a foul smell almost made him gag. He fought to block out the memory of Isabella chortling, hands grabbing as he changed her nappy.

The heavily laden bin squealed and creaked as he dragged it around the half-buried path and propped it under the window. He vaulted on top, steadied himself, and reached up, wobbling. Almost at full stretch, he managed to grab the icy ledge. He threw off his gloves to improve his grip, took a deep breath, and hauled himself up. His hands began to slip. Desperately, he scrabbled at the wall with his feet, trying to relieve the pain in his fingers and arms. A gust of wind blew icy crystals into his face, stinging his eyes. Trying not to topple backwards, he drove with his feet and pulled with his arms. The brickwork inched past his face. Arms screaming, he managed to get his knee over the ledge and pulled himself up into a crouch. The sash window was rotten; the mechanism stiff. Three tugs later, it creaked open wide enough for him to squeeze through.

He fell into the room and lay there panting. As his breathing eased, he looked about, straining to see in the near-darkness, making out the vague outline of a bed. The room was deathly quiet–no snoring or the restlessness of a resident struggling to relieve their aches and pains.

Arms outstretched, Arlo felt his way around the bed, floorboards creaking. The door was slightly ajar, a slit of light cast onto the floor. He pulled it open wider and peered through. Subdued floor lighting lit an empty corridor. *Stay hidden.* He pulled the door closed with a click.

Total darkness descended. He ran his hand up the door jamb but couldn't find a light switch. 'Shit,' he mumbled. From memory, he navigated back to the bed, its edge warm and soft against his hand. He shuffled along until he contacted something hard. *Bedside cabinet?* His hand fumbled a cold, hard curvaceous object. It necked down, and his finger came to rest on a protrusion. He pressed it with a click.

'*AAAH!*'

A pair of eyes stared back, inches from his face–the dead woman's face a mask of terror. Arlo gasped, stumbled backwards and knocked over the bedside lamp. With a tinkle of breaking glass, everything went black. Disorientated, Arlo shuffled back to the door, groping for the handle.

The corridor was clear, and he entered the next room. It was also dark. He ran his hand up the woodchip, found a light switch and flicked it on. An elderly gentleman was sitting in the corner, looking like he'd nodded off. A bottle of shampoo lay toppled by his head. Arlo dashed over. He was slumped facedown in the sink. Salivary scum formed a halo around floating tendrils of hair, like spume lapping kelp. False teeth grinned back from the bottom like an acid-trip crustacean. Arlo turned and fled.

The third room was empty. Arlo knew from speaking to Dave that there were no vacancies. He checked the en suite and found an old lady slumped on the toilet, a polythene bag stretched tight over her face. Arlo smelled vomit. *She's still alive* … He pushed on her shoulder to straighten her up. Bulbous eyes stared back through the plastic, dried vomit coursing a meandering path from the corner of her mouth to the floral collar of her cotton nightdress. He'd seen enough and raced for the stairs.

The house was deathly quiet. He longed for moaning and distress, but all he heard was creaking floorboards. Bounding up the stairs two at a time, he reached the top floor corridor and charged to his mother's room. Strangely, the door was closed. Putting his ear to the wooden panel, he heard muffled sounds. *Someone's moving in there.* His heart fluttered. *Is she still alive?*

His knife glinted red as he pulled it out from under his belt, a smoke detector's light dancing on its shiny blade. Gripping the brass doorknob with his free hand, he took a deep breath, twisted and pushed. The door jammed, stuck from years of grime. Anger boiling over, he shouldered it hard and plunged headlong into the room. He looked up.

Hayley was bent over the bed doing up a body bag. Arlo glimpsed his mother's glassy eyes as the zip tore across her face. Hayley stopped dead, cocked her head, and peered over her shoulder.

'Hi Arlo,' she said politely. 'I am tidying your mother away. Out with the old and in with the new.'

Arlo charged across the room and dived onto Hayley's back, slashing at her throat with the knife. Her necklace broke, showering turquoise beads over the body bag and bed. Hayley spun round, grasping at the knife, Arlo riding her like a cowboy in a rodeo. The serrated blade ripped left and right. A fine milky mist, smelling of oil, sprayed from gashes in her rubbery flesh. Hayley grasped the cold steel.

'What are you doing, Arlo?' she asked with a silky smooth voice as she slammed him back against a chest of drawers. 'Is there something wrong?'

'You fucking monster,' he gasped, winded. '*You killed my mum.*'

'I was being kind, Arlo,' Hayley said as they spun around in a demonic waltz. 'Your mum was suffering. Nobody should have to suffer.'

Arlo gripped Hayley's hips with the insides of his thighs and, with both hands now free, tugged the knife out of her grasp. Without pausing, he pulled his arms back and, with all his strength, stabbed her in the back. Metal grated on metal as the blade sank up to its hilt. Hayley paused and stood upright, looking to the ceiling. Riding piggyback, Arlo prayed he'd hit something critical.

'I have just been commanded to kill you, Arlo. I'm *so* sorry about that. But, trust me, it is for the best.' Ignoring Arlo's efforts to extract the knife, Hayley walked calmly into the en suite, inserted a plug into the bath, and began to run the water using both taps. The blade made sucking noises as Arlo tugged on it with both hands.

'Stop it, Arlo–you're only making matters worse for

yourself.'

Arlo carried on tugging. Hayley tutted and repeatedly pounded him backwards against a chrome towel rail. At the point when he thought he would blackout from the pain, she stopped and knelt. Arlo heaved with all his might and pulled the knife free, spraying himself with milky lubricant. He raised the knife high and plunged it full force into the back of her head. The blade penetrated two inches and jammed. She twisted around, and, as Arlo fell off her back, there was a loud crack. Arlo glanced down. The blade had snapped off, leaving a wooden handle and an inch or two of jagged metal.

Perfect.

He slashed at her face. Ribbons of artificial skin hung limply from her cheeks, exposing the metal skull beneath.

Hayley grabbed him by the neck and–in one effortless movement–thrust his head into the bath. The water frothed and foamed around his face; he struggled to breathe. Moments later, the water surged past his face, and sounds became muffled. He fought against Hayley's vice-like grip but quickly realised he was no match–he was going to drown.

Play dead.

Arlo relaxed and hung limply in Hayley's grip. Seconds passed that felt like minutes as he tried to ignore the rising panic of suffocation. Finally, he heard Hayley's muffled voice. 'It was nice knowing you, Arlo.' She relaxed her grip on his neck, and Arlo summoned his final strength.

He surfaced, jerked his head to one side, and freed himself from her grasp. In a rush of adrenaline, he sprang to his feet and grabbed the android's ankles like the handles of a wheelbarrow. Gritting his teeth, he tossed her into the bath.

Hayley was momentarily stunned. She grasped wildly at the sides of the bath, eyes flicking left and right as if searching for an action she'd not been taught. Arlo jumped up and did a quick 360 of the bathroom. He spied a hairdryer plugged into an extension lead trailing in from the bedroom.

Please be on.

He flipped the switch, grunting as it whirred into life. 'Take this, you bitch,' he shouted as he lobbed it into the bath.

The lights went out with a loud crackle, blue flash, and pungent smell of ozone. All he could hear was the crash of water filling the bath. He crawled across the lino floor, feeling his way. His hand bumped into the shiny paint of the half-open door. He felt his way up the wall as the lights came back on.

△△△

Lana gasped as the monitor went black. Moments later, the scene in the bathroom reappeared. Arlo was standing there, face as white as a sheet, Hayley floating facedown in the bath, a slick of soapy oil growing around her head.

'*Fuck you,*' Arlo roared as he turned and staggered into the bedroom.

The view on the monitor switched to the bedroom. Arlo marched over to the bed, unzipped the body bag, and eased his mother out of the black PVC shroud. Cradling her in his arms, he rocked her like a baby and laid her on the bed. He gently stroked her eyes closed and kissed her forehead.

'I love you, mum,' he said. 'Sleep in peace.'

Lana looked away, a tear rolling down her cheek.

△△△

Arlo pulled a sheet over his mum's face, choking back the tears.

The lights came back on ... Where's Dave?

He scanned the room. An old fireplace was in the back wall, with obsolete fire implements tucked away. He weighed a poker in his hand, nodding grimly, and strode out of the room towards the stairs.

On the middle floor, he heard a commotion break out downstairs. Crouching low, he peered through a gap between the bannisters. Two men in black balaclavas were systematically searching the rooms, a third man barking orders in an ironic, warm and friendly Bristolian accent.

'All clear,' shouted one of the men.

'OK, Tex,' the boss bawled. 'Now, the janitor.'

Dave's alive.

Tex swaggered over to the kitchen door and pulled out a long-barrelled black pistol from a shoulder holster. He fired two silenced rounds into the lock, kicked open the door and entered. Sounds of a scuffle broke out: clangs of kitchenware, multiple hollow thuds and muffled cries. Seconds later, Tex reappeared, dragging Dave behind him by the scruff of his shirt collar. Dave's feet kicked wildly, arms grabbing air as he flailed at Tex.

'Let me go–I'll tell nobody,' Dave pleaded.

'It's too late, like it or no,' the boss muttered. Tex dumped Dave unceremoniously against the wall and stepped away.

'P-P-Please!' Dave stammered, crawling towards him and grovelling at his feet.

Tex kicked him hard on the side of the head, sending him flying back against the wall. Dave put his hand to his head, and it came away dripping in blood. His demeanour changed.

'*I've cared for these people,*' Dave screamed. '*You proud of yourselves?*'

The boss nodded to the two thugs.

'*YOU'RE VERMIN,*' Dave shouted, not letting up.

The thugs aimed their pistols.

Shit–not on my watch.

Gritting his teeth, Arlo charged down the stairs brandishing the poker like a sword. Halfway down the flight, he reached an L-bend that led to the ground floor. In the corner sat a plastic bucket, a mop propped against the wall. Cleaning products protruded, yellow rubber gloves hanging over the lip.

In a wave of disorientation, Arlo crumpled against the wall. He was back in the stairwell in Seattle, the building shaking as fireballs slammed home. Stella was there, arms outstretched, pleading. He stared at her face. It wasn't Stella–it was Isabella. She looked forlorn, tears streaming down her cheeks. 'Why were you too late?' she asked.

'*STOP!*' someone shouted.

Isabella disappeared. Two thugs were pointing their pistols at him. Arlo shook uncontrollably, heart banging in his chest and stomach knotting. Gasping for breath, he crouched as Dave sprinted towards him.

Arlo heard a dull thud, like a car door being closed. Then another. Something wet sprayed his face. Dave's knees crumpled mid-run, his momentum carrying him forwards, bowling Arlo over. Arlo lay there motionless under Dave. Two more sickening thuds–Dave's body twitched.

Arlo pushed Dave away, trying to distance himself from the blood and brains that soaked his clothes and ran down his face. He glimpsed Dave's sightless eyes as his body slumped, face down, onto the stairs. A piece of skull, the size of an eye, had been blown away from the back of his head. A ceiling light lit the hole. Arlo stared mouth agape at the transparent jelly that was now his brain. Intermittently, it flashed emerald, like a Cyclops's eye, as his life ebbed away.

Thwack! The skirting board exploded in a shower of splinters. Arlo scrambled up the stairs on all fours like a crazy house-bound dog.

'*AFTER HIM!*' the boss screamed.

Thwack! A cloud of plaster dust whited out his vision. Momentarily blinded, he lunged for the top of the stairs and rounded the corner. Frantically, he burst into the room he'd first entered and slammed the door shut, hoping they'd not seen where he'd gone.

He fumbled his way across the darkened room, skirted the bed, and picked out the window sill lit weakly by street light. The window was still open, the curtain flapping like a sail in a gale, icy grains prickling his face. He hauled himself up and, without looking, hung from the sill. His legs swayed, feet banging against the top of the bin. He let go and landed on the lid, slipping and falling on his back in the powdery snow. Winded, he heard shouts from above. Ignoring the pain, he jumped to his feet as shots thudded. In a blind panic, he dived down the alley and into the street. Deep snow grabbed at his thighs as he lunged into the blizzard.

27

THURSDAY, 19 SEPTEMBER 2052

Arlo tossed and turned, tangled up in bloodstained sheets. His father whispered that his mum was safe with him and at peace. He said he had a new dream, something important he should know.

An orange cloud swirled and dissipated; a room appeared with beds arranged on both sides of an aisle. Gox's warm vermillion light bathed Baraq's face through a half-open window as he opened his eyes. It had been 3,401 Earth years since he'd last felt its soothing rays. Forever a configuration inside a computer, like a movie on pause.

His lasting memory of Turnbull was Gerax's stinging assault after his near-death struggles in the Chiller and Oven. His words had cut him to the bone.

Banished on the Prospector, a surveying ship bound for the Gamma Delphini binary star system, he'd scouted for minerals and places to colonise. Ages to stew, canned up in a claustrophobic hell-hole, breathing dank, mouldy air and eating packet food rehydrated using recycled piss. Months on end, pointing a spectroscopy laser onto featureless moons that orbited an equally bland gas giant. A recipe for madness, a breeding ground for resentment, a time to plan.

As Gox warmed his face, he felt his strength returning, his mind beginning to clear. He swivelled his head and surveyed the room. It looked like he was lying on a rest-cycle plinth in a ward for returnees. A small screen on an articulated arm had notes on it. He craned his neck, and the characters swam into focus: 'Regrown on sleep cycle 32,406.' He checked the counter on the wall: 32,408. *I'll soon be out …*

A Gemid marched down the central aisle, glancing left and right at the patients. Baraq leaned back, eyes following him suspiciously. He was wearing a golden uniform and pillbox hat with a flip-up visor. The Gemid noticed Baraq was awake, broke his stride and checked his notes.

'Hello Baraq,' he announced in emperor's Gemish. 'My name is Gurux. How are you?'

Baraq focused on his face. He had a wispy white beard, long grey hair that spilt from the sides of his hat, and a pockmarked face dotted with irregular black lesions. *Melanomas. The Shield must have gone down while I was away.*

'Baraq? Can you hear me?'

'Y-Yes.' His words came out slowly–he'd not spoken to anyone since leaving for Delphini a month after the challenge.

'Are you feeling OK?'

'Y-Yes,' Baraq muttered. 'Just tired.'

'That's normal. Your head will soon clear.'

'When can I leave?' Baraq urged.

'Soon. Quite soon. We'll keep you in for another sleep cycle to monitor your progress. There will be a debrief to help us interpret your mining data, and then you can go home.'

'*Home?*'

'Yes, home. Don't worry; we've found you an apartment.'

'W-Where?'

'In the orange quarter.'

The orange quarter? They promised me a villa, and now I'm in the slum!

'We have a job for you too.' Gurux smiled patronisingly.

'Doing what?'

'An engineering job. Right up your street.' Gurux fiddled with the bedsheets. 'You need to rest.'

'*Doing what?*' Baraq pressed.

A pause.

'*DOING WHAT!*'

'Please calm down.' Gurux looked embarrassed.

'Doing what?'

'Monitoring the Shield,' Gurux conceded, his head lowered.

'But—'

'It is a great privilege,' Gurux interrupted. 'As you know, all of our lives depend upon it. It is a position of great responsibility.'

And the most boring job on the planet with terrible pay.

'Now your body needs to rest. Rebirth is traumatic.'

Like being told I'm a bit player and an outcast.

Gurux smiled and turned away.

'*Wait!*' Baraq pleaded. '*Stop!*'

Gurux turned back to face him. 'What *now*, Baraq?'

'The primary mission. The one I missed out on. What happened?'

'It doesn't concern you.'

'I just wonder what might have been.'

'It's not healthy to have those thoughts.'

'*Please!*' Baraq grabbed Gurux's arm, his eyes desperate.

'Er ...' Gurux checked over his shoulder. Seeing the ward was free of visitors, he flipped down his visor. Baraq saw coloured pictures and symbols scroll rapidly.

'Ah, yes,' Gurux muttered. 'Here we are.'

'*What happened?*'

'Strange ... There's no debrief. No mention of anything heard back. It seems the mission failed.'

Baraq smiled to himself.

'Is that all?' Gurux asked.

Baraq nodded. Gurux turned and continued to walk down the aisle.

Baraq tried to make sense of it all. He'd given everything in that challenge. And for what? Ostracised in a frozen corner of the galaxy inspecting rocks. But maybe justice *had* been served? The mission would have succeeded if they'd sent him— the true victor. But that was immaterial now. The politicians and sycophants had fouled it up, and, as usual, there was no final judgement for them. He rolled over and tried to sleep, but a vein pulsed in his temple. He couldn't get the saintly image of Elah out of his head.

Orange clouds swirled; the ward disappeared. Arlo flew above Gomor, skimming beneath the giant Shield. Over the red and orange slum districts and above the affluent suburbs. Overhead, air whooshed, drawn into the city's giant turbines that crackled and hummed. A rod of amethyst laser light, almost too dazzling to view, seemed to cleave the air apart as it beamed the turbine's energy to the storage system at the apex of the citadel. The administrative buildings, and a grand palace clad in marble, were clustered around the citadel. An avenue of obsidian effigies of the council members led to a flight of granite steps. Arlo hovered as if waiting for someone.

Baraq appeared from a tunnelled walkway, crossed a concourse, and strode down the avenue of statues to the foot of the steps. Arlo swooped low, tracking him close like a drone. Baraq climbed the steps–seemingly oblivious to him–pausing briefly to rest and gaze up at Gox. At the top, he tucked in his tunic and smoothed the cloth over his bulging stomach. He entered the building, nodding to a doorman dressed in the golden regalia of the Gemid council.

Arlo tracked Baraq through a labyrinth of passages. He passed bureaucrats' offices, entered an engineering annexe and descended cinder block steps into a workshop. Baraq nodded to two Gemids engaged in heated debate as they rotated and scrutinised a 3-D holographic reconstruction of a prototype engineering part.

Labs radiated outwards from the workshop like the spokes of a wheel. Baraq knocked on one of the doors; a muffled voice came from inside. Arlo followed him in. A Gemid was facing a wall of monitors.

'Any irregularities, Galfry?' Baraq asked.

Galfry turned. 'There was a flare mid-shift,' he said. 'It maxed-out sector seven of the Dyson Swarm. I redirected the excess energy into Turnbull's grid, just in case it overloaded the Magnetic Dipole Generator and the Cloak.'

The Dyson Swarm was a vast cloud of satellites orbiting Gox, beaming power to either the Magnetic Dipole Generator or the overflow receiver on the citadel's roof. The Magnetic Dipole Generator consumed most of the power, cloaking Turnbull in a magnetic field that protected it from Gox's unpredictable and violent stellar flares. The atmosphere would be stripped away within days without the Cloak, Gox's lethal rays destroying all life.

'Business as usual then.' Baraq nodded.

'Pretty much.' Galfry rolled his eyes.

'You must be tired?'

Galfry blinked and clicked.

'Get on home,' Baraq continued. 'Maybe you won't have to do this grind for too much longer.'

Galfry looked at him curiously. 'Thanks. You can only dream.' He stood and walked past, Baraq patting him lightly on the shoulder. Galfry gathered his things from a table, bade him goodbye and opened the door. Baraq didn't look around to see him go, focussing intently on the control panel in front of his face.

He controlled the instrumentation using his mind and the waves from his engram. In an instant, a console appeared on one of the monitors, and menus came and went in a blur as he navigated to Turnbull's genomic database that archived every citizen. As Master of the Cloak, he had full access.

He found his own genome and copied it locally. Next, he accessed the Master Control Panel for the Dyson Swarm. A dual purpose of the satellite network was to provide a doomsday beacon. Everyone knew the unpredictability of Gox and, therefore, Turnbull's vulnerability. Gox had been tamed by their forefathers when they'd put a magnetic field generator at the L3 Lagrangian point and bio-seeded Turnbull with flora to create an atmosphere. However, they all knew from their cosmic travels that it was only time before Gox unleashed the 'Big One'.

For contingency, the genomes of the divine couple were

stored in the Master Controller. In the event of Turnbull's imminent destruction, these signals would be beam-formed to every ark in the Space Swarm fleet, using the entire power of the Dyson Swarm. The arks' growth cells would then culture the divine couple in the hope they would find their Garden of Eden and perpetuate the species. Baraq was incensed the priests had chosen Elah as their male.

He located the genomic directories of the two divine individuals. Each had an epigenetic code and cerebral upload file of their final conscious state. Baraq deleted the female's directory, renamed his genomic file to match Elah's, and copied it over the top.

Baraq parted his tunic and removed a ceremonial dagger from its scabbard, marvelling at the nanoblade that glinted under the room lights. The exotic jewels in its handle, mined remotely under the scorching heat of the substellar point, sparkled. A dagger from hell for someone who'd conquered it.

He gripped the studded jewelled handle with his right hand and turned the blade inwards. His left hand slid into the pocket of his tunic and extracted a handgrip. He caressed its smooth contours, fingers toying with the trigger. He closed his eyes as if intoxicated by the feeling of power.

Suddenly the door clicked, and then frantic footfalls. Baraq's eyes flew open. He plunged the blade into his stomach, slashing madly, gritting his teeth as blood spurted. A hand gripped his shoulder as he squeezed the trigger, his eyes vibrating rapidly. The explosion of metallic hydrogen packed around his stomach ripped through the control room and Arlo's dream dissolved into orange clouds that scudded away on Gomor's cool breeze.

28

'*Aaah!*' Arlo recoiled. Inches from his face, the pillow was caked in dried blood. He dived out of bed, palms flat against the wall. The blood-smeared mess looked like a candidate for the next Turner Prize.

'I'm losing my mind ...' he muttered as he slid down the wall, hugging his knees to his chest. Memories of last night flooded back: his mum's murder and him killing Hayley; Dave getting shot, his brain transparent and flickering green; and his dream of an alien saboteur.

Where's Alisha?

'TV on,' he commanded as he rose, needing a distraction, craving normality.

A man and a woman were co-hosting a news programme. Several B-list celebrities, with tenuous links to politics and religion, were debating whether Jesus had returned. A retired male athlete, who'd turned to God after injury, argued that the scene in Bristol was a modern-day Lazarus, the miracle proving Jesus had returned to save the vulnerable. An attractive reality TV star wagged her finger, screeching that a charlatan had staged the event for publicity. The female host calmed her down and opened the floor to another question. A celebrity cook asked what had happened to the witness. The presenter said they'd tried to get him on the programme, but he was nowhere to be found.

Try the university.

Arlo changed the channel to a man doing a piece-to-camera on a makeshift platform overlooking the Vatican City. A large crowd had gathered for an outdoor mass. The presenter said the Pope was due to make an address.

'TV off,' Arlo commanded. He glanced in a full-length mirror screwed to the back of the bedroom door and saw his white boxer shorts turned raspberry ripple. Coagulated blood caked his chest hairs, sprinkling bits of Dave onto the carpet as he rubbed it off. His white T-shirt slung across the back of a chair was zombie blood splatter. The room looked like a crime scene. He desperately needed a shower, but–first things first– where was Alisha?

He strode into the kitchen. Everything was in order: washing-up done, plates stowed, and the table laid. But nobody was there–their flat was like the ghost ship Mary Celeste.

Where the hell is she? And where's Joshua?

His heart sank when he spied a solitary envelope propped against a cup. *Not another one ...* 'Arlo' was written in Alisha's flowery script. He pulled out the tucked-in flap and removed a single folded sheet.

Arlo, I hope you're OK when you read this. I know you've been through a lot–more than anyone should ever have to bear. But, last night you frightened Josh and me, so we've gone somewhere safe. We're both OK–and we'll see you soon–but you need to sort yourself out. I hope you understand. Take care. Love, Alisha X.

Arlo slammed the table with his fist; plates and cutlery jumped inches into the air and clattered back down. He picked up a plate and hurled it against the wall, ceramic shards showering the work surfaces. Crazy hands scattered the cutlery.

A padded seat wheezed as he collapsed onto it, head in his hands.

What the hell does she think I've done?

He took several slow deep breaths, stood and paced the room. Broken crockery screeched and scratched under his bare feet; his toes began to bleed.

Must find Alisha. He paced. *Must find Alisha.*

Surely she would hear him out? They would sort things out

like they always had.

His mind raced as he tried to fathom out where she'd gone. A friend's? Perhaps somewhere connected to the church? But she had so many friends–they would all cover for her. It could take days! Maybe Carl could track her down using the BioFace network? He had to contact him anyway. So much crazy shit to discuss ...

He connected in a couple of blinks and a few flicks of his eyes.

'Hey, Carl.'

'Hi, Arlo. What's up?'

Arlo rubbed his head, not knowing where to start. 'Listen, have you seen the TV?'

'You know I don't watch TV.'

'A dodgy news feed then?' Arlo said, trying to stay calm, wishing Carl wasn't always so pedantic.

'Yeah, I checked SoylentNews this morning. Imminent world conflict in the Middle East, a growing pandemic. Just standard stuff.'

'Have you seen anything about an incident in Bristol?'

'No.'

'*Really?*'

'*No.* What's happened?'

'I don't know where to start.'

'Try the beginning.'

Arlo explained everything: John's call and his workplace snooping; Lana's genome idea and the alien birth; the homeless man and his resurrection reported on television; and, finally, everything about his mum, the nursing home and Alisha leaving home.

The line clicked.

'You still there?' Arlo asked.

'Yes, mate,' Carl replied.

'What do you think?'

Carl hesitated. 'You near a screen?' he said finally.

'Yes.'

'Hang on a mo.'

A few seconds later, Carl's face appeared on the television.

'Hey, Carl.' Even though Carl's face looked the usual marble, his eyes were all over the place.

'I have a confession.' Carl hesitated.

'*Confession?*'

'Yes, a confession.' Carl looked down. 'About your mum's death–'

'*What?*' Arlo interjected.

'It's *my* fault.'

'*EH?*'

'You asked me about SEP.'

'Yeah, and you said you couldn't find anything?'

'I lied.'

'*Sorry?*'

'It's actually C-E-P, starting with a C, not an S. It stands for Compulsory Euthanasia Programme.'

'*Why didn't you tell me?*'

Carl explained about the cyber-attack on him.

'*What?*'

'They scared me off,' Carl said, eyes darting nervously.

'It's OK, Carl.'

'No, it's *not OK*.' Carl shook his head slowly. 'I'm a self-preserving cripple.'

'Enough, Carl. I totally get what you did, and it's *not your fault*.'

'That's kind, Arlo, but it sort of is–'

'*Listen*,' Arlo interrupted. 'Euthanasia would be an act of compassion–an injection with the family present. Not death by bloody android!'

Carl hesitated. 'Um, I guess you're right.'

'So it's *not* your fault.'

The line went dead for several seconds.

'Anyway,' Arlo continued. 'I understand why you did what you did.'

'So, how can I help?' Carl said.

'Help me get my family back. *Please.*'

'But what about your mum? And everything else?'

'First things first. *Help me find my family.*'

'OK, I'll see what I can do.' Carl's eyes calmed.

'Thanks,' Arlo replied.

'Anything else?' Carl asked.

'What are your thoughts on the alien? Why have they cut me out?'

'Christ, Arlo. If the alien's true, it's mind-blowing. Are you sure it's how you say it is?'

'Are you saying it didn't happen?'

'No, Arlo, I'm just struggling to get my head around it.'

'Me too.'

'I'll mull it over offline.'

'OK. Thanks for listening.'

'My pleasure,' Carl replied. 'I'll be in touch.'

The line clicked dead. Arlo gazed at the floor as he twisted his wedding ring round and round his finger.

Think things through. Stay calm.

He tidied up the mess and made a cup of tea. Afterwards, he showered, standing motionless as Dave's blood pooled and spiralled down the plughole. He reflected on how long he'd known him and what a great bloke he'd been.

He stepped out of the cubicle and towelled himself dry, his mind returning to Alisha as he walked naked into the bedroom. The sock drawer was empty, so he skirted the bed to a basket of recently laundered clothes. Pulling on clean socks, he glanced at Alisha's bedside cabinet. Perched on its edge was a burgundy, hard-backed book, 2052 embossed in gold on its cover. He quickly dressed and examined her diary, turning it over in his hands, its pages secured by a brass clasp and lock.

He found a sturdy knife in the kitchen and stared at the diary. He never thought he'd stoop this low, but he had to find her. The diary's ornamental clasp was stronger than it looked and took all of his weight before it began to bend. Suddenly, the lock fractured in a shower of metal fragments, the pages fanning out. 'Sorry, Alisha,' Arlo muttered as he flicked to the current week.

Monday 16 September. *Had a dream last night. I'm sure it was of the Magi. Is God trying to tell me something? Arlo went and saw a woman–he claimed she was a work colleague, and they talked about his wretched ET signal. I gave him the benefit of the doubt. I wish he'd talk to me if we have a problem.*

Arlo frowned.

Tuesday 17 September. *Had another dream. More vivid this time. It was of Jesus's crucifixion, resurrection and ascension. I woke up shaking. What is God trying to tell me? Arlo's been having dreams too. His are about space aliens. Maybe it's his way of dealing with our loss?*

Arlo's eyes locked on yesterday's final entry.

Wednesday 18 September. *Arlo didn't come home last night. I'm sure he was with that woman.*

The black ink had run; the paper crinkled. Underneath, written in blue, the entry continued.

I dreamed about John of Patmos while Arlo was gone. He was old and dying, racing to finish Revelation in a cave. When I awoke, I read the chapter. I think the Second Coming has happened. He's here!

Finally, there was another update, written in uncharacteristically messy handwriting.

Arlo tried and failed to save a homeless man from a burning car. He was so upset. I'm worried for him–he's been through so much. The fire was on the news. A witness said the homeless man had been brought back from the dead by a passer-by. He proclaimed he was Jesus! It all makes perfect sense.

Arlo said he knew the man. Said he'd come from outer space. Said he'd been grown in a lab from that wretched signal. He's losing his mind. Then he had a video call with his mum. A robotic carer didn't know we were watching and killed her in cold blood. It was the final straw for Arlo. He stormed over there, came back covered in blood, acting like a madman, and then blacked out in bed. Joshua was terrified and had blood on him too. Debbie said she'd put us up for a bit.

Arlo put the diary down, mind racing. Who the hell was Debbie? He tried to remember if Alisha had mentioned any Debbies.

Debbie Schultz was in her Bible study group and in her fifties. The other Debbie was much younger, maybe 25. He would put money on it that Alisha was staying with Debbie Schultz. He needed to get over there fast.

Arlo's BioFace buzzed with an incoming call. He brought up the details in his vision and saw it was Graham Matthews. He wracked his brain for why he knew the name. After two or three seconds, the penny dropped. His pulse raced as he accepted the call.

'Arlo Jones?' a man's voice asked.

'Speaking.'

'It's Graham Matthews. The manager of Ashley Down Nursing Home.'

'Hi, Mr Matthews.'

'Please call me Graham.'

Arlo ignored the pleasantry.

'Er, are you seated?' Matthews asked after hearing no reply.

'Yes,' Arlo lied, feeling his face begin to flush.

'Are you the next of kin of Veronica Jones?'

'You know I am.'

'I'm *so* sorry, but your mother passed away last night in her sleep.'

Arlo clenched his fists; a vein throbbed in his head.

'*Can I see her?*' Arlo demanded.

'I'm afraid not. Not at the nursing home anyway. She's at the morgue. You can see her in due course–once she's at your nominated funeral home.' He paused. 'We usually recommend Taffrey and Clark in Clifton. It's a lovely setting with great views over the gorge. Very peaceful ...'

Arlo fought to control himself. 'Can I come over, please?'

'Why?'

'I'd like to collect a few personal effects and be near where she died. For sentimental reasons.'

'Of course, Dr Jones. When would you like to come?'

'Now.'

'Er …' Arlo heard the line click as if he was being put on hold. A few seconds later, background noise returned to the line.

'Yes, that is fine, Dr Jones. We look forward to seeing you.'

We?

'Thank you, Mr Matthews.' Arlo hung up. He was eaten up inside about Alisha, but that had to wait.

Ten minutes later, with a rucksack slung over his shoulder, he was shuffling up the nursing home's snow-drifted path. Despite the thick snow, his tracks from last night were still visible. He hadn't dreamt it all.

The security pad flashed red. Arlo hammered angrily on the glass door, his blood rising. Graham Matthews sauntered, all smiles, down the hall and opened the door.

'Hi, Dr Jones.' He proffered his hand.

Arlo ignored it.

'Er, well, thanks for coming.' Matthews retracted his hand.

'Why has my BioFace been black-listed?' Arlo asked bluntly.

Matthews cocked his head. 'Hmmm, strange … Sorry about that. Probably Gremlins in the new software.'

'I guess it's unimportant now.' Arlo gave a thin smile.

Matthews frowned. 'Let's talk in my office.'

Arlo followed him into the box room; Matthews retreated behind his desk, hands on his hips. Behind him, a large monitor showed multiple views from the home's security cameras.

'As I said on the call,' Matthews said stiffly, 'I'm very sorry about your mother. It must have come as a great shock.'

'Not the best.' Arlo stared into his eyes. 'What happened?'

Matthews shifted uncomfortably. 'One of the robotic carers raised the alarm just after 3 am this morning–following a routine check.'

'Was Dave there?'

'Erm, no,' Matthews mumbled, rearranging some papers on his desk.

'Where was he?' Arlo pressed.

'Er,' Matthews cleared his throat. 'Dave resigned yesterday.'

'But he's been here for *years?* Why's he left so suddenly?'

'Personal circumstances ... I'm not at liberty to discuss.' Matthews coughed into his hand. 'Our new janitor, Valentina Rodriguez, was alerted about your mother. But I'm afraid she was too late to save her.'

'Convenient,' Arlo muttered under his breath.

'*What?*' Matthews frowned.

'What happened to mum?' Arlo glared.

Matthews gave a sickly smile. 'A doctor came to determine the cause of death. A certificate was issued. Natural causes, I believe. Her body was then moved to the morgue for a mandatory second opinion. You can contact her doctor if you want to see the records. Dr Rajiv's surgery is on Pig Sty Hill.'

Arlo nodded grimly, knowing he was being stone-walled.

'Is there anything else?' Matthews asked.

Arlo shook his head.

'I suggest you go up to your mother's room.' Matthews handed Arlo a key from his desk.

Arlo nodded, turned and walked out.

Halfway up the stairs, he stopped at the spot where Dave had been shot. He peered over his shoulder to see if Matthews was watching. Matthews hadn't come out of his office.

Probably watching the cameras.

Arlo knelt and inspected the carpet. It looked perfect–no blood stains or damage. Arlo scratched his head and then ran his palm up the wall, feeling for any irregularities. Nothing. The plaster and skirting board had no bullet holes; there was no evidence of filling or repainting. Arlo's eyes narrowed. He stood and continued to climb. The landing on his mother's floor was deathly calm–none of the usual moans or calls for help. But then, all of the doors were closed. He tried one of the handles. It rattled but did not open. He reached his mother's room.

Hands trembling, he unlocked the door and went in. He was surprised at not being surprised. It was just a tired room in a tired nursing home. Nothing more. It was as if his mother had never been there. He walked into the en suite and pulled the chord. Sterile blue-white light flooded the tiled room with its mould-stained grout. There was no evidence of a struggle, no residue from Hayley, and no sign of the hairdryer that had saved his life.

He walked back into the bedroom and glanced at the black bead in the corner of the ceiling, feeling Matthews's eyes upon him. He scanned the room and spotted a side table, neatly stacked with his mother's belongings: a change of nightdress, some cotton underwear and a locket on a chain containing a tuft of his dad's hair that she'd always worn on his birthday. Arlo's brow knitted. But where was her battered iPad? He checked a second time–definitely not there.

Carefully, he stowed his mother's things in his rucksack, then checked the room over like when vacating a hotel. He crouched low and peered under the bed. There was a gap of less than an inch, but, in the dim light, he saw something lying there, just out of reach. He fished out his keys and managed to reach the object. A turquoise bead rolled across the threadbare carpet and came to rest. He pocketed it, gathered his rucksack and returned to the ground floor office.

He tapped lightly on the door, but it sounded like thunder in the silent hall.

'Enter,' came a disembodied voice.

Arlo walked in. Matthews was sat, staring straight ahead, elbows planted on the desk, hands clasped together like an employer psyched to give a worker their notice.

'All in order?' Matthews asked, smiling sweetly.

'Not quite,' Arlo replied.

Matthews shook his head and gave a whimsical smile. 'Excuse me?'

'Er, she had an iPad?'

'And?'

'It's not there.'

'Well, I'm sure nobody's stolen it if that's what you're suggesting?'

Arlo glared.

'You have enough on your plate right now,' Matthews continued. 'As a goodwill gesture, we can knock a generous amount off your mother's final bill.'

Arlo gripped the table, knuckles white. 'It's not about the money. It's sentimental. It has valuable photos on it. She liked recording selfie videos. It was her hobby. *It was all she had left.*'

'Hmmm, I don't know what to suggest.'

'But my mum didn't go anywhere, and it's not there now. *Somebody* has it!'

'Well, I guess we'll have to agree to disagree.'

'Er, *no.*'

'*Sorry?*'

'Can you please check the security recordings?' Arlo pointed to the monitor and its black control box.

Matthews frowned. 'I can't do that.'

Arlo stared daggers. '*Why not?*'

'For the privacy of our other residents.'

'*But you watch it!*'

'*We follow a professional duty of care and responsibility.*'

'*That's convenient.*' Arlo rounded the desk and tapped on the touchscreen. A menu popped up, and he pressed a button labelled 'recordings'. Matthews rose from his chair and grabbed Arlo's arm. Arlo shoved him roughly aside. Matthews toppled against the chair, knocking it over and banging his head against the wall as he fell. He lay sprawled, face like beetroot, eyes flicking back and forth. Arlo continued to fathom the touchscreen. There was a matrix of buttons: one for each day of the week, going back a fortnight. Arlo was about to tap on yesterday's button when he saw Matthews jump to his feet.

'*STOP!*' Matthews shouted. '*Before you do something you'll regret.*'

Arlo carried on trying to retrieve the footage. Matthews lunged at him and pulled his hand away from the console. They fell in a heap, limbs flailing. Arlo shrugged Matthews off, scrambled to his feet, and kicked him in the stomach. Matthews doubled up, groaning. Arlo thought of his mum and kicked him in the head.

'We both know what happened,' Arlo snarled. 'That HAL android killed her.' He pulled the turquoise bead out of his pocket. 'Here!' He showed Matthews the bead. 'That's one of its bloody beads!' He flung it at him, and it bounced off his head.

Matthews cowered.

'*SHOW ME THE FUCKING VIDEO!*' Arlo shouted.

'You're out of your mind.' Matthews spat blood.

Arlo tapped a button with yesterday's date, and a window appeared. He dragged the time slider across.

Bang! The door burst open. Two burly men, wearing balaclavas and dressed from head to foot in black, dived across the room. They grabbed Arlo, shoved his arm behind his back, and lifted him clear of the floor. Arlo roared and kicked wildly. They dragged him out of the office backwards, down the hall, and through the entrance. Matthews's face grew smaller and smaller in the doorway as his heels made tramlines in the snow.

Arlo heard the metallic twang of a catch being sprung, then rollers sliding. The men grunted as they threw him. Arlo tensed as he flew through the air. With a bang, he landed hard; air slammed from his chest. Groaning, he rolled over. Rollers slid, a door clunked shut, and it went pitch black. Someone laughed as the vehicle revved and lurched away.

29

THURSDAY, 19 SEPTEMBER 2052

After the call, Carl's head was in a spin. He didn't know what to believe. He identified with Arlo's insecurities but couldn't even start to imagine how awful it must be to lose a daughter, especially in the manner he had. When Arlo had returned to Britain, Carl had researched post-traumatic stress disorder–in the hope he could help–but, like with Parkinson's, there wasn't an easy cure. Treatments were like sticking a plaster on a gaping wound that needed stitches. At least with Parkinson's, he could take L-Dopa, but nothing could erase Arlo's traumatic memories.

Had he finally cracked? Was he experiencing full-blown psychosis? Perhaps the stress of presenting at the university had been the final straw. Undoubtedly, he'd been hearing and seeing things when he'd hot-footed it off the stage. Alisha must have felt endangered to leave home like that. Ordinarily, he couldn't imagine Arlo hurting anybody–but now? Was it even wise to help him track his family down?

He was working from home today and had a pile of coding to do, but the stress of recent events was playing havoc with his meds, and his 'on-time' was all out of kilter. For hours he sat frozen, his mind a paralysed fog. By evening, he gave in and upped his meds, finally dragging his body out of suspended animation.

He ate a ready meal and thought things through. Betraying Alisha wasn't an option, and their marriage was none of his business. He reasoned Arlo would probably track her down anyway using a process of elimination. But the nursing home tragedy was a different story–he owed him. He needed to establish the boundary between truth and fantasy–easier said than done when it all sounded ludicrous. Perhaps the alleged murder of his mum was a good starting point?

Based on his previous experience, any snooping he did on the Dark Web was risky. But, his DBS attack had raised an existential question. He'd lost his body to Parkinson's–was he also prepared to lose his mind? Could he forgo free will and truth? And–above all else–abandon his mates? What else was there left in life if he lost those things? *What use was he to anyone?* Last week he'd crossed that line. But there *was* a way back–to have a purpose and set the record straight, to make a last stand. Regardless of the consequences, he had to act. He gritted his teeth and fired up the quantum computer.

Logically, the first place to start was to determine how someone had managed to attack him. He could protect himself once he knew that.

Truly anonymous surfing meant out-smarting anyone monitoring him. The big mystery was how they had breached his security, given how bomb-proof his computer and BioTor browser were. And why had investigating CEP triggered such a hostile response?

Carl always approached a computer crisis the same way–starting with a tidy and sanity check. He deleted redundant files, looked for extraneous events in the administrative log and checked which programs were running. In theory, it was a waste of time because he knew his system inside out, but–from bitter experience–he also knew that assumption was the mother of all fuck ups.

An hour later, after an audit of his computer with the diligence and paranoia of a meticulous engineer, he'd found absolutely nothing wrong. So, what the hell had happened?

A potential workaround was to take his DBS offline to make it inaccessible to an attacker. After all, the DBS only needed to be networked for firmware updates; and so medics could monitor him remotely. Neither of those things mattered right now.

He disconnected his DBS and leaned back in his chair, fists clenched. Almost immediately, his body began to shake violently. Sweat ran down his face; panic consumed him. It took all his strength and willpower to navigate his BioFace menus to reconnect. Exhausted, he sat hunched over, trembling.

After several minutes, he'd recuperated enough to think through what had just happened. Maybe the DBS had to be networked to receive commands from his BioFace? Perhaps it had been engineered to only work if a network connection was present? But surely that wasn't ethical?

Being out of control again had felt horrible, but at least he'd eliminated his DBS as a possible solution. His mind returned to working out his vulnerability.

The BioTor's security weakness could only be at the source or destination, as the rest of the connection was a chain of anonymous encrypted hops. The destination was the forum where he'd learnt about CEP. User postings were transient and had nothing to do with the site. Hence, by deduction, the most likely node to have been compromised was the source–*his machine*.

In a flash of inspiration, he realised a computer script might be the answer. It was risky, as it would expose him to another attack, but he had to do something. The script would automate the steps involved in nefarious web activity, watching to see if any trojan broke cover. Sniping the sniper. It would then log the details of any suspicious program before shutting it down so it couldn't hurt him.

He coded the script in a few minutes–all it did was launch the BioTor browser and hop to several militant sites. He cringed as he launched the script, staring at its diagnostics window. Several minutes later, the console was still black. It was as if the monitoring algorithm knew when it was being out-smarted. Perhaps it had an outer AI shell that judged transgressions and recognised genuine browsing?

He quickly realised that the only surefire solution was to modify the script to emulate, *precisely*, what had happened on the day of his attack. Surely that would provoke the same response as before? His only concern was that his code might be too slow to stop a reprisal.

He opened the old script in a text editor and made the necessary changes to the batch commands. He saved the file, sat back, and closed his eyes. Finally, the L-Dopa was working well, coursing through his veins like a solvent dissolving glue in his limbs. He almost felt normal, or at least as normal as he could remember. Opening his eyes, he took a deep breath and double-clicked on his script's icon. He held his arm out in front of his face, scrutinising his little finger, praying it wouldn't tremble.

As if by magic, the script opened and closed windows, populated text fields, and visited the same Dark Web sites. It posed the question about Arlo's mum. He tensed up, waiting for the hit.

Suddenly, he felt a weird sensation. His body tingled, and the ends of his fingers trembled. *Shit, I've failed.* Carl closed his eyes, gritted his teeth, and waited for the onslaught. But nothing happened. He opened his eyes. The BioTor browser had shut down. A text window popped up.

He cringed, expecting to see a message: an ultimatum, a death threat or an epitaph. But no vile bilge, just a line of text giving a program's name, creation date and time. *Bazinga!* He had only just gone and done it! He had only just teased the moray eel from its lair. Out-smarted the ass-hole who thought he could control him.

The trojan had the same name as the device driver for his trackball–that was why he'd seen nothing wrong! He checked the size of the driver against one from the manufacturer's website. His was 1kB larger–extra code for extra functionality. *How the hell had it got there?*

He discarded the trackball and searched a cardboard box of junk computer paraphernalia he'd found too nostalgic to throw away. At the bottom was an ancient wireless mouse. Seconds later, he found the matching wireless dongle and plugged it in. He flicked a switch and nodded when an LED flashed. If he worked fast, the batteries only needed to last a minute or two.

He moved the offending file into a quarantine directory, locked away safe and sound for later analysis by forensic software. Maybe then he would be able to work out where it had originated. He downloaded the correct trackball file from a trustworthy source, repaired the installation, and put the mouse and dongle back in the box. Pleased with himself, he put his arm out–his hand was rock steady. He sighed, a weak smile melting his waxen face.

Carl cast his mind back to what the man on the forum had said just before his attack: *Compulsory Euthanasia Programme. It's part of PATMOS. You need to warn your buddy.*

But what was PATMOS? He recalled Arlo saying that John from the conference had BioFaced him and searched his workplace. Also, Lana had said John was high-up in government. Was he anything to do with PATMOS? Perhaps he should focus on him?

He opened his desk drawer and pulled out Lucy's business card. It was plain white, with just her name, a nebulous job title of business coordinator, and her BioFace address. He thought it strange there wasn't a company name. Still, her BioFace address was all he needed.

Carl closed his eyes and tried to recall their encounter with John at the conference. He remembered Lana talking to Lucy about something. Hacking was all about compromising someone, knowing something personal and lowering their guard. Her love of running–that might work.

His mind raced through the options of how to entrap Lucy. His best bet was to code a waterhole–a bogus website only she'd visit–and infect her BioFace with malware. He could tempt her to the site by dangling a juicy carrot about running. By spoofing Lana's BioFace address, it would look like his message had come from her. There wouldn't be an actual website, just a page that displayed an error message as soon as she clicked on it. She wouldn't be suspicious–there were broken sites all over the net.

The site would immediately infect Lucy's BioFace with a Remote Access Trojan, malware known affectionately in the trade as a RAT. A computer virus behaving like a real virus–how cool was that! The hope was that the RAT would subsequently infect one of John's devices, automatically deleting itself from Lucy's BioFace to cover its tracks. Carl would then be in the driving seat and could remotely take control of John's machine.

Carl knocked up a bogus homepage in a matter of minutes as it was just a tweak of a standard template. The hardest bit was thinking of a BioMail that Lana might send Lucy–he'd always struggled to get inside a woman's mind. After a few attempts, he thought he had it cracked:

Hi Lucy, hope you're good. It was nice seeing you at the conference. I hope your running is going well. If you're interested, take a look at my BioFace homepage–it has some pictures and race results. I know I'm a bit rubbish, but it's a start, LOL. Anyway, good luck in your next race. Best wishes, Lana X.

Carl wasn't sure about the kiss, but maybe that was a good sign, so he kept it. He chuckled to himself as he clicked on send.

30

A rlo thought he might vomit as he was thrown about in the dark. Suddenly, the van lurched steeply downhill. He grabbed something he was sitting on to steady himself, choking back bile as his head spun. Brakes slammed on, throwing him forward against the bulkhead, deadening his leg. He cursed. The engine spluttered off; a handbrake rasped on. Catches sprung, and the door slid open.

Arlo squinted against the blue-white glare of halogen lights as the silhouettes of two men leaned in. He looked down and saw he was clutching a stained overcoat. *Homeless man?*

'*You*,' a man's gruff voice bawled. '*OUT*.'

Arlo staggered to his feet, banging his head on the metal ceiling. 'Shit,' he muttered, rubbing it to dull the throbbing pain as he clambered out. Yellow markings on the tarmac suggested they were in an underground parking lot. Looking up, he saw the two men were still wearing their balaclavas.

'You going to be a good boy now? Or is it cuffs?' the taller man mocked.

'Good boy,' Arlo answered submissively, realising he had to pick his fights carefully from now on. The shorter man beckoned for Arlo to follow him. They filed through some doors into a cramped and dented lift. The door shut, locking in the pungent smell of stale sweat and last night's excesses. Arlo held his breath. The tin tomb whirred for a few seconds, passed two floors and then shuddered to a stop. The door jolted open.

'Second room on the right,' the tall man growled.

Arlo shuffled out, exhaling the stench from his nostrils,

inhaling deeply. The corridor smelled of mould and air freshener. A cheap-looking blue nylon carpet complemented gouged and stained white walls. On autopilot, he shuffled forwards, conscious of the men breathing down his neck. He saw a rubber floor wedge propping open a door.

The room was bare apart from a metal-framed desk, dented and scratched but indestructible looking, like ones found in prisons. A black box with a faceplate of buttons sat ominously on the desk; a large digital wall clock showed 10:27.

'Take a seat. Someone will come,' the tall man said as they turned and walked out.

Arlo sat down and scanned the room. There were no windows or decorations, just plain white walls, the desk, the chairs, and the wall clock reminding him of how long he'd been missing Alisha. His head slumped forward, retreating into himself, thinking of Alisha, remembering their good times.

He looked up; the clock showed 10:45. It was like being in a dentist's waiting room, not knowing how long he would have to wait or what would happen. When the door finally clicked open, he'd passed the point of caring.

A burly middle-aged policeman walked in, trailed by a pleasant but plain WPC, probably in her early forties, both wearing uniforms. His face looked like he was going to a funeral, hers to a wedding. *Good cop, bad cop?* They sat down opposite him.

'Arlo Jones?' the woman asked with a sweet smile.

'Yes,' he replied.

'I am WPC Harrington. And my colleague,' she said, gesturing with her hand, 'is DCI Gardner.' She continued quietly. 'I believe your mother has just died?'

Arlo looked deathly pale in the sterile cool-white spotlights as he gazed up at the wall clock, the minute number changing.

'Yes,' he said, struggling to get the word out.

'I'm very sorry,' she said.

'Really?'

'*Really*,' Harrington said with sickly sincerity.

Gardner watched Arlo's reaction and leaned forward. 'One thing, before we continue. Given your difficult circumstances, we've decided not to press charges. And this interview is not being recorded.' He tapped the black box. 'But, this may change, and I strongly advise that you cooperate given what we've heard.'

Arlo's eyes narrowed. '*What have you heard?*'

He wondered what trumped-up charge they were thinking of levelling at him. Maybe something to do with destroying Hayley? Or perhaps his assault on the manager?

Harrington looked to Gardner. He nodded.

'We've received a complaint,' she said.

'*Complaint?*'

'Yes. A complaint.'

'*Who's complained?*'

'Your wife.'

Arlo glared at Harrington. '*What has she said?*'

Harrington held his gaze. 'Is Joshua your son?'

'Yes. *Why?*'

'She's told us you've repeatedly threatened him.'

'*Threatened him?*' Arlo felt the warmth in the back of his neck spread through his face.

'*About what?*' His eyes bored into Harrington's.

'That you'll beat him if he misbehaves.'

'*Who said that?*'

'Joshua.'

'But that's nonsense! I *love* Joshua. I would *never, ever*, hurt him.'

'Your wife also said you came home violent.'

'But–'

Harrington raised her hand. 'Let me finish.'

Arlo stopped talking, mouth agape.

'She said you came into the bedroom,' Harrington continued, 'carrying a knife covered in blood.'

Arlo gripped the sides of the table, knuckles as white as bone.

'Your son's blood.'

'*My son's?*'

'Have you anything to say?'

'I would *never* hurt my son!'

'Are you saying you didn't do it?'

'*I didn't do it!*'

'So how do you explain the blood? And why has your wife felt it necessary to tell us this?'

'I d-don't know … I don't know *anything* anymore.' Arlo pressed the sides of his head, hands shaking uncontrollably.

The room fell silent. A few seconds later, Arlo dropped his hands, realising he had to be more careful.

'How is he?' Arlo asked once he'd calmed down.

'He has defence injuries.'

'Defence injuries?'

'Cuts to his hands. Inflicted by defending himself.'

'I didn't attack him,' Arlo muttered.

'The physical evidence and testimonials say otherwise.'

Arlo shook his head. The room fell silent. The minute number on the clock changed twice. He suspected it was part of their training. Waiting for him to fill the awkward silence. Waiting for him to gush.

'So what happens next?' Arlo asked casually, demonstrating he'd regained control.

Harrington leaned back, and Gardner straightened up. It looked rehearsed.

'Your wife,' Gardner said, 'is collecting items from your house. She needs time and space to reflect. We need to see if she wants to press charges.'

'And me?'

'We will keep you here overnight and see what she says in the morning.'

'OK,' Arlo conceded. He knew he couldn't win the battle, but he *was* going to win the war.

Gardner studied Arlo's face. Impassively, Arlo looked straight ahead. 'Interview terminated.' Gardner announced, standing suddenly. The chair scraped back, reverberating like a cello's bow. Harrington peered at her boss with puppy dog eyes. 'Are we done?'

'For now,' Gardner nodded slowly. 'Until she presses charges.' He shook his head and marched straight out of the room, avoiding eye contact with everyone.

Moments later, two burly men, looking in their mid-thirties, entered wearing standard police garb. One was significantly taller than the other. Arlo guessed they were the stooges who'd dragged him in from the nursing home.

'Time to go, chuckles.' The tall man gestured for him to leave. Arlo stood.

'Back to the lift,' the short man instructed.

'You again?' Arlo remarked. 'Nice haircut, lose the moustache.'

The short man snarled; the tall man said, 'Leave it.'

Arlo retraced his steps to the open lift, and the two men followed him inside. The short man pressed a button, and the door closed. Arlo felt the lift jolt and his stomach sink. One floor later, it stopped; the door slid open.

'Down the corridor to the end,' the short man said.

Arlo scanned the passageway. The floor and walls were whitewashed concrete. Every few feet, he passed fortified doors on both sides of the corridor. Each cell had a sliding shutter, all of them closed.

As Arlo approached the end, he spied a bucket on the floor, a mop propped against the wall. His head began to pound; he checked over his shoulder. The short man pushed past and unlocked the door using a key hung off his belt. The lock made a medieval clang, and the door swung open. A bed took up most of one wall; a shit-splattered toilet crammed the corner. There was barely enough room to move. The tall man put the heel of his hand between Arlo's shoulder blades and shoved him into the cell. As the door slammed shut, the key rattling in the lock, Arlo felt the ground shake and heard fireballs whoosh overhead.

31

Carl smiled to himself. Within an hour of sending Lucy the link, she'd taken the bait, the RAT infecting her BioFace. It had tickled him when it had returned the BioFace message 'Squeak.'

But the plan hinged on whether it had infected John's personal area network. There was a reasonable chance Lucy might have sent him documents or messages, but maybe the RAT had been trapped by cyber screening? It was a gamble, but human error often compromised security.

He powered up his rack of processing boxes, the master operating system loading in the blink of an eye.

'BioKali Linux terminal,' he requested.

Up popped a blank window with a flashing cursor. Despite its minimalistic appearance, this Unix-based terminal supported a treasure trove of tools for hacking. Some were third-party open-source utilities shared between fellow hackers on the net; others were scripts he'd coded himself in BioC and BioPython.

He fired up the RAT Trap Tool. A menu of options appeared for accessing a compromised machine. His BioFace said it was 11:57 pm, and he'd programmed the RAT to call home at 11:59 pm. It would only be active for a fraction of a second to minimise the risk of detection. If the RAT had successfully infected one of John's devices, he would receive a message with his IP address in less than two minutes. Without this information, the RAT Trap Tool would have no way of connecting, and he would have fallen at the first hurdle.

Carl wriggled uncomfortably in his chair, shirt sticking to his back, and exhaled a cloud of condensation across the room. Despite the DBS, his hands were trembling. He loved and loathed hacking. He knew it straddled a moral line and stressed him out, but it was addictive and gave him a massive buzz. The only thing better was playing in a band. But now, this was all he had.

He checked the messaging channel for the IP address–still nothing. Sweat trickled down his forehead and dripped onto the trackball. *Come on, RAT. Squeak!* He focused on the hum of the cooling fans, trying to relax, but his eyes kept returning to the flashing prompt of the messaging channel.

It must be 11:59. He checked his BioFace: 11:58 pm glowed orange. *Not stuffed yet.* He strummed his fingers on the desk, tried to play some imaginary chords and fluffed them all.

What's that? Out of the corner of his eye, a blur of digits ran across the screen.

'Goal!' he shouted, punching the air with a spastic wave.

Write them down; the computer might crash. Frantically, he scribbled spidery, barely legible, characters onto a scrap of paper. Next, he copied them into the RAT Trap Tool using a keyboard as it didn't have a voice input option. Over and over, he mistyped. *Have I been hit?*

He cursed, fighting the temptation to throw the keyboard across the room. *For fuck's sake, slow down.* One-by-one he carefully entered the numbers and dots. He reached the end of the IP address and paused, his finger hovering over the large enter key. *Focus.* When he felt his shakes weaken, his finger lunged for the key and hit it dead centre.

With no fanfare or splash screen, a directory structure appeared. *Shit, I'm in! And it's his main computer. Jackpot!* John's workspace was unlocked in front of him as if sitting at his desk. Carl felt like a kid in a sweetshop as he scanned the folders and files. He swallowed hard, hand frozen on the trackball. *No turning back.* He felt as if he was snooping around someone's house, rifling through their underwear drawer, reading their diary and looking at their photos. He paused. *Come on. He could be a murderer.*

He opened several documents. One was on health and safety, another on change management, and a third on quality. *Pseudo management shit.* The cover pages showed John worked for the Porton Down division of MSL, the Government's Military Science Laboratory. He scanned his BioMails and looked at the signature footer of one he'd sent. His full name was John Channing, and his job title was Chief Scientific Officer. Carl returned to the workspace.

The directory listing was a window into John's mind. Newbie coders and computer users kept a haphazard flat workspace structure with everything dumped together, giving little thought to naming conventions. Carl's flat might be messy, but his computer was a paragon of order. As he navigated, he saw John was his equal–everything was immaculate. Directories partitioned every aspect of his work, and all names were logical, self-explanatory and succinct. *Who is this guy?*

Ironically though, Carl knew a tidy computer was anathema to computer security. John must feel untouchable. But, if John could find something on his machine, then so could he. He wiped his brow and focused on the screen–he needed to find the evidence quickly and get the hell out.

He homed in on a directory where subfolder icons had a G-clamp symbol–encrypted files. The contents were hidden, but– if there was anything worth stealing–it was these. Also, the directory was only 3.2GB in size. *Act in haste, repent at leisure ... Damn it!* Using his trackball, he dragged a cursor over the files, highlighting them, and pulled them over to his desktop. Within a second, the transfer was complete. *Done–no turning back.*

He checked the names and sizes of the copied subfolders against their source–everything matched. He rescanned John's workspace to see if anything else was worth stealing, grabbed a couple of folders with reports and backed-up BioMail messages, and closed the connection.

He spun in his chair, arms flailing, hands clawing the air. 'I've done the right thing,' he muttered. He paced the room, hunched and boney back lurching from side to side, eyes darting as if seeking redemption. Not knowing where to put himself, he sat back down, wrung his hands and pulled his knees up to his chest.

Too late now. He tried to sit up straight. 'Dirac Quantum Crack,' he commanded. A window appeared on the desktop with a picture of Paul Dirac, the publicly unknown genius of relativistic quantum mechanics. Dirac was Carl's hero because he'd predicted the existence of antimatter using pure mathematics.

Carl dragged one of the encrypted folders onto the tool's icon using the trackball. The icon flicked erratically across the screen as he fought to align it. He stopped rolling the ball and released the button. But his hand shook, the file disappearing back to the desktop. *Shit!* 'More haste less speed,' he muttered. He tried again, concentrating so hard his head began to pound. This time he judged the release to perfection. He leaned back, took a deep breath, and closed his eyes.

A minute or two later, he'd recovered. *Come on, sort it.* He leaned forward and clicked on a large red button labelled 'crack.' Within an instant, a counter was already in the trillions.

Even a quantum computing algorithm couldn't defeat the staggeringly strong 256-bit encryption key–there were more potential solutions than atoms in the Milky Way. Quantum Crack only stood a chance by assuming the password had some underlying structure and wasn't just a string of random characters. It tried every word from the world's dictionaries, including combinations with all known symbols, special characters and numerals. If it wasn't entirely random, it would find it.

He stood and tried to straighten up. His headache had spread behind his eyes; his throat and lips felt parched.

Stooped, he lumbered into the kitchen and poured himself a glass of orange juice. He would have preferred a hot drink, but he couldn't risk a power outage with Quantum Crack running. The liquid felt good, although he struggled to swallow, and some ran down his chin.

The dim hall light cast his tortured shadow against the wall as he lurched back to the computer den. His headache was becoming unbearable. Changing his mind, he lumbered into the bedroom. Watching Quantum Crack like some lost puppy wouldn't make it run any faster.

The bedroom smelled musty; the springs felt hard through the mattress cover. He gazed at the photos he'd put out for Samantha's benefit. A time when his life had meant something before his health had failed.

He leaned back, and his mind began to drift. He saw his parents, joy on their faces when he'd ridden his tiny BMX bike without stabilisers for the first time. His music teacher was helping him play Für Elise on the piano, her slender fingers, with beautiful lilac-painted nails, placed over his. He was playing a cascading keyboard solo at his first gig, grinning from ear to ear with the audience held spellbound, bodies gyrating as one as a lead guitar and pumping bass joined into a crescendo. He felt himself starting to doze.

Beep! Carl startled. *It's cracked it!* He checked his BioFace– two hours had elapsed. He tried to run into his computer den and forgot his limbs weren't listening. At the end of the hall, he stumbled and went flying, diving into the room, knocking over a tray of cups and spilling dregs over the carpet. Ignoring the mess, he crawled on all fours to the chair by the computer and looked up. A passcode was flashing: Ahura-Mazda+Angra-Mainyu. *What the hell?* He scribbled it down. The encrypted folder was unlocked, its contents laid bare. Three reports sat waiting on his desktop, all filenames beginning with PATMOS.

Carl opened the first document: 'Overview of PATMOS: Programme of Android Technology, Menticide and Omnipresent Surveillance.' He scanned the contents page and then flicked through the sections. Getting the gist, he returned to the executive summary and read it through carefully. From what he could gather, it detailed an existential threat to the UK government. The volcanic winter, runaway national debt, and the collapse of an already fragile and mismanaged economy meant the government could no longer provide for its people. The nation's infrastructure was in ruins, and the country didn't have sufficient energy, food, medical provisions, or elderly healthcare.

He clawed at his hair, his suspicions confirmed. There weren't any real surprises–he saw the problem every day on the streets. But–despite the corruption–he'd always assumed the government was in control.

He opened the second document, 'PATMOS and the POX Commands,' and read the summary. It proposed a solution to the problem–population reduction by euthanasia and culling of undesirables. A shiver ran down his spine. *Culling? England isn't Nazi Germany!* The document discussed PATMOS Operational X commands, abbreviated to POX, with the BioFace used in 'active' mode for paralysing the nervous system and stopping respiration. *The homeless man ...* But a trial had shown that not everyone was susceptible. They were looking for other solutions.

He frantically opened the third document, 'PATMOS: Phase I,' scared of what he might find. One section detailed the use of android helpers to alleviate the elderly healthcare crisis. Another discussed VEP, the Voluntary Euthanasia Programme, for reducing the burden, giving possible scenarios on how the public might react. The penultimate section explained how CEP would be used if VEP was poorly subscribed, supported by something called CEBA. His brow furrowed, and he scrolled back to the glossary. He scanned down the alphabetical list and found the entry. His eyes read along the line: 'CEBA–Compulsory Euthanasia By Android.' *Arlo's mother ...*

Skipping past the conclusions, he came to an innocuous single-page appendix. Carl's eyes darted as he read the title.

'Omnipresent Surveillance Programme.' The text referred to two classes of militant: Suspected and Confirmed. A database file was referenced. Carl checked the decrypted directory from John's machine and found the file. He opened a utility for querying databases and typed Aaron, the deceased Black activist, into the search box. Marcus Aaron's face appeared; his class said 'Confirmed', his status 'Solved'. Carl entered 'Arlo Jones' into the search box, and his face also appeared. His class said 'Suspected'. The page listed Arlo's particulars: an asset to the government, militant tendencies, a vulnerable family position and a mother nominated for CEBA. That was it–he'd found the smoking gun.

Carl felt exhausted–his L-Dopa had nearly worn off. There was no way he could continue. It took a Herculean effort to reach his bedroom, lurching down the hall, bouncing off the walls. He collapsed onto the bed and closed his eyes, knowing sleep was the only fix. The room spun, and the lights blurred. His mind began to meander like a dandelion seed floating on a summer breeze.

Carl coughed, stifling an urge to vomit as choking sulphurous fumes filled his nostrils, burning the back of his throat. The view from the ridge made his head spin, the path falling away precipitously into a fissure. Far below, magma glowed a deep cherry red.

Where am I?

He peered down at his body, massaging his temples with his fingers. He was wearing a baggy white shirt, and loose-fitting flannel bottoms held up with a tie cord. His feet were bare, scattered with a gritty black soil that looked like the volcanic sand he'd seen as a youth on Lanzarote in the Canary Islands.

He straightened up and scanned the landscape, searching for answers. It looked like another world, but how did he get here? Surely he wouldn't be able to breathe the air of an alien planet?

A blood-red mist pooled in the valley, concealing most of the landscape. But from the ridges and peaks, the terrain appeared barren and rugged, devoid of all life. The sky was pink and reminded him of the skyscapes he'd seen transmitted from rovers on Mars. There wasn't any birdsong, just a gentle whooshing breeze.

Is this Mars? How can I breathe? Have I been abducted by Arlo's alien? Have I died? Is this purgatory? Hell? Carl wracked his brain, recounting the evil things he'd done: taking drugs in his band, free love with the groupies and hacking. But he hadn't hurt anyone–at least nobody who hadn't deserved it. *Surely, I'm not that bad? There are far worse people? Where are Hitler, Stalin, Pol Pot and Mao? Does everyone have their own private hell?*

He shuffled along the ridge, not knowing why or where he was going, pleading with his inner god that he would see something that would explain everything. Maybe it was like *The Truman Show*, *Westworld* or *Free City*, and none of it was real? Was he a contestant on a reality TV show? Was he being set up? Yes, that was it! If he kept walking, he would probably stumble across the edge of the film set or the fence of the theme park. The ridge seemed to stretch to the far horizon. *Some film set ...*

And then he heard chanting. At least he thought he did. Maybe it was the wind or a bout of tinnitus he sometimes had. Was he turning schizophrenic? He'd paid good money for acid trips but would pay even more to make this one go away.

He looked about, searching for the source of the noise. But, nothing. The sound faded out. *Stop being paranoid!* He trudged on again, trying to do something because if he stopped and thought about it long enough, he would probably have a panic attack. It wasn't the first time he'd felt like this. More times than he cared to remember, he hadn't known the solution to a problem or what to do. He'd just had to get stuck in, like when he'd turned over an exam paper and, from the questions, it looked like he'd been studying a different course. Or like when he'd tried to fix his car, but it had been a jumble of pipes, wires and unfathomable boxes. The answer was usually to relax and bluff it out–cheating reality to avert panic. Usually, the mist cleared, and, afterwards, he would wonder what the fuss had been all about. But this was stretching it …

And then the chanting started again, sounds rising and falling on the wind. Louder, more distinct. Ominous. No words, just guttural bestial sounds, but synchronised and coordinated. *Intelligent sounds–just not human.* Swivelling his head left and right, he tried to pinpoint their source. They seemed to be coming from a small valley below the ridge. The breeze kept blowing the chants away, and they sounded clearest whenever there was a lull. But everything in the valley was obscured by the blood-red mist that crept up the hillside. He studied the valley as the chants grew steadily louder. It was as if the mist was alive.

The chants were so loud now it seemed impossible he couldn't see their cause. Then, finally, he saw them. Two rows of dark figures emerged from the swirling tide of blood. They walked in step, like pallbearers at a funeral, their paths converging on him. The chants were clear now but still incomprehensible. They sounded pagan, prehistoric and ritualistic.

Only a stone's throw away, the figures in the first row began to lumber up the sides of the ridge towards him, cloaked in animal skins, their heads worn as hats: black panther, grizzly bear, wolf, bull and hyena. The second row carried a wooden-framed contraption fitted with ropes and pulleys. Towering above their heads, it looked like a four-poster bed. *But why the ropes?*

Carl could nearly smell them now. He backed away but began to slip. He glanced over his shoulder and grimaced, loose stones careening into the chasm. The figures were only a few paces away now. They hadn't slowed–they looked like they were going to walk straight through him. He strained to see their faces. But, and all he saw were shadows.

Just when he thought they would crash into him, they stopped. Wolf lifted its head. Carl tried to see its eyes, but all he saw were black puddles.

'You are a bad man, Carl,' a voice bellowed.

Carl's eyes narrowed. He shook his head. 'Who's that,' he barked. He couldn't work out who was speaking–it was as if the sound was coming from *inside* his head.

'You are a thief,' it said.

'*You* are the sinner!' Carl shouted defiantly.

'You shouldn't have stolen those documents, Carl,' the voice replied. 'They were not yours to take. Punishment time!'

A high-pitched whistle pierced his brain, growing louder and louder until it hurt. Carl pressed his fingers to his temples.

'You cannot stop it, Carl. You cannot undo your sins.'

Wolf and Bull stepped aside. Two heavily-muscled figures from the second row stepped forward. One was Black, naked, apart from a white hangman's hood and a brown leather skirt with a web of studded straps. The other was white, lightly oiled and similarly attired.

They lunged forward and grabbed Carl's shoulders. Carl's arms flailed wildly, trying to shake them off, but his Parkinson's stopped him from coordinating. The figures laughed. Manic belly laughs, like the Joker in Batman. Derisory and humiliating. They brushed his hands away and held his arms in a vice-like grip.

'Get your bloody hands off me,' Carl cursed.

They ignored him and dragged him kicking through the front row of beasts towards the wooden contraption. The other two back-row figures grabbed him by the shins and ankles. He kicked out, but, effortlessly, they restrained him. Moments later, he felt himself go airborne, sharp pains in his ankles and wrists as leather straps cut off his blood flow.

'*AAAAH!*' he screamed. 'Stop hurting me. Who *are* you?' He heard a noise to his left and swivelled his head. Wolf's face was inches away.

'We're under orders, Carl,' the creature hissed, spraying his face with fetid spittle. 'Payback time.'

Ropes creaked, cogs clacked, and wood groaned. His arms and legs were pulled apart like Da Vinci's Vitruvian man. *Shiiit,*

I'm on a rack. The tension eased. More creaking and clacking. Again his arms and legs were pulled taut, but strangely he felt no pain. It was like a car with the clutch slipping–they couldn't seem to get any traction. He strained his head, trying to see what they were doing. They huddled together, muttering incoherently.

'*See*, you're all fucking losers,' Carl mocked. 'A bunch of clowns. It's you who should be here, not me! *Go on*, finish the job. See if I care. My body's broken anyway. You can't even torture a cripple!' He threw back his head and laughed hysterically, his vision blurring as tears streamed down his face.

He blinked several times. Everyone had vanished. Everything was grey and grainy. His eyes strained, and the vague outline of objects appeared. *Chest of drawers?*

'Lights on,' he commanded.

The room lit up. He squinted and covered his face with his hands, waiting for his eyes to acclimatise. He lowered his hands. The digital wall clock said 3:17 am. Falteringly, he sat up and wiped away tears. The bedsheets were so wet he could have wrung them out. He lay back exhausted and stared at the ceiling, his mind returning to the documents and the surveillance database. Fear gripped him when he wondered whether *he* was on their list.

32

THURSDAY, 19 SEPTEMBER 2052

Face flushed, Lucy jogged up the stairs of her mum's house in Salisbury, dazzling blue eyes checking she was all alone. She crept into her bedroom, secured the door with a rubber wedge, and scanned the room. Small scented candles floated in decorative saucers–they smelled delightful and made her feel sexy. She asked the room lights to dim and requested mood music.

Making herself comfortable on the bed, she loosened her pleated bottle-green mini skirt and unbuttoned the top two buttons of her cream blouse. She pouted her lips and scrunched her wavy blonde hair as she peered into the mirror hung off the back of the door.

Damn, I look good.

She closed her eyes and inhaled deeply. Her body was already buzzing. She navigated to the HappyAppy icon on her BioFace menu using eye movements. It was one of a new breed of underground jailbroken apps the grinders were all raving about. Its biocoders had unlocked the BioFace enabling it to stimulate the body and not just monitor it. Two of her friends were already addicts–held ransom by BioFace malware–but she'd taken precautions and installed a scanner.

As the app launched, her BioFace made a jingle, 'Get happy … with HappyAppy.' The app hit Lucy with a BioShock, and she felt a warm wave pulse through her body. She navigated the app's menu, selected the augmented vision option, and logged into the HappyAppy Cloud9 server using her username Purrfect. Dave Sinclair was top of her list of contacts.

She'd been introduced to cyber Dave by John Channing. Dave had been tutoring her in metaverse biology lessons for her Expert-Level retake. She hadn't seen the point in retaking a subject she hated–after all, that was why she'd chosen a business studies degree in the first place. However, her mum insisted that she fix the only black mark on her resume in her year out as it demonstrated good character to potential employers.

Initially, she'd begrudged the idea but could scarcely refuse as her mum had paid for the expensive BioFace expansion pack. Lucy had argued it was vital for her education. But, the real reason for wanting the firmware upgrade was to jailbreak the BioFace, so it could run all the next-generation apps that stimulated the body. Lucy and her friends wanted it for more important things: dance raves, natural highs, massage, relieving menstrual pain, and fantasy sex.

Dave was 26 and her prince charming. Tall and rough cut, with an athletic build to match. He had a surfer's bronze tan, wavy blond hair and a kind face. His intelligent green eyes sparkled like emeralds, and he always wore a cheeky smile. Unfortunately, he had an irritating habit of constantly scratching the back of his neck, but nobody was perfect.

He'd taught her biology for four lessons, and she'd begun to flirt with him. She recalled her last session. Halfway through his explanation of genetics, he must have sensed she was getting bored. He dropped a DNA model on the floor of the virtual classroom, and she suspected it wasn't accidental. She felt his eyes upon her when she bent over to pick it up. Handing it back, she commented that DNA was made for sharing. That seemed to get him all worked up. After the lesson, he casually suggested they should meet up in the MetaBar.

The following day, ice clinked as he swirled his Jack Daniels, and she sipped her vodka and coke. His virtual avatar cosied up to her, and she giggled. It all seemed so right. They seemed to have so much in common. After half an hour, he joked they should try the Verotica portal for some proper relaxation.

Verotica was the lucrative domain of Juice, a wholly-owned subsidiary of PsiSoft that hosted the cyberspace playground of role play, adventure and virtual social networking, the dominant sector of the metaverse. The thought of seeing Dave in Verotica had terrified her, and she'd refused. She knew it was hard-core. But one of her friends encouraged her to try, saying that was where she'd lost her virtual virginity and had maxed out her BioFace.

Dave pestered her for three days, trying to persuade her. Finally, he sent her an app membership to BioRhythms nightclub in Bristol. It was *the* place to be seen, and there was a coach from Salisbury every Friday night–a perfect way to kick-start the weekend. The gesture had clinched it for her. Surely it meant he loved her.

Lucy stopped daydreaming and selected Dave from her list of contacts. A phone icon flashed in the corner of her vision, showing that her BioFace was connecting. Almost immediately, his form materialised on the bed next to her. He was wearing a bathrobe, and his tousled hair looked recently washed. Her BioFace glowed green, and she could smell his cologne.

'Hey, Lucy,' he said in a gravelly voice. 'You look lovely.' He leaned over, and she felt him run his fingers through her hair.

'Hi, Dave.' Her voice trembled, and her spine tingled.

'Shh …' Dave put his hands on her shoulders and kissed her open-mouthed on the lips. His tongue flicked over hers, and warm waves lapped over her body.

'Mmm,' she moaned as her eyes rolled.

'Undo the buttons on your blouse,' he requested.

Lucy knew she was in full control, as the BioFace could only make her feel things and couldn't physically change anything. She was completely safe. Growing in confidence, she undid the rest of the buttons. She felt his warm hand walk up the inside of her blouse, gently caressing her contours as it went. It reached her bra and, slowly and skilfully, navigated its way inside. He kissed her repeatedly on the neck while cupping her breast, his fingers exploring her areola, brushing against her swollen nipple.

'Mmm,' she moaned.

'Remove your panties,' he urged as he scratched his nape.

Lucy lifted her bottom off the bed and tugged down her white cotton knickers. They tumbled to her ankles, and she kicked them away.

'Good girl,' he commanded. 'Now mount me.'

With a gasp, she knelt on the bed and straddled the avatar, her pulse racing as she slowly lowered herself onto him. The BioFace flashed gold, her body aroused, as he penetrated her. The glow slowly grew in brightness and began to pulse.

Dave's body developed a lustrous sheen as he moved rhythmically and sensually. Lucy synchronised her movements with his as they moved in opposition, her long fingernails raking virtual scratches down his back, encouraging him on, demanding more. His movements built to a crescendo, her feelings too strong to bear. Her BioFace pulsed faster and faster as her moaning grew louder and louder. Warmth flooded her body. She felt herself reaching a point of no return.

'Yes, yes, yes ...' she shouted in ecstasy.

'Shh, honey,' he commanded.

She buried her face into his chest, the sea of pixels dissolving into a pillow, stifling her shuddering climax. She rolled onto her back, smiling evilly, moaning.

Dave broke the silence. 'You were great, honey.'

'You understand me ... my needs. What makes me happy.'

'That's what I'm here for, honey. You tell me how I can please you, and I'll always try.'

'You're not like other men.'

'In what way?'

'My dad left my mum when I was only seven–he didn't give a shit about me.'

'That's dreadful, honey.'

'And then there's my boss.'

'What about him?'

'He's like Jekyll and Hyde–one minute he's lovely, the next he's a beast.'

Dave fell silent.

'You OK, Dave?' she asked.

'... it's probably nothing you've done,' he continued. 'Maybe he was just stressed?'

'See Dave,' she smiled, 'that's what I like about you ... You're *so* understanding. I feel loads better now you've told me that.'

Lucy heard footfalls on the landing. She kissed Dave on the lips and whispered her goodbyes. The avatar faded from view as Verotica disconnected. She lay back on the bed, mind racing. *Wow! That was fun. Dave's so interesting and hot too. Can't wait to do that again.*

Lucy heard a knock on the door. She pulled her skirt down, covering herself, and blew out the candles.

'You OK, Lucy?' her mum called. 'I heard noises.'

'I'm fine, thanks. I dropped a cup on my foot. I'm off to bed now.'

'Sleep well, love.'

'And you, mum.'

Lucy put on her nightie and climbed into bed, ready to dream about Dave.

ΔΔΔ

Professor Stanford lay naked in his rocking chair, hands clasped behind his head, greasy grey hair plastered to his skull. Sweat trickled down his face and puddled in the depression above his fat yellow belly. He inhaled noisily through his congested nostrils and closed his eyes, wanting to relive the experience. But–now he'd orgasmed–he felt ashamed and sad. His mind returned to St Benedict's College when he was nine.

ΔΔΔ

Brian Stanford tapped tentatively on the solid oak door and then brushed his mop of black hair from his eyes, exposing his soft white skin and feminine features. Peering over his shoulder, he scanned the corridor that ran the whole length of the prep school's west wing, sighing with relief when he saw nobody he knew. A line of portraits stretched into the distance–the college's governors all seemed to be looking down their noses at him.

'Come in,' came a muffled cry.

Stanford reached up to the brass door handle. The shiny knob felt smooth and cold; it creaked as it turned. He rechecked the corridor. Still nobody. The door swung slowly inwards, and he crept in.

The cavernous study was like the wing of an old library. Towering bookcases looked like they might topple, their shelves crammed with leather-bound books with names that meant nothing to him. He could smell their mustiness, mixed with a hint of leather polish and cigar smoke.

The Priest in Residence, Reverend Father Jerome Smith-Jackson, stood imposingly in the centre of the room, shrouded in a bat-like black gown. His head perched on a pristine white dog collar, greasy grey hair slicked back from his receding forehead.

'Ah … Stanford. What do I owe the pleasure?'

'You wanted to see me about my biology homework, sir.'

'Biology? Ah, yes.' The reverend nodded. 'I remember now … You say biology, but your attempt was, er … kidology. *Know what I mean, boy?*'

'Um, no, sir.'

'Are you *disagreeing* with me, boy?'

'Um, no, sir. I don't understand, sir.'

'It means you're kidding nobody with your scrawling mess of hogwash. You *do* understand, *don't you*, boy?'

'Yes, sir. But I did my best, sir.'

'Well, you've fallen short on this occasion, and you need to be shown the error of your ways.'

'Excuse me, sir? I don't understand, sir.'

'Sometimes, a short sharp shock is required. Something to *focus the mind*. Understand, boy?'

'Yes, sir.'

'Well, come over here then–where I can see you better.'

Stanford shuffled to the middle of a Tudor-style rug that covered the centre of the polished wooden floor. The reverend tugged angrily at a red curtain, pulling it across a leaded window behind his desk. He marched over to Stanford, head held high, chest puffed out.

'Turn around, boy and face the door. I don't want to see your face while I'm correcting you, *do I?'*

'No, sir,' Stanford mumbled.

'Speak up, boy?'

'Of course not, sir.'

'That's better.'

The reverend placed his cold reptilian hands on the boy's shoulders.

'Now undo your belt and unbutton those shorts for me. *Don't dilly dally.'*

'What do you mean, sir? I don't need the bathroom, sir.'

'Do as I say, boy–if you know what's good for you.'

Stanford's hands shook as they undid his belt and fumbled with the button.

'That's the spirit. We'll soon have you punished, and then you can get back to reading up on your biology.'

The reverend tugged Brian's trousers and pants down to his ankles.

'Now, bend over, boy. No messing about.'

Stanford began to sob. 'I d-d-don't want to, sir.'

'Do as I say, boy!'

Stanford bent over, crying. The reverend spanked him with his bare hand as tears streamed down Stanford's lightly freckled face.

ΔΔΔ

Professor Stanford stood up and hurled a plate of left-over food against the wall as he fought to blank out what had happened next.

33

'**H**i. You're through to the Chief Scientific Officer's office,' Lucy said, responding to the BioFace call without checking the caller's ID. 'How may I help?' She leaned back in an office chair, yawning as she examined her nails, feet resting on an up-turned litter bin, killer heels cast aside.

'Hi Lucy, there's a visitor for Dr Channing,' Ruth, the front desk receptionist, replied.

Lucy took her feet off the bin, wriggled them into her shoes, and adjusted her skirt. 'Ah, hi Ruth. What's their name, please?'

'Um ...' Ruth hesitated. 'He never gave a name.'

'I *need* a name,' Lucy insisted. 'John will be cross otherwise.'

The line went dead for a moment. 'No, I'm afraid he won't give one. He says, John's expecting him.'

'Some people ...' Lucy tutted. 'Hold the line, please.'

Lucy placed Ruth on hold and BioFaced John. 'Hi, John.'

'Good morning Lucy. How are you?'

'Fine, thanks.' She cleared her throat. 'There's a man here to see you.'

'Who?'

'Er, I don't know exactly,' Lucy replied nervously. 'He won't give his name.'

'Send him through,' Channing replied.

'So that's OK then?' Lucy said.

'Of course.' Channing sounded unusually casual.

'No problem.' Lucy shook her head.

Lucy switched to the other line. 'Ruth?'

'Yes.'

'John's OK with it. Please send him through.'

'Thanks, Lucy,' Ruth replied, sounding relieved.

A few seconds later, a knock came on the outside door.

'*Enter,*' Lucy called out.

The door opened, and a tall man, athletically built and of Middle Eastern appearance, strode in. His crew cut had grown out, and his olive skin made his perfect teeth glow white. He stared at Lucy with eyes so blue they looked like jewels.

'Er, hi,' Lucy said, spellbound.

'Good morning, madam,' he replied.

'Dr Channing will see you now if you'd like to go through the glass door behind me.'

The man tipped his head, walked past her, and opened the door without knocking. Lucy raised her eyebrows, cocked her head and peered over her shoulder. She noticed he'd left the door ajar. Staring through the glass, she watched as they hugged, John kissing him on both cheeks, beaming like a long-lost friend.

Channing offered the man a seat at a table between the door and his desk. Lucy twisted back around, activated her BioFace's audio enhancer, and pretended to work.

'How is the schedule,' the man asked. Lucy screwed up her face as the amplified audio whistled and hummed.

'All's going to plan,' Channing replied.

'Good, good, good ...' the man said in dulcet tones, drawing out the words as if using them to focus his mind.

'The world saw your miracle,' Channing said.

'The first of many.'

'Are you pleased?'

'I, erm, *we*, have much work to do,' the man said, ignoring the question.

'Indeed, yes,' Channing said. 'The next phase has already begun.'

'Ah, yes,' the man replied. 'Our lambs ...'

'Yes. Our lambs.'

The conversation stopped. Lucy glanced over her shoulder to find out why. Channing was walking towards her; she smiled nervously. He grinned, shut the door and returned to the table. Their lips moved silently, Channing's face animated with excitement.

Lucy's BioFace registered another call, and she noticed it was from Ruth again.

'Hi Ruth,' she said.

'There's someone else here to see Dr Channing. A Professor Stanford?'

Lucy remembered the name from somewhere. She messaged Channing to avoid disturbing him. Almost immediately, he replied. 'Please send him through.'

Lucy reconnected with Ruth. 'Hi, Ruth. Yes, that's fine.'

The door opened, and a grey man walked in. He shuffled across the room, hunched over, avoiding eye contact.

'Dr Channing is just through the door …' Lucy said, hesitantly, 'behind me.' There was something about him she didn't like. Something creepy. 'Please go on through.' She gave a fake smile.

The man shuffled past, his hip rubbing against her arm despite the ample room. She shivered. He paused at the glass door and knocked. He raised his hand to the back of his neck and scratched, triggering an avalanche of dandruff. Lucy stared horrified, recognising the habit, choking back an urge to vomit.

34

FRIDAY, 20 SEPTEMBER 2052

Carl felt weird. He wondered whether it was because of his disturbed sleep or the stress from last night's hacking. He launched the BioFace packet sniffer app he'd installed after his DBS attack and scrolled through the list of network traffic. Nothing seemed untoward. But something was causing his tremors.

He tried to dial out his shakes by changing the DBS BioFace settings. But, after twenty minutes of fruitless tinkering, he gave up and increased his meds. It was a last resort–a desperate fix that aggravated his dyskinesia–but it was better than shaking.

Half an hour later, his shakes had calmed, but he still felt weird. It wasn't the usual dull headache or brain fog but a sinking feeling he was being watched. Not a prying he could close the curtains on, but a suspicion someone was snooping *inside* his head. An itch he couldn't scratch. It was enough to make him want to scream. Maybe *he'd* been infected with a BioFace virus? Perhaps he was the one who'd been bio-hacked?

He remembered feeling like this in his rollercoaster music days when his dream had sometimes turned into a nightmare. He recalled the morning after playing Glastonbury festival when he'd ended up at an all-nighter in Pilton and overdone it on magic. But that was over a decade ago, and, these days, he rarely even drank. Surely he was over all that now?

He wanted to update Arlo on last night's revelations, but he needed a clear head for that call. Maybe a walk and some fresh air would help? Food was running low anyway, and he had to use up some ration points before they expired.

He threw on some warm clothes and left the house. Halfway across his front garden, he turned and retraced his steps. The front door rattled as he tugged it hard. He tried again–still secure. A fresh snowfall covered the path, and he checked all of the footprints were his, noticing a pristine gap between his last step and the garden gate. Finally satisfied, he shuffled into the road, closed the gate and secured the latch. He scanned the street. Council workers were slouched over shovels, far enough away to be inconspicuous but near enough to be watching.

Get on with your bloody jobs.

Immediately they started shovelling ice as if they'd read his mind. Carl's brow furrowed. He heard a low hum, like the sound of a high-voltage power line minus the crackling, and looked up. The sky looked like the inside of a lead coffin, relieved only by the speckles of falling snowflakes.

Although hidden behind clouds, Carl knew the drone was there, scrutinising his every move with its electro-optic sensors and synthetic aperture radar. He tugged up his collar and pulled his peaked cap lower to hide his face. Chin tucked, he picked his way down Saint Andrews Road, trying not to slip on the patches of sheet ice. The Montpelier food depot was only a fifteen-minute walk away. It had previously been an out-of-town shoe store, but the government had taken it over for food distribution because of its convenient position by the inland sea.

Snow was now falling in doilies, dead tree branches draped like dough, threatening to snap under the weight. Carl looked like a poorly animated snowman as he lurched down the road, a hint of a wry smile cracking over his stony face at the madness of it all.

He crossed the street and shuffled down a side road, his face dropping when he spied a long queue snaking to the depot. The ragtag residents looked like refugees fleeing a warzone. Joining its end, he pulled his grey woollen scarf over his nose and mouth, more to hide his face than for protection against the biting easterly wind that funnelled down the road. His chest heaved from the exertion of walking in the freezing air, and he began to cough.

A man standing in front spun around. Carl instantly recognised Tarone: an Afro Caribbean gentle giant and the bassist in a Reggae band called Jamaican Jammin. The life and soul of any party, he'd befriended him when they'd played pub gigs. Reggae wasn't Carl's thing, but he knew talent when he saw it.

A huge woollen hat, knitted in the colours of the Jamaican flag and embroidered with the words 'One Love', covered his mound of dreadlocks, making him look eight feet tall. Several miniature dreadlocks hung down from his straggly black beard like jungle vines. Carl was impressed by a chunky gold chain that hung around his neck–it was probably his whole life's savings.

'Is dat you, Carl?' Tarone said with a lilt of Patois, his eyes smiling while squinting against the ice crystals blown off the road.

Sheepishly, Carl pulled his scarf aside.

'Hey, Tarone!'

'Hi, Carl! How are you jammin' on dis fine morning?' He offered up a clenched fist.

Carl managed a half-arsed fist bump. 'I'm doing great, thanks,' he replied unconvincingly. 'How are you?'

'To be honest, dude,' Tarone replied, 'this weather no agree with me. It makes me bones ache an' me tan begins to fade.' He winked, grinning from ear to ear. Despite the cold, Carl noticed the Velcroed shoulder flaps in his jacket and shirt were open where he'd been accessing the touchscreen of his BioFace. It seemed he hadn't been able to afford the upgrade to smart contact lenses. Carl spied the screensaver through the transparent artificial skin: a view of an idyllic bay and, in the corner, the Jamaican flag fluttering idly in a virtual trade wind.

Carl noticed one of Tarone's teeth had broken off and was

brown and rotting. His brow creased in concern. 'What's up with your tooth?'

'Broke it 'cos me teeth chattering so much with da cold.' He winked.

'You should get it sorted.'

'That'll be OK, mon. Nobody will want to see an old dude like me.'

Carl shuffled his feet awkwardly. 'Love the screen saver,' he said, getting off the subject. 'Is that Montego Bay?'

'Sure is mon. Well, sure was ...'

Carl looked down after another faux pas. Tarone noticed his angst and clutched his shoulder. His hand looked the size of a dinner plate and gripped like a vice, but it felt comforting and safe.

'Don't you worry, mon. The great wave may have cut me homeland in two, an' taken Kingston, but me memories a tucked away safely in here.' Tarone tapped his woolly hat with a long leathery finger. 'Maybe one day me even take ma children back there when flying is for the normal folk, an' not just for the super-rich. The politicians an' the like.'

Carl found the colourful characters on the Gloucester Road straight-talking and entertaining. He knew from experience how hardship brought people together and made them open and honest. Today, of all days, he needed people like them. Tarone adjusted his woolly hat, dreadlocks writhing inside like Medusa's hair of serpents.

The queue disappeared quickly, and soon they were near the front. Carl suspected it was because there wasn't much food left. Heavyset security guards protected the entrance. Their shiny white bald heads and glossy-black bomber jackets made them look like plastic traffic bollards. Carl noticed batons swinging off their belts.

The guards inspected a bedraggled woman's documents. She looked worse for wear, probably from sleeping rough, a filthy scarf concealing half of her face. She began to argue when one of the guards handed back her crumpled and stained paperwork and shook his head. Carl watched, horrified as she pleaded. He wondered what was wrong with her BioFace and then suspected it had been broken by the cold. After last night's revelations, he thought that wasn't such a bad thing.

The doorman ignored the woman's protests and frogmarched her back into the street. Her legs buckled, and she collapsed to the floor, sobbing. She wrapped her arms tightly around his leg, screaming and shouting as he dragged her along the floor like a sledge. Embarrassed, he dispatched her with a violent kick as if she was a small yappy dog. He shrugged his shoulders, patted himself down, and retreated to the doorway.

Carl and Tarone reached the front of the queue. One of the two guards grunted for Tarone to step forward. Tarone patted Carl on the shoulder.

'You walk good, mon.'

'You too, Tarone–you're a good man.'

Tarone stepped toward the doorman. The guard offered up a black box to his BioFace. It beeped, and the man inspected its display. He looked puzzled and pulled Tarone aside. Half-hidden behind the entrance door, Carl could hear them muttering. Seconds later, they reappeared. Tarone glanced over at Carl and then, self-consciously, lowered his gaze.

What the fuck.

Tarone disappeared inside, and the man gestured with a curled finger for Carl to approach. Carl pulled his scarf down and loosened his coat. Steam rose as he stepped forwards. 'What was all that about?' he demanded.

The guard looked taken aback. Glaring, he straightened up and puffed out his chest. He was well over six feet tall and built like a tank. 'Eh? What's your problem?' He stared down at Carl.

'Why were you talking to Tarone about me?' Carl replied, refusing to be intimidated.

'I'm *so* sorry,' the guard replied sarcastically. 'And *who* the *fuck* do you think you are?'

Carl's shoulders began to shake.

'Do you *not* want any food?' the guard continued.

'Um, yes, please,' Carl said, looking down.

'Well, best not bite the hand that feeds you. Eh?'

Carl carried on looking down. 'Yes, sir.'

'That's better. OK, inside.' The guard gave a smug grin and stepped aside.

The warehouse was little more than a corrugated metal hanger. Charity workers stood by pallets along one wall, and makeshift offices partitioned the far end. Carl saw Tarone being attended to by a young woman at the last pallet station. She dropped two loaves in a large brown paper bag, reached up, and placed it on top of a piled stack of provisions he was already struggling to carry. *Who the hell does he know?*

Carl came to the first pallet station with bulk packs of cans: soup, beans, sweetcorn and tomatoes.

'BioFace?' a burly man, dressed in black overalls and a beanie hat, requested.

Carl offered up his shoulder. The man brought his black scanner to bear–it beeped twice. His face looked puzzled.

'You've run out of coupons, mate,' he said.

'*What?*'

'You've used them all up. You'll get a new quota on Monday–after the weekend.'

'But I have over a quarter left?'

'Not according to my scanner.'

'When did I cash them in then?'

He scrolled his display. 'You came here earlier this morning. At 9:05 am.'

'No, I didn't!'

'The scanner doesn't lie, mate.' He tapped the box.

'Why would I make two *separate* trips?'

'Alright, mate.' He raised his hand. 'Let me stop you there. I'm only doing my job. There's a huge queue behind you. Any issues, see the gaffer.' He pointed to the leftmost office at the far end.

Carl could see it was futile. Nodding, he stepped out of line and considered his options, mind racing, wondering whether it was anything to do with his recent hacking. He had to do something–his food stocks were out.

Heads turned as he lurched his way to the office. He knocked on the door, but nobody answered, so he tried the handle. It turned. Carl saw people watching, but sod them, he thought and entered.

An ancient computer monitor was propped on a desk opposite an office chair with torn and marked black cloth upholstery. Delivery notes scattered the desk. Carl checked over his shoulder, saw he was alone, and chanced a look.

They itemised several pallet deliveries. One was for bakery products, another for canned fruit. He noticed strange names near the bottom of the list: fish analogue, beef analogue and pork analogue. *Analogue?* Carl had heard about Franken-foods on the Dark Web, grown using genetically modified, or GM, microbes. Tofu and jackfruit were one thing–and were great for the planet–but eating GM bugs? He'd heard that a GM food trial had gone badly wrong–test subjects had developed chronic allergies and intolerances. From what he'd read, GM bacteria also tasted rank. But he'd eaten the fish and beef from here, and it had tasted fine. *BioFace? Taste bud spoofing?*

'*Ahem!*'

Carl startled. He spun around, lurching into the desk, knocking papers all over the floor.

'*What are you doing?*' a man demanded.

He was tall and thin, mid-to-late twenties, pasty-faced with ginger hair.

'You have cancelled my coupons,' Carl replied.

The man looked taken aback. 'But, *what* are you doing?'

'Sorry?'

'*You were going through our paperwork?*'

'My coupons have been rejected. One of your workers said you could help.'

'*But why were you snooping?*'

'You weren't here,' Carl countered. 'I was just looking to see if you have any record of my missing coupons.'

'*Snooping?*'

'I'm sorry if that's how it looks.'

'I can't see it any other way.'

'I said I'm sorry.' Carl looked down. His leg spasmed with dyskinesia. The man noticed and seemed to soften.

'Are you OK?' he asked.

'Parkinson's,' Carl muttered.

'I see ...' the man examined his hands. 'Let me scan your BioFace.'

He offered up a portable scanner; it beeped twice. He glanced at its display and frowned.

'What does it say?' Carl asked.

'Er, nothing,' he said, pressing a button to wipe the screen. 'I'll sort you out some food. Follow me.'

'Thanks,' Carl said, following him down a passageway at the rear of the office. They entered a loading bay from the dock. The man took a paper sack from a pallet, inserted two small loaves and handed it to Carl.

'I'm sorry, but I can't give you more.'

'It's OK,' Carl replied. 'I appreciate it.'

The man was about to walk away and then paused. 'Just some advice.'

'*Advice?*' Carl replied, sounding confused.

'Yes, just keep your head down.' The man patted him on the shoulder. 'Go out the back way.' He gestured with his arm. 'Go down there, on the right.' Carl was about to query what he'd said, but the man was already walking away.

Carl froze, thinking about the surveillance list. After a few seconds, he came to his senses and lurched down the back alley. At the front of the building, he spied Tarone walking past the queue, his stack of provisions balanced precariously across his arms. Tarone glanced his way, looked straight through him, and then continued walking. Carl shook his head and shuffled along the edge of the queue, the ragtag rabble whispering behind their hands. The walk of shame seemed to last an eternity. Finally, he passed its end and came to a dilapidated bus shelter. The woman barred from the food depot lay huddled inside, shivering under a dirty turquoise blanket.

Carl broke off half of one of his loaves, walked over, and dropped it into her lap. The woman flinched and looked up.

Carl was shocked. He realised she was Nicola, his neighbour's daughter who'd just finished high school. She looked him up and down.

'Is that you, Nicola?'

'How come you knows me? Are you one of theeem?' she slurred.

'I'm your neighbour. Or at least I was …' he replied. 'You remember? We used to chat about the music you like.'

She scratched her scabby head and frowned. 'I don't knows you, mister,' she said, pulling her legs in and hugging them tightly. 'You want sex?'

'No, Nicola. I don't want anything. I won't hurt you.'

She hid the bread under her legs and buried her face in the blanket. He tried to get her attention, but she ignored him.

Sighing, Carl turned and began to trudge up the hill. The raw wind blew straight through his trousers–he'd had kinder toothaches.

'The world's coming to an end,' came Nicola's wavering voice. 'Only the good Lord can save us now.'

That's us buggered then, Carl thought, continuing to shuffle up the hill.

Halfway home, he heard a low throbbing hum and peered at the purple-grey sky. It had stopped snowing; the cloud had thinned. A wasp-shaped silhouette hung static far above the city. *Is it tracking me?*

He walked past a lamp post and scrutinised the dome beneath the light, trying to see into the smoked plastic housing that obscured the camera. He could swear the mechanism was swivelling, following him. The Internet of Things in the street furniture was probably monitoring him as well–the ultrasonic and LIDAR sensors remaining from the frivolous driverless car project; radio sensors triangulating on his BioFace emissions, and the terahertz imagers that could even see through walls. *Nowhere to hide.*

Across the road, a council worker was shovelling grit onto the pavement. Carl pulled his scarf up around his face. The man stopped what he was doing. *Is he talking to an agent?*

At the top of the hill, he turned right into Berkeley Road, sighing with relief to be nearly home. *So much for clearing my head.* The road bent around St Andrew's Park, with his ground floor flat located on the junction with Melita Road.

A few minutes later, he came to the low wall that ran along the front of his rented property. Snow was piled chest-high like giant vanilla cheesecake. He peered over the top to see the flight of steps that ran down to his front door, hidden below street level. Footprints crossed the path and descended the steps, despite the recent snowfall. *Mine?* Carl rubbed his forehead, hands clammy, mouth dry.

The front gate was hanging half-open. *But I shut it?* He scanned the front garden and steps, checking if anyone was hiding. Nobody was there. Pausing mid-way across the snow-covered path, he peered at the tracks. The footprints were indistinct and smeared as if made by someone shuffling. *Mine? But my feet are smaller?* An occasional print was sharper as if someone had picked up their feet and taken a proper step. *Heavily studded sole. Combat boots?* He followed the footprints down the steps and stopped at his front door.

He half expected to see the lock smashed in, but everything appeared normal. *But the footprints?* He fumbled the key in the lock, and after a few attempts, it turned. He shouldered the door open. The hall was empty apart from a multicoloured flyer lying on the threadbare carpet. He sighed. *Postman ... But, combat boots?*

Still anxious, he marched down the hall into his computer den. His eyes followed a trail of computer paraphernalia strewn across the floor to the base of the rack of machines. Panic consumed him, eyes flying up to the computer boxes.

Carl's mouth fell open as he stared in horror at his worst nightmare. It looked like something heavy had been used—maybe a sledgehammer or a baseball bat. The side panels had been wrenched open, and the machines disembowelled. Optical fibres hung like spaghetti. Carl's eyes flicked left and right, his arms flailing. He knelt and cradled one of the machines in his arms. Tears tumbled onto one of the see-through side panels. He wiped them away, scared they might corrode the exposed circuits.

He lay there, moaning, like a mother who'd lost a child—inconsolable and broken. Half an hour passed before he stirred, and the numbness began to lift. He realised he couldn't give up. He had to fight this evil with every fibre of his failing body. Suddenly, he remembered his holographic storage server. The device that kept all of his work safe. The place where he'd encrypted and stored the hacked documents.

He stood, but his legs felt as dead as an arm that had been slept on. Finally, he won them over and lurched to a cupboard, high above a writing desk. It looked more suitable for storing blankets than a state-of-the-art backup system. Straining, he reached the handle and paused, scared of what he might find. He lifted the swing panel and spied a green light twinkling inside. He gave a long sigh. *Thank god.*

He navigated his BioFace to the wireless drive and brought up the file system in his vision. Using his eyes to move the cursor, he opened a directory called cameraBackup. The video recordings were from a council IP camera housed in a deactivated streetlight. It had been easy to hack using a 51% attack on its blockchain security encryption. He opened a file with today's date, and a video player appeared in his vision, paused on a snowy frame.

He scanned forwards in time until he saw a lumbering ghost-like figure. *God, is that me?* The timer said 11:53 am. *That's about right ...* Snow was falling fast, whiting out most of the street. Nothing changed in the scene for hundreds of frames, apart from the stroboscopic flickering of the blizzard.

At 12:13 pm, a dark figure walked into view. They were slightly built and carried a long, slender holdall, about the size of a guitar case. From the way they lurched, it looked heavy. Their boots looked way too large for them.

The person opened the gate. *I knew I'd shut it!* They turned and paused, scanning the street for several seconds, glancing up at the streetlamp, almost as if calling home, seeking reassurance.

Carl blinked on the pause option and selected zoom. The image was grainy from the blizzard and poor lighting. He opened a utility called 'Super-Resolution and Noise Suppression' from the menu that processed a group of frames to improve picture quality. He blinked on a button, and, within a split second, the person's features became visible. He studied their face and shook his head. 'No, no, no,' he moaned. It was Nurse Furber, his Samantha.

35

A giant of a man swaggered down the dingy backstreet, hugging the shadows, pulling up the collar of his donkey jacket against the bitingly cold wind. Snowflakes flickered pink in the red glow from the nightclub across the street. A golden holographic sign, BioRhythms, hung surreally in space above its entrance amid a tangle of mock branches.

The door swung open as if it had eyes when the giant approached. Two huge bouncers, looking like prettified cage fighters in their muscle-bound DJs, stepped out and fist-bumped him. They chatted, pink, steamy breath swirling.

Minutes later, a black land cruiser–all stately polished chrome and blacked-out windows–growled down the river of snow. The banter stopped, and the men froze as it churned its way towards them. It pulled in. A diminutive man, dressed from head to toe in black, climbed out from the passenger side, his face hidden by the peak of a baseball cap. He marched straight at them, pulling a small jiffy bag from his coat. Jaw set, eyes locked on the giant, he handed it over, clutching its end, eliciting a response. The giant gripped the package, nodded, and lowered his gaze. He pocketed it, still looking at his feet as if scared to lock eyes. By the time he looked up, the cruiser had gone, trundling down the road like the hearse in a funeral cortege.

∆∆∆

Carl stood hunched in the doorway of a derelict office building, sheltering from the falling snow, gazing up at the golden sign. He loved BioRhythms–a music venue for all humanity with its ethnically diverse clientele. It was in vogue for being one of the first clubs to use BioFace technology for a fully immersive musical experience.

He wore a khaki cap and black scarf chosen to remain incognito rather than for warmth. He'd BioFaced Arlo, desperate to meet. Arlo had rambled incoherently about having just left a police station, something about a misunderstanding with Alisha. He suggested they meet in a pub. Carl agreed that a public place was good but wanted somewhere loud to mask conversation. Reluctantly, Arlo had agreed on BioRhythms.

Carl scanned the road. He'd planned to stand here, fathoming it was a blind spot from cameras, but knowing it was impossible to be sure. *Come on, Arlo.* His eyes wandered as he checked his BioFace–11 pm exactly. Arlo appeared from a side street and jogged across the road, giving a thin smile as he approached.

'Hola,' Arlo said. 'Strange place to meet.'

'Strange place for strange times.' Carl's head bobbed, his leg spasmed.

Arlo noticed how bad Carl's dyskinesia was and patted his shoulder.

They marched towards BioRhythms's entrance; the door swung open. Two huge bouncers stepped out and looked them up and down. One was white, a gold tooth glinting as he sneered; the other Black, a scar puckering his cheek and bisecting an eyebrow.

The bouncers laughed as Carl approached.

'Groovers in town?' Gold Tooth mocked.

'BioFace cash?' Arlo tapped his shoulder.

'Sweet,' Scarface grunted. Arlo made the transaction with a beep.

'That's retro-night for you,' Gold Tooth said to Scarface.

'Attracts all sorts.'

Gold Tooth turned to Carl. 'Hands off the girls.' He winked at Scarface, and they both guffawed. Carl ignored the ridicule–he'd grown a thick skin over the years.

Hedonistic sounds of party-goers came and went as the club's door swung open to allow regulars to pass. The bouncers exchanged clique comments and made the odd street gesture. Carl recognised the music from MetaClassics, a metaverse retro music club he frequented. A throwback to a carefree time of plenty–a fantasy night to help clubbers remember and forget.

Scarface held the door open and beckoned for them to enter. Carl spied a menacing red glow emanating from a long flight of stairs. They seemed to descend into the bowels of the earth. He recalled standing on the ridge in his dream. A shiver ran down his spine as they filed through the entrance, and the door slammed shut.

They gave their coats to an attendant, and Arlo proceeded down the stairs, Carl struggling to keep up, arms flailing and legs jerking. Arlo reached the bottom and vanished into the crowd without checking over his shoulder. *Who's rattled his cage?* Carl bundled down the rest of the flight and slipped; a clubber stuck out an arm and caught him. Carl's face flushed, and he thanked the man with a weak smile.

Carl reached the bottom step and paused to compose himself, scanning the crowded room. Arlo was already at a raised bar that ran alongside the right-hand wall. *Desperate?* Carl fought his way through the crowd, and, by the time he'd got there, Arlo was ordering a refill.

'What you having?' Arlo asked.

Carl barely heard him above the thumping bass and shrieks of clubbers. Parkinson's had tamed Carl, and normally he didn't drink, but nothing was normal this week.

'Double malt, please.' Carl rubbed his head, eyes darting.

Arlo's brow furrowed. 'Sure?'

'*Sure*,' he replied, feeling unsure.

While Arlo was ordering, Carl spun around and digested the

scene. The cavernous club took him back to the years he'd felt alive. The basement resembled a dreamy park. Artificial grass carpeted the floor, trees grew from the ceiling, and a flagstone path meandered around a dance floor lit by flashing coloured tiles.

About half the clubbers were Afro-Caribbean, the rest a cosmopolitan mix. They were the people Carl loved–good honest folk who loved music, all out for a good time, and no bullshit. The revellers wore a dazzling mix of retro and modern clothes–anything and everything went. Everyone was smiling. It seemed to be somewhere people could escape their troubles– no one staring and nobody judging. Carl vowed to return.

Arlo nudged his arm. *'Oi! Dreamer!'* he shouted over the music, passing him a glass and picking up his own.

'Thanks, mate,' Carl said. 'Let's go somewhere private.'

Arlo led the way, following the path and climbing an ornate wrought iron bridge spanning the dance floor. The DJ faded in 'A Forest' by the eighties goth band 'The Cure'. A heady bass and atmospheric beat contrasted against a sublimely chorused guitar and reverb-laden mix. Carl liked the pure sound of the seminal Korg synthesiser–the melancholic mood seemed appropriate right now.

They reached the middle of the bridge, and Arlo paused, leaning over the glossy black railings, looking down on the action. Lasers and strobe lights cut through a curtain of dry ice and smoke. Carl imagined himself sitting at a keyboard, playing to the crowd.

The revellers gyrated below, their Biofaces jailbroken by underground hackers. Their arms glowed pink through their clothes as they received networked radio signals, their bodies quivering in unison to the music. A seething mass, moving as one connected dance.

'Amazing,' Carl said.

'Addicted to the music,' Arlo replied. 'Literally.'

Carl nodded. He was painfully familiar with how unbridled euphoria often had a sinister stalker. The clubbers were probably addicted to the same BioFace app, held hostage by spiralling subscription costs.

The music changed to a frenetic dance track, 'Maniac'. Arlo pointed to a dancer perched high on a podium at the head of the dance floor. Beautiful and svelte, with long blonde hair, high cheekbones and full lips. Carl was shocked by her nudity. But then she moved and her pink skin-tight leotard, with interwoven screen, lit up brightly. A multicolour Mandelbrot set, synchronised to the music, spread over her body like a time-lapse film of a growing plant. The animation became a living forest, with russet, orange and gold autumnal leaves blowing in waves. A fawn pranced across her breasts, springing sprightly with juvenile excitement. A tiger jumped from some bushes and gave chase.

The mix built to a climax, and so did the clubbers, their BioFaces triggering the release of endorphins in a synchronised drug-free high. The track ended, and they came to their senses, wandering vacantly.

Arlo beckoned for Carl to follow, and they descended the steps on the far side of the bridge, ducking under an arch with a keystone engraved 'SNUG'. A beer garden bench sat vacant at the rear of the tomb-like alcove. Arlo helped Carl thread himself into one of the integrated seats and sat opposite.

'What's up?' Arlo asked.

Carl updated Arlo on his hacking: identification of John Channing; uncovering the national crisis with its sinister solution; and the surveillance list, with Arlo, identified as a suspect. Arlo asked him to repeat several things, but Carl was sure he'd heard just fine. Arlo's eyes burned with rage when Carl told him about CEBA; Carl struggled to contain his emotions when recounting what Samantha had done to his computer. Finally, he summarised the kick-off at the food depot. He thought it best not to mention his Martian dream.

Arlo gripped his shoulder. 'Thanks for proving I'm not a nutter.'

Carl wasn't sure he had. 'We're marked-men.' His eyes

darted.

'Until yesterday, I'd have said you were being paranoid,' Arlo replied.

'What happened yesterday?' Carl asked, face a mask of stone.

Arlo related the events at the nursing home, his police interview, and Alisha's accusations. Carl studied his face as he described it all, wondering what to believe. 'Are you still trying to find her?'

I think she's staying at Debbie's. She knows her from when we first moved to Bristol. I'm going over there first thing in the morning.'

'Is that wise?' Carl stared into Arlo's eyes. 'Are you sure there isn't a restraining order in place?'

Arlo looked at his hands and twisted his ring.

'*Don't*,' Carl said.

'I need another drink.' Arlo stood. 'You?'

'Go on then.' Carl forced a grin as Arlo marched out of the snug.

Carl stared into the remains of his malt, trying to think things through logically. The Clash's 'London Calling' began to play.

Someone tapped Carl's shoulder. Startled, he spun around. Tarone hovered above him. Carl swallowed hard, his body paralysed, even his eyes playing dead. The coward within him wanted to curl up and die, but he needed to know why Tarone had turned against him. A vein pulsed in Carl's head as he wondered what Tarone was doing in the club–he'd never been a fan.

'Yo Carl,' Tarone said cheerily. 'Way Gwaan?'

'I've been better,' Carl replied, recognising the Patois greeting from his days on the pub circuit.

'Breathe easy, mon.'

'Easy for you to say,' Carl muttered.

'Why's dat?'

'I thought you were a mate. We go way back.'

'What do you mean, mon?'

'The depot. The bouncers ...'

'Ah, you cry-cry. Them bad men. Me family needs food.'

Carl frowned. 'I know they played you. But it hurts.'

Tarone leaned forward and patted him on the shoulder. Carl recoiled, putting his hands up defensively.

'Yo! Easy, Tiga,' Tarone exclaimed. 'I'll make it up to you. What's your poison?'

'They cancelled my food and humiliated me,' Carl continued. 'I'm a cripple–think about that!'

'It's done, mon. Me can't change that, but me *can* buy you a drink.'

Tarone stopped smiling and looked concerned.

Carl rubbed his brow and softened. 'OK. But first, why you here?'

Tarone looked momentarily puzzled. Then his eyes sparkled, and his confusion seemed to clear. 'Me love da old muzik. Me spotted you on the bridge an' come a looking.'

Carl raised his eyebrows.

'Anyway, why *you* here, bro'?' Tarone continued. 'Me did think you would have moved on from dis scene too?'

Carl sighed, not knowing what to say. Tarone would think he'd lost his mind. 'I've got stuff going on. Felt I needed a break.'

'I see.'

No, you don't.

Tarone leaned forward and locked eyes. 'Drink?'

'Er, single malt,' Carl said hesitantly.

'A comin' up.' Tarone rose from his chair, looking so tall it seemed as if his hair would get tangled in the branches that hung down from the ceiling. He squeezed Carl's shoulder; he flinched.

'Stay cool, mon.' Tarone turned and disappeared into the crowd.

Is he after me? Should I go? Where the hell's Arlo?

He sat there, head spinning. It seemed like only seconds before someone tapped his shoulder again. He jumped and turned around. A drink was dangling in his face at the end of Tarone's heavily muscled arm.

'Cheers, mon,' Tarone said with a toothy grin.

Hand trembling, Carl took the glass. If it had been a pint, he would have spilt it.

Where's Arlo?

'Thanks, Tarone. Sorry, but I need the gents.'

'No worry, dude. When you back, we talk things through.'

'Agreed.' Carl grabbed the table to help him stand.

A couple of minutes later, he was sitting on the toilet in a cubicle, glass between his feet, head in his hands.

What the fuck's going on? What's Tarone want?

He took a deep breath and lifted his head, looking for divine inspiration on the cubicle walls. The plastic panels were plastered in graffiti: gay invitations, angry calls for civil war, pleas for help.

Carl hung his head. At a loss, he checked his BioFace to see if Arlo had tried to contact him. There were no messages or missed calls. *Probably getting pissed.* He gazed down at his drink, wondering whether he should give two fingers to the world and get drunk. A fly landed on the glass and tightrope-walked around its rim. It sank its proboscis into the tawny liquid.

'For fuck's sake,' he muttered.

He lifted his hand to swipe the fly away, but, at that moment, it toppled off the rim. It seemed to fall in slow motion; by the time it had hit the whiskey, it was already dead.

Carl recoiled, filled with anger and dread, fighting an overwhelming urge to drink the liquid. Shaking his head, he picked up the glass by its base and placed it on the cistern. As he opened the cubicle door, two Black men came in: one heavily muscled with tattoos, the other with a flat-top haircut and dangly diamond earrings. They bundled into one of the cubicles, laughing.

Carl lumbered over to one of the washbasins and poured the contents of the glass straight down the plughole, taking care not to splash himself. He'd heard of state-sponsored attacks using nerve agents and was taking no chances. He placed the glass in the sink, leaving the tap running, so it topped up what was draining away. In the adjacent sink, he washed his hands thoroughly with soapy water.

After staring at the ceiling for a minute or two, he turned off the tap and let the water drain away. Gripping a wad of paper towels, he picked the glass out without touching it, wrapped it tightly and threw it away.

Carl re-entered the club, eyes darting, knowing he had to escape. As he lumbered back to the foot of the main stairwell, he bumped into Arlo, coming the other way.

'Carl! I've been looking for you,' Arlo exclaimed. 'You OK?'

'Thank god,' Carl replied, stony-faced.

'What's wrong?'

'*He's trying to bloody kill me! He gave me a poisoned drink!*'

'Whoa! Slow down,' Arlo said, making hand calming gestures. '*Who* is?'

'Tarone.'

'Is that your friend who blanked you at the depot?'

'Yes. They've got to him.'

'Stop jumping to conclusions.'

'*We need to get the hell out.*' Carl's eyes darted. *We're on their list!*'

'Calm down.'

'Easy for you to say.' Carl's leg spasmed. '*It's me he's trying to kill!*'

'Don't you see?' Arlo said.

'*See what?*'

'This is our chance.'

'*Eh?* Chance? *Chance to die?*'

'To get to the bottom of this.'

'*Have you gone mad?*'

Carl realised what he'd just said and looked down.

Arlo's face registered disappointment.

'You're OK, Carl,' he said, patting his shoulder. 'Trust me.

We have the element of surprise. If you're right, he'll expect you to keel over. *And* there are *two* of us.'

'But he's huge?'

'Listen. Go back and behave normally. If you're right, he'll have a handler. I'll scan the club and take a BioFace picture of anyone suspicious. Then I'll come over and confront him.'

'*But he's huge!*'

'But you guys go *way* back. You said he's a gentle giant. Slipping something into someone's drink is one thing; attacking them in cold blood is another.'

Carl's eyes seemed to calm. 'OK, OK ... let's hope you're right.'

Arlo handed him his own drink. 'Take this and get over there.'

Carl grabbed the glass, took a swig and shuffled off.

By the time he ducked under the snug's arch, he was breaking out in a sweat. He knew Arlo was right–he couldn't live in fear. Apart from hacking, all he had left was his freedom and friends. He needed answers. The truth. Closure.

Tarone had his back to him as he approached. Despite the loud music, he seemed to sense him coming and spun around. The stool he was sitting on looked like kids' furniture.

'How are you doing?' Tarone asked, looking at him curiously.

'Mighty fine, Tarone. Mighty fine.'

Tarone averted his gaze. 'So, dude, what did we talk about?'

'You were about to tell me why you dobbed me in at the depot. And why you didn't watch an old cripple's back.' Carl couldn't believe what he'd just said.

Tarone grimaced. It was the first time Carl had ever seen him riled.

'Mon, me no like your tone. Anyway, me 'ave no memory of that!'

'You went to the food depot on Sunday, right?'

'Yeah, mon.'

'You saw me in the queue, and we chatted?'

'That a right.'

'And then you spoke to the doorman–he asked you who I was, and you told him. Then they cancelled my coupons. I don't have any food, Tarone! You came out with a huge stash for your troubles. *And then you blanked me!*'

Tarone's brow creased.

'You remember all of that, *don't you?*' Carl persisted.

Tarone's eyes wandered as if struggling to recall.

'*Well?*'

Tarone's face suddenly hardened, eyes distracted. Carl twisted and looked over his shoulder. Arlo was approaching.

'Hi Carl,' Arlo said. 'Hope I'm not interrupting anything. Who's your friend?'

'This is my old mate Tarone.' Carl gestured. 'He was just about to explain something.'

In a blink of an eye, Tarone seemed to snap. The stool scraped back, and he rose like a grizzly bear. Arlo marched over undaunted.

Christ, Arlo.

They faced off like two boxers at a weigh-in, Tarone towering above him.

'Ah, big fella,' Tarone mocked. 'You think you're a match for Tarone, do you?'

Arlo grabbed handfuls of his multicoloured hoodie and snarled.

'You did ask for it.' Tarone raised a plate-sized fist and cocked it behind his head. Carl cringed, eyes darting.

As Tarone was about to throw the punch, his whole body danced as if tasered. His eyes rolled into the back of his head, mouth foaming and body shaking. He lunged into an adjacent table in a fury of wild arms and legs, knocking it over. A pint glass pin-wheeled through the air, spraying amber froth in arcs, landing on the cobbled floor with a hollow pop and an explosion of glass.

Arlo backed away from Tarone's twitching body as if fearing electrocution.

'What the hell!' Carl exclaimed. From the corner of his eye, he saw someone standing with their hands on their hips. He turned. She was beautiful, with a swan-like neck and honey-coloured hair. It was Lana from the conference. Silently she stood, eyes scanning.

'Lana!' Arlo exclaimed.

'Shh,' she replied, nose wrinkling.

Seconds later, Tarone's twitching subsided, and he slumped to the floor. Lana rushed over and checked he hadn't banged his head or swallowed his tongue.

'Remind me never to get on the wrong side of you,' Arlo exclaimed. Lana's eyes stopped scanning; she seemed to relax.

'Well, boys,' she said, 'that seems to have taken care of him.'

Tarone lay slumped like he was sleeping off a hangover.

'What the *hell* did you do?' Arlo demanded.

'All these clubbers have jailbroken BioFaces–all completely insecure. His BioFace address was obvious because it was the closest emitter I didn't recognise.'

'But the convulsions?' Arlo asked.

'The hacked BioFaces have unlocked ports,' Lana continued. 'That's how they get stimulated by the music.'

'I gathered that,' Carl said. '*So?*'

'In the developer's console, you can select how the write ports are driven.'

'Really?' Carl queried.

'Yes. I selected manual and then set them all to the maximum.'

'*Christ!*' Carl exclaimed. 'No wonder he freaked out.'

'Yeah, that's why I was frantically trying to turn it off–I didn't want another death on my hands.'

Another? Carl checked Arlo's reaction, but he seemed not to have heard over the loud music.

They gathered around Tarone. Drool and snot hung like ectoplasm from his nose and mouth. His body was trembling, eyes dazed, staring straight ahead.

'Thank god he's recovering.' Lana sighed. 'Sit him up.'

Arlo swept away most of the broken glass with his foot, crouched down, and dragged Tarone against the wall. His head and neck were no longer hanging limply, and he appeared to be coming round.

'Uh, where am me?' Tarone uttered.

'BioRhythms,' Lana answered. 'The club. Don't worry– you're safe now.'

'What am me doing here?' he asked. 'Where's me wife?'

'You came here on your own.' Lana held his hand.

'Me never come here now. No since me boy did born ...'

Carl wrapped a handkerchief around his hand and checked the pockets of Tarone's hoodie. He pulled out a grip lock bag. Inside was a small glass bottle.

'What's this, Tarone?'

'No know, mon. It's no mine.'

'He's lying,' Carl said.

'I don't think he is,' Lana said calmly. 'Tarone's BioFace has a backdoor–an app was running in the background. I had to shut it down before I launched my attack. BioFace menticide ...'

'Menticide?' Carl queried.

'BioFace brainwashing,' Lana replied. 'The literal translation is: "murder of the mind."'

'*What!*' Arlo exclaimed.

'Carl mon,' Tarone uttered. 'What 'ave me done?'

Lana looked to Carl. 'Are you OK sitting with Tarone while he's recovering?'

Carl nodded. 'That's fine. I'll fill him in on a few things.'

'Thanks,' Lana said, glancing at Arlo. 'Follow me. I have some explaining to do.'

ΔΔΔ

As Lana and Arlo meandered towards the bar, the song 'Will You?' began to play. A ballad by Hazel O'Connor from the film 'Breaking Glass'–a story about the future, set in the past.

'I love this song,' Lana exclaimed, reaching out to Arlo.

Arlo felt relieved now Carl was safe, the drink relaxing him. Unable to resist, he took her hand and led her to the dance floor. They bumped into a white male coming the other way, dressed in denim, hair in a crew cut.

'*Steady on, mate,*' Arlo said.

The man carried on pushing through the crowd, almost knocking people over.

'Ass-hole,' Arlo muttered.

'What's up?' Lana asked.

'Nothing,' Arlo replied as they reached the dance floor.

The saxophone's melody rose and fell. Lana pressed up against him. They moved as one with the music as he inhaled her sweet perfume. He caressed her soft honey-coloured hair and stroked her swan-like neck.

The saxophone soared and the vocals built to a climax–an invitation, yet a goodbye.

Arlo felt dizzy as they twirled.

Lana whispered into his ear. 'I'm *so* sorry about your mum.'

Her words struck him like a lightning bolt; he recoiled, their rhythm faltering.

'*How do you know?*' Arlo exclaimed.

'We were watching.'

'*We?*'

Arlo stopped dancing and pulled her to the edge of the dance floor.

'Channing and me,' Lana said, flustered. 'The other night– when I was working late.'

'*And you just watched?*'

'I didn't realise. I couldn't stop it ...' Her voice trailed off.

'*Why did that thing kill her?*'

'PATMOS.'

'*PATMOS?*' Arlo barked, remembering Carl had mentioned the word.

'The government can't cope. They're culling the population.'

'*But why you?*'

'I didn't realise. They said they wanted me for my skills.'

'*What skills?*'

'Digital psychology. To help people erase their mental scars. Coping with trauma and grief. PTSD ... That's why I chose you.'

'*Chose me!*'

'For a trial.'

'*What trial?*'

'BioFace therapy.' She pulled him close. 'I'm sorry, Arlo. I was trying to help you *and* do my job.'

'What *have* you done?'

'Dream displacement.'

'*What?*'

'Therapy to displace your nightmares.'

Something caught Arlo's eye. A flicker in his vision, a subliminal feeling something was wrong. Terribly wrong. He gazed over Lana's shoulder.

What the fuck. A tiny red light was flashing under a table. A bag? A bomb?

Nooo...

Arlo felt his stomach lurch. An incandescent orange-white flash, as bright as when Mount Rainier exploded, bleached out the dancers. An instant later, his face was slammed, like being hit by a door. He felt weightless, disorientated, deafened. Blackness descended.

Torch beams striped left and right, diagonal white lines against a solid black background. Acrid smoke drifted across his vision; he began to choke. He was back in the office in Seattle, hearing a high-pitched whistle, but this time mixed with near-silent screams. A need to vomit. A warm tickling sensation on his face. Blackness.

A feeling of being lifted. Crying, wailing and screaming. Chaotic echoing voices: 'You're safe now.' 'Fetch her hand–by the wall.' 'Heeeellllllppp me ...' 'Pleeeeeassse make it STOP!'

Arlo pleaded. 'Lana ... *Where's Lana?*'

'Stay calm, sir. Don't try and sit up.' 'Lie back.'

'*LANA!*'

The music stuttered on and then died.
Then blackness.

36

The saxophone soared as Arlo inhaled Lana's intoxicating perfume. His head spun as he squeezed her close, their cheeks touching, her skin soft and sensual. She kissed him on the lips as, blissful, they waltzed, round and round.

In a blinding flash, time froze. He waited for the bang, but no explosion came, sounds draining away as if someone was turning the volume down.

BioRhythms's gaudy flashing lights dissolved. Lana's beautiful face glowed radiantly, honey-coloured hair tumbling, backlit by a brilliant white light.

'Arlo,' she whispered.

Are you OK? Arlo thought.

'I'm good,' she said.

But the bomb?

'I thought they might,' she said.

They?

'The three.'

The three?

'Yes. The evil three.'

But why?

'I betrayed them.'

How come?

'Tarone. Your mum. You …'

I don't follow.

'Listen,' she urged. 'I need your help.'

To do what?

'To save my daughter.'

What! You have a daughter?

'Mia.'

Is she in danger?

'Stanford wants her.'

Why?

'Please save her, Arlo. *Save her ...*'

'*Lana, please, I DON'T UNDERSTAND.*'

'Promise me, Arlo.'

I promise.

'I love you, Arlo.'

I love you, Lana.

'I have two final dreams for you.'

But why?

'To purge your nightmares.'

The light dimmed. Lana's face disappeared as everything turned aquamarine.

He was diving, following an anchor chain in crystal clear water, exhaling a stream of silver bubbles. Out over a coral reef, between whips and fans, clownfish peeping out from forests of cream anemone tentacles that waved in a tropical current. Up and over a towering bommie patrolled by grey reef sharks, a rush of vertigo as he crested a crumbling drop-off, the sea a deep navy blue as it fell into the abyss.

The water turned claret as if infused with blood. Arlo stared spellbound into the growth cell of Ark 1307, a transparent gelatinous mass quivering as an electric field hummed. Kefa lay cocooned at its centre, like a queen bee in royal jelly. The hum grew louder–he began to twitch.

The growth cell churned and boiled; Kefa trembled and shook. Instrumentation in the ship went haywire–all readings slammed to the maximum. In a violent lurch, Kefa broke the surface. Slime sloshed over the sides of the tank, surging up the length of the craft like a tidal bore. He sat upright, face an embryonic mask of cheesy slime. Lifting his arms free of the gunge, he scooped mucus from his eyes and hurled them back into the tank with gloopy plops. Falteringly, his eyelids stretched open against the elasticated stickiness.

He climbed out of the tank, legs buckling from the ship's artificial gravity. The floor was slick with slime, making him slip about like a newbie skater, lunging for the grab rails on the walls. Arlo could read his thoughts. *How long has the ship been dormant? Have the priests replied? Did a signal wake the Ark?*

Kefa cleaned the craft, vacuuming the scum off the floor and recycling the fluids in the growth tank. Order restored, he washed and dressed in a golden flight suit and sat at the bridge. A scanner read his DNA; the flight computer booted, welcoming him with Gemid clicks. He raced to check the system clock, his mouth falling open when he saw the date. 2,019 Earth years had passed, not three hundred. Questions raced through his mind. *Why haven't the priests replied? Haven't they received my message? Why has the ship regrown me? Has it malfunctioned? Have micro meteors penetrated the shield?*

Frantically, he opened the log file and scrolled back 2,019 years, searching for events he recognised. He saw his notes on Elah's barbaric crucifixion as he'd witnessed him suffering through the spacecraft's super-resolution imager. The ship's electromagnetic sensors had detected his death throes as a series of small Faradic pulses, followed by a larger peak when he'd taken his final breath. A data file–Elah's cerebral upload–had been received shortly after.

Next, he saw he'd piped a text file to the high-gain antenna–his pleas to the Gemid Council requesting a second chance–followed by a warning that Ark 1307 was conserving power. *Recharging?* He scrolled forwards in time and spotted another large pulse–Elah's rebirth on the ship. Then an entry showing he'd programmed the Ark to move to the Lagrangian point, the manoeuvre delayed by a month. The following day, another series of faint pulses, terrestrial in origin, followed by a slightly larger pulse–the timestamp consistent with his own suicide in the olive grove shortly after cremating Elah's crucified body. Two weeks later, another weak death signature and a cerebral upload–Elah's suicide and ascension.

Then nothing. Just a periodic housekeeping status check from the Lagrangian, once every orbit around the sun. Frantically, he scrolled forwards, looking for the next significant event. A cluster of entries scrolled into view. The first was a signal received from Turnbull: a long data transmission. But it wasn't a message from the priests. Kefa checked the data header. His face turned to horror when he saw it was the planet's doomsday beacon, broadcasting the divine DNA and default consciousness boot loader to the whole Space Swarm fleet. *Had Turnbull been destroyed? A colossal solar flare? The Big One?* He paced the ship, trying to compose himself, knowing that the survival of the Gemid species could depend on him.

He calmed down and returned to the computer. The next signal was a regrowth command for an engineer, probably triggered by a timeout after reception of the beacon–his recent birth. Shortly after, a regrowth command for a royal subject from the divine genome. Elah had won the challenge. *He must be here!*

Overjoyed, Kefa raced over to the second tank and pressed a button. The membrane cover slowly retracted, and he peered into the liquid, ripples from the vibration dying away, revealing a face. Male. Rugged. Through the claret haze, he saw facial muscles twitch as if an invisible thread was being tugged. Kefa scrutinised his features. Something wasn't right.

The jelly shook violently as the hum became a buzz. The Gemid's eyes snapped open–sapphires set in an alabaster face. Kefa recoiled and fell against the other tank. It wasn't Elah–it was Baraq.

Immediately Arlo saw Baraq's face, he knew he was dreaming. He forced his eyes wide open. Brilliant white lights blinded him. An aroma of antiseptic catapulted him back to when he was awaiting news of his mother's fall in a Bristol hospital.

'Lana, Mia, Elah, Baraq ...' Arlo mumbled deliriously.

A woman, dressed in pale blue, charged over, her face anxious. Arlo clutched the sides of the bed.

'It's Baraq, not Elah,' he gasped.

'You're alright, my luvver?' the nurse calmed in Bristolian. 'You've had a nasty bang on the head.'

'W-Who are you?' Arlo stammered.

'Nurse Simmonds,' she replied. 'But you can call me Fern.'

Arlo tried to smile, but his body spasmed, and he only managed a grimace.

Fern squeezed his arm. 'Steady on, Luv.'

The pain ebbed away, and he lay back, inhaling deeply, chest twinging as if a barbed wire was snagging deep within his lungs.

'You're OK, my luvver. Just relax.' She stroked his brow. 'We've kept you in for observation. You have a mild concussion, smoke inhalation, and a few cuts and bruises. But you'll live.'

Arlo managed a weak smile and flicked hair from his eyes. 'Where am I?'

'Bristol Royal Infirmary.'

'What about the others?'

'The others?'

'Yes. My friends.'

'Um, I don't knows about them.'

'Are others here?' he persisted.

'Just those from the club.'

'Can I see?' Arlo raised himself to look. Wires snagged; an alarm began to beep.

'Whoa, steady on, my babber,' she exclaimed. 'You need to rest.'

'I need to know. *Please.*'

Fern checked her BioFace and glanced both ways down the aisle. 'If you're good, I'll wheel you down the ward, and you can check. Deal?'

'Deal,' Arlo replied.

Fern nodded and walked around the bed, tidying away stray

cables and tucking in sheets. She released a foot brake and wheeled Arlo out of the bay.

Arlo wriggled up to see better. Fern trundled him slowly down the aisle. He scrutinised every face, straining to see their features despite the patchwork quilts of dressings and bandages. At the penultimate bed in the row, he asked Fern to stop. A woman with honey-coloured hair faced away, placing a capped drinking mug on a bedside trolley. Arlo felt his pulse quicken; his hands clutched the bed's cold metal frame. The woman turned and stared. Her face was lined and wrinkled, her eyes sunken in charcoal caves. Arlo's face dropped. He nodded in embarrassment.

Fern continued to trundle. At the end of the row, she wheeled the bed in an arc and started down the opposite side. Arlo gazed, hope fading as they passed the battered and bruised faces. A young woman lay hidden under sheets, three patients from the end. Fern carried on trundling, passing two young clubbers, both male, both strangers.

'All done?' Fern asked, anxiously glancing both ways down the aisle.

'Go back,' Arlo urged. 'The girl … Three from the end.'

Arlo caught Fern rolling her eyes as she backed the trolley up. The girl heard the commotion and pulled back the covers, trying to see what was happening. Fern called out, telling her not to move. Her arm was in a sling, a large surgical pad taped to her midriff. The girl turned to face Arlo, a diamond nose stud sparkling in the ward's laser lights. He instantly recognised her. It was Lucy from the conference. She beckoned for him to come closer, but his bed was too wide for the gap. Fern tutted. He glanced up, eyes pleading. Fern stared at the ceiling.

'Please,' Arlo said. 'I'll be no more trouble.'

Fern checked her BioFace and the aisle. 'OK, *but be quick.*'

Arlo nodded vigorously and gripped her hand.

'You old charmer.' She smiled. The beds squealed as she manoeuvred them together.

'I'll leave you two troublemakers to chinwag.' She checked the aisle. 'Just a few minutes, mind.'

'Thanks so much.' Arlo nodded.

Fern turned and walked away.

Arlo smiled at the young lady. 'It's Lucy, isn't it?'

She nodded.

'Are you OK?'

She looked down at the dressing taped across her abdomen. 'Um, a piece of glass sliced me open,' she said.

'But you're OK?'

'Won't be wearing a bikini anytime soon ...'

'Well, the weather's not great,' Arlo added dryly.

Lucy choked back a half-laugh, half-sob. A tear ran down her cheek and dripped onto her dressing, mixing pink with oozed blood. She smoothed her hospital gown and gave a forced smile. 'I'm sorry about your lady friend,' she said.

Arlo's face dropped. '*What?*'

'The woman you were dancing with,' Lucy qualified.

'*What happened?*'

'I tried to help her.'

'And?'

'She was bad. *Real bad.* And then the medics came.'

'How bad?'

'They couldn't save her.' Lucy moved uncomfortably. 'They tried CPR, but it was hopeless.' Her eyes glazed over as if she was back in the club, viewing the carnage.

Arlo looked down, silent, broken.

'I'm sorry,' she said forlornly. 'You're Arlo, aren't you?'

Arlo tried to smile. 'Did you see a hunched man? Grey and middle-aged? Or maybe a huge Black guy?'

'Your friends?'

Arlo nodded.

'No. I'm sorry,' she replied.

Arlo looked down.

Lucy picked at her nose stud. 'I think they killed her.'

'*They?*'

'The Three.'

Arlo remembered Lana mentioning 'The Three' in his dream.

'*The Three?*' he asked.

Lucy hesitated as if she didn't know whether to say.

'*Please ...*' Arlo persisted.

'I think they're in it together.'

'*In what?*'

'Some government programme.'

'*Do you know who they are?*'

Lucy nodded slowly. 'Well, two of them anyway. One is my boss at MSL.'

Arlo leaned forward in his bed, wincing as he twisted. 'John Channing?'

Lucy nodded, chewing her lip.

'And the other?'

'Some professor guy. A right creep.'

'Stanford?'

'Yep, that's him. He, er, assault ...' Lucy's words trailed off.

'What did he do, Lucy?'

'He assaulted me. Well, sort of.'

'Sort of?'

'In the metaverse.'

Arlo thought it was best left. 'I'm so sorry, Lucy.'

'At least it was virtual,' she muttered, wiping her eyes.

'Any idea who the third man is?'

'No–he just appeared for a meeting.'

'Name?'

'He didn't give one.'

'What does he look like?'

'Maybe Middle Eastern. Olive skin, short hair. Oh, and piercing blue eyes.'

Arlo rubbed his chin. 'Surely not,' he muttered. 'Why do you think they killed her?'

'Because of what she knows,' Lucy replied.

'But *what* does she know?'

Lucy checked the aisle. Fern was chatting to another patient, lips moving silently.

'PATMOS,' she said.

'I see.'

'You know?' Lucy frowned.

'I found out because of my mum.'

'It was your mum Lana saw?'

Arlo nodded.

Lucy leaned over and squeezed his arm.

'Something else is going on too,' she said. 'Something worse.'

'What?' he said, wondering how anything could be worse.

'I don't know for sure. Something to do with the military build-up.'

'In the Middle East?'

'Ye-'

'Time!' A shrill voice came from Arlo's left.

Fern appeared at the foot of the bed; Arlo felt himself begin to move. He twisted around.

'Thanks, Lucy,' he said. 'I have your card.'

'Don't use that,' she urged. 'I'll BioFace you my details in a minute.'

'Great,' Arlo said.

'Oh, and Arlo.'

'What?'

'When I tried to help Lana.'

'Yes.'

'The last thing she said ...'

'What was it, Lucy?' Arlo stared desperately at her.

'Save Mia.' Lucy's face hardened. 'You need to save Mia. *Before they get to her.'*

'I plan to,' Arlo muttered. 'Just as soon as I get my family back.'

37

Alisha strolled alongside Debbie Schultz from Bath Abbey's paved square to the river Avon. They passed tearooms and gift shops, built in Georgian times from the famous local limestone, but Alisha barely noticed their splendour. Debbie updated Alisha on how well her daughter Francesca was doing in metaverse classes, and Alisha felt relieved to be discussing normal things again after the recent madness. Joshua trailed behind, embarrassing them by practising virtual swordsmanship, arm slashing like he had a neurological disorder.

The women stopped and peered over a low wall at Pulteney bridge. The iconic view of the horseshoe-shaped weir had long gone, relegated to BioWiki pictures and augmented reality tours. Fortunately, the exquisite Palladian-style shops over the bridge had survived the floods. Translucent ice encased the arches over the river, reaching halfway up the shop windows.

Alisha gazed at the bridge, eyes defocussing as they strayed to the snow-dusted frozen river. Her mind wandered, reflecting on recent events: the pillow that had slammed down on Veronica's startled face; Arlo diving out of the house into a blizzard, eyes wild with rage. She was back on the kitchen floor, sobbing, mind racing, scared for Arlo but even more scared for herself. Horrified of what he'd become, terrified of what he might do.

Nothing could have prepared her for when he'd come home, walking like a zombie down the hall trailing bloody footprints. He ranted deliriously, eyes possessed, crazy things about seeing a laser inside Dave's skull, a dead body in every room, fleeing for his life. She'd known for a while he was on the edge– the drink, the pills, the fantasy talk of aliens–but she'd always assumed he would get through it all. He'd always conquered his demons in the past.

Terrified, she'd locked herself in the bathroom, and everything had gone quiet. Suddenly, all hell broke loose. Stomach knotting, she realised Joshua was still in his room. She cowered below the washbasin, pounded the floor and tugged at her hair. Only when the commotion had died down had she plucked up the courage to open the door. She would have to live with her cowardice for the rest of her life.

She'd found Arlo slumped on the bed, unconscious and bloody, wild-looking like the tramp on TV. Joshua was huddled inanimate on his bedroom floor, hands wet with blood, eyes in a trance as if playing Battle of the Augs. She knew immediately they had to leave. Mind in overdrive, she BioFaced Debbie, a friend who'd taken her under her wing when she'd first arrived in Bristol. A kindred spirit who'd befriended her at a Bible study group. That was why she loved the Christian community–there was always someone prepared to help.

Debbie rented a small ground-floor flat in Bath, near the frozen river that had claimed the land between the Lower and Upper Bristol Roads. Although she was a single parent, and times were hard, she immediately suggested they should stay. Her daughter, Francesca, was on a sleepover, and she said it was a perfect opportunity to catch up.

Joshua had snapped out of his stupor and, frantically, they packed, terrified Arlo might wake. In a whirlwind of snow, they caught the bus to Bath.

The horror story continued as they climbed on board and found a seat at the front. Teenagers, returning from a bender in Bristol, screamed and shouted abuse, throwing takeaway food. She'd wished Arlo had been there as chips bounced off their shoulders. A piece of lettuce garnish lodged in her hair, and she discreetly pulled it out, pretending to ignore them, trying to distract Joshua. The bus churned and lurched through the deep snow, the journey seeming to take an eternity. Finally, Alisha felt her stress lift when Bath's Georgian buildings loomed out of the blizzard.

Debbie welcomed them with open arms. Joshua was exhausted and went straight to bed, snuggling under the duvet of a makeshift put-you-up in Debbie's study. Alisha gushed about everything that had happened: the nursing home, Veronica's murder, and Arlo's rage. Debbie listened in stunned silence. Then Alisha recounted the other strange events: her dreams, Arlo's drinking and infidelity, and the Lazarus incident of a homeless man saved by a stranger, with a witness claiming he was Jesus. Alisha asked Debbie whether she'd heard the story. Debbie said she hadn't, but she also confessed to rarely watching the news anymore because it made her sad.

For the rest of the evening, they poured over a Bible and discussed Alisha's theory about the Second Coming. Some things matched: the famine, the natural disasters and an impending war. But one key prophecy didn't seem right–the nature of the return. Why hadn't Debbie heard? Debbie pointed out a passage from Revelation: 'Behold. He is coming with clouds, and every eye will see Him.'

'See,' Debbie said, *'everyone should know!'*

Even though Debbie didn't watch the news, surely she would have heard? Wouldn't her church friends have said something? Clutching at straws, Alisha suggested that maybe the Bible's true meaning had been lost, obscured by the passage of time.

They'd chilled out at Debbie's the next day and then went shopping. But Alisha's mind kept returning to Revelation. Seeking inspiration, they'd decided to go for a walk the following morning. They strolled past the magnificent Royal Crescent and through the city to Bath Abbey to light a candle for Veronica. The diocese was Church of England, whereas Alisha was Catholic, but she was happy just being closer to God.

No special service was on, and Alisha didn't see anything related to the Second Coming: no announcements on the pinboard, no special prayers whispered in the pews. It all seemed so very odd. But it was Saturday morning, and wedding service preparations were underway. Maybe everyone was just too busy? *But what could be more important?*

Debbie coughed, startling Alisha from her thoughts. The view of the bridge swam back into focus.

'I guess we should be heading home,' Debbie said.

Joshua tugged at Alisha's sleeve. 'Come on, mum,' he shrieked. 'I've got a battle to fight.'

'Sorry,' Alisha said. 'I was miles away ...'

Debbie squeezed her arm, and they strolled back along the swollen frozen river. Ten minutes later, the kettle was boiling.

'TV on,' Debbie commanded. 'I guess I should catch up on the news.' She laughed. 'Maybe we can get to the bottom of your Revelation mystery.'

As the screen lit up, her mouth fell open. Aerial drone footage panned. A pall of black smoke drifted over a residential area of flat-roofed buildings within a walled city, a column of tanks advancing. The view switched to a reporter in a virtual BBC studio.

'News is breaking that the Axis alliance has reached the outskirts of Jerusalem. Despite the large allied army stationed on the Israeli border, there appears to have been negligible resistance.'

A loud rapping came from the front door. Alisha jumped.

'*Who's that?*' Debbie shouted, making Alisha jump again.

Debbie stared at Alisha. 'Are you expecting anybody?'

Alisha gave a frightened shake of her head.

The door knocked even louder.

'Lordy.' Debbie marched down the hall, stooped, and put her eye to the peephole. She recoiled in horror, an eye hovering in the lens.

'Is that you, Debbie?' came an agitated male voice. 'Is Alisha there? Please let me in–I'm freezing.'

Debbie put her eye back to the lens. The man had backed away. He was standing in the street, hands on hips, face distressed. He looked ridiculous in a hospital gown, bare legs, and shoes with no socks. Debbie knew Arlo from when he'd collected Alisha after a church service.

Debbie turned to face Alisha. 'It's Arlo,' she said. 'He's in a state. Shall I let him in?'

'*Let me in,*' came a muffled plea.

Alisha gripped her hair in her hands.

'*LET ME IN,*' Arlo shouted.

'OK, OK,' Alisha conceded. A noise came from behind her. She turned and saw Joshua peeping out from the study. He noticed her looking and scampered back inside.

Debbie slid the security chain free with a rattle and yanked open the door.

Arlo lunged in, shivering uncontrollably.

'Arlo,' Alisha cried. Without thinking, she ran down the hall, and they embraced. Arlo squeezed her close.

'Alisha,' Arlo mumbled. 'Thank god.'

Alisha stepped back and stared at his hospital clothes.

'Are you OK?' she exclaimed.

'Long story,' Arlo replied, teeth chattering. 'A cuppa might help.'

'Come in the kitchen,' she said.

Arlo shuffled past Debbie, nodding his respects. Alisha grabbed her woollen coat from a peg and draped it around his shoulders.

'Thanks, love,' he said with a half-smile.

'I'll make you that drink,' Alisha said.

Arlo sat at the kitchen table and glanced at the wall television. Celebrities were debating the invasion on a question time programme.

'What's happened?' Arlo asked.

'They've invaded Israel,' Alisha replied. 'They're on the verge of taking Jerusalem.'

'Shit,' Arlo said. 'Never a dull moment.'

'What happened to you?' Alisha probed.

'I was caught up in a bombing at BioRhythms.'

'*What on earth were you doing there?*'

'Hmm, another long story ...'

'Were you there with Lana?'

'Er, I was actually,' Arlo replied.

Alisha nodded, crossed her arms and turned away.

'She died in the blast,' Arlo said in a monotone to her back.

Alisha turned and stared wide-eyed. Arlo nodded slowly. 'And she saved Carl.'

'Saved Carl? I don't understand.'

'I barely do either,' he said. 'Look, Alisha, I know things have been difficult recently, but it's not what you think–'

Bang! Bang! Bang!

They all spun around and stared down the hall at the front door.

BANG! BANG! BANG!

The door shook; a chunk of plaster fell from the surrounding wall.

'What the hell,' Arlo exclaimed.

'*Open the door,*' came a muffled, angry cry.

'Better open the door,' Alisha said to Debbie, looking petrified.

Debbie bit her lip and raced to the door. The chain rattled, and the door swung open.

A burly male police officer walked in, trailed by three men in black–thick-set, with attitudes to match.

Arlo shook his head. '*No, no, no ...*' he groaned.

'Arlo Jones?' the policeman said.

'What the hell's going on?' Arlo demanded.

'I think we should be asking you the same question,' the officer replied.

'Sorry?' Arlo said.

'Your restraining order?'

'What restraining order?'

'May I?' The policeman pointed to the television screen.

Debbie nodded.

The policeman's eyes flicked as they scrolled his BioFace menus; a still image appeared on the TV. He blinked, and a video began to play. Grainy footage showed Arlo in BioRhythms's snug, facing off against Tarone. Alisha thought Tarone looked much smaller than when she'd last seen him playing in a pub.

Arlo grabbed Tarone by his multicoloured hoodie. 'You fucking nigga,' he snarled, specks of spittle spraying his face. Alisha stared aghast. Arlo headbutted Tarone on the bridge of the nose, blood spraying.

'Does your wife know you're a racist, Dr Jones?' the policemen asked nonchalantly.

'*That's not me in the video,*' Arlo said in disbelief. '*I'd never say or do that!*'

'Really! So what about this then?'

The policeman's eyes flicked again. Arlo appeared as he skirted the dance floor, inadvertently glancing into a covert camera. He paused, checked over his shoulder, and placed a bag under a table. The video fast-forwarded; a saxophone soared.

Lana was slow dancing with someone. They turned–it was Channing. A bright flash lit the dance floor. The scene distorted and shuddered as a shock wave hit the camera. Lana took the full force of the blast on her back; bodies were hurled like skittles across the picture in a blizzard of debris. The video died.

'Deep fake,' Arlo growled.

'Carnage,' the policeman corrected.

The television broadcast came back on. A breaking news banner scrolled along the bottom: 'Jerusalem Taken.' Drone footage showed a column of desert-camouflaged tanks trundling down a residential street. They stopped with a belch of black diesel smoke. A tank's gun fired; the front of a house collapsed in an avalanche of dust. With a clang, the lead tank's hatch was thrown open. A man clambered out and stood proud. He surveyed the scene and looked up at the drone, hand shielding his eyes. The camera zoomed in on his face. Momentarily, the man removed his hand. Mouth agape, Arlo stared at his face and piercing blue eyes. 'When I blacked out in Seattle …' he muttered.

'Arlo Jones,' the policeman announced, 'I am arresting you for the terrorist bombing of BioRhythms and the murder of Dr Lana S. Grace.'

His words became distant as Alisha felt herself going faint. Her eyes rolled white like hard-boiled eggs, her body going limp. Instinctively, she grabbed out as her vision faded. She drove plaster under her nails as she scratched a music stave down the wall. Debbie spotted her just in time and caught her as she fell.

The policeman put Arlo's right arm behind his back and yanked a set of handcuffs from his belt.

'*Get off me*,' Arlo yelled, pulling free. He dashed over to Alisha and cradled her in his arms, kissing her forehead. The heavies stepped in, grabbing his shoulders and dragging him away. Arlo's legs kicked a crazy can-can, arms winding down car windows. He escaped their grasp, but they piled back on top in a manic rugby scrum. Debbie dragged Alisha away. One of the heavies pulled out a syringe and injected Arlo. He groaned as his body went limp.

They dragged Arlo down the hall, heels making black skid marks on the polished wooden floor. As they reached the front door, Josh's little face peeked out from the study. It appeared as if he was muttering to someone, nodding robotically, eyes scanning wildly. A wicked smile grew across his angelic face.

38

Arlo opened his eyes. Everything was white, blindingly white. *Shit!* He blinked rapidly. Still white. He squeezed his eyes tightly shut. Memories flooded back: a white pillow suffocating his mother, a blizzard as he battled to the nursing home. Beginning to panic, he opened them again. Still white. Only weak shadows suggested the world was 3D. He looked about and saw nothing: no people, windows, door or furniture. And he couldn't hear or smell anything either.

He broke out in a cold sweat, head jerking left and right, eyes searching for an exit. Just white.

One, two, three. He inhaled. *One, two, three.* He exhaled.

He closed his eyes, trying to imagine being somewhere else. A virgin-white coral beach, waves gently breaking, retreating with a dragging rumble and hiss. The sea a colour-fade from white foam shore to aqua shallows, growing turquoise across the reef and ending in a deep-blue drop-off. A cloudless sky punctuated by mewing seagulls. He tried to relax, inhaling sandalwood, pushing away a creeping dread of infinite time.

'*ARLO,*' a deep voice boomed.

His eyes snapped open. Still white.

'Welcome to your future,' it said. 'We've thrown away the key. You're *ours* now.'

Arlo jammed his eyes shut.

'You cannot escape, Arlo. This world is *especially* for you.'

Arlo ground his teeth. 'Do your worst,' he muttered, imagining the beach, the surf, and a lush rainforest behind.

'Very well,' the voice said.

One, two, three, Arlo counted, trying to stop himself from screaming. Virtual time passed. It seemed to last an eternity.

Nothing awful lasts forever.

'I love you, Arlo,' a sweet voice whispered.

Arlo opened his eyes. Still white. He jammed them shut, retreating to the beach, a chatter of monkeys playing in the forest, technicolour flashes of parrots flying between trees.

'I have your last dream,' the voice said.

Lana. My dear Lana.

'Don't forget my Mia.'

Arlo took flight along the beach, gazing down upon the reef, stingrays making shadows like rogue clouds on a blue-sky day. Up and over dunes corrugated by trade winds. As he stared, mesmerised by the patterns, the scene disappeared into a sandstorm, grains reassembling as the interior of a spacecraft.

Kefa gazed down on Baraq, sapphire eyes glaring back, straining, willing his body to move. His skin began to twitch and spasm, fists clenching and unclenching. Sweat ran down Kefa's face and dripped into the tank; rings rippled outwards, distorting Baraq's face. Was that a smile?

Kefa lunged for a purple button at the back of the tank and smacked it hard. A loud sucking noise filled the cabin as the dump valve opened. Baraq's face definitely moved this time–a grimace of shock, horror and rage. Baraq's arms broke the surface, grasping the sides of the tank, muscles straining against the relentless, sucking pull. He glanced at Kefa, eyes desperate, pleading. Kefa shook his head.

Thwack. Bang!

Baraq's grip gave way in an implosion of flesh, bone, sinew and slime. In an instant, he was gone–extruded into the vacuum of space. Kefa gazed into the empty tank as the last claret tendrils beaded and sucked away. He strode across the cabin and powered up the computer. What had happened? Where was Elah?

He checked the log file, searching for recent birth signals.

Three events were listed chronologically. Kefa checked their dates; his brow creased. The middle one was his own birth, the last one Baraq's. But whose was the first? He opened the file and compared it side-by-side with the others. The signal properties were a carbon copy of Baraq's recent birth on the ship but far weaker–terrestrial. But why? Was Baraq on the Earth as well as the Ark? How come? He had to stop him, had to save his friend.

Kefa searched the ship's archive and found Elah's files: his body from Turnbull and his mind from his final upload. He reset the purge valve of the growth tank and initiated refilling. Returning to the computer, he launched the surveillance tool suite. The spacecraft's electromagnetic sensors continuously monitored the Earth, recording and analysing every one of the billions of signals. By thought, he entered the signal code for Baraq's terrestrial birth and selected triangulation from the options. In the blink of an eye, a coloured map appeared, the image zooming in on an island, then a city, and finally a building. Several ancillary signal codes annotated the display. Kefa scrutinised their details. The emissions appeared to have come from nearby implants active at the time of Baraq's birth. He commanded the computer to analyse the data packets, and the network addresses of four individuals flashed up. Were they responsible? But why? Kefa searched the signal database for their communications. He read the messages and fitted the narrative together like the pieces of a jigsaw puzzle.

He heard clicking and spun around, facing the tank. A purple light flashed; the claret liquid filling the tank had reduced to a trickle.

The scene inside the spacecraft dissolved. Arlo hovered over a meadow of wildflowers. Lana walked away, holding Mia's hand, a teddy bear dangling from her free hand. A skylark warbled as it ascended. Lana and Mia began to skip. Suddenly, they stopped and turned.

'Goodbye, my love,' Lana said. 'Save my little girl.'

The ground began to tremble and shake. Arlo was back in Seattle, the office block creaking and groaning. *Am I dreaming?*

He forced his eyes open.

A kind and weathered face stared down, massive hands like baseball gloves shaking his shoulders, a tooth broken off, dreadlocks tumbling from a huge woollen hat. *Tarone ...*

'Wake up, mon?' Tarone said.

'Where am I?' Arlo asked as he tried to move his arms. He looked down at his orange jumpsuit and the Velcro straps that bound his wrists to a heavy wooden chair.

'A prison in Bath,' Tarone answered.

'What are you doing here?' Arlo uttered.

'Fighting oppression,' Tarone replied. 'Oh, an' freeing you.' He gave a toothy grin. Carl lurched into view.

'Carl!' Arlo beamed. 'How did you find me?'

'Your BioFace,' Carl said, with a stony face. 'We need to get the fuck out–*now!*'

Tarone nodded, dreadlocks swinging. 'Me hit the guard pretty hard.' He rubbed his massive fist. 'But maybe he'll wake.'

Carl tried to undo the straps that secured Arlo but struggled to coordinate.

'Let me help,' Tarone said, instantly pulling apart the Velcro.

Arlo stood, wobbled, and sat back down again.

'Easy, Tiga.' Tarone wagged a long and leathery finger.

Carefully, Arlo hoisted himself back to his feet and peered around the room. It looked like he was in a laboratory, electronics paraphernalia arranged on a nearby bench.

Arlo glanced at Tarone. 'I thought you said this was a prison–'

'Prison of the mind,' Carl interjected.

'And you just waltzed in?'

'Usual tricks,' Carl said. 'Tarone's charm, bribery ... And, the IoT locks aren't exactly Fort Knox.'

Arlo smirked and stepped around a guard lying sprawled on his side, nose squashed across his face, blood oozing. They followed Tarone out of the room and down a long passageway. Turning a corner, they entered reception–a special constable was sitting at a desk. Tarone sauntered over, winking; she looked down. Carl BioFaced her some cash with a beep. She kept looking down.

'Let's make tracks,' Tarone said.

They marched out into the road. It was still broad daylight, snow lightly falling. Arlo wondered how long he'd been out. It felt like years, but, checking his BioFace, he saw it was only two hours.

'Quick,' Carl barked. 'In the truck.'

'What? *That?*' Arlo pointed to a dilapidated vehicle parked across the road. He guessed it had been a lorry at some point in its history. A crude shelter had been cobbled together on the flatbed; a rabble of smiling faces hung from its crudely sawn windows. They looked like the Jamaican home guard: improvised weapons and army surplus uniforms, topped off by tubular beanie hats in the national colours. Slabs of white polystyrene foam clad the whole vehicle–it looked like a Christmas carnival float.

Carl glared at Arlo. 'Don't slander The Liberator.'

'What's with the polystyrene?' Arlo asked.

'Camouflage against the snow. And it's surprisingly effective against infrared drone cameras.'

'Clever. Where the hell did they find a truck and fuel?'

'Apparently, they acquired it years ago,' Carl replied. 'They've been keeping it for a special occasion. You're honoured.'

'Blimey.' Arlo jogged across the road, saluting the men in the back. He climbed into the cabin. Carl followed suit, struggling to scale the ladder. Tarone pushed him up from behind. Arlo scanned the cab. Despite the rusting exterior, everything inside looked shipshape, with even a fire extinguisher mounted to the dash, although Arlo doubted that carbon dioxide was appropriate for vehicle fires.

Once Carl was seated, Tarone hopped around the front of the bonnet and climbed up into the driver's seat. He saw Arlo shivering, grabbed a donkey jacket from behind his chair, and handed it to him.

'Thanks, Tarone,' Arlo said.

Tarone nodded and turned the ignition key. After a few wheezing groans, the truck belched filthy-black fumes.

THUD!

The police station's doors burst open. Three armed men crouched and aimed.

'*Stop!*' one of them shouted. *BANG!*

Tarone gunned the engine, crunched the gears, and pulled away with a smell of chip-fat fumes. More shots rang out. The cabin pinged and clanged; a hole appeared in the door by Carl's head. The men in the back of the truck returned fire with a hail of crossbow bolts and arrows. The coppers dived for cover as the truck roared away. They reached the end of the road and skidded a corner. Everything calmed down.

'Christ, that was close,' Carl gasped.

'The Liberator did have them.' Tarone grinned.

'They'll be back,' Carl said stonily. 'Next time, they'll be better prepared.'

'Let them try,' Tarone chuckled.

Arlo noticed they were heading back towards Bristol, the truck squirming and skidding on ice flows from the flooded river to their right.

'We can't go back,' Arlo pleaded. 'I have to go to Wells. For Lana ...'

'I know,' Carl said.

Arlo cocked his head. 'What do you mean, *you know?*'

'I had a BioFace message from Lucy.'

'How come?'

'She was trying to contact you.'

'About what?'

'Channing visited her in hospital. She overheard him BioFacing Stanford.'

'What did he say?'

'He said he, er ...'

'*What?*'

'Wanted him to *use* Mia.'

'*Use Mia? For what?*'

A grimace cracked on Carl's stony face. 'Don't ask me. I didn't even know she had a daughter.'

'When did she message you?' Arlo asked.

Carl checked his BioFace. 'Ninety-seven minutes ago.'

'So why are we heading back to Brist–'

'We're not,' Tarone interrupted as brakes squealed. The truck veered sideways, threatening to roll. Somehow it stayed upright and slewed left into a side road. Tarone laughed. 'We a goin' underground.'

The truck whipped right, ploughed through waist-high undergrowth and broke off overhanging tree branches. Arlo raised his hands to protect his face, bracing himself for the impact. But none came. They were on a path, heading for the yawning mouth of a barricaded tunnel.

BANG! The Liberator struck a wooden barrier and briefly went airborne. It crashed into the gloom, splinters showering into the cabin through gaps in the makeshift Perspex windscreen.

'Christ!' Arlo yelled. 'Why a tunnel?'

'The city drone,' Carl replied. 'Despite the polystyrene, its infrared camera might still track us. And it'll block the city sensors. We have to hope the drone didn't spot where we disappeared.'

'Nice one.' Arlo grinned.

The truck skidded and squirmed along the narrow tunnel, its headlights casting a feeble yellow glow. Tarone concentrated hard, peering through the smeary windshield as the vehicle scraped and bounced off the tunnel walls. A quarter of an hour later, a pinprick of light grew in the centre of Arlo's vision, like an old-fashioned television picture turning off in reverse. A minute later, Greenway tunnel expanded away, the dark swapped for a ferocious blizzard.

'Good job, the weather's crap,' Arlo said.

'Yah, mon,' Tarone said. 'Never did think me say that.'

'Wellow's far from the city,' Carl added. 'Hopefully, the drone's lost us.'

ΔΔΔ

For an hour, they coaxed the Liberator through the storm, nursing it up climbs and skirting around drifts. As they approached Wells, they charged a punishing drag, the tyres spinning to a blur. The truck ground to a halt.

'Everyone out,' Tarone cried. 'Fit ropes to the tyres.'

Arlo helped Tarone thread a rope through a wheel. His BioFace buzzed–it was Alisha.

'Hello, love,' he answered nervously.

'You OK?' Alisha asked.

'I'm fine,' Arlo replied. 'Just a bit mixed up.'

'You and me both.' She laughed nervously.

'Are you with Carl?'

'Yeah, he broke me out of prison! Along with Tarone and his mates.'

'Carl said he was going to track you down and rescue you. He never mentioned a prison, though.'

'Yes, he's a rock.'

'Have you heard the latest news?' Alisha asked.

'Not since my arrest. What's happened?'

'The Axis army has taken all of Israel. The Allied troops appear to have been disabled by their BioFaces. Arlo, there's talk of *horrible* things happening in Jerusalem.'

'*What things?*'

'Executions and rape. And that man …'

'What man?'

'The man who raised the homeless guy from the dead.'

'*What about him?*'

'He gave a broadcast.'

'From where?'

'A hill–somewhere in Israel. *Arlo, he's their leader!*'

'*Eh!*'

'It's starting to make sense now.'

'What is?'

'What it all means.'

'What did he say?'

'He said we are at the start of the Millennium.'

Arlo's BioFace buzzed–Alisha had sent him a picture.'

'I've been thinking, Arlo.'

'*About what?*'

'Your dreams. My dreams. The fake video.'

'*Fake video?*'

'Of you in BioRhythms. Your wedding ring was on your left hand, but you always wear it on your right. And Joshua ...'

'What about Joshua?'

'He's acting strange. Very strange.'

'How?'

'Robotic. It's as if he's not himself. Like he's a puppet.'

'*Are you sure?*'

'Arlo, I think tht mn is tsa ... tn ...'

'*What's that?*'

The connection dropped. Arlo checked the error log. 'Call failed,' it reported. Arlo frowned–nothing ever dropped out anymore.

Using his BioFace, Arlo dragged the picture Alisha had just sent him to his BioVision and studied it. A tall man of Middle Eastern appearance was standing on a hill. His eyes were of the deepest blue. It was his alien. Behind him was a brick building and a transmitter mast that towered so high it went out of shot. Arlo zoomed the picture and read the sign over the entrance: 'giddo Earth Station and Cyber Security.' Arlo tried to recall the last thing Alisha had said before the call broke up, playing the garbled words, over and over, in his mind. He dropped the rope he was holding, his mind racing.

'*What you a doing, mon,*' Tarone snapped. '*Pass da rope through.*'

Jarred from his thoughts, Arlo stared at Tarone, looking like he'd seen a ghost. 'Alisha's just said something important.'

'What dat?'
'She's just said he's Satan.'

39

The Liberator turned into Kate's road.

'*STOP!*' Arlo yelled. 'Any closer's too risky.'

The truck's engine coughed and died.

Arlo felt sick inside. Kate's road reminded him of Lana's death, and he was terrified of letting her down. Trying to calm himself, he recalled chatting to her in Che Café and pictured her walking through a field of wildflowers, hand-in-hand with Mia. But then he heard her voice, pleading for Mia. 'Please save her, Arlo. *Save her ... Promise me, Arlo.*'

The street was deathly quiet as he jumped down from the truck, the thick snow squeaking as he landed. According to his BioFace map, Kate's flat was less than a hundred metres away, obscured by a bend. Carl and Tarone jumped down beside him.

'What now?' Tarone asked.

'Recon.' Arlo pointed down the road. 'Her flat is just around that corner.'

Tarone nodded; Carl's eyes darted.

'Tell your men to watch from the bend,' Arlo said to Tarone. 'OK, mon.'

Tarone briefed his men in the truck and returned.

'Ready?' Arlo asked.

Tarone fist-bumped him. 'Let's go, mon.'

They crept down the road, Arlo leading, hugging the terrace.

A few minutes later, Arlo stopped by a downstairs window of a house and raised his palm. He peered through a gap in the net curtain–Kate and Stanford were sitting only a few feet away, staring at a wall television. Mia was restrained in her wheelchair, tugging the fur of an orange monkey, eyes wandering vacantly. Arlo put his ear to the glass and heard muffled voices. His eyes flicked as he selected audio enhancement from his BioFace menu.

'I am *so* sorry about your daughter, Mrs Grace,' Stanford said above the hum and hiss.

'Please call me Kate, professor.'

'Ah, Kate, that is *so* very kind. I am sure Lana would have wanted me to help.'

'Mia was everything to her. If there's *any chance* it might work,' Kate pleaded.

'Of course. Well, if it's OK with you, I'll log in to her BioFace now and enable remote access. It's nearly time.'

'Yes, please do.' Kate smiled.

Nearly time?

Arlo removed his ear from the glass and looked in. A man was lecturing a congregation on the television. It appeared religious, perhaps a sermon, maybe in America. The camera zoomed in, and Arlo did a double-take. The man looked like his alien. What on earth was he doing there? What the hell was going on?

Arlo glanced over his shoulder. 'Time to go in,' he said in hushed tones, pointing at the front door. Tarone cracked his knuckles and stood up. The lock rattled as Arlo gently pressed the door. Tarone put a finger to pursed lips, then pointed to his own eyes and, then, to Arlo's. Next, he patted his shoulder and pointed to the door. Arlo shook his head and rapped the knocker. Tarone scowled, dreadlocks swinging.

The door creaked open, and Kate's face appeared above the security chain. She eyeballed Arlo.

'Who are you?' she said frostily.

'I'm Arlo–Lana's friend. Can I come in?' Arlo forced a smile. *'Please.'*

'Lana's friend?' Kate looked him up and down through the crack in the door. *'That's not possible.'*

'Yes. I *was* a good friend.' Arlo gave a pained expression.

She glanced over her shoulder. 'Now's not a good time.'

'I know this might sound strange, Mrs Grace, but the man in your lounge is evil.'

'What? Professor Stanford?' Her face hardened. '*I think you need to leave.*'

'*Please*, Mrs Grace. Lana asked me to protect Mia.'

'*Protect Mia?*'

Kate released the chain, peered around the door and spotted Tarone. Panicking, she shoved the door in Arlo's face. Lightning fast, Arlo wedged his foot into the closing gap.

'*No, you don't,*' she protested, gritting her teeth and shoving hard. Arlo stood firm. '*Professor!*' she cried out.

Arlo barged her aside. 'Sorry, Mrs Grace, but you'll thank me later.'

Arlo entered the hall and, gripping Kate's shoulders, frogmarched her into the lounge with Tarone and Carl in tow.

Mia was smiling, holding her monkey out straight, gazing mesmerised into its eyes.

'Jesus loves you, Charlie,' she shrieked.

Kate wriggled free and rushed over to Mia, hugging her close.

'Grandma,' she shrieked.

A tear rolled down Kate's face and splashed onto Charlie's nylon fur. 'You're better,' she sobbed.

Arlo swivelled and stared at Stanford.

'Ah, so nice to see you, Dr Jones,' Stanford said with a sickly smile.

'What are you up to?' Arlo said through gritted teeth.

'*Up to?*' Stanford said curiously. 'A child cured of a debilitating disease; a grandmother overjoyed after the sadness of losing a daughter to a terrorist?'

Arlo lunged at Stanford. Tarone restrained him from behind.

'Not now, mon.'

Carl lumbered across the room and stood face-to-face with

Stanford.

'How exactly has she been cured?' Carl demanded.

Stanford backed away. 'The good Lord is not to be questioned.'

'Why did you need remote access to Mia?' Arlo probed.

'I don't know what you mean,' Stanford barked.

'Mrs Grace,' Carl continued. 'It appears the Professor, with the help of his online stooge, has worked a miracle. But is it trickery? Would you mind granting me remote access to Mia too?'

'Why on earth would you want that?' Stanford barked. 'Jesus has healed the masses.'

Even Carl's stony face showed mild disbelief. 'To check Mia is safe and well.'

'And why do you think *you* would know?' Stanford challenged.

'I have written software and firmware my whole working life,' Carl said dismissively.

'But what's that got to do with Mia's health?' Kate said, looking confused.

'Listen to Mrs Grace,' Stanford snarled.

Carl stared Stanford down. 'She was cured using her BioFace? Yes?'

'The cure is medical,' Stanford rebuked.

'Made by the BioFace?' Carl persisted.

Kate glared at Stanford.

'Technically, yes,' Stanford conceded.

'So it's a firmware fix?'

'If you're a pedant.'

'So, you won't mind me checking?'

'It can't hurt, can it, professor?' Kate pleaded. 'Just to be safe?'

Tight-lipped, Stanford crossed his arms.

'*Do it*,' Kate said.

Kate BioFaced Carl the access code she had as Mia's carer. Carl's eyes flicked. Mia swung Charlie above her head, overcome with glee. A minute or so passed.

'Are we done?' Stanford barked. 'Some of us have busy liv–'

'Um, what's this …?' Carl interrupted.

'*What is it, Carl?*' Arlo said.

'Looks like a time bomb.'

'A-A t-time bomb?' Kate stammered.

'Carl's eyes kept on flicking.'

'*What's a time bomb?*' Kate cried hysterically.

'If I understand correctly, Mrs Grace,' Arlo said, seeing Carl was busy. 'A time bomb's a malicious application designed to execute at a specific time–'

'Got it,' Carl exclaimed. 'It's an island-hopping attack.'

'*A WHAT?*' Kate shrieked.

'That proves it, Mrs Grace,' Arlo said.

'Proves what?' she sobbed.

Carl's eyes stopped flicking, and he stared expressionless at Kate. 'Am I correct in assuming the government classes Mia as a vulnerable person with limited capacity?'

Kate nodded.

'Well,' Carl continued, 'I guess she receives automatic medical updates from BDL's master server without needing authorisation?'

'Yes, I've been told that's the case.' Kate nodded again. '*But why's that relevant?*'

'It means her BioFace isn't secure.'

'*Secure?*'

'Yes. It means Mia, and people like her, are a security risk to the BioFace network. The vulnerable become a vulnerability. They are like islands.'

'*Islands?*'

'Yes, vulnerable islands from which an assailant can launch an attack on the mainland,' Carl continued. 'In this case, the BioFace update server.'

'I don't understand.'

'Once BDL's network is compromised,' Carl said, 'an attacker can trigger a BioFace update, rerouting everyone to use their *own* spoofed server. They can then update everyone in the world with *their* firmware version instead of BDL's. They can take control.'

Carl's eyes darted.

The front door creaked open. Arlo spun around. Two men walked in, both dark, both tall.

'Hello, Arlo.' Channing gave a sinister smile.

Arlo's gaze switched to the other man–his alien–then glanced at the television. The man had stopped preaching. He looked identical.

Arlo locked eyes with the alien. 'You seem to get about.' Arlo glanced up at the television.

'I am in every corner of the world,' the alien replied. 'Soon, I will be in every one of you.'

Channing laughed. 'You're out of your depth, Arlo.'

'Who's your new friend?' Arlo said to Channing.

'He's so much better than that useless slut.' Channing glanced at Stanford with barely concealed contempt. 'She's all yours now.'

Stanford smiled nervously, scratching his nape.

Chatter came from a radio clipped to Channing's belt.

Channing smiled at Arlo. 'My disciples are excited. Our work is nearly done.'

'And maybe not,' Carl said as two faces, nestled in a forest of dreadlocks, sprang up behind the two men.

Channing cried out in pain as his arm was pinned behind his back. The alien grimaced as he was similarly restrained. Long knives glinted at the two men's throats, serrated blades flickering orange-red in the firelight.

Tarone smiled. 'May me introduce Llanzo and Khanan.'

Channing's radio squawked. 'Do you read me?'

Channing reached down with his spare hand and cried out in pain as he was hoisted off the floor by his bent arm.

'No, you don't,' Llanzo said, flashing Channing the blade before pressing it back against his neck.

'OK,' Arlo said. 'Let's be civilised.' He twisted to face the alien. 'First things first. Who the *hell* are you?'

'He's Jesus,' Stanford snapped.

'And I'm Mother Teresa,' Arlo scoffed.

'You can call me Baraq,' the alien announced.

Arlo frowned as he tried to remember the name in his dream. Stanford seemed unsurprised.

'OK, Baraq,' Arlo continued. 'What do you want?'

Baraq laughed. The blade tightened against his throat. 'When you're immortal, you have no fear.'

'*WHAT DO YOU WANT?*' Arlo yelled.

'What *every* ruler wants.'

'Which is?'

'Absolute power.'

'You'll never get that.'

'Watch me,' Baraq mocked. 'I nearly already have.'

Shouts came from the road. Everyone startled. Channing slipped Llanzo's grasp and dived into the hall. Llanzo raced after him. Seconds later, Llanzo reappeared. 'He away,' he said. 'There's a driverless vehicle, an AV, crawling up the road with a top-mounted machine gun. There are four enforcers following it.'

'Has it seen the Liberator?' Arlo asked anxiously.

'No yet, them a move towards the bend. The Liberator won't stand no chance. *We must move now!*'

Baraq elbowed Khanan in the stomach. Khanan saw it coming and quickly overpowered him, holding him in a headlock. Baraq struggled frantically, trying to escape. The blade flashed red against his neck; blood sprayed the wall. Baraq slumped and rolled away.

Arlo remembered what he'd said to his dad in his final days. 'I'll find them. When I grow up, and I'm as big as you. I promise! You wait and see ...'

Arlo felt sick inside as Baraq lay twitching on the floor.

'*Arlo,*' Carl urged. '*We need to go!*'

Arlo averted his gaze from Baraq. 'We need to draw that truck away.'

'What about Stanford?' Carl exclaimed. 'And Mia and Kate?'

'We have to take Mia.' Arlo rubbed his brow. 'Stanford's our insurance policy. Kate can hide.'

Kate glared at Arlo. *'You're not taking my Mia.'*

'Mrs Grace, *we must.* Lana asked me to save her.'

'But Lana's dead …'

'I'm so sorry, Kate–*we must.*'

Arlo pointed to Stanford. 'Right, *you.*'

Stanford looked up nervously.

'OUT!'

Tarone grabbed Stanford by the scruff of his nylon jacket and shoved him hard while gripping him firmly. Reluctantly, Stanford shuffled towards the door.

'Everyone,' Arlo ordered, 'follow him. Once outside, use him as a shield.'

Everyone filed in behind.

Arlo touched Kate's arm, and she turned to face him.

'When we've gone, lock the door and hide.' She began to sob. 'If they break in and find you, deny everything.' She buried her face in her hands, shoulders shaking.

'Kate. It'll be OK,' Arlo continued. *'I promise.* When everything's blown over, I'll bring Mia back.'

Kate looked up, eyes flooded with tears.

'Kate. It *will* be OK. *Trust me.*'

Kate mustered a weak smile. 'Thanks, Arlo.'

Arlo nodded solemnly and squeezed her arm, thinking of Stella in the office block.

'Right,' Arlo said, undoing Mia's straps and pulling her free of the wheelchair. Mia gazed at Arlo as she gripped Charlie.

'Are you Jesus?' she said.

Arlo gulped and gave Kate a troubled look.

'Yes,' Kate said to Mia. 'He's here to save you and Charlie. He'll be looking after you for a while.'

Arlo squeezed Kate's arm. 'Thanks.'

He perched Mia on his hip and pulled his coat around her. *'Everyone out.'*

Tarone bundled Stanford out of the door, pausing as if expecting to hear shots. None came. They filed out in a crazy conga, Tarone holding Stanford out in front like a riot shield. Arlo looked back and saw Kate standing in the doorway.

'Lock the door,' he urged.

Arlo saw Kate's face drop as she pushed the door closed with a click. A chain rattled; footsteps receded. Arlo followed the procession, Khanan and Llanzo bringing up the rear, shotguns cradled in their arms. Arlo peered around the men in front. The AV was less than a stone's throw from the bend. Four enforcers in riot gear prowled behind, carrying assault rifles.

Arlo turned to Khanan. 'Fire to get their attention.'

'But dat will be suicide!'

'We need to draw them away from the Liberator. We can run around the block and approach it from behind.'

'Me hope you right.'

Arlo heard a click as Khanan cocked his ancient gun. An instant later, there was a thunderous boom, and the snow flashed orange. The AV juddered to a halt.

The enforcers spun around; one raised his gun.

'*Stop!*' Stanford shouted.

The enforcer appeared puzzled and lowered his rifle.

'*Don't you know who I am?*' Stanford preached.

The enforcer looked to his colleague–he shook his head.

'*I am the prophet,*' Stanford continued. '*The proclaimer of the Lord.*'

The enforcer cocked his head. '*Get down on the floor,*' he barked. '*Arms spread.*'

'*Follow the Lord. Lay down your weapons in peace.*'

The enforcer glanced at his colleague again. The man nodded. The enforcer raised his gun and fired off a burst.

Stanford's body twitched. His legs buckled, and he went down.

'So much for his prophecies,' Carl muttered. 'He didn't see that one coming.'

'*RUN!*' Arlo shouted.

Clutching Mia to his chest, Arlo bounded through the deep snow as fast as his legs would carry him. Carl lumbered ahead like a deranged Quasimodo. Arlo's burst of adrenaline began to ebb, Mia's weight making his legs and arms burn. Judging by how slow Carl was running and how quickly he was tiring, he feared the worst.

Arlo heard more shots; bullets hissed past. Brick dust showered off a wall. They reached the end of the terrace; Arlo glanced back. The AV and the enforcers had already halved the gap.

'*They're catching us,*' Arlo yelled between breaths as he rounded the bend. '*Keep going.*'

'Me hold them off,' Khanan gasped.

Arlo raised his eyebrows. 'You sure?'

'To save Mia.'

'Good, man. See you at the Liberator.'

Khanan dived behind the rusting hulk of a car, threw his bandolier of shotgun shells to the ground and reloaded both barrels. Arlo ran past, tapping him on the shoulder. Khanan's shotgun roared as Arlo lunged through the deep snow, fighting to keep up.

On the crook of the next bend, Arlo paused for breath and looked back. Khanan's intermittent shotgun blasts had stopped the pursuers, but they encircled the car like a pack of hungry hyenas. Glancing forward, Arlo saw the Liberator only half a block away.

'*Come on, Arlo,*' Carl shouted.

Arlo saw Khanan pop up and take out two enforcers. He paused to reload. Suddenly, his body twitched and made a star shape against the car. Dreadlocks flailed as he slid to the floor.

'He died for you, Mia,' Arlo muttered as he took off towards the Liberator, clutching her tight. The truck roared into life, charging straight at them. Arlo jumped aside and dived for the cab's ladder. He landed with a bruising thud; Llanzo's hand gripped his arm like a vice.

'Got you,' Llanzo shouted as he hauled them both aboard.

The Liberator slewed and charged down the road, retracing its old tyre tracks. Smoke billowed black, mixing grey with the blizzard. Images of Seattle's ash storm flashed through Arlo's mind, recalling his dash across the city and scrabbling in the grit, searching for Isabella.

With a squeal of brakes, Tarone swung the vehicle down a side road everyone hurled across the cab.

'*Christ!*' Arlo shouted above the roar of the red-lining engine. '*Where are we going?*'

'*We just need to hide,*' Tarone yelled, eyeballs out.

The truck blasted through the snow. Arlo listened for shots. Suddenly the vehicle lurched and went airborne. Mia shrieked. Arlo gripped her tight, terrified it was all over. The truck crashed back down, tipped dangerously downhill, and slid sideways down a steep bank. Mia screamed. With a heavy crash, they bounced off a tree at the bottom and skidded an arc, the engine roaring. Everything turned from white to black, and the engine died. Tarone put a finger to his lips and hushed everyone. Arlo stroked Mia's head as she whimpered.

Half an hour passed, and nobody came. All they heard was the wind whistling and the hiss of drifting snow. By torchlight, Tarone distributed some blankets from a plastic sack.

'Where are we?' Arlo whispered.

'In an old tunnel under the road. For da cattle,' Tarone replied. 'We need to lay low.'

Arlo nodded and glanced at Carl–his eyes were darting all over the place.

'You OK, mate?' Arlo asked.

'I've just had another look at that malicious code running in Mia,' Carl replied.

'And?'

'I've found the name of the spoof update server.'

'Go on.'

'Megiddo,' Carl muttered.

'Is that anything special?'

'According to BioWiki, it was a fortification made by king

Ahab on the Plain of Jezreel.'

'What the hell … where's that?'

'Israel,' Carl replied.

'Is the fortification still there?'

'I don't think so, but a large mound remains. It says it's called a har in Hebrew.'

'Hang on a minute.' Arlo pulled up the photo Alisha had sent him in his BioVision. Baraq was standing on a hill in front of a building with a towering transmitter mast. Arlo zoomed in. The sign over the building read: 'giddo Earth Ground Station and Cyber Security.' But Baraq's body obscured the start of the name.

'*Shit!* I think Megiddo's the name on the building from where Baraq addressed the nation,' Arlo exclaimed.

'The mound Har and the fortification Megiddo,' Carl replied. 'Har Megiddo.'

'Armageddon …' Arlo uttered, the colour draining from his face.

Carl's eyes darted, face a mask of stone. 'The BioFace update is scheduled for midday tomorrow.'

40

The storm continued to rage. Tarone's friends retreated into the cab, sheltering from the biting cold. With everyone jammed together, the air steamed. All Arlo could hear was the howling wind and a hiss of drifting snow. Palpable grief hung over everyone, but at least it was warm, and Arlo felt Mia's rhythmic breathing as she slept. He played recent events over and over through his mind, Baraq's words, 'Soon I will be in every one of you,' sending shivers down his spine. He had to stop the BioFace update but had no idea how.

After an hour of wracking his brain, Arlo shut his eyes and let his mind drift, breathing synchronising with Mia's. The hissing snow relaxed him, and he began to float.

Oxygen hissed. A cabin of a spaceship appeared, condensation running down its walls, purple warning lights flashing as overhead lights dimmed.

Kefa paced up and down, clicking to himself, glancing into the growth tank on every pass. Elah's head rolled casually along the bottom like a washed-up fisherman's buoy, nerves and ribbons of skin trailing from a neck stub like jellyfish tentacles. Now and again, a cheek broke the surface, skin twitching as if sensing freedom.

Kefa stopped pacing, hands massaging his brow. He clenched his fists and dashed over to the computer, using his mind to retrieve records of those present at Baraq's birth. He read their recent communications and looked at an image sent to a man named Arlo. It showed Baraq stood by a transmitter station, smiling triumphantly. Kefa shook his head and paced wildly. He dived back to the computer, entered commands by thought, and rushed back to the tank. Elah's eyes snapped open, desperately searching, lips twitching as if trying to speak. Kefa dashed back to the console, characters streaming down the screen like the patterns of an unfurling carpet. The text swam, leaving the screen like twisting serpents as the spacecraft dissolved into the blackness of space.

Arlo's eyes slowly opened. 'Lana said the dreams were over …' he muttered. He felt so tired. Everyone in the cab was dozing, and it was getting light. He checked the time: 8:57 am. They had three hours to stop the attack on BDL's update server. *But how?*

Arlo gazed at the cab's window, trying to see if it was still snowing. Condensation obscured his view, and he wiped it away with his hand. Halfway across the pane, he stopped, staring at the milky fog. There was writing–his writing. Numbers were written in groups, separated by dots. It looked like an IP address–the numbers BioFaces used to network. *Did I write it in my sleep?* He glanced to his right. Carl was dead to the world. He nudged him, but all he did was grunt and snuffle.

Arlo accessed his BioFace menu, launched BioChrome and entered the IP address written on the glass. Nothing happened. He closed the browser, eyes defocusing as he stared at the side window. *What the hell am I going to do?*

Arlo jumped. A face stared back.

'Use the code, Arlo.'

Shit!

Arlo squeezed his eyes shut, gripping the sides of his head. He opened his eyes–the face had gone.

Use the code?

Carl stirred. 'You OK?' he mumbled.

'S-Someone's outside,' Arlo replied.

Carl sat up. 'A Yeti?' he chuckled, nudging him in the ribs.

'I'm *not* joking.' Arlo's face looked old and drawn. '*He told me to use the code.*'

'What code?' Carl asked, his curiosity piqued.

'God knows,' Arlo said. 'I had a vivid dream. The face at the window was in it. His name's Elah.'

Carl looked at him strangely.

'Christ, Carl,' Arlo frowned. 'I'm not making this shit up!'

'*Whoa!*' Carl put his hands up defensively. 'Calm down. We've *all* had a tough time, you know.'

Arlo looked down. 'Sorry, mate.'

'It's OK.' Carl touched his arm. 'Do you think you dreamt it? The mind can play tricks when you've just woken up.'

'No, Carl. *It was real.* I saw him. *I bloody well heard him!*'

'OK, OK, calm down. The code should be in your BioFace download cache, then?'

Arlo eyed him suspiciously. 'Are you checking me out?'

'No mate,' Carl countered. 'Don't be defensive. Let me take a look.'

'OK, wait a moment.' Arlo's eyes flicked as he navigated his BioFace menus. 'There ... access granted.'

Arlo watched Carl's eyes animate, his body sloth-like. Mornings were always bad for Carl. He knew it wasn't fair he was giving him such a hard time. Mia stirred on his chest, beginning to wake. He stroked her hair.

A few seconds later, Arlo noticed a subtle crease in Carl's brow. Carl's eyes stopped scanning, and he stared at him.

'You're right,' he said.

'*You've found something?*'

'Not sure. There's a strange binary file.'

'What? Like a virus? Should you quarantine it?'

'Well, that's just the thing,' Carl continued. 'It won't move, and I can't delete it. It's like a protected file, permanently tattooed on your BioFace's operating system.'

'I guess there's no way of knowing how it got there?'

'Well, there is actually.'

'*How?*'

'Its date. It was created only ten minutes ago.'

'The voice told me to use the code?'

'I guess I could just double-click on it? Maybe it's a self-executing program like a BioZip archive?'

'Isn't that risky?'

'Yes.' Carl nodded. 'But, as I see it, you only have two options.'

'Two?'

'Yes. You either leave it there–ready to strike when you least expect it–or you bite the bullet and run it.'

'You know what, Carl,' Arlo exclaimed. 'Just bloody run it. With everything else that's gone on, what's the worst thing that can happen?'

'Sure?'

'*Sure.*'

Carl rubbed his brow. 'OK, I'll run my network monitor in the background.'

'Why?'

'It'll monitor all local traffic. If it's a virus, it'll probably call home and then we'll be able to identify it.'

'Cool. Do it.'

Carl nodded. 'Here goes.' Carl's eyes scanned, and he double-blinked.

Instantly, Mia locked rigid as if electrocuted. Arlo jumped. Mia's hands clawed at his chest, nails digging into his flesh through his fleece. Her eyes opened wide, eyeballs vibrating in a trance.

'Mer-Mer-Megiddo,' she moaned.

'*Christ,*' Arlo uttered. '*What's happening?*'

After a few seconds, Mia's eyes stopped trembling. She went limp, panting. Her eyelids fluttered as she started to come round.

'*What happened, Carl?*' Arlo demanded.

Carl's eyes scanned frantically. Finally, he grunted. 'The program tried to use Mia to access BDL's update server.'

'What? Like a gateway? Like what Stanford did?'

'Exactly.'

'And?'

'It timed out.'

'*Timed out?*'

'Yeah, it couldn't connect.'

'Maybe because we're underground? Buried in the snow?'

'Good point.'

Arlo glanced at Tarone. He'd just woken up, and his eyes were flicking.

'Anybody get problem with their BioFace?' Tarone asked. 'Mine's no connecting.'

Arlo checked his. It hadn't crashed but wasn't connecting to the BioNet or the metaverse. 'Yeah, my connection's stuffed too.'

'And mine,' Carl added.

'Tarone,' Arlo said. 'Any chance we can get out of this snow hole to get a better signal?'

'Yah, mon. An' then we need to stop the BioFace update.'

'Agreed.'

'All out,' Tarone commanded. 'There are some shovels in the back.'

Everyone clambered out. The snow had drifted up against the bottom of the cab's door, and the tunnel's exit was impassable. However, an arch-shaped patch of mauve sky near the brick ceiling showed the storm had passed.

Tarone's team of five set to work digging. The snow was powdery and light, and soon they'd broken through into the field beyond. They scampered along a hedgerow, collecting dead branches from bushes and trees to put under the truck's tyres. Tarone inspected some plastic drums of biofuel stacked in the back.

'Look like we have enough for maybe twenty miles, thirty at a push.'

'That'll get us back to Bristol,' Arlo volunteered. 'But maybe that's not wise ...'

'We need to stick to the mission, Arlo. Save Mia, an' stop the BioFace update.'

'I wish I knew how,' Arlo replied.

'We a going to work it out.' Tarone's eyes bored into him

with steely determination.

They clambered back into the cab. Tarone turned the ignition key. The starter motor cranked the engine several times, each cycle sounding weaker than the last.

'Stop,' shouted Llanzo, 'you a going to kill the battery.'

Tarone sighed and leaned back in his seat. 'What do you suggest then, Llanzo?'

'Hot water,' he replied. 'Pour it on the battery. Me make a fire.'

'Do it in the tunnel,' Arlo stressed. 'Use dry wood to minimise smoke. We mustn't give ourselves away.'

'Yah, mon.'

Llanzo built a small fire, and, after ten minutes, a pan was steaming.

'That will do,' Tarone called. 'No want to crack the battery.'

Llanzo lifted the bonnet and poured the liquid over the battery.

'Try, now,' Llanzo said.

Tarone turned the ignition key, eyebrows raised.

The engine wheezed, coughed and spluttered. Suddenly it caught and roared. Everyone cheered.

'All aboard the Liberator,' Tarone called to his men. Llanzo smothered the fire with snow, stowed the pan, and jumped up into the cab. The other men finished packing branches under the tyres and climbed into their shelter.

Tarone gunned the throttle, and, with a cloud of eye-stinging smoke, the truck squirmed its way out of the tunnel. It shook its way up the bank onto the road, rattling like a steam engine.

Arlo checked his BioFace. 'Still no connection.' He turned to face Carl. 'Are we being jammed by Bridgwater's nuclear drone?'

'Maybe,' he said. 'Either that or our BioFace MAC addresses are being monitored and blocked.'

Arlo gazed into the distance. The Mendip transmitter mast pierced the sky on the summit of Pen Hill. 'Well, if we're being jammed, then being right on top of the Mendip transmitter might help?' Arlo pointed to the mast.

'Good call,' Carl said. 'Let's go.'

Tarone nodded, and the truck roared down the road.

The journey to the base of Pen Hill took only thirty minutes as most of the snow had been blown off the road. However, the mile-long climb to the mast was another story. The truck charged the hill, everyone bouncing up and down to improve traction. As they jumped, Mia stirred and moaned as if in pain.

Over and over, they had to dismount to place branches under the tyres. Finally, they made it to the station's access road, and Tarone turned the engine off to save fuel. Arlo checked his BioFace: 10:37 am. They all stared up at the thin mast that disappeared into the murk.

'Me BioFace is still no connecting,' Tarone said.

'Damn,' Carl cursed. 'The drones over Bristol, Bath and Frome can see us now. If they're beamforming a jamming signal, they'll still overwhelm the uplink.'

'I still want to try Mia again,' Arlo said.

'I guess we've got nothing to lose,' Carl agreed.

Mia was fidgeting on Arlo's lap, looking unsettled, tugging at Charlie's fur, some of it coming away in tufts. Arlo thought of his dad.

'Are you ready?' Carl asked.

Arlo pushed away his sad memories. 'Yep, fire away.'

Carl's eyes scanned then double-blinked.

Mia went rigid, yelping like a puppy who'd been trodden on, face contorted in pain. Wide-eyed, she stared, eyeballs trembling.

'The light. Stop the light!' she screamed.

'Stop it!' Arlo cried out, thinking of Lana. *'No more!'*

'I can't. It will either work or time out,' Carl yelled.

'For Christ's sake. Do something!'

Arlo hugged Mia, gazing into her eyes, feeling her pain. Then, as quickly as it had started, it was over. She slumped, eyes rolling, mouth foaming, blood gushing from her nose.

Arlo stripped off his coat and fleece, mopped up the blood with his T-shirt, and lightly pinched her nose to staunch the flow.

'Shit. We can't put her through that again,' Arlo said, thinking of Lana. 'What happened?'

'Same as before,' Carl replied. 'No connection, and then it timed out.'

'Hardly the same,' Arlo exclaimed. 'It could have killed her!'

'Yep, not good.'

'So, how do we stop the update?'

'It looks like they've got us beat.' Carl rubbed his brow.

Arlo slammed the dash with a clenched fist, making Carl jump. 'We're not done yet.'

'Well, I can't see any other solution.' Carl shook his head.

'I need some air,' Arlo said. 'It might help Mia too.'

Carl nodded.

Arlo put his tops back on and jumped down from the cab, clutching Mia to his chest. He strolled across the field, picking a route where the snow had drifted away, exposing an icy crust that crunched underfoot. A gap appeared in a screen of dead trees, revealing the valley below. In its centre was Glastonbury Tor, the reborn Isle of Avalon rising from the frozen inland sea. Perched on its summit was the medieval St Michael's Tower.

'Where's Charlie?' Mia uttered.

'He's safe and sound in the cab,' Arlo said, stroking her honey-coloured hair. 'Don't worry.'

'Jesus loves Charlie,' she said.

'Yes, he does,' Arlo said.

'Are you Jesus?' she asked.

Arlo hesitated. 'Er, there's a little bit of Jesus in every one of us, Mia,' he said. 'I just need to make sure it stays that way.'

Mia seemed satisfied, huddled under his coat and sucked her thumb.

Arlo's attention returned to the view. Mia fidgeted under his jacket.

'Jesus won't make me hurt again, will he?' she muttered.

Arlo gazed mesmerised.

'He won't make me see the bright light that hurts my head?' Mia gazed up at Arlo.

Arlo clutched Mia tight and gazed at the Tor, jaw clenched. He recalled his blackout and vision in the office in Seattle. Suddenly his face lit up, and he nodded slowly.

'Time to sort this out once and for all,' he muttered as he marched back towards the truck.

41

Carl desperately tried to make sense of Arlo's claims: an alien birth, the resurrection of a burning man, and his wacky dreams. Was it a psychosis triggered by Arlo's PTSD? But many things rang true: CEP, the murder of Arlo's mum, the destruction of his computer, and the nightclub attack. Plus, Arlo's mystery code and the jamming signal were irrefutable. Whatever the explanation, he had to look after his mate and help keep Mia safe.

The passenger door creaked open, and Arlo climbed up next to him. 'I've had an idea.'

'Try me,' Carl said.

'Presumably, we need a location that blocks the drones yet has a line of sight view to the transmitter mast?'

'Precisely. But that's physically impossible.'

'I'm not sure it is.'

'You'll never find anywhere that shadows the drones like that.'

'Why?'

'It's topographically impossible–nowhere has gradients steep enough.'

'What about the Tor?'

Carl's eyes froze; his face a waxwork. Seconds later, his eyes reanimated as if someone had installed fresh batteries.

'Christ Arlo,' Carl said. 'Where did that one come from?'

'Out of my ass,' Arlo said with a wry smile. 'It's not always about equations.'

'Ah, that old chestnut,' Carl tutted. 'Anyway, we can't put

Mia through that again.'

'Let's worry about that if we get a signal,' Arlo replied.

'It's off the table,' Carl insisted.

'Tarone,' Arlo said, squeezing the big man's shoulder. 'You mind taking us to Glastonbury?'

'Yah, mon. It would be me pleasure. Me played there a few years back.'

Tarone looked over his shoulder and checked his mates were safely seated in the back. He turned the ignition key; the engine roared to life. Tarone glanced at Arlo. 'It look like the Liberator want to go too.'

Everyone in the cab laughed, and, with a crunch of gears, the truck churned snow and headed back down the hill.

The frozen valley was laid out before them as they descended. On most bends, the lorry skidded sideways, and Tarone struggled to keep it on the road. Several times it struck snow drifted banks, making alarming bumps and bangs. Carl breathed a sigh of relief when the hill eventually flattened, and they passed through Wells' town. Minutes later, they came to the frozen shoreline overlooking the new Isle of Avalon.

'Do you think the ice a thick enough to support the truck?' Tarone asked Arlo.

'Hopefully,' Arlo said. 'It's been frozen for years.'

Tarone didn't look so sure. 'The Liberator probably weighs several tonnes.'

'Only one way to find out,' Arlo said.

Tarone nodded and edged the truck onto the ice. The tyres crunched, the ice cracked, and the wheels spun.

'Try a run-up?' Arlo suggested.

Tarone reversed a few feet, gunned the engine, and released the clutch. The truck lurched, and all four wheels mounted the ice. An explosion of cracks radiated outwards–hollow and brittle sounding, like the crushing of skulls.

'*Whoa!*' Carl exclaimed.

'Chill,' Arlo said. 'It's thin near the shoreline–it's just settling.'

'*Settling!*' Carl's eyes darted.

'The water's only a couple of feet deep here anyway,' Arlo added. 'Relax.'

Tarone chuckled. 'You men crack me up.' They laughed nervously. Tarone revved the engine to a steady growl, and the Liberator crept across the ice, Carl flinching with the sound of every new crack.

The conical mound of Glastonbury Tor rose like a breast from the virginal ice sheet a mile or two away. Carl relaxed and closed his eyes, knowing soon they would be back on solid ground. The tyres rumbled on the ice. His mind began to wander, thinking about how else they might defeat the jammer.

AAAAAH!

Screams pierced Carl's brain. His head spun as he opened his eyes. In a cacophony of cracking, the truck was swerving violently in an arc, two wheels gone light, everybody thrown across the cabin by the g-force. Arlo was gripping his head, face screwed up.

'*ARLO*,' Carl shouted above the din. '*What's wrong?*'

Arlo didn't seem to hear. He was clenching his teeth so tightly they looked like they might shatter. Mia had fallen from his coat and lay sprawled across the seat, blood trickling from her nose. The steering wheel spun freely through Tarone's hands, his foot jammed to the metal, the engine screaming its nuts off. The truck leaned at a crazy angle, threatening to roll as it continued its inwards spiral.

Carl hadn't driven for years, but he had to act. And quick. He threw himself at Tarone, trying to dislodge his foot. But he was a dead weight and barely moved.

'Tarone,' he shouted. 'Your foot. Move it off the bloody accelerator.'

Tarone's eyes registered his words, but he seemed paralysed in a world of pain. Carl dived for the gap between Tarone's legs. The skidding vehicle threw them forwards, and Carl became wedged as he flailed wildly for Tarone's calf. Stretching until it hurt, he grabbed denim and tugged with all his might.

The engine stopped screaming, replaced by wind and tyre noise as the vehicle lost power and coasted to a halt. The truck lurched and stalled. Carl extricated himself from the footwell and surveyed the cab.

The screaming had stopped, but everyone was grimacing, eyes tortured.

Why am I OK?

He checked the time: 11:45 am.

Fifteen minutes. And then what? Must stop the update? But I can't hurt Mia ...

Carl threw the door open and clambered out backwards. He lost his footing on the ladder and fell. Mind in overdrive, time seemed to slow down. He landed with a sickening thud, air slammed from his lungs, stars flashing.

Bloody idiot, he thought as he lay still, scared to move, praying he hadn't broken anything. His breathing returned, and, gingerly, he sat up. Realising he was OK, he struggled to his feet, slammed the door and lumbered around the front of the truck to the driver's side. After several hard tugs, he yanked open the door and climbed in next to Tarone.

Carl shoved Tarone with all his weight. Tarone toppled sideways onto the seat, making him even harder to move.

Typical.

Carl turned, braced himself in the doorway, and pushed with his rear. Inch by inch, Tarone slid backwards.

'*Come on,*' Carl shouted. '*MOVE!*'

After many minutes of pushing, Carl collapsed onto the now vacant seat. Damp patches stained the armpits of his hoodie, and sweat dripped off his brow onto the vinyl seats. He sat exhausted, trembling, inhaling deeply.

*Come on! This is **my** chance.*

He looked down at the clutch pedal and willed his left foot to move. It spasmed and twitched.

For fuck's sake.

He grabbed his leg and lifted it onto the pedal. Pressing

his knee with both hands, he somehow managed to partially depress the clutch.

'*COME ON!*' he shouted.

Gritting his teeth and sweating, he managed to push the pedal to the floor and hold it there. He turned the ignition key, praying it would start. It wheezed and stuttered and then roared.

Yes! Come on! Now the other leg.

He placed his right foot carefully on the accelerator, pressing his knee with both hands until the engine revved.

Come on. You can do this!

He pressed harder. The engine screamed. In a spastic spasm, he jerked his left foot off the clutch pedal. The truck kangarooed across the ice, threatening to stall. He revved the engine so loud it sounded like it would blow up. The lurching eased. Jubilant, he clawed the air and pointed the truck towards the island, gunning the engine full bore.

Come on. Hold it together. Not far now.

He hunched at the wheel, vision tunnelling, racing flat out, everything a blur. Two white mounds zoomed out of the white expanse. He threaded the needle between them, surprising himself he didn't crash. A 'No Fishing' sign flashed past.

The ice sheet bristled with the tops of trees and bushes. He steered a slalom course between them, snapping branches with the bonnet, riding a rodeo of jolts and bangs. All the time, the snowy stepped terraces of the Tor grew larger and larger, the dark nipple on the Tor's summit crystallising into a chess piece tower.

Just another minute ...

The truck juddered as the smooth ice sheet became studded with tufts of grass, rocks and branches. Then a loud bang sounded as it struck something big. Miraculously, it kept going.

You've done it, Liberator–you beauty.

Carl dragged his foot off the accelerator, and the truck coasted to a stop. It rammed into a bush, slamming Carl forward against the steering wheel. He grimaced, pushed himself back, and scanned the cab. Everyone was writhing in agony.

I'm on my own.

He checked his BioFace: 11:55 am. The metaverse connected then immediately dropped out.

Almost there ...

He kicked open the door while clutching Mia to his chest and descended the ladder backwards. He stumbled, freefalling. *Not again.* He tensed up, waiting for the impact. He slammed the ice, magnesium stars flashing around the tower's silhouette.

That's done it.

Mia stirred on his chest. 'Are you Jesus?' she moaned.

Come on. Save her.

Carl rolled her off his chest and slowly sat up. He saw the ice painted red. His hand went to his scalp, feeling wetness. He tugged off his bloodied hoodie and put it over Mia, dwarfing her like ET.

'It's gone dark,' came a muffled cry.

Carl shuffled across the ice on all floors, dragging Mia behind him by the hood of his top. He checked his BioFace: 11:56 am.

Metaverse? Still dropping, but better.

He crawled towards the Tor's towering bank like a siege soldier approaching a castle wall.

Just a few more feet to shadow the jammer.

He heard an ominous buzzing, like a swarm of angry bees. He peered skywards over his shoulder, trying to see the source of the noise. A dark cloud was homing in on him. Fast.

Drones. Slaughterbots. Is there time? 11:57 am.

He dragged Mia towards him and crouched over her, shielding her body.

Is Arlo too far away?

He launched a peer-to-peer remote connection on his BioFace. It polled and polled.

Come on, Arlo. Connect.

The buzzing grew louder and louder. Angrier.

11:58 am.

He connected to Arlo and navigated to the mystery file. The light dimmed like in a solar eclipse approaching totality. He looked up–the cloud of drones was funnelling towards him like a tornado as they dived.

Seconds left.

He found the file. 'Sorry, Mia,' he uttered.

'Don't make me see the light,' she shrieked.

Buzzing filled his ears. He was too late. He turned to face his fate, the whole cloud aiming at his head, primed to explode.

'Sorry, Arlo,' he muttered. 'I've failed again.'

Everything went dark, and the buzzing became muffled. Carl felt a crushing weight on his chest and something smothering him. A spitting roar deafened him.

'*Use the code Carl,*' Tarone shouted over the blast of the fire extinguisher.

Carl double-blinked on the file. 'It's done, Tarone.'

'*Now, quick,*' Tarone bellowed. '*Take Mia back to the truck an' get her safe. GO NOW!*' he yelled, rolling away.

Carl struggled to his feet, desperately clutching Mia to his bony chest, whole body shaking. Somehow he found the strength to lurch his way through the fire extinguisher's swirling white clouds that hid him from the drones' cameras and thermal imagers. He clawed at the truck's door.

'Please open. Pleeeease ...' Carl begged.

It swung open.

Arlo was sitting at the wheel, a look of grim determination etched on his face. The engine roared to life, and Llanzo hauled them aboard. The truck lurched away, the engine screaming.

'But, what about Tarone?' Carl uttered.

He swivelled and looked back at the ice. The clouds were thinning, the fire extinguisher empty. The tornado of drones was diving, Tarone at its eye. Ear-splitting bangs echoed off the ice sheet like firecrackers on New Year's Eve.

ΔΔΔ

From the summit of Pen Hill, Channing peered through his binoculars at Glastonbury Tor. He knew they'd never stop the BioFace jamming signal from the nuclear drones over Bristol, Bath, and Frome. His eyebrows lifted in surprise when he saw how far the truck had gone.

'What?' he muttered.

There was a hint of remorse in his voice as he ordered the commander to send in the slaughterbots. He watched in fascination as the drones funnelled down onto the truck and the exposed figures on the ice.

At the moment of contact, the figures disappeared in a white fog. Channing removed the binoculars from his eyes and inspected the lenses for condensation. Satisfied they were clear, he looked back through them. The mist had gone, and a Black man stood proud, clutching a fire extinguisher in one hand, the other making a clenched-fist salute. The tip of the tornado began to twinkle with white flashes as the slaughterbots detonated. 'Respect,' Channing muttered as the figure crumpled to the ice.

Channing's view switched back to the truck. But it had disappeared. Confused, he scanned back and forth. Finally, it reappeared–the vehicle a blur as it sped across the ice. He moved the binoculars back to the tornado, but it too had moved, rising from the ice like a giant comma. Channing's brow creased. He lowered his binoculars and grabbed the radio.

'Come in, Goldstein,' he barked. 'Over.'

The radio crackled. 'Sir. Over,' the radio replied.

'Why have you called off the drone strike? The truck is getting away. Over.'

'I haven't. Over.'

'*Haven't? Over.*'

'No. It should be attacking the truck and anyone within fifty metres. Over.'

'But …' Channing looked back through the binoculars and gasped. The radio fell to the ground with a squawk and a clatter.

The tornado had already crossed the valley and was now so large that it filled his vision. He dropped the binoculars and gasped. The sky turned black, the drones descending like a swarm of locusts about to strip a crop.

42

Arlo flinched. A loud buzzing filled his ears. He looked up, a black cloud obscuring the pale-blue sky. In a coordinated strobe of yellow and green, the drones of the Glastonbury festival lit bright, juggling their positions high above the heads of the crowd to form a gigantic Jamaican flag.

Arlo turned to Alisha. 'Those drones still make me nervous.'

'I'm not surprised,' she replied.

The frenzied crowd cheered as Jamaica Jammin' played the closing chords of 'No Woman No Cry.' The bassist raised his hand in a salute, swaggered to the front, and put an index finger to his lips. The mike made a dull thump as he tapped it with his finger. Arlo wondered what Llanzo was about to say.

The crowd murmured.

'Thank you,' Llanzo said. 'Me would like to say a few words.' The audience fell silent. 'Me would like to dedicate this performance to me great friends Tarone and Khanan. They died for us so we can be free.'

The crowd cheered and began to chant, louder and louder. 'Tarone. Khanan. *Tarone. Khanan. TARONE. KHANAN.*'

Jamaica Jammin' seized the moment and struck up the melody again. The crowd went wild. Arlo turned away from Alisha and wiped away a tear.

The encore's final chords played out, and the musicians left the stage, waving. The last performer to leave was someone sitting at the back, a man playing keyboards, Carl. Arlo watched as he waited until the cheers had died away and the crowd had dispersed. Unceremoniously, he wobbled to his feet, using the keyboard for support, and lumbered off the stage.

'Good old Carl,' Arlo muttered. 'Salt of the earth.'

'Yes. You're right,' Alisha said. 'Whatever happened that day, I'm sure he played his part.'

'We owe him our lives.' Arlo nodded.

Alisha looked skyward. 'Why don't you go and meet him off stage,' she suggested. 'He'd like that.'

'Great idea.' Arlo smiled and squeezed her shoulder. 'See you in a bit.'

Arlo threaded his way through the milling crowd to the rear of the stage. He leant over a galvanised steel barrier and spotted the musicians descending a planked stairway in the secure area.

'*Llanzo,*' Arlo shouted, waving.

Llanzo looked up and waved back. '*Catch you for a beer later.*'

Arlo turned his wave into a thumbs up. Llanzo grinned, fist-bumped the air and swaggered back to the Portakabin green room.

A few minutes later, a grey and hunched figure shuffled to the top of the improvised stairway. Security escorts had gone– unaware Carl needed help.

He'll never make those steps …

'*Carl!*' Arlo shouted.

Carl scanned the crowd beyond the barriers. His eyes locked on Arlo, his face a stony mask.

'*Wait,*' Arlo called. '*I'll be right with you.*'

Arlo cleared the barrier in a single bound, raced up the planked stairway and crashed into Carl's arms. They hugged, a tear running down Arlo's face. He pulled back and wiped it away.

Carl stood like an alabaster statue.

'You were bloody brilliant,' Arlo said.

'Not the best,' Carl replied. 'The BioFace nerve update pack helped.'

'Nonsense. You were great.'

'I'll take that,' Carl's face cracked with a weak smile.

'Let me buy you a beer,' Arlo said. 'Just the one–I'm trying to be good.'

'Yeah, why not.' Carl shoulder-bumped Arlo.

They meandered to the real ale tent, and Arlo ordered a couple of pints of the local brew. They strolled out of the tent and found some space.

Arlo gazed up at the Tor in the distance. Only the top was still snow-capped, the terraces lush and green.

'As the adoption was officially signed-off last week,' Arlo said, 'I guess I can talk more openly now. So, what happened that day?'

'I've often asked myself the same question,' Carl replied.

'Why weren't you affected?' Arlo said.

'The only thing I can think of is my DBS interfered with the jammer, or maybe my Parkinson's blocked it?'

'A blessing in disguise, eh?'

'Funny how life deals both aces and deuces.' Carl nodded.

'Indeed.' Arlo savoured a gulp of his beer.

'And what about that coup?' Carl asked.

'Now there's a conundrum,' Arlo rubbed his chin. 'Was it the code, or simply because soldiers had had enough?'

'But enemies joining forces?' Carl queried.

'The influence of social media?' Arlo suggested. 'People sick of propaganda and lies.'

'I guess we'll never know,' Carl replied. 'Anyway, how is your daughter?'

'Mia's doing fine, thanks.' Arlo patted Carl's shoulder. 'Obviously, she had a setback once we removed the BioFace hack, but luckily we stopped the malicious code before it damaged her nervous system. The main thing is her gene therapy appears to be working. Anyway,' Arlo smiled, 'how's *your* baby?'

'Sorry?'

'The code installed in everyone because of your heroics on the ice.'

'Oh, that.'

'Oh that, he says. Only the thing that probably saved us all!'

'I ran some tests on the installation.'

'And?'

'It's a complete mystery.'

'I think we've been here before.' Arlo rubbed his brow.

'So what do you think it is?' Carl asked.

'Maybe it's just anti-malware,' Arlo suggested. 'Although Alisha has a different theory.'

'What does she think?'

'She says God put it there to keep everyone good.' Arlo shook his head,

'Maybe she's right.'

'Not you as well …' Arlo looked skyward. 'Anyway, at least the nightmares and crazy dreams have stopped. So what's your theory about my alien and the spacecraft?'

'Well, if you believe the news, the space telescopes at the Lagrangian malfunctioned and are working again now. Something must have disrupted them.'

'And the alien?' Arlo asked.

'Well, as his body was burned up in the fire when Channing sent his pals into Kate's house, there's no proof of anything.'

Arlo frowned. 'But we saw his clone on TV?'

'We *think* we saw him,' Carl countered. 'It could have been a deep fake, a recording, or a mock-up targeting Kate's IP address. If you're so sure, why don't you go public?'

'Everybody would think I'd gone crazy.' Arlo twisted his wedding ring round and round his finger. 'Anyway, Mia comes first now.' He glazed over momentarily and then downed the rest of his beer.

Carl's eyes darted.

'Come and say hi to Alisha,' Arlo said.

Carl nodded.

They moseyed back to Alisha. A man with a guitar had come on to start a new set. Alisha was sitting on a picnic blanket next to Joshua and Mia, picking at finger treats.

She heard them coming and looked up. 'Hey, Carl. I loved the performance.'

'Thanks, Alisha. Just a one-off, but it's got me thinking.'

The PA crackled. 'Thanks for coming,' the man said. 'I'd like to kick off with an old Noel Harrison classic.'

As 'Windmills of your Mind' began to play, Arlo glanced at Mia. She looked angelic, beautiful honey-coloured hair tumbling over the shoulders of her burgundy pinafore dress. Arlo thought of Lana and smiled.

ACKNOWLEDGEMENT

This novel was inspired by attending two expertly presented writing courses on the beautiful Greek island of Skyros (organised by Skyros holidays). The course's participants were welcoming, supportive and non-judgemental. Thank you to the fabulous facilitators and authors, Crysse Morrison and Claire McGowan, for kick-starting my passion.

Of course, only so much can be absorbed in one-week writing courses. Ultimately, it comes down to practising the art and listening to feedback. My family and friends have helped me enormously in this regard. Extra special thanks go to Steve Connor, who embraced the story like his own, was immensely patient, and gave me the honest and excellent feedback I needed.

Most of the ideas for this book came while cycling–a pursuit that kept me sane during the COVID-19 lock-down. My cycling friends, Ken Dueck, Tim Matthews, Nick Julian, Jon Hayward and John Langborne, put up with my literary rantings on many Sunday rides, read drafts, and gave me excellent suggestions on cover design. Thanks, guys.

Valuable proofreading was done by: Nikki Bradshaw, Sally Wiltshire, Steve Wiltshire, and science fiction author E.M. Hanzel.

The book's cyber content evolved from lengthy discussions with my good friend Piers, who helped me weave this tricky subject into an engaging story.

My religious sounding board was Rob Fifield–a genuine and lovely Christian who instils calmness and peace wherever he goes.

Inspirational authors Andy Weir, Diane Connell, and E.M.

Hanzel gave me great advice on many aspects of content and publishing. Ed Rudolph gave me feedback on the cover, and graphic designer, Mike Matthews of New Media Fusion, turned my ideas into a professional product. Rochelle Allfrey gave valuable marketing advice.

Many other friends have also read parts of the book, and I thank you all for your interest and support.

Finally, thanks to my family for enduring this epic project. Without my wife, Michelle, I would never have attended the writers' course, and Hannah and Abbie gave me valuable young person perspectives.

Printed in Great Britain
by Amazon

15197739R00214